Juilliard or

Else

by

Nichele Reese

Dedication

I dedicate this book to my wonderful husband.
For always being so patient with me in this process.
For always being there, for always loving me.

Our Love is for always.

One choice can make you or break you.
That one choice can be life changing.
Choose right or choose wrong.
What's more important...Fun or Happiness?
That one choice is yours.

~Nichele Reese

Chapter One

~Tucker~

"This going to be enough?" the stranger asked, looking at what I had given him, opening his hand and then closing it fast again.

"Should be," I answered quickly, then glanced down the street because I heard police sirens getting closer to us as they headed our way.

One police car rounded the corner, and I watched as it pulled over to the curb to stop in front of us with its lights flipped on. "Stay still, man," I told the stranger who complied. "Whatever you do, don't run." I turned my body and looked at the lit up vehicle. Of course, I was pretty sure I knew who was driving it: the one and only Officer Daniels. He always patrolled this area and knew me pretty well, including all the shenanigans I had gotten myself into over the years.

Sure enough, it was Officer Daniels who stepped out of the patrol car. He slowly walked over to us, taking his sweet time with one slow step after another. He had on his usual policeman attire, but today he had on an extra jacket. The weather took a turn for the worse, making it a very cold and windy during this early morning. The wind was so cold that it almost felt like tiny paper cuts on my face. In Brooklyn, it always got really windy around the beginning of September to remind us that winter was coming.

"Tucker," Officer Daniels growled and nodded his head. My body went stiff as a board when he used my name like that. He already knew what I'd been doing this morning.

"What, Daniels?" I snapped, shoving my hands in the front pocket of my hoodie.

"I hope you're not selling your product out here to this guy...or should I say boy."

I glanced over my shoulder at the kid, who slowly backed away from me. I knew he was young, but he was old enough to know what the hell he was getting himself into by contacting me and coming into this part of town. Watching him back away from me some more, I already knew what he was planning to do, and before I could say anything to stop him, he took off down the sidewalk at full speed.

"Goddamn it, Tucker! You promised you were done with this shit!" Officer Daniels yelled at me while pulling off his Walkie Talkie to give out the description of the kid who took off and which direction he was headed in.

I heard the sirens of the rest of the cop cars that always patrolled this area with Daniels. No matter what, the kid was going to get busted; he didn't stand a chance against the cops around here. He was a noob in the drug world – even I could tell that. But if I didn't get rid of it fast, my buddy would be in even more trouble – life or death kind of trouble.

Daniels just glared at me. "You said you were done, Tucker, or should I just finally take your ass into custody?" Daniels knew my situation at home. He knew I didn't have any money to get myself out of jail; my mother wouldn't bail me out either. She didn't have a dime to her name, and even if she did, it would evaporate faster than water.

I put my hands up, defending myself as I heard more sirens coming in our direction. "I'm done, Daniels, swear."

He let out a big breath that I could see in the cold morning air. "Get outta here," he warned me and jerked his head to the side.

"Alright, man," I muttered at him, turning around to leave, cutting through the alleyways to head back where I belonged: Bushwick, Brooklyn.

The morning sun was beginning to shine through the spray painted buildings, which were marked up in graffiti. The sound of beer cans echoed through the empty alleyways as the cold wind blew around them.

I made my way back to the run-down apartment I shared with my mother. The cold air was hitting my face harder than before, so I pulled up the hood from my gray hoodie to help keep warm, wishing that I had worn something heavier.

As I rounded a corner, I kicked an empty pop can most of the way back. Thinking about what Officer Daniels just told me, I really did need to stop dealing, or I was going to find myself in a situation I would regret. As I passed more buildings, black trash bags lined most of the front walls – just another day to show that the garbage man could give two shits about our trash. Most people considered where I lived an unwelcome part of the neighborhood, and it was. You shouldn't be caught walking around here after dark, carrying any money or wearing any sort of jewelry on you. It was simple; you shouldn't come to this part of town, but if you did and you were smart, you'd carry a gun.

A screaming woman on the sidewalk shouting at her husband didn't make me move any faster as I buzzed myself into my cold, dirty building and walked up the creaky four flights of stairs to my apartment. The screaming woman reminded me of my mom and my dirt bag of a father always fighting. When I was eight, I would scream at them to stop, but my dad just ended up beating me until I stopped or passed out. They could never get along and my dad finally left us. He left me and my mom dirt poor and in a shitty apartment. He never came around at first, but then he started coming around sporadically to beat my mom and take what little money she'd had. But I haven't seen him in a couple of years now, so I don't know what's happened to him.

As I climbed the stairs, my eyes scanned over the dirty green and brown flowered wallpaper stripping away. The holes in the walls seemed to grow larger by the day, and the broken banister looked like it had its day a hundred years ago when the building was first built. The hallway lights flickered as if they were trying to stay on, but the electricity was deciding on something else. This building was so run-down and old that you had to watch your every step on the stairs or you might just fall through the boards; each step almost felt like it would be your last.

A little warmer now that I was inside, I pulled my hood down as I reached the top of the dirty stairs. I paused a moment as I heard loud bass music coming from the end of the hall where my apartment was.

Groaning, I knew when that type of music was playing, it meant Skinner was with my mom. I made my way down the hallway to my apartment and reached above the doorframe for the little copper key. When I stepped into the apartment, all the lights were off. The music pounded away as if the speakers were ready to blow, and my eyes scanned the room, looking around for evidence of Skinner.

Inside the apartment was shittier than the building itself. Garbage was everywhere; fur stuck to the carpet from my mom's three cats, and the crappy furniture looked even trashier since she never vacuumed. Dishes with old food stuck to them flooded the sink. Newspaper was crumbled up all over the counter and table. I stomped my foot hard at one of the cats, making it hiss and skitter away fast as lightning.

God, I hated cats.

I turned down the stereo in the living room and walked into the kitchen to get a beer from the fridge. When I opened the fridge door, it smelled as if something had died in there because of all the rotting food. Mold contaminated a full loaf of bread; I don't know which revolted me more – the rotting food smell or the loaf of bread that had just gone to waste.

When I was a kid, that bread would have lasted me at least a week. When my dad left us, my mom stopped trying to take care of me. I taught myself to make peanut butter and jelly sandwiches for my main meal of the day and wash my own clothes in the bathtub. Sometimes it was days before I could eat because she went on a drug spending spree. Now sitting here in the fridge was a loaf a bread, just fucking rotting away.

Out of anger and pure disgust, I slammed the door shut, causing the fridge to rattle and bang into the wall behind it. I stalked my way to my mom's room and turned the doorknob, but it was locked. I banged on the door with my closed fist and yelled for her, but no one answered... no sounds... no movement. I tried again...nothing.

With my hands clenched in fists, I yelled, "I'm gonna break down the damn door if you don't answer!"

Nothing.

5

"Mom!" I pounded on it again, hoping Skinner or my mom would finally answer.

I hated to cause more damage to this shithole of a place and have Skinner bitch at me for more money that I didn't have...or so I told him. I banged on the door once, but no one answered. Grabbing the doorknob, I slammed my body into the door. It gave away fairly easily and I watched as the door fell back into the wall, barely hanging by its broken hinges.

My mom, who was beautiful at one point in her life, was motionless; her body was sprawled out on the bed in her dirty pink nightgown, which just barely covered her body. Her eyes were closed as Skinner crouched over her right arm.

Heat blazed my face as I saw the rubber strap wrapped tightly above her elbow. Skinner was drawing a needle out of the vein from the crook of her arm. He whispered to her, "Sleep now, baby girl," and then kissed her cheek.

I walked over to her in two short steps and pulled her nightgown down to cover her more modestly. "Damn it, Mom." I pulled on her free arm but she didn't move. I expected her eyes to flutter open, but when she was high like this, she never opened them. I looked up at Skinner, who was now injecting the same crap in his own arm, using his belt and the same damn needle he just injected into my mom's arm.

Shit!

He inhaled a rush of air and looked up at me. "Now that's some good shit."

I watched as his eyes rolled into the back of his bald head. He deeply exhaled and opened his eyes to look back over at me. I just wanted to punch him in his stupid fucking face for always doing this to my mom...to us. So what did I do? The answer was simple; I punched him in the face.

He didn't even see it coming. I reached over my mom, grabbing the front of his white shirt, and punched him straight in the nose. Blood sprayed across my gray sweatshirt and onto my mom's pink nightgown. The punch didn't even faze Skinner because he was so out of it. All he did was smile in my direction with his nose dripping blood. And it covered his teeth, which for some reason pissed me off even more. So, I punched him again and he fell backwards on the bed, and then landed onto the floor. My mom stirred and mumbled something; I tried to shake her awake, but nothing happened.

"Damn it, Mom, every time," I yelled, hoping she would be her old self and talk back to me for yelling at her.

I heard groans coming from the opposite side of the bed and Skinner stumbled to his feet. He dabbed his face and glared across the bed at me. "Did you hit me?" he asked through clenched teeth.

"No. You're a clumsy ass who fell off the bed," I said, turning to leave the room, but Skinner grabbed the cowl of my hoodie, tugging me backwards and spinning me around in the process so I would face him directly.

"You hit me!" he yelled, while spitting blood in my face. I quickly wiped away the splattered blood with my sleeve.

I shoved him hard off me, but he came back swinging, hitting me in the jaw. I heard and felt a pop in my head. Skinner tackled me with a blow of his shoulder, slamming me back through the open door of the room and into the wall in the hall. The wind burned from my lungs and I could hardly breathe.

"You fucking hit me, Tucker!"

Now more than ever, I was really angry. I could feel the rage boiling through my veins; my face burned and my heart started to race faster. "You fucking hit me, too!" I shoved at his shoulders to release the hold he had on me. He stumbled back into the room and fell on his ass, his head hitting the metal bed frame as he went unconscious.

I fixed my sweatshirt and made my way towards the front door. I couldn't stay another damn minute with that jackass; he was a loser. I locked up the apartment and went back down the crappy stairs. I banged on the manager's door and waited for him to answer. Bouncing with rage, I felt like I was going to explode. When he finally answered, he looked at my bloodied hoodie and shook his head.

"Skinner is causing problems again," I said through gritted teeth. Then I started explaining what had happened.

He shook his head some more. "Your problem, Tuck," he told me, then slammed the door in my face.

Shit!

I raked my hands through my long brown hair. Normally, he would call the cops to get Skinner to leave the building; I guess Sam was done helping me and my deadbeat drug addict mother.

Finally leaving the dirty building, I decided to take the subway and two buses to get to Central Park to a little hideout I always hung around. Some of my friends that I'm not proud of hung out there with me. I'll admit that they're not good people, but it's where I belong. They felt more like brothers to me. They came from the same outskirts as I did and always understood my problems with Skinner. Pulling out a fresh pack of cigarettes from my back pocket, I grabbed one and lit it up. Smoking was a bad habit – something I wished I could break, but never could. I sucked the tobacco down in record time and flicked my butt in the street.

Of course, in the main part of the city close to Central Park, cabbies honked their horns non-stop. So when I crossed the street and a cab honked at me, it was an instinctive reaction to flip him off. I kept my head down as I walked down the street; the cold air turned warmer with each passing hour, but out of habit, I pulled my hood up and decided to take a shortcut through an alleyway...and that's when I saw *her*.

A car with the darkest tinted windows was parked up against the curb, and a girl like no other was standing next to it. Suddenly, an urge came over me to watch her – to stay still. Everything about her looks screamed innocence as she stepped away from the black *Bentley Mulsanne*.

My eyes took in her pale skin. Her blonde hair was pulled back in a tight bun thing that girls do. She wore jeans that clung to her body with black boots that made her legs look twice as long, and a black leather jacket. I was too far away to know what color her eyes were, but whatever color they were, I'm sure they were perfect. I could clearly see her smile from the alleyway; it was simple, yet wonderful. It brightened up her pale face.

When she walked toward the moving truck, I felt like I could hear every step her black boots made against the asphalt. One of the moving men met her at the back while the rest opened up the big lift and handed each other pieces of furniture.

Everything screamed out to me in a rush of words: *spoiled, rich, snob, brat, daddy's girl,* but I brushed it off. She was the most gorgeous girl I'd ever seen. What was a guy like me doing, checking out a high class rich girl on the Upper East Side of town? And in Central Park West, no less...I had no idea.

She moved back to the *Bentley* as a window was rolling down. She was speaking to whoever was inside, and for some reason this bothered me. Whoever was in the car didn't show much respect to the vision of this beautiful girl I was looking at. They should have walked her to the door of her new place in New York, or at least made sure she had a key or something.

As she stepped away from the car, it sped off. She was alone now with a big purple bag in one hand, just staring at the back of the *Bentley's* taillights. She walked over to the three movers and pointed up to an apartment in the building. The man spoke to her and nodded. She looked back up the street to where the *Bentley* was disappearing around the corner.

Looking up towards the sky in the morning light, she inhaled a deep breath and began smiling like at that very moment, she didn't have a care in the world. She was too breathtakingly beautiful, even for her own good. I couldn't help but stare.

Turning, she lowered her head, the beauty of her neck stretched gloriously around as she looked down the alleyway. I couldn't tell if she saw me. Most of my body was behind a dumpster, and my gray sweatshirt hood covered my head, but I swear I saw her innocent little smile curve up on the corner of her mouth before she turned back to the movers who were starting up the stairs to her new apartment.

Chapter Two

~One Month Earlier~

"YES!" I screamed out as I jumped up and down, scanning the letter again for the hundredth time.

Dear Miss Abigail McCall,

We would like to take this opportunity to welcome you to The Juilliard School of Dance for Ballet. Enclosed is your dance schedule and apartment information.

Those were the most wonderful words that I'd ever heard concerning my future. Not only was I accepted into the most prestigious dance school in New York, I was also leaving the parental units' nest. With my letter in hand, I immediately left my room, looking for my mother.

When I found her, she was in the kitchen, shadowing our maid Isabelle. She always made sure to do everything perfectly because my mother was constantly watching her every move. Considering my mother grew up with the "proverbial silver spoon" in her mouth, she'd watched my grandmother hover over their maid the same way. I didn't want to follow in either of their footsteps. Simply put, I wanted to live my own life and my dream was finally coming true.

After applying and being denied twice by Juilliard, I figured why not apply again...third time's a charm, right? As luck would have it, I was right. I knew my mother was going to be thrilled I'd finally been accepted...or so I thought.

Rushing to her side, I beamed a smile. "Mother, I got in, I finally got in," I said, pretty much screaming the announcement as I jumped up and down, flinging the acceptance letter in her face. I looked over her shoulder towards Isabelle, and she had a big smile plastered on her face for me, sending me a secret congratulations.

"Abigail! That's not how a young lady presents herself in a room," she scolded, her blue eyes narrowing. "You should be ashamed. Have I not paid enough for your etiquette schooling?" she spat out, hands on her hips, waiting for me to answer her in a more proper manner.

"Mother," I started, choosing my words very carefully as I repeated my announcement. "I have been accepted into The Juilliard Dance program for Ballet," I said more calmly this time while handing her the letter. She snapped it from my hand, almost giving my palm a paper cut as she scanned it over, her face completely impassive.

"Stand up straight," she mumbled towards me, her diamond wedding ring shimmering as I pulled my shoulders back, fixing my posture.

With hands in front, legs erect, spine perfectly straight, I stood there just like I was taught. I stared at her, waiting for a response. She and my dad paid top dollar for my schooling and even etiquette classes on the side, so I knew posture was the key in garnering her full attention and hoped it worked this time.

My mother was a gorgeous woman with short blonde hair that framed her face perfectly and ocean blue eyes. She only wore cream, tan, or beige colored outfits, but occasionally black to a fancy charity event or black tie dinner with my dad.

As I stood there waiting, a memory from when I was ten years old flooded my mind. I had passed a classroom full of ballerina dancers. It was amazing. My eyes watched their long arms stretching gloriously in front of their bodies, circling and bending at their knees. Their feet were delicately wrapped in ballet shoes as they balanced on their toes, wearing their pink leotards with matching tutus. They were gorgeous, moving rhythmically in formation with each other. It was then that I found my passion in life. I wanted to be a ballerina; I wanted to dance to music and make songs that much more beautiful for the eyes and ears of others.

When I first told my mother of my dreams, she actually laughed at me. I was only ten. She said dancing would ruin my feet. At the time, I didn't know what that meant, but I begged my father to reason with her, pleading to change her mind. She never did. However, one day she came to my room and saw me in front of my mirrored closet door, practicing what I saw the ballerina dancers doing. It was then that she finally gave in.

She sat me down and explained that she was allowing me to be a ballet dancer since that was the path I so desperately wanted to follow. She did have a few prerequisites, though. On top of completing any necessary homework, I needed to keep my grades in good standing. When I answered her in the proper manner of "Yes, mother," she then explained that she'd signed me up with the best instructors, and that I was to treat them with nothing but kindness, just as I would a teacher in school. If she didn't get good reports back, I could no longer attend dance class. I did everything I could do in order to get straight A's. I never hung out at friends' houses, basically just staying home and practicing until my toes would bleed.

Clearing her throat, my mother looked into my caramel colored eyes. "Well, it's about time. You need to go practice your routine; that way it's perfect for your new instructor. Now go," she clipped, moving her hands in my direction, essentially swooshing me out to go practice. "And don't forget to pull your hair back off your shoulders."

"Yes, mother," I said, holding my hand out for the letter.

She thrust it at me and turned around to Isabelle, whose back was facing my mother.

"No!" she yelled at her, causing Isabelle to jump and drop the spoon she was using to stir whatever was in the pot. "You're missing the third and most important step; we've talked about this, Isabelle!" she spat, slamming her fist on the table.

Hurrying, I left the room before I could hear what my mother was so upset about. Isabelle probably forgot to stir the onions and mushrooms for the fifth time or something absurd like that.

I walked down the hallway to my dance studio, which my mother designed just for me. We had it added onto our French Gothic House on the corner of 5th Avenue and 79th Street...like this house needed to get any bigger. However, my father didn't have a say in the matter because my mother controlled his money, buying whatever she wanted.

I changed into my leotard and stockings, and then wrapped my feet up in my ballet shoes. I pulled my blonde hair back in a tight bun and turned on Pyotr Llyich Tchaikovsky's music to *The Nutcracker* in the first act, Scene 1 No. 2 the Marche. *The Nutcracker* was my favorite to dance to, especially during Christmas time.

I walked on the points of my toes, passing the wall length mirrors on my way over to the ballet barre to stretch out my legs. When my warm-up was complete, I started on my routine for *Dance of the Sugar Plum Fairy*, which blended nicely with *Pas De Deux* for the ending.

My legs stretched to their max and my arms didn't bend unless they were supposed to. I had perfect posture and I made my way through the entire routine without missing a beat. With my back bowed and toes pointed perfectly, I moved gracefully like an elegant swan across the room. When I danced, I felt as if I was the only person who mattered. I was in control – not my mother, not school, not even my etiquette. I was free.

When the music ended, I felt proud that I had this routine down. When I looked at my reflection in the mirror, I saw my father standing in the doorway. He had his arms folded and was leaning against the doorframe. He looked so tired and I could clearly see the bags under his eyes. His tie hung loosely around his neck and his suit jacket was unbuttoned, completely rumpled up.

I sighed, out of breath, "Oh, Daddy."

He held his arms open for me and I made my way over to him, crushing our chests together. He was the complete opposite of my mother. I could call him daddy instead of father and he wouldn't mind. The only name I'd been allowed to call my mother was...well...mother. She always said mom never fit her, whatever that meant. I loved my dad more than anything, so I guess you could say I was a daddy's girl.

"Abigail, you dance so gracefully," he said, kissing the top of my head. "I'm so proud of all your hard work."

I pulled away from him to look at his face. "Did mother tell you that I received my acceptance letter today for Juilliard?"

"Yes, she did – that's why I came to find you," he said, smiling as he placed a kiss on my forehead. "When do you start?" he asked, stepping into the room to shut off the surround sound music.

Watching him move around my studio, I studied him. My dad was very handsome, tall and fit; however, he was balding at the top, so he shaved his head to a buzz cut. The look suited him. I got most of my looks from him.

"I have to move into my new place in one month's time." I nodded, remembering what the letter explained.

My dad rolled his eyes at my words, knowing they didn't come from the real me as he walked back over to look deep into my caramel eyes. "I'm so proud of you," he said, giving me another hug. "I know your mother and I don't tell you enough, but we are." With that, he left the room. My dad told me how proud he was of me all the time; it was his significant other who didn't. I turned the music back on and started my routine over again.

Later that night, my mother and father argued about my new school. My mother wasn't happy about me living in the dorm rooms because of the lack of space and security. She disagreed with my father about contacting the school and having the other two girls move in with me in a secure apartment building; they would cover all the costs. Seriously, the babying would never end.

My mind always went blank when my parents would argue. It's like nothing mattered except for their words, back and forth; my mother would fight until she got her way. There was no "or" in the matter; her feelings were the only ones that mattered.

Listening to them altercate with each other, I picked, poked and prodded at my food and ate very little. I kept my head down and sighed.

"Sit *up*, Abigail," my mother said, glaring at me from across the table.

Pushing my shoulders back, I sat up and met her eyes.

"Leave her alone, Carol," my dad said in a displeased tone. "Our daughter was just accepted to the finest Ballet school; we should be celebrating tonight." He put his fork down and waved Isabelle over. "Isabelle, please bring a bottle of champagne – one of Mrs. McCall's favorites."

With a nod, Isabelle left the room like the devil was at her heels.

"We don't need champagne, David," my mother snipped, eyeing my father as she finished her bite of food with elegance.

"Can I please be excused?" I shut my eyes, knowing that as soon as I said that, my mother was going to scold me on saying "can" instead of "may" I.

"Abigail, you disappoint me yet again today." She put her fork down with force; it made a glass breaking sound, even though nothing broke. Picking up the napkin in her lap, she dabbed the corners of her mouth.

Another one bites the dust, I thought.

"Carol, stop," my dad abruptly cut in.

"She needs to learn. It's *may* I be excused, Abigail. You are nineteen years old; it's time for you to act like it."

I couldn't take anymore tonight. I had to leave the table before she would scold me more for my immaturity. "May I please be excused?" I asked my mother, careful not to give her anymore attitude.

"No, you may not. You haven't..."

Before she could finish, my dad reached over and patted the top of my hand. "Of course, sweetheart," he said, giving me a reassuring smile.

I rose from my chair and made my way up the stairs to my room. Once inside, I stripped my clothes off, slid into my pajamas and padded into my bathroom to brush my teeth. Stopping myself before I grabbed my toothbrush, I stared in the mirror for far too long. I'd made up my mind, and with that, my body followed my bare feet over to the white porcelain bowl, so clean and sparkling. Yes, it was clean. Isabelle had scrubbed it that way. I wish she could scrub away how dirty I felt.

Lifting the seat, I stuck two fingers down my throat and easily heaved up my dinner with skilled practice. It was easier than learning to point your toes; you just stick your finger down your throat and let the gag reflex take over.

I remembered when I was five, throwing up and crying for my mother to come rub my back. I had the flu and was constantly feeling the bile rising in my throat. I prayed the burn wouldn't come, but it always did and my mother never came. I still wasn't used to that burn. Would I ever get used to the burning in my throat the purging caused?

I started sobbing, hating what I was doing to myself. I looked at the remains of my dinner. I laid my head against the side of the cool porcelain, trying to calm myself and catch my breath. My dad would be so ashamed of me if he knew. His perfect little girl couldn't quite measure up. I was sixteen when I first purged. It's been three years since then, and without doing it, I wouldn't be the right weight. I had to get up and move before someone came in and found me this helpless. With a warm rag, I cleaned my face, brushed my teeth and went to bed.

The next couple of weeks flew by. I was working on a new routine, and my mother called Juilliard to explain my living arrangements to the headmaster of the program...like they could care and they didn't. My mother then did research on whom my roommates were going to be and contacted their parents.

Both sets of parents agreed that for the safety of us girls, we needed to be in a more secure place. We no longer had to stay in the dorms, which made me mad. I was excited to start school and live in the dorms like a normal, regular college student.

Mother went apartment shopping the very next day, but without me, of course. I didn't get any say in where I lived. I overheard her talking with my father about the apartment she did find on 22 West, 66th Street. It was across the street from Central Park, which put me just down the way from the Lincoln Center, where Juilliard was; I could easily walk there.

But mother not only looked at the apartment, she *bought* it, and without my father's approval. The apartment itself was over three million dollars. My stomach literally fell out my butt when I overheard that. I gasped in the hallway of my father's study, hearing footsteps walking closer to me, and then the door click shut. My father was very displeased about that, but didn't voice his opinion. He always told me that he would rather keep my mother smiling than fight with her.

My bulimia went from once every couple of nights to twice a day. I could no longer stop myself. The burning in my throat helped with the pain I couldn't release – the pain caused by my own mother...by how controlling she was...by her lack of caring. It was apparent all she cared about was the fact that I might end up embarrassing her. I was getting more and more upset with her. I couldn't wait to leave here and get out on my own. With the stress she would put me under, I didn't need to use my fingers to help the bile come; it just came on command. Whenever she would yell or be displeased, you could find me in the bathroom, kneeling in front of the toilet.

I stood up from the toilet on shaky legs and leaned on the door frame to check the time, noticing it was three minutes before my private instructor, Ramón, showed up to teach me new choreography. When I finished brushing my teeth and wiping my face off, the doorbell rang right on time.

I meet Ramón down in the studio. I was already changed into my black leotard with light pink tights and had my hair pulled back tightly. When I entered the studio, he applauded me. I stopped to curtsey at him.

"My flower, I heard about Juilliard," he cooed as he grabbed for my hands, pulling me into the room. "Felicitations," he said, telling me congratulations in French and kissing both my cheeks in a traditionally French way. Thanks to my mother, French was my second language, and Italian my third. Did I even like Italian? I'm not sure; it honestly never mattered.

He held open my arms and looked at me. "My flower, you look a bit pale, are you alright?" He brushed my cheek with his fingers, and then gave my hand a little squeeze.

Of course, I lied to him. "Yes, Master Ramón, just tired," I muttered. If Ramón ever found out about my bulimia, he wouldn't let me dance. Even though he didn't agree with my mother half of the time, he would go straight to her about it.

He dropped my arms and walked over to the stereo, turning on the classical music to *Swan Lake*.

"You must learn a new dance today, my flower," he said, walking to the center of the room as he faced the mirrors, raised his hands, inhaled deeply, and then bent at the waist to touch his toes.

I made my way over to the ballet barre and went through my stretching routine.

Ramón walked up behind me and placed his hands on my shoulders. "The fun begins, my flower. *En' Face*. Let's start with some positions." I faced the front of the room and made eye contact with Ramón in the mirrors. The sweet and friendly Ramón had left the room, replaced by uptight, pain-in-the-ass Ramón instead. "First position; arms and legs," he commanded.

I positioned my arms at a curve in front of my body, forming a circle, the balls of my feet turned out completely so my heels touched each other and my toes pointed outward.

"Very nice," he rewarded. "Second position, arms and legs."

I positioned my arms open to one side with my elbows slightly rounded like the first position; on the balls of both my feet, I was completely turned out, but my feet were spread apart.

"Again, very nice Abigail," he said, nodding. "Fifth position; arms and legs," he demanded.

I positioned my arms and lifted them over my head. My arms rounded with the elbows slightly bent, and my hands held close together, but without my fingers touching. I placed my foot in front of the other, both of my feet touching as my toes aligned with my heels.

"Straighter on the legs," he said, bumping my calf with his toes. "*Mieux*." He nodded in approval at my correction. "Let's do an *Adagio* together," he said, placing his hand on my lower back. We made very slow movements together, looking graceful and effortless, floating as we performed slow lifts, turns, and other supported steps to warm us up for what was going to come.

"*Très bon*, my flower." Ramón praised. I smiled back at him. "Now, the real fun begins."

Swan Lake is a tough ballet to dance to. Princess Odette is turned into a swan by an evil sorcerer's curse. To capture that and make Princess Odette come alive through the dance, you had to make all the turns perfectly and give the right emotions through the turns. Trying to emulate Odette's beauty while remembering not to fall, I kept my neck straight and head held up high.

Odette's evil double, Odile, is harder for me to grasp because she's evil. Instead of smiling as if I was Odette to show my beauty, my face had to stay passive. Ramón told me to think of my mother and glare, as if I would be glaring at her. I tried not to smile at that.

"*RAPIDE*, ABIGAIL, *RAPIDE*!" Ramón kept yelling at me to move faster. "*Tête haut*, head high,

Abigail!" He snapped his fingers. "*Sourire*, big smile for your audience."

I corrected my face and smiled; my feet were starting to get sore, but being a ballerina, this was nothing new.

"Now, *Allegro*, Abigail." I leaped into the air as high as I could go.

"ENCORE!" I tried again. "ENCORE!" I leaped again, feeling that I went higher than the first time.

"Now, *Arabesque* and *Arabesque penchee*."

I stopped while standing on one leg with the other leg extended straight back. I lifted it as high as possible while tilting my upper body forward to maintain my balance.

"*Pirouette*, NOW, ABIGAIL!" I started turning over and over, rising *en pointe* as I did each turn, and maintaining my balance so I didn't get dizzy and fall on my face.

"Stop! *Echappe'*, ABIGAIL!" I stopped and jumped from the ground with both my feet together and separated them in the air, finishing my leap with my legs apart. I knew when I landed, my feet ended up together when they were supposed to be apart.

"ENCORE, ABIGAIL!" I did the leap again, but corrected myself on what I did wrong. This time when I was in the air, I felt weightless and landed perfectly with my feet apart.

"NOW, *Plié* and *Chassé*." I bent my back and moved my foot forward, and the other foot quickly followed behind, chasing it. Keeping my body bent backwards, I continued to maintain my balance.

"*Fermé*, too close, Abigail. Now, *Pirouette* again," he yelled, again. I was *en pointe* and started to turn repeatedly. I lost my balance on my toes, and it became my focus to correct myself, which caused me to fall flat on my butt.

I was exhausted and out of breath.

"Abigail!" My mother's high heels clicked loudly on the wood floor, alerting me of her approach. "Get up! When you fall, pick yourself back up." I stood up on shaking legs and faced my mother. "You never fall again, young lady." She pointed at me, pushing at my chest with her finger and causing me to step backwards; she always became furious with me when I fell.

"Yes, mother." I faced Ramón once she left the room and he had a look on his face as though he could spit needles at her, very displeased with my mother on how she always treated me when I made a mistake. However, that "one mistake could cause the most damage to my future," was what she always told me.

"We're done for today, my flower," Ramón said, turning off the music. "You've done well as Odette, but you have yet to master Odile. She needs some work." He handed me a bottle of water and I took a long pull from it, hydrating myself. It was very refreshing.

"I can do it, Ramón," I assured him, taking another sip from my water.

"*Oui*, I know, but I won't push you too hard." He rolled up a towel and pointed to the ground. I obeyed and laid down flat on my back, resting my head on the rolled-up towel. Ramón then unlaced my slippers and started to rub my feet. I winced at the pain in my foot. "Oh, you bleed," he whined.

I looked down at my sore and swollen feet. I had blood between my toes and under my toenails. He put another towel down and poured some water on them to wash the blood away. Having the cold helped; I would have to remind myself to soak them later. When

Ramón was done rubbing my feet and legs so I wouldn't cramp up, he packed up and left.

After three hours of hard-core dance plus a new routine I had never done before, I really wanted a shower. I shut the studio down and walked into the hallway, almost running right into my mother. She was standing there with her arms crossed, tapping her high heel on the tile floor, disappointment written all over her face.

"Abigail, you disappointed me in the worst way just now," she huffed, her hands and arms flailing about. She looked more pissed than disappointed. "You had Ramón yelling at you for three hours; you could have done better. You better not embarrass me when you go to Juilliard or else there will be consequences." She pointed, slowly walking towards me. "You better get the leading role in every dance while you're there or so help me, I will pull you out of that school in a heartbeat."

That hurt worse than telling me I weighed one hundred and eight pounds and was overweight. With that said, she turned and left me in the hallway where I dropped to my knees, holding my head in my hands, and for the first time in three years, I cried instead of making myself throw up.

Chapter Three

With the last of my room packed and ready, I came to a stop and glanced around once more. I had to admit, in some ways, it screamed "baby girl arrival". Despite its juvenile décor, I had mixed emotions over leaving it behind. When I wasn't dancing in my studio, I spent most of my time in the pink, girlish space. I stood in my childhood room, considering the many memories it'd brought to me playing by myself, alone. My bed had fluffy, white pillows and a beautiful matching comforter that I would hide underneath when I was scared of my mother. I was actually more anxious about moving in with girls my age than about my audition for Juilliard.

I moved into my bathroom to get ready to go through my bedtime routine, but before I could make my way to the toilet, I heard a soft knock on my bedroom door. When I answered, my dad stood on the other side, wearing his burgundy robe and reading glasses. With his hands behind his back, he rocked back on his heels. "May I come in, angel?"

I didn't say anything to him; I just held the door open. He brushed past me and in just a couple of steps, sat on my bed and padded the spot next to him. He seemed nervous; I could feel the bed shaking which meant that he was shaking.

What was his deal?

"Abigail," he started, but stopped. I tilted my head to get a clear look at his face, and that's when I realized that his eyes were glossed over. My heart started to break for him.

My dear, sweet daddy – what has him troubled enough to start crying? My throat began to tighten and squeeze shut as I felt my own tears pricking away at the corners.

"Abi..." He couldn't even finish his sentence. His sob caught in his throat as he took off his glasses, pinching the bridge of his nose. I couldn't stand seeing him like this; it broke my heart. Something very troubling was eating away at him.

"Dad," I croaked out, but he didn't answer me; he just silently cried and trembled, the heel of his hands pressed into his eyes.

I couldn't take it; I slid my arms around his neck and pulled him snug against my side. I felt the wetness of his tears on my own cheeks as I cried into his shoulder. In all my years, my father had been a kindhearted person to everyone. He had taken more crap from my mother than I had, and not once had I ever seen him cry. He was supposed to be the strong one – the one who I could go to with my problems, and he would pound them into the ground for me, making them all go away.

When both of our tears were dry and our hiccups stopped, he cupped my face. His dark brown eyes rimmed red from the salty tears. "Abigail, I'm so proud of you." I started to cry again. "I want you to be your own person when you get there. Remember to have fun." I shut my eyes and felt my tears cascade down while I nodded in his hands. I felt his thumbs wipe the tears away from my face.

To be very honest, I had the greatest dad a child could ever ask for. He knew I didn't like the whole glamour or the extra schooling my mom put me through. I just wanted to dance. He was proud of me for becoming a ballerina – his ballerina – and for following my dream.

"I have something for you...more like a good-bye gift," he said, reaching into the pocket of his robe as he pulled out a velvet box.

I smiled weakly at him. "It will never be good-bye, daddy. Just...see ya later." I wiped my nose on my sleeve with more tears sliding down.

"If you don't like it, we can find something else," he sniffed, handing over the little black box.

I noticed as I held the velvet box in my hand that it was smooth against my fingertips. I usually only received gifts on my birthday or Christmas, but never as a reward. Mother said she didn't want to spoil me with worthless presents, especially since I already had everything I could want or need.

I opened the lid and sitting there was a perfect, elegant, little heart, covered in tiny diamonds and dangling from the silver chain. It was perfect and simple – very me.

I gasped at the sight of it, "Oh, Daddy, it's beautiful."

I took the sparkly necklace and held it up as it shimmered in the lamplight. He took it out of my hand and held the two loose ends open towards me. Leaning forward, he clasped it behind my neck and locked it into place, making it mine. My hand went up to touch the cool metal that was now placed perfectly on my chest.

I threw my arms back around his neck. "I love it," I said gratefully into his shoulder.

"I'm glad to hear that; I was nervous."

I pulled back and looked at him. "Nervous? Why?" Why would he be nervous to give such a gorgeous gift to me?

"Well, your mother has to pick out everything," he said, shrugging his shoulders as if it didn't bother him. "Get some sleep. Tomorrow is going to be a busy day." He kissed my forehead once more and then left my room without another word.

I walked back into my bathroom. I didn't have the nerve to kneel in front of the toilet. I didn't feel disappointed in myself, nor did I have anger towards my mother. I was too happy, and all thanks go to my dad. I brushed my teeth and went to bed, falling into a relaxing, dreamless sleep.

The next morning, I woke before my alarm went off at seven. I laid there fumbling with my new necklace from my dad, sliding the heart back and forth along the chain. It was such a thoughtful gift. You wouldn't catch my mother doing anything nice like that for me. When I was little, I overheard one of the servants saying she didn't have a heart and that it was blackened. I asked my dad what that meant, but he just chuckled and then said I would understand one day – but I never saw that servant again.

I lay there for far too long, and when I checked the clock again, it read seven thirty-five. I knew my mother would be annoyed at me for wasting the day away in bed. Right then, my bedroom door burst open and in walked Mrs. Queen Bee herself.

"Abigail! What are you...get up." She clapped her hands. She walked over and threw open the drapes that I had closed to block out the sun. *It's too early*, I wanted to shout at her, but couldn't find the courage. I never found the nerve to do so; I'm such a wimp.

Squinting my eyes at the devil sun, I tossed my arm over my face, shielding myself from the dangerous light.

"Abigail," my mother snapped at me.

I sat up, rubbing my tired eyes and glanced at my perfectly put together mother. Not a hair was out of place, her nails were perfectly manicured, and her penciled skirt and blouse didn't have any wrinkles in it. This woman was nothing but perfection on heels, covered in pearls. I climbed out of bed and padded over to my bathroom to brush out my morning breath. My mother followed me and scrunched up her nose in disgust as she entered my bathroom.

"Has Isabelle come in here to clean lately?" she asked. I continued to brush my teeth, knowing that if I answered her with a mouth full of paste, another notch would be on my belt for the morning.

I spit out and rinsed. "I don't know, mother," I stated, rolling my eyes in secret so she wouldn't see.

"Unbelievable!" she shouted and I jumped. My mother threw her hands up in the air with a "displeased with Isabelle" look on her face, which I'd seen many times before.

Watching her pace in my mirror, I started stripping for my shower. My mother then walked over to the door and screamed "Isabelle" at the top of her lungs. I covered my ears as her voice echoed off the bathroom tiled walls and not even twenty seconds later, Isabelle was at the door with a frantic look on her face. She was looking around my room to find her mistake before my mother told her what she did wrong.

"Follow me," my mother commanded through her gritted teeth. I knew when my mother talked through her teeth, you should turn around and run the other way as if hell itself was trying to swallow you whole.

That was never a good sign. Her temper would only rise higher.

When they both appeared in my bathroom, I was only in my white cotton bra and panties, but continued to strip and climb in the shower as if they weren't even there. I didn't even wait until the water was warm. I stepped into the freezing line of water to put my head underneath and ignore what was going to come, making me focus on the cold water, but unfortunately, I still heard her.

"Isabelle," she started to say cuttingly, "why does it smell as if something has died in this bathroom?" She commanded an answer from Isabelle. I could hear her high heel just tapping away on the tile, waiting impatiently – something she always did.

I was thankful for the spray of the now warm water to cover my face, so my mother couldn't see the guilt that was smothered all over it. I tried to ignore the conversation for Isabelle's sake, but couldn't help myself. I was actually afraid of my mother's shrieking voice, and before Isabelle could even started to explain, my mother interrupted her.

"I do not want any excuses, Isabelle. Clean the bathroom and I want it to sparkle." She emphasized the last words through her teeth, making me shutter. I felt Isabelle's pain; I knew exactly what she was going through at that moment.

I could see my mother's figure through the shower door, waving her hands about in front of Isabelle's face. I picked up the shampoo and started scrubbing my hair, letting the menthol suds soak into my scalp.

"You're on very thin ice, Isabelle!" I heard my mother yell.

When I was done, I padded back into my room with a towel wrapped around my body. I found that my mother had already selected an outfit for me to wear along with black leather boots that killed my feet every time I wore them. My ballet feet were made for flats or something without heels. Some girls could do it, but my feet were always too sore. Besides, I hated wearing heels, because being five feet six inches, they just made me even taller.

When I was dressed in my mother's choice of outfit, I stuffed my necklace underneath the sweater for my sake, so mother wouldn't bring up how unfashionable it was – plus she would just call it tacky and tell me to take it off.

When I walked back into my new, sparkling clean bathroom, it no longer smelled as if something "had died" as my mother put it. But trying not to ruin the cleaning job that Isabelle had just done, I still found my way back to the gleaming white porcelain to complete my morning ritual.

Eventually, I finished making myself feel dirty and pulled my blond hair back in my usual ballerina bun. Then I put on a light amount of mascara and lip gloss to complete my simple look. I was never one to wear makeup; I was lucky to know how to put mascara on.

On one hand, I was happy to get out of this house and leave my mother, but on the other, I felt sad to leave my father behind to deal with her every day.

Brushing away the confusing feelings that were eating away at my conscience, and my heart, I turned around, leaving my childhood buried in my past. Finally ready to be on my own and become my own person, I was no longer the person who my mother saw; I was me.

I found my father in his very spacious office, surrounded by stacks of paperwork. The walls were lined with an array of books, but most of them pertained to law. My father owned his own law firm and was the top Criminal Justice attorney in New York...plus he had the best team around. He's even had celebrities hire him to handle some of their cases. He was sweet and loving at home, but in the courtroom, he was ruthless, cruel, and emotionless; he could eat you alive for breakfast and make you feel like you were nothing your whole life.

I couldn't believe my eyes and ears when I observed him one day in court. I was terrified of him and he saw that. Later that day, he pulled me onto his lap to have one of our talks. I ended up confessing how mean he sounded. He kissed my cheek with an apology and explained to me that it's his job to win and to be cruel no matter what. It became a lot clearer the older I got. He's had thousands of cases but has only lost three in his eighteen years of being a lawyer.

Ruthless.

He always buried himself away in his work, but in a way, he had to become a workaholic in order to keep my mother's shopping habit up to her standards. We had to have the finest things that topped New York living. Not only did my parents have a prime house on 5th Avenue, but everyone knew who we were. I could understand why my mother was so worried I would drag her name through the mud about attending Juilliard. She was the Queen Bee of New York high society. Every woman wanted to be her. She was cold and heartless, just like my father when he was in the courtroom, but she has always been that way; he has not.

I watched my dad highlight some paragraphs in a law book before he noticed me standing there, watching him. He looked up over his glasses and set the highlighter down before he spoke.

"Yes, Angel?" My father sat back in his chair, stretching out his legs beneath the desk and folding his arms over his chest.

"I just wanted to say 'see ya later' before I left," I answered. I reached in my sweater and pulled out my new necklace, sliding the little heart back and forth across the chain.

When I met his dark brown eyes, they clouded over with sadness, and I wanted nothing more than to comfort him. Walking around his desk until I was standing in front of him, he grabbed my hand to pull me into his lap, coddling me one last time. He kissed my head and I pulled back to look at him. He reached out to take hold of my stunning new necklace, which I already cherished.

"This is perfect, just like you." He smiled as it slipped from his grasp and landed back on my chest, the perfect brilliant silver shining against my black top.

"Thank you, Daddy. I love it." I smiled at him. "Let's take a pic." Pulling out my iPhone, I opened the camera, making sure to turn on the front facing camera feature so we could see our faces on the little screen.

"Smile," I said quite cheesily. My dad chose that moment to dig his fingers in my side. Making me giggle and squirm, I almost fell backwards off his knee. I heard the camera click as I laughed and tried to move out of his reach. He started to chuckle and held me up in his strong arms. Once we settled down from our excitement, I reached down to pick up the phone which I had dropped in the process of our enjoyment. It landed on the Persian rug below our feet.

When I looked at the screen, I was in awe with the results. It was really a picture-perfect moment of me and my dad together. He was looking up at me with a big grin, his dimples showing the wrinkles on the corners of his eyes. I, on the other hand, looked like I was in complete disarray. My head was thrown back in happiness and I looked like I was about to fall backwards. I smiled and saved it as my wallpaper so I could see it every time I looked at my phone. Kissing his cheek, I left his office with a new memory of us.

Entering the empty kitchen, I went to the fridge for some orange juice and something small to eat. Digging around, I finally found some cut strawberries and blueberries. *Perfect.* Making my way over to the granite countertop to set the bowl of fruit down, I started to eat the delicious, juicy fruit. The fresh strawberries mixed with blueberries were so refreshing; I was enjoying every single bite. After eating only a couple of bites of my food, I heard the footsteps of Queen Bee's heels on the tile floor entering the kitchen.

I took a deep breath and groaned. I was never prepared for whatever was coming my way. I felt like I had a checklist whenever she walked into a room; back straight, feet and legs together, elbows off the counter.

"Abigail. There you are," she huffed. "We need to get going. Andrew already put your belongings in the truck and I want to leave before the traffic hits," she explained to me while moving about in the kitchen, not really doing anything – just moving around, making me dizzy watching her.

After taking a refreshing drink of my orange juice, I set my cup down. "Mother, it's New York; there's always traffic." I shrugged my shoulders like it wasn't a big deal. Anyways, it was New York. It was one of the many reasons why this city was so famous: the traffic.

After taking another bite of strawberry, I set my fork down in my now empty bowl and glanced up at my mother. Her blue eyes turned angry as they were staring daggers at me, making me want to run into a corner and hide. That's when I immediately regretted my choice of words. Shockingly, my mother didn't point out my wrongness, but the look she had in her eyes was terrifying; her expression alone was threatening.

Oh crap, not good.

Everything was screaming at me to run for my life, to turn away as she silently stalked towards me. But I couldn't – my feet were plastered to the floor. Her high heels didn't make any sound on the tile floor. Her eyes never parted from mine as she got closer and closer to me. This moment, I didn't see coming; it was one of those moments a child always feared.

It was then I felt the sting hit my cheek. The loud smack echoed through the kitchen. My head snapped sideways as the heat bloomed across my pale cheek, and my eyes watered at the corners as tears slowly dripped down my face. My mother had never hit me, but then again, she had never hugged me either. My hand went up and cupped my inflamed cheek, and my mother chose that moment to get right up in my face.

"You *never* speak to me like that again," she hissed, her blue eyes, fierce and angry.

Footsteps then rushed up behind me, and a pair of warm hands covered the tops of my shoulders.

"Carol, enough!" my father barked. I saw my mother's eyes fume with rage as they met my dad's. She didn't look back at me when she turned and left the room.

My dad turned me in his arms and gathered me into his chest. Breathing in his fatherly scent, I let my tears fall onto his white shirt, soaking it through. I still cupped my cheek. *She hit me.* So many emotions were running through me all at once. I pitied my mother at the moment. I didn't want to see her, to be around her. I wanted so bad to just tell her off to her face for touching me like that.

She hit me.

But do I have the courage to do so?

I pulled away from my father's embrace and staggered backwards, just recognizing that I was trembling...and so badly that I could barely hold myself up.

"Abigail," my father said, reaching out to enfold me back into his warm, safe embrace, but I ran out of the kitchen before he could catch me. "Abigail."

She hit me.

I stumbled up the stairs as I made my way down the hall and slammed the door to my room. I barely made it to my bathroom before I vigorously shoved two fingers down my throat, causing myself to gag hard into the toilet bowl. Today, I did this out of anger; normally, I only did it because I was sad.

She hit me.

I usually hated when the burning of the acid would come, but now, more than ever, I embraced it. I wanted the pain – wanted the burning of my stomach coming up my throat. I coughed into the bowl as my breakfast made its way up and out of my mouth, hitting the water below me.

The normal burning I experienced when purging was intensified because of the orange juice. It was too much; I couldn't handle it. I sobbed into the toilet, trying to catch my breath, but I kept on gagging because of the smell. I finally had to move, because it was making me sicker. The pain hit me with crushing force in the pit of my stomach as I collapsed on my soft rug, tired and worn out, and it was only nine thirty in the morning. I screamed and pounded my fist into the rug, not caring who heard my cries.

She hit me.

I don't know how long I laid there crying. However, I do know I'm utterly alone in a deep darkness that feels like it's swallowing me whole. I couldn't shake this cruel feeling running through my veins. I'm completely alone in my mind and I'm too scared to disappoint them all. No one understands the pressure my mother puts on my shoulders – all the weight I carry to make her happy, but it never works. All I told her was that there was always traffic and she hit me. The sound of her flesh hitting my cheek replayed in my head like a CD stuck on skip. It was playing over and over again.

Several minutes passed while I laid there grieving on my rug, and the only thing I could think about was how lonely I am. How pathetic I must be for thinking that. But I needed to focus on the coming days – on my new roommates, finally having friends, and my dancing which I loved so much. It was really the only thing that kept me going.

I stumbled up on my wobbly legs, but managed to rise to my feet. I looked in the mirror like I did every day to see the same face. Now dark pools formed under my eyes, and deep inside me, my inner child cries at the choices I've made about myself. I know it's not healthy what I'm doing, but they'll never understand the pain that my mother puts me through.

I heard a knock at my door, which startled me. I quickly tried to recover from my episode as I heard my dad's voice just on the other side, calling my name. But hearing his voice made me think about how many times I had put him through my pain. Even though he didn't know about my purging, I knew it would destroy him if he ever found out.

I gave him a weak smile as he entered my bathroom. He pushed his glasses up on his nose as he asked, "You alright?" and placed a hand on my shoulder. I didn't answer him and reached for my toothbrush and cleaned off my face with a warm washcloth.

"Abigail," my dad started, "one day, you will understand how your mother is." He rubbed the back of his neck in a stressful manner.

I spit in the sink. "Why are you taking her side?"

His brown eyes met mine in the mirror. "I'm not, angel."

"Yes, you are," I snapped.

His eyes were hidden behind his glasses, but I could see that he was upset. "I'm not happy about what she just did. It's just...you'll understand one day is all."

I rolled my eyes. His words slashed at my insides and didn't bring comfort. I didn't believe him. I'll understand her one day? That's just another excuse, just like when a husband beats the crap out of their wife and she defends him. I was sick of living in fear of my mother. She was my mother. Mothers are supposed to care for their children, protect them, and not make them live in fear of their own parent. I was sick of being so hurt by her, and she could hurt me so easily, too. Her words and her actions always pierced through my chest to my heart, making me feel nothing but worthless. No matter how hard I tried to please her, it never worked

I left my bathroom in a rush to search for my mother. I had taken enough crap for one day. I couldn't back down now when I finally had the courage to confront her. I found myself almost running through the house, searching for her. When I opened her bedroom door, I was enveloped with the smell of her perfume. *Chanel Number 5* never smelled so evil.

"Abigail," my father said right before I slammed the door in his face, locking him out. I made my way around the fancy gold and beige room. I was livid now; my fists were clenched together so tightly. I felt my nails dig into my skin as my lips held tightly together in a hard line, making my brows pull inwards. My heart raced against my chest as I pulled my thoughts together about what I was going to say when I found her.

Should I just tell her to shove everything up her glorious snob butt?

Forget it; I was just going to let the words flow.

Taking a deep breath, I screamed, "Mother!" My face burned with my rage. My heartbeat pounded in my ears as my blood raced through my veins.

I waited on pins and needles for her to emerge from her bathroom. I knew she was in there; where else could a rich snob hide? My patience was starting to wear thin when the door finally opened. My mother was standing there, looking perfect as usual and I didn't move. She stared me down as we made evil eye contact.

"Yes, Abigail?" she gritted through her teeth.

Now what should I do? I thought to myself. I got myself in here. *Do it... say something, anything.* But I couldn't get any words to come out of my mouth.

The elastic holding me together finally snapped. I finally felt it – that deep down rage, like a volcano ready to explode, and then I yelled, "I hate you!" Every nerve in my body was making me shake as anger exploded throughout my body. Tears cascaded down my face in fury. "I hate you," I said to her. She still didn't move – didn't hesitate at the evil words I threw at her. She was motionless and empty, just like her soul...heartless, just as the servant said when I was younger.

"I hate you," I said to her one last time with shaky breaths.

She pushed some hair away from her face and swallowed. "I'm sorry to hear you say that."

What? I'm stunned. Didn't she care that her daughter just told her, "I hate you"? She cleared her throat.

"Is that all you can say?"

"I'm sorry you feel that way, but I don't know what to say to you, Abigail." She clasped her hands in front, lacing her fingers together.

"You're so ungrateful," I said to her. "I have done everything – *everything* to make you flippin' happy, and not once have you ever acknowledged that I've done well. You've only pointed out my faults." I couldn't stand anymore how she treated me like a child. I was shaking so bad with my ruthless anger and she *still* didn't move a muscle.

Narrowing her eyes, she tilted her head as though she was having a hard time processing my words.

I wasn't quite sure if it was minutes or seconds that passed before she slowly walked up to me. This time, I prepared for the blow that was to come. "Are you going to smack me again?" I spat out at her.

Finally, here was a reaction that made her shrink back from me as if I burned her.

She stared down at the ground and started twisting her ginormous diamond ring around her finger. When she looked back up, her blue eyes were filled with tears. I didn't feel one speck of remorse for the words I had spoken to her. It was finally nice to see her get upset, considering how long she had done the same to me. She extended her arms out, but I stepped back. I didn't want her touching me. She dropped her arms back to her side. Whatever emotion she was feeling right then, whether it was sadness, sorrow, regret, or shame – it was all gone in a blink of an eye.

She smoothed down her blouse. "Be down in the car in twenty minutes and then we'll leave," she sniffed. She then turned around and slammed the door to her bathroom, locking herself back inside her hidey little hole.

Still standing in her room, I thought about what she tried to do when her arms came up. Did she want to hug me? Try and push me out of her room? You never knew what she had planned up her sleeve.

I was proud of myself for finally telling her how I felt.

I turned and left her room, but when I opened the door, my father was across from me with his hands deep in the pockets of his slacks, ankles crossed. I could see disappointment in his eyes behind his glasses. He stood up straight and held out a hand to mc. "Abigail, we need to talk. Now." Hearing his stern voice, I knew this wasn't a request. So I took his hand while he led me through the house. I didn't say anything to him, just followed his steps.

We took the stairs outside into the morning traffic and passed our doorman, Jack. He gave my father a firm nod and shot a small smile in my direction. I softy said hi to him. My father walked me down the busy sidewalk, still holding my hand tightly as we crossed the street and made our way down a little path through Central Park.

We'd walked for only a couple of minutes when he finally let go of my hand. The sun was shining high in the morning sky, and the park was filled of the fresh cut grass smell. He sat down on a park bench and looked up at me. I was still standing, not moving. This was the first time my dad had done anything like this. He usually ignored everything that went down between me and my mother, not wanting to get in the middle of anything between us or make it worse by voicing his opinions. He'd told me that before; now I wondered what was going on in that lawyer brain of his.

He pinched the bridge of his nose. "Abigail, I know you haven't had a normal childhood," he started.

Yes, he was right. I'd been so focused on my ballet that I hadn't made friends or gone out to have fun as a teenager. I'd never gotten to experience a high school crush, have a boyfriend or even a best friend. I didn't want to let my parents down, and now it seemed like that was all I was doing to my mother. I let her down in everything, even with my communication skills, the way I stood, and my ballet.

Making my way over to the bench, I sat down next to him. He stretched out beside me and put his arm around my shoulders, making himself comfortable, and I could feel him start to relax, which helped me relax.

"The thing is, angel," he said, letting out a big breath that he was holding in. "Before you were born, I had an affair." I whipped my head around to stare at him in shock; I didn't see that coming.

A ringing sounded in my ears at the word...affair. Did I just hear him right? He had an affair?

Holy crap!

"I didn't cheat on your mother. I was married before, to a woman named Shannon. She was so beautiful, and I didn't deserve her." His head dropped.

Was beautiful? I let out a breath, ready to hear the story my dad prepared himself to tell me.

"We were married for about eight months when we got into an argument one night about work, school, and buying a house with no money. I was going through law school at the time. Yale didn't give a damn about giving you time off if you had personal problems. It was either be there or quit. After our fight, I went out to a bar and got rip roaring drunk. I met a woman named Caroline, who at the time was trying to 'find herself' by living it up, as she put it." He chuckled at the memory. "We danced our asses off, and in the end, I ended up going home with her and we started having an affair."

I had never heard my father speak so freely with me before, and I had no idea what to say to him. I was in shock for sure. I could never picture my dad having an affair; he wasn't the type to do that...or so I thought.

"I couldn't let Shannon know I was sleeping around with Caroline, so I slept with both of them, but it was starting to become too much to handle. I was leading two lives. One was with Shannon, with the fighting, house hunting, law school, studying, and more fighting. The other was with Caroline; she was free to do whatever she wanted. I didn't have to worry about school. We drank, had crazy sex wherever, danced and had a great time with each other; she took all my worries away and I fell in love with her. I was planning on dropping out of school and leaving Shannon, but when I decided to tell Shannon this, I found her on the bathroom floor crying. And then I noticed the five pregnancy tests lying around her feet – all of them positive."

He eyed me over his glasses. "I was full of regret and decided not to tell Shannon about Caroline. So, I stopped seeing her."

I shifted uncomfortably on the bench; hearing my dad talk about having sex wasn't my cup of tea, but the pieces were starting to fit together like a mixed up puzzle. Carol wasn't my mother; she was the "other woman" in my dad's life. I looked away from my dad who had tears running down both cheeks as he quickly swiped them away. My mother wasn't my mother. I didn't even know what to say. I know that I should be livid, but taking in all this information, I couldn't form the right words.

"I knew you would be a blessing to us – help us survive our problems so we could make our marriage work. I never heard from Caroline after I gave her the news. She understood I couldn't leave my pregnant wife, so she got up from the table and never looked back."

Another tear escaped from my dad's eye. "When you were born, you were absolutely beautiful. Weighing in at six pounds three ounces, you were so tiny – just a red-faced, little princess, wrapped up in my arms. I was the first to hold you."

I covered my mouth with my hands to muffle my soft cries. I had never known much about my warm welcome to the world. Carol always changed the subject whenever I asked about when I was born.

"Then, machines started beeping." I looked back up at him. "You were ripped from my arms and I was shoved out of the room. I had no clue what was happening. My wife and baby were in a room with loud, beeping machines. I lost it. I started pounding on the door and shouting to be let back in. I was then escorted to the waiting area because I was scaring the other soon-to-be mothers." My dad took another big breath of Central Park air. He shut his eyes to gather more thoughts and when he opened them, he continued on.

"I sat in the waiting room for about an hour before your mother's doctor came to tell me she died as she suffered from hemorrhaging. There was just so much blood that they couldn't stop it. So up until you were six months old, it was just me and you, kid," he chuckled and nudged my shoulder. I softly smiled at him. A little family with a small boy walked in front of us; they were all laughing without a care in the world. The mother called out to her son as he ran fast ahead of them. The dad playfully scooped him up to give a raspberry on his stomach, and the little boy giggled and screamed. They were a picture perfect family. Did I ever have that?

"I ran into Caroline again at a charity event and she was a completely different person; she was all dolled up, just like a woman of New York City. She even talked differently...more proper sounding. She no longer went by Caroline – just Carol."

The final pieces came together; I didn't have my dad's dark brown eyes or his thinning brown hair, and Carol had bright ocean blue eyes and white blonde hair. I had more of a softer blonde with caramel eyes. I wondered what Shannon looked like and if I received any of my looks from her. My dad must have been thinking the same thing, because he pulled a small picture out of his pocket and handed it to me. I peered at the old, worn-down photo and realized that I was looking at my birth mother.

I had her hair color with the same caramel eyes and her nose, too. My dad always took my nose away from me when I was little saying, "I got your pointy little nose." She had that same little nose. I couldn't help my tears as they trailed hot streaks down my cheeks. This woman right here in this little photo was my mother and my dad was right – she was so beautiful. I traced her face with the tip of my finger, trying to connect with her somehow. I wish I could have met her.

"She loved the name Abigail and wanted to call you Gabby. Believe it or not, she also loved going to ballets." He reached out and took my necklace between his fingers. "This was Shannon's as well." My heart sank and then shattered into a million pieces. I had something to keep close to my heart – something of hers that I could always cherish. I couldn't believe he gave me something like this.

"Why didn't you tell me?" I kept my head down, wanting to know why he could keep something like this from me.

"Carol couldn't have children and she didn't want to adopt. We wanted to wait until you were ready, angel."

"Don't you think you should've told *your* daughter that her mother isn't really her biological mother? Dad!" I felt angry, but I couldn't get my anger to boil up. I just kept still as possible, staring at the picture of my biological mother. The thought crossed my mind as to why Carol couldn't have children. Plenty of lonely children needed homes; why not adopt?

"I know I should have told you earlier on, but I couldn't."

"That doesn't make it okay, Dad."

"I know – I'll always regret not telling you sooner," my dad huffed and checked his watch. "Come on. Carol is probably wondering where we are, and you need to get going to your new place soon." He stood up from our bench and grabbed my hand, not waiting for a response from me. I tucked the picture of my mother in my pocket. Kids laughing throughout the park made me wonder that if Shannon was still alive, would my childhood have been happier?

When we came out from the park, I saw Carol standing with the door open to her *Bentley Mulsanne*; of course she had to have the flashiest car in town. She had my giant purple bag containing my ballet slippers and leotard, and she carried my black leather jacket across her arm. As we approached her, my dad took my jacket and slipped it on my shoulders for me.

"Thank you, Daddy." I smiled at him. Carol cleared her throat at me, knowing very well I used daddy instead of father like I learned in my etiquette school. I looked directly in her eyes, "Yes, Caroline?" Her eyes widened in shock and she looked at my dad with a disturbed gaze. "Yes, he told me everything," I snapped as I stepped towards her. "You never lay another hand on me." Finally, I felt like I had some sort of power over her.

I turned back and stood up on my toes to kiss my dad's cheek. I gave him a small smile and then climbed into the car. I shut the door and looked out the tinted window, seeing neither of them saying anything to each other. Carol turned away and walked to the other side and slid in next to me. Tension filled the expensive car along with Carol. She usually brought it wherever she went. I don't know how long I stared out the window until Carol finally started talking to me.

"Abigail," she said in a whisper.

"Don't, Carol," I barked at her as the car pulled away from the curb.

"No, Abigail, listen to me."

"You're not my mother." I glared at her.

"You're right, I'm not. I wish I was. I very deeply wish I was." I snorted; her expression went a little more miserable than usual. Carol's eyes were pleading with mine, asking for forgiveness. "I'm sorry I smacked you; I don't know where that came from." She reached over and brushed my cheek with her fingertips. I tensed up at her soft touch.

"It doesn't make it right, Carol."

"I know. I'm very ashamed of myself that I stooped that low to do such a thing."

Silence then remained in the car until we reached my apartment. My apartment was about a seven minute drive from my parents' house, plus it was close to the school, so I didn't have to worry about a driver taking me there. As the car came to a stop, Carol reached over and grabbed my arm. "Your roommates should already be here or on their way. It's apartment 22A with a gorgeous view of the park; you'll like it." She held out a key to me and I took it.

"I'll like it because you won't be there to yell at me all the time." I glared at her once more and ripped my arm out from her grasp. Not bothering to say good-bye, I turned my head and climbed out of the car, seeing Andrew at the back of the moving truck waiting for me.

"Hey, Andrew." I smiled as I approached him and his waiting crew. "It's apartment 22A; here's the key, just go on up." I pointed above me. The other men opened the big truck door and started unloading my things out of it. I looked back at the car to see Jordan, our driver, wave me over. Carol's window rolled down and she had her laptop open on the armrest in front of her, her manicure fingernails clicking away on the keys.

"Your father has a dinner for his firm next Saturday. I will email the information to you. Good luck, Abigail." The window rolled back up and the car sped off, and just like that, she was gone.

Finally feeling free, I tipped my head back to breathe in deeply, and for once, I actually took the time to smell the scent of freshly baked bread in the air. I listened to the cars honk at each other and the squealing brakes as the taxis passed by me. While the workers unloaded my things, I turned my head to have a glance around at my surroundings in my new neighborhood. I saw a guy wearing a hood standing in front of a dumpster a little ways down in the alleyway, watching me. Before I knew it, I smiled at my first stranger with kindness.

I was dead nervous as I made my way inside the building where I saw our own doorman whose name was Michael. I introduced myself and he asked if I needed anyone on the approved list of people who were allowed up to my apartment, and I just told him my dad, David, for now. Carol could soak in my anger a little longer. I knew if I let her come up into my apartment, she would definitely change it around and voice her opinion on my décor skills, unless she had already decorated it herself.

I stepped into the waiting elevator Michael held open for me. I was a nervous wreck to meet my roommates who must think I was a spoiled brat because Carol wouldn't let us stay in the dorms on campus. I shut my eyes and focused on the motion of the elevator that was taking me up to the twentieth floor.

Chapter Four

I stood in front of the white apartment door and stared hard at the gold numbering of 22A. I heard the other two girls' muffled voices inside the apartment as they waited for my arrival. *Take a deep breath, Abigail. They won't bite*, I told myself, but this was a huge deal for me. I'd never hung out with girls before; I was never allowed to have friends if I wanted to dance. Now I had roommates. I gripped the cool gold knob and gave it a twist to reveal my new place.

As I stepped inside, I was taken aback by the large amount of space. Right in front of the entryway was the living room with a red couch facing a big flat screen TV on the wall and some black sitting chairs on either side of a black coffee table. I approached the gorgeous floor to ceiling windows that covered the entire living room, showing me a breathtaking view of Central Park. We were on the twenty second floor and this is what Central Park looked like from up here? I could live with this, even though Carol the bitch picked it out.

A sliding door led out to the balcony with three lounging chairs ready for us, thanks to Carol's doing, I was guessing. She'd want to make sure we got nice and cozy in *her* living arrangements. However, an ashtray sat on the little table with one cigarette burning away the last bit of tobacco. I knew Carol didn't put that there.

Taking a deep breath through my nose, I looked out at the top of the green trees of Central Park and heard the girls hush each other. It was all quietness now in the living room. I was sure they were listening for me, so I continued to walk around, knowing my boots were making noise as I moved around the spacious living room and then ended up back at the window.

Then I heard them talking. "Do you think that's her?" one asked.

"Yes, and be nice, Jade," the other answered in a loud whisper.

"I always am, dumbass," the other scoffed.

I stifled my laughter as they came out of the hallway and around the corner to stand in front of me. Butterflies ran through my veins and landed in the pit of my stomach as they both stared me down.

They were both striking in their own individual way, and with very different types of faces. The girl who stood right in front of me had red hair with brilliant green eyes. Her hair wasn't the kind of bright red you'd usually expect, but softer. She was thin like me, but had legs that looked miles long in her white skinny jeans and black heels.

The other girl had black as night hair with a pale face and wore black clothes. She was standing behind the redhead with her arms folded at her waist.

"Hey you, we've been like dying to finally meet you," the gorgeous redheaded girl said to me with a little smile.

"Yeah, you took freaking forever to get here, too," the black-haired girl said while moving out from behind the other to stand at her side. I was shocked at her beauty. Who knew darkness could give off so much light?

Dressed in complete black from head to toe, her skin was very pale with beautiful, shiny black hair that framed her face. Black eyeliner was drawn around her ice blue eyes, making them stand out clearly from her pale face; they reminded me of the Caribbean ocean against the white sand.

Ignoring her friend, the beauty in front of me started talking again. "Just ignore Jade." She gave Jade a shove at the shoulder. "I'm Rachel Dawson or Ray as Jade here calls me. We've been friends since we were toddlers." She smiled happily at me again, showing off her pearly straight white teeth through her pouty lips.

Giving a small wave, I said, "Hi, I'm Abigail."

"Abigail?" Jade raised a brow, "Oh, hell no. That won't work for me, you sound like a grandma. You got a middle name or something?"

Rachel elbowed Jade in her side. "She's Jaiden Monroe by the way. She's just the daughter of Satan; ignore her PMS stage." Rachel smirked.

"Too far, Ray, plus it's a dude's name," Jaiden whined. "Just call me Jade."

I'm definitely going to need to get used to them if they bickered like this back and forth. I was only used to Carol's bickering at my dad and me. Now I had roommates. I thought of what my dad told me not too long ago about my name. "She loved the name Abigail and wanted to call you Gabby," my dad's voice rang through my ears.

"My mom wanted to call me Gabby," I muttered. Still in shock a little bit about saying mom and not meaning Carol.

"What do you mean *wanted* to call you?" Jade asked plainly at me.

"She died." It wasn't as hard to say as I thought. I bit my bottom lip, waiting for them to respond.

Rachel's brows shot up and she looked at Jade. Quietness roamed the living room. "Awkward," Jade mumbled under her breath, "but Gabby it is!" She then yelled through the open space of the apartment, raising her hands in the air like she just discovered something remarkable. It was obvious she was trying to ease the tension I had just created with the little tale of the death of my mother.

"Chill, chick," Rachel said while grabbing Jade's arms to put them back down to her sides. "Have you already seen the place?"

I shook my head.

"So, the lady who bought this place is what...your stepmom?" Rachel questioned me, raising yet another curious brow.

"Yeah, stepmom." For some reason, that didn't feel weird to say at all; it felt right more than wrong. She had always felt out of place in my life – never comforted me when I was sick and didn't praise me for anything. Only punishment came from her mouth.

"So your stepmom didn't show you the place before?"

Why did I feel so embarrassed about that question? Shifting from foot to foot, I mumbled, "No, she just bought it without me or my dad seeing it." I gripped my purse tighter. My knuckles were turning white from death grip I was giving it.

"No shit," muttered Jade and tilted her head to the side.

I looked over and met Jade's gaze; she was staring at me with this dumbfounded look in her blue eyes. That made me relax just a little more and I eased my grip on my purse.

"No shit," I said quietly, ending with a smile and swearing for the first time. Friends could change you in a blink of an eye.

Carol would be furious if she heard my mouth just now. I was actually swearing in front of people without feeling the restriction of having to watch my language, I was going to take advantage of it and enjoy it.

"Well, I'm going to go finish my cig." Jade turned and left the room, leaving Rachel and I alone.

"Let's have a look around," I stated.

Rachel backtracked through the apartment and showed me the kitchen first. It was to the right of the front door. The cabinets were gorgeous mahogany with black countertops and stainless steel appliances. I walked over to the fridge and pulled open the door, wondering if it was empty, but I was wrong. It was very well stocked to the brim with water, juice, fruit and all the necessities to cook something. When I opened the pantry door next to the fridge, we saw that it was also well stocked with everything you could imagine from the regular things: flour, sugar, crackers, noodles and lots of water.

"What you going to Juilliard for?" Rachel asked.

"Ballet. You?" I asked, shutting the pantry door and facing her.

"I'm going for acting – going to be a Broadway star like my mom, but I'm going to LA to make the big bucks. And Jade is studying artistic drawing and plays the cello."

The gothic girl played the cello...didn't see that coming. Wonder how she sounds.

"So how old are you?" Rachel asked me unexpectedly. I could tell she was trying to get me to open up as much as possible.

"Nineteen," I answered, not meeting her eyes as my fingertips brushed against the cool countertop.

"Nice. Jade and I are nineteen, too."

Looking up, I said, "You two seem close."

Rachel shrugged her shoulders. "Yeah, known each other as long as we can remember, she's...special."

Michele Reese

"What do you mean by *special*?" I asked, raising an eyebrow in surprise.

Rachel held up her hands "Oh, she's not slow or anything like that, just...special."

I was still confused as to how she meant Jade was "special". Clearly seeing the confused look written all over my face, Rachel let out a long breath through her mouth and approached me slowly; we didn't say a word to each other as she reached for my hand to slide my sleeve up to my elbow.

Watching her move in slow motion while all you could hear was our shallow breaths, Rachel turned my arm so my wrist was face up. She dragged her French tipped fingernail across the veins on my wrist. I let out a gasp in shock, my head snapping up to meet her saddened green eyes.

"You're serious?" I questioned her gesture. Rachel didn't answer me; she just nodded and then turned around and left the kitchen.

Jade hurt herself – like physically cut herself. Didn't that hurt or bother her at all? I was surprised someone could do that, but in a way, I wasn't one to talk. I made myself throw up to feel the burning pain of the acid coming up my throat. I'd always heard people complain about throwing up, like it was the worst feeling they could ever feel, but yet, I embraced it every time I did it. I was the one who was the biggest baby when it came to getting a paper cut. Cutting yourself was entirely different, but not much from my situation. I felt sick for Jade; maybe she and I could get to know each other better and help each other out.

I found Rachel in the living room, looking out the window at Jade. In just a couple short steps, I was at her side. I felt strange watching Jade sit out there, smoking alone.

56

"She's my sister," Rachel whispered, her voice going into the high pitch squeak as if she was going to break down any second.

Looking up at Rachel, I witnessed tears in her eyes. Feeling a little uncomfortable, I decided to take a chance, placing my arm around her waist to give her a little squeeze of comfort. She looked over at me and placed her arm around the tops of my shoulders, and just like that, we became good friends. Something inside of me bonded to this girl I only met five minutes ago.

"You're a good friend, Rachel," I told her. She dropped her head and dabbed under her eyes, trying not to let the tears fall.

"Let's find your room," she said as she patted my hand on her waist.

The dining room was in the same room as the living room; the wall that I passed into the hallway contained our fine dishes and glass cups. Around that were shelves holding many, many books. Walking past it and down the little hallway, I could see a room straight in front of us, but Rachel turned to the first door on the left and moved inside.

"We didn't choose any rooms, yet. We wanted to wait for you, but this room shares a bathroom right through that door."

The room was very big with hardwood floors, tan walls, red bed sheets and a fluffy white comforter. A door to the right led to the bathroom that had another door on the other end leading into the next room. The bathroom was very nice as well; it featured red tile work and mahogany cabinets just like the ones we had in the kitchen, a glass shower, and a big Jacuzzi bathtub in the middle. There was also a toilet in the corner closest to the first room. Carol really outdid herself picking this place out.

I moved into the next room and the decor was just the same as the first. I went across the hall into the third room to find Jade laying in the middle of the bed with her feet up on the wall. This room was decorated just the same.

"Hey Gabs," she greeted me. "I call dibs on this room. You freaks were too slow to choose." I looked around and Jade had already put a couple of posters on the walls. They were of dark bands I never heard of; I definitely had some catching up to do to get to know each one. All I knew of was Pyotr Llyich Tchaikovsky and some country, but that wasn't saying much.

"Okay, babe," Rachel said to her. "This is the only room that has its own bathroom."

"Ha! That's right and I took it from you bitches."

I burst out laughing at Jade and her upfrontness.

She really was a funny girl with all her cursing; I knew I was going to like just being around her. She made me feel at ease with everything and didn't take things so seriously.

Rachel nudged me to stop laughing, but I couldn't help myself; I kept laughing. She then pushed me and I toppled on the bed right next to Jade. Rachel crashed on the other side of Jade, and just like that, the three of us were sharing a bed within the first day of meeting each other. It was a nice feeling, being able to click with certain people right away.

"Oh holy balls! One of you really stinks," Jade stated very loudly and I started laughing again.

"Way to ruin a good moment, Jade," Rachel replied. Sitting up on the bed, I examined the poster in front of me of the dark group; one of the band members was wearing black eyeliner with glasses hanging off the end of his nose. I got up and walked over to check out the amazingly good looking male who was giving a smoldering look as he stood at the front of the group.

"Who's this?" I pointed to the hot guy who had my attention.

Jade arched her neck up to look where I was pointing. "That nice piece of ass is M. Shadows. He's the lead singer of Avenged Sevenfold. They're comin' to town soon – October, I think. They are coming along with Black Falcon, Korn and some small new band."

"Oh, I love Black Falcon," Rachel said with a growl in her voice. "We should get tickets."

Jade nodded in agreement. "I'll look up tickets."

I never found tattoos sexy, but after seeing them on this guy who was wearing a tight black shirt to show off his bulging tattooed arms, I could easily change my mind. He even had a lip ring that I found attractive; it looked good on him. Some guys either looked good with them or it didn't do anything to enhance their body.

I left the sexy poster and went back to room number one, which I liked. It had the most windows of the three, and I wanted as much light as possible. I was now in my new home and in my new room. Life felt good so far.

I sat on the red couch in the living room and watched Andrew and his men bring in the rest of my things. I offered to help them, but Andrew told me they had specific instructions from Mrs. McCall to handle everything. Hearing the back door open and Jade sitting down in one of the chairs outside, I hopped up from the couch and followed her out to the sunshine filled balcony. I smiled when she looked up at me.

"Hey." I gave her a small wave while shutting the door.

"What up, dawg," she said; I shook my head and giggled. I could really get along with Jade and I really wanted to get to know her some more. I hadn't quite figured out what I liked about her so much...just how relaxed she was, I guessed...not caring about what people thought. She proved you could just be your own person, and that's exactly what I was aiming for.

Jade unwrapped a new pack of cigarettes and banged them on the palm of her hand.

"Why are you hitting them?" I questioned.

"It packs the tobacco down. You want one?" She held the pack out to me with one sticking out the top. Being curious, I took it. I held the small white stick in between my fingers and glanced back at Jade. She put one in her mouth and flicked the lighter to light up her cigarette. She tipped her head back to blow the smoke out above us; it looked easy enough.

I put the cigarette between my lips; Jade stretched her arm forward and flicked on the lighter. I leaned forward until the tip hit the little yellow flame. I sucked in and felt my mouth fill up with smoke and puffed it out in one giant breath.

"You didn't inhale and if you waste that cigarette, I'll beat your ass," Jade scolded at me.

"How do I inhale?" I nodded at the cigarette burning in my fingers.

"Don't you know how to breathe?" Jade took another drag of her cigarette. "You inhale it, suck it in like a big breath so it goes in your lungs and blow it out."

As I watched Jade tell me this, I took notice of the smoke coming out of her mouth as she spoke to me. I put the burning cigarette back up to my lips and to take another pull from it just as Jade explained.

HOLY MOTHER OF...

I felt the lining of my lungs being burned away. It burned worse than the acid from my purging. I coughed and the smoke went everywhere, hitting me in the face, burning the crap out of my eyes. I covered my mouth with a closed fist and kept on coughing. I felt Jade pound on my back. People really do this?

"That a girl," Jade said, hitting my back some more. "That's when you know you did it right." I glanced up at her, still choking and trying to catch my breath.

Still choking, I croaked out, "What?"

"The coughing – you'll get used to it, though. Take another drag."

I didn't want to; it was just plain nasty. But remembering Jade's warning about wasting her cigarettes, I put it back up to my mouth and inhaled again. However, I was expecting it this time and coughed very little. I still felt my lungs being burned away while my stomach turned in nasty circles. I ended up blowing out the smoke too fast which burned the crap out of my nose, making me start to feel lightheaded.

"Keep it up, Gabs; you're doing awesome," Jade praised me.

By the time the cigarette came to an end, I was just getting the hang of it and it didn't burn as bad. When there was just a little left, I raised the cigarette to my mouth, but Jade reached over and plucked it out of my fingers before I could finish it off.

"I wasn't done," I told her.

"You'll just hit the bud and get a lungful of filter; trust me, you're done." Jade put the cigarette out on the ashtray and tossed the bud over the balcony railing. Silence lingered between us for I don't know how long, but Jade huffed and when I looked at her, she was staring. I raised my brows and shifted my body to face hers.

"What?" I asked and she just shrugged her shoulders at me without a word. I stood up from my chair and went to lean over the rail. I peered down at the busy street and passing taxis. I could feel Jade's eyes burning holes into my back.

"You're easy to read, chick." I heard Jade stand from her chair and felt her stand beside me. "Parents are rich and you're lonely. Am I right so far?"

Did my body language really give me away that easily? I was lonely, but now that I was out from under Carol's dirty nose, I could be my own person. I finally felt free, and Jade teaching me how to smoke was a bonus.

"Evil step mama?" I eyed her, but she was right, of course. I turned my head back down to the street. She continued on, "Yeah, I've got one of those, too." Jade looked back down at the busy traffic with me. "My mom killed herself four years ago."

My heart sank and broke for her. Jade had lost her mother; was that why she cuts? I didn't have the nerve to ask her as that would be stepping out of line. We had just barely met and I didn't feel comfortable going down that road. You never knew – she could completely turn on me and become my mortal enemy. She had that mortal enemy glare down to a T when she gave it to Rachel.

"My dad remarried the biggest bitch in New York. God, I hate her."

"I bet she isn't as big of bitch as Carol," I huffed out.

Juilliard or **Else**

"Explain, Gabs." Jade turned around and rested her elbows on the railing, crossing her feet at the ankles, waiting for me.

"Well, about two hours ago, I found out she's actually my stepmom and my birth mom died when I was born."

Her brows shot up in surprise. "The bitch just told you?"

Shaking my head, I replied, "No, my dad did."

"Whoa...now that's messed up."

I nodded in agreement.

"I can tell you've been living in a black hole. We need to loosen you up – show you what you're missing. And first things first."

I started to giggle at her. "What?"

"You need to get rid of that nasty ass bun at the back of your head."

I didn't have time to reach up myself before Jade was already undoing it for me. When my blonde hair curtained around my face in little waves, the sliding door opened and Rachel poked her head out. "Jade, are you being a good example?"

"Shove it up your ass, Ray," Jade snapped.

I chuckled and shook my head. Jade gave off the vibes of being an honest, up-front person when it came to confronting Rachel. She didn't give a crap what people thought, and so far, it's what I liked most about her. I wanted to be that person and take charge, so I said the first thing that came to mind.

"Yeah, up your ass, Rachel." Rachel's face dropped at my foul words. Jade's head faced me with a huge grin, her blue eyes gleaming in approval. Maybe talking that way wasn't my style. "Sorry," I mumbled, but broke out laughing right after. Maybe that was a little much, but I couldn't help myself. My body folded in half at Rachel's saddened face. I laughed so hard my stomach started to hurt. My face heated up and my cheeks were starting to hurt from my smile. I looked back towards Jade; I knew she was letting me enjoy my moment of happiness and she was.

"I can see Jade has taught you well so far," Rachel murmured, "and took your hair down."

I shrugged my shoulders and muffled my laughter with my hand.

"What shall we do tonight, Ray, to help Miss Tight Wad loosen up her panties?"

By the way Rachel's eyes looked, I could tell she was up to no good. "Show her porn?"

"No," I protested as I held up my hands. "I'm good. I know all about Sex Ed."

"Porn isn't Sex Ed unless you watch a naughty student mixed with a nasty teacher with a ruler," Rachel told me. "I'll order Chinese. Jade, get the laptop ready." Rachel pulled out her phone from her pocket while shutting the glass door to call the restaurant.

Jade nudged my arm with her elbow. "You're already loosening up a lot. Want another cig with me?"

"Sure."

The more Jade and I talked, the more and more comfortable I felt being around her. She explained that her mom killed herself after her boss accused her of stealing money from his company – a lot of money. Her boss had tons of evidence to use against her, framing her to shield himself, they later found out. Jade said that the day her mother died, her grandma came to take her away to stay at her house, but gave her no explanations as to why she was staying with her. But Jade never saw her again until the funeral. They even had to have a closed casket service because her mom shot herself in the mouth and Jade's dad couldn't fix it.

"Couldn't fix it?" I asked, wondering what she meant by that.

"My dad's a plastic surgeon – best in the biz."

We both heard Rachel yell from the inside that the food was here. When we walked back into the living room, the first thing I heard was loud moaning from the laptop sitting on the coffee table. I definitely blushed at the loud sex noises the couple was making...well, mostly the screaming girl was making, as she was clearly enjoying herself.

Rachel had paper plates, napkins, and plastic forks for us, surrounded by Chinese food. Eating my food in utter silence, I watched the couple on the screen go at it like dogs. Well, technically I think I stared at the floor or at my food more than at the erotic couple. This is what they really did for entertainment? Jade explained that the porn was a good touch just to lighten me up and help me come out of my shell more. I couldn't help but smile at her for that. She knew I had a stepmom who was hard on me. I explained very little to her about Carol other than she was not my birth mother.

I was loosening up some, but still felt tense. I didn't like the videos; porn was just nasty. Jade quickly helped with the mood in the room. "What would happen if Big Bird walked in right now as they were going at it on the desk?" she asked, growling around the egg roll and taking a nasty bite out of it.

Rachel choked on her food and rice sprayed everywhere. I burst out into loud laughter.

"Where did that come from, Jade?" Rachel asked when she settle down and had control of her breathing.

Jade winked at me and said, "I don't know. I had a Sesame Street song stuck in my head." She shrugged her shoulders and I knew she was trying to distract me. It very much helped. I no longer pictured it as strangers having sex for money and being taped, but more along the lines of a sexual fantasy they were trying to get. But no way was Big Bird involved.

"When have you ever watched Sesame Street, Jade?" Rachel asked and Jade ignored her. I silently thanked Jade for helping me.

After five porn videos and more Sesame Street sex talk, we were still laughing. Rachel speculated what would happen if Elmo walked in and used his high-pitched voice asking, *'Hey guys, whatcha doin?'* I had to admit, she did a perfect Elmo voice. Jade was making us laugh with a Big Bird impression of a couple having sex, clucking around the living room like a chicken, while moaning up against the wall.

I was lying on my back with my legs under the coffee table, feeling dizzy from our rambunctious laughter. My stomach was aching from all the fun and laughter we were having. Why was I afraid to meet these two girls? They were awesome. I loved them.

After we settled down, I slowly sat up, not wanting to feel anymore dizzy than I already was. We went through the fast basic questions you do when you meet someone new: favorite color, TV shows and so on. I really wanted to watch this *Client List* Rachel raved on about.

I found out Rachel loves to shop and invited me along to go with her and her mom tomorrow. Of course I agreed. At the beginning I was so afraid they wouldn't like me enough because I came from a rich family, but it turned out that their parents were wealthy as well.

Jade stood up and announced she wanted coffee. "It's coffee time! Coffee, coffee, coffee! Coffee time," Jade sang while picking up our dirty paper plates.

I looked at the clock on the DVD player to see it was five thirty and couldn't believe it was already so late in the day. I was having so much fun with Rachel and Jade. We all put our coats on and left the apartment arm in arm. Rachel and Jade's favorite coffee stand was just a block away from our place.

"I bet you anything Ray will order hot chocolate," Jade whispered in my ear as we walked in. And Rachel went right up to the cashier and ordered her hot chocolate just as Jade predicted. "Hot chocolate, Ray? It's a coffee stand." Jade rolled her eyes and ordered hers next: Venti regular coffee, extra light and extra sweet with a pumpkin scone on the side. I couldn't stand pumpkin anything; something about the spices made my nose turn up just at the smell. I studied the menu, reading over the mixed drinks. I didn't ever drink coffee, so I just ordered the first thing I saw – a Mocha Frappuccino.

I usually liked the smell of the coffee Isabelle made for my dad in the mornings. I remembered when I asked if I could taste his one morning; he shrugged at me and pushed his coffee cup towards me. I winced at the memory because it turned out that I didn't like it. I'd have to see how this tasted.

When our drinks were made and we spotted an empty table in the back of the darkened room, I studied my surroundings of the small coffee shop. Above the table we headed towards was a balcony with a pool table and a group of laughing guys leaning against the railing. They were watching us as they stood there, holding their pool cues, some of them nodding in our direction.

We sat down at the table when Jade started talking, "So this Big Bird thing." We all busted out laughing. I took a sip of my mocha coffee; the warmth of the smooth drink went down my throat and warmed my belly.

Oh holy hell. I'm in love.

"Good, huh, Gabs?" Jade asked me and I nodded, taking another drink of my mocha. When I set my half empty cup down, a little ball of rolled up napkin landed in front of me... then another, and then another.

"What the hell? It's snowing napkins up in this shit!" Jade shouted. Rachel and I snorted and looked up to the boys still leaning against the metal railing as they rolled up the napkins and tossed them down at us.

"Hey, Red," one guy called down. "Come on up here. I bet you can't beat me in a game of pool," he challenged and balanced a pool cue in front of his face and over the railing. I just hoped he didn't drop it on us.

Rachel looked back at me from across the table and winked. What the hell? Was she really going to go up there with them? Rachel stood up from the table, hot chocolate in hand, and made her way to the set of stairs, which led up to the pool room. More napkins started falling around Jade and I, and when we both looked back up, one guy with long black shaggy hair and a lip ring remained. He sent a wink towards Jade. She snapped her head back at me so fast; if looks could burn, Jade would be up in flames.

"What?" I asked, staring at her.

"He's freaking hot," she mumbled, then started chewing on her lip while her cheeks turned crimson.

"Hey cutie," he called out and did a little whistle, but Jade didn't turn her head back up to him; she just slowly sipped on her coffee and picked at her scone.

More napkins started falling around us again, but when I looked back up, my eyes met with another guy wearing a gray sweatshirt with his hood up on his head. He gave me a jerk of his head with a wink, clearly telling me that I should join Rachel and come up the stairs.

I looked back at Jade who was still chewing on her lip. I reached over to pat her hand to get her attention. When she glanced at me, I smiled, feeling very brave and ready to try something that I've never done before. "Come on, I'll go too," I said, standing up from the table as I pulled on Jade's hand to come with me.

Every step we made to the top of the stairs, Jade stumbled. I couldn't picture her being this way about anything.

When we reached the top of the stairs, the guy with the black hair met us. He stuck out his hand. "Hey, I'm Jett."

Jade pressed into my side; I gave a little push with my shoulder into her side to get her to introduce herself, but she just stayed silent. When I did it for a second time, she finally mumbled out, "I'm Jade." I smiled at her, knowing she didn't see me. Jett reached for her hand to shake it, then he pulled her away from my side. I nodded at myself in approval with a side smile while my inner self clapped.

I watched Rachel as she bent forward on the pool table and the guy that challenged her was behind her, teaching her how to hit the ball on the cue just perfect. I spotted an empty table by the rail and sat down, taking in my surroundings of the pool room.

Feeling the presence of another person next to me when they filled the empty chair, I turned my head to find the guy wearing the gray sweatshirt occupying the now taken seat. His hood was off his head and he was smiling at me. My knees started bouncing with my nerves.

Wow. Now he's cute.

I was immediately drawn to his bright, ocean blue eyes; his smile was hot as the one deep dimple in his left cheek deepened the more he grinned. I wanted to trace that dimple with the tip of my finger. His brown shaggy hair was styled in a messy look, like he just ran his fingers through it; it was long and flopped over one side of his head. His jaw line was strong and he had a perfectly shaped nose. He was the hottest guy I'd ever seen in person.

He reminded me of the guy on the poster in Jade's room minus the lip ring and tattoos.

"Hey, I'm Tucker," his voice strong and masculine sending chills up my arms.

"I'm Abigail," I thought I whispered that to him, but I guess I was wrong because Jade yelled from across the room, "Grandma Gabs." I laughed at her and hit my head with my hand, dumbfounded.

I heard Tucker chuckle next to me. When I looked back over to him, I could tell that I blushed, which made his smile widen and the dimple deepen.

Holy crap, his smile is to die for.

"Umm...Grandma?" he asked as his brows pulled together at Jade's nonsense statement. Of course that didn't make any sense to him at all.

"Jade thinks my name sounds like a grandma's name, so she started calling me Gabs."

"Gabs, I like it." He nodded.

"I like Tucker; it's different."

He leaned in, resting his elbows on the table as he looked deep into my eyes. My stomach dropped as my heart began to race. I tried to concentrate on my breathing, which wasn't helping my heart; it was only pacing faster. Right away, I could tell he was trying to read me, just like Jade had done earlier. But the way he was looking at me with his eyes boring into mine gave off this strong sense of power; I really liked it.

Tucker's eyes flickered down to my lips, then back up to my eyes. My breathing hitched in my stomach, giving me the worst case of butterflies. My head dropped and felt my face flush again.

"It's adorable that you blush so easily, but don't drop your face when you do. I'd rather see it." His statement made me look back up to him. "You should smile; it brightens up your cute face."

Right after he said that, I immediately smiled. Goosebumps raked up my arms and chilled down my spine. And here sat a deep draw I had for him to touch me...a brush of his fingertips against my hot skin. I couldn't help this giddy, happy feeling that started in the pit of my stomach and tingled throughout my body.

Tucker stood up from the table and held a hand out in front of my face. "Come on, let's put some music on and play some pool."

I actually hesitated and looked at his hand. I glanced around to see Rachel facing the guy who wanted to play pool with her; they were standing close to each other just talking. When I saw Jade over by the jukebox machine, she was also standing very close to Jett, who now was tucking a piece of her black hair behind her ear and dragging his finger across her cheek.

Tucker cleared his throat, then wiggled his fingers in front of my face.

"You shouldn't worry. Brad won't bite and Jett is a romantic at heart. Your friends are safe," he reassured me.

When I met Tucker's gaze, our eyes locked onto each other. The magic pull was back and drawing me to him, to be in his arms. I had never felt this way before, but Tucker was the first guy that I had ever been around. He was the only guy I wanted to be around in this way.

I slowly placed my hand in his. His hand was so strong in my little one and he led us over to one of the empty pool tables, his skin is soft against my palm, giving my hand one squeeze before he let go.

Picking up the two pool cues that were laid out on top, I watched him as he chalked both tips, then handed one to me. I had no idea how to play pool. I watched Tucker place a triangle rack at the top of the green felt table and start putting all the pool balls in the middle. Every once in a while, he would shuffle them around and then finally took the wooden piece off, leaving the pool balls in place. He walked around to me and placed a white ball where my hip was resting and faced me.

"Okay, you get to break."

"Break what?" I asked curiously. I didn't know I got to break something.

Tucker chuckled and shook his head. Realizing that wasn't what he meant, I was mortified to realize I was actually having a blonde moment .

Great, now I'm a dumb blonde. I needed to recover myself quickly.

"Sorry, I don't know how to play. Don't the balls just go in the hole?"

"THAT'S WHAT SHE SAID!" Jade yelled from behind us.

Everyone in the room with us started laughing at her little joke. I shook my head at the silly girl and felt the heat rise again to my face. After Tucker leveled out his breaths, he continued on with his instructions to the game.

"You hit the white ball into the group, and that's called breaking," he explained as he smiled.

I leaned over the table and felt Tucker's presence right beside me. My hands started to shake and I could smell his faint cologne on his body. Being right next to me, his height was overpowering. Taking a deep breath, I pushed with force on the pool cue and completely missed the white ball.

Disappointed, I stood up straight to stop my hands from shaking. I looked up from under my lashes at Tucker, and of course, he was smiling. His dark blue eyes in the dim light seemed so bright and I was lost in them. I bit my lip and looked down, hoping he would touch me.

"Hey, don't look down." His fingers tipped my chin up and our eyes locked once again.

This was the moment I thought he would lean in and kiss me. Then his thumb gently stroked my jaw line, and my cheeks heated back up as I gazed into his memorizing sapphire eyes.

"You're so beautiful," he whispered. His breath hit my face in a soft whirlwind. My eyes fluttered shut as I felt his body move closer to mine. I had never felt this way before with the sudden rush of being this close to a person and having an attraction to them. I mean, I had seen it happen in movies, but never had it happened to me.

When he didn't kiss me, my eyes drifted open to find his eyes tightly closed. Almost as if he was fighting himself, trying not to kiss me. Another disappointed feeling washed over me as I stepped back. His hand slowly dropped back to his side and he cleared his throat. Sadly, whatever shockwave passed through us was now gone.

Chapter Five

We had already played four rounds of pool when Carol called my cell. The ringtone for her wasn't music to my ears. I hit ignore and shoved the phone back into my pocket, watching Tucker place the pool balls in the triangle for another round...and this time, Rachel and Brad were betting against us. I already knew that Tucker and I were going to lose; it didn't matter who would be on my team. I sucked no matter what. I saw Jade sitting on a stool with Jett right next to her side. Even though I hadn't been around a group of people like this before, I was at ease around them, having fun and letting go.

"All right, it's on," Brad said clapping his hands and rubbing them together. "You goin' down, blondie," he said, pointing at me.

I rolled my eyes when Tucker leaned in to whisper in my ear, "It's all right. Watch this."

I turned my head towards Tucker's face; our mouths were so close together. I could feel his breath against my lips. The instant attraction was back with full force this time around. His hand brushed up against my hipbone, sending strong electric waves through my veins in the best way possible.

He turned away before anything could happen. I don't know if I was grateful or disappointed, but I was leaning more to the disappointed side. Tucker had treated me with nothing but kindness, even though I sucked at playing pool. I was lucky I made two shots each game. Tucker would just shake his head at me and laugh.

My cell started ringing again with Carol's annoying ringtone. I knew if I didn't answer, she would just keep calling. I held up my finger to Tucker who was taking the first shot into the game; he sent me a wink.

"Hello."

"Abigail, could you meet me for lunch tomorrow?" Carol asked me in a very calming tone. She usually just demanded that I would have lunch with her right there on the spot. So with her asking me, it was very different. Maybe my dad had a talk with her and she wanted to mend things with me.

"I think that would be okay. I'm going shopping with Rachel and her mom tomorrow though."

"All right, just email me a place and time. Good-bye, Abigail." Then she hung up. I pulled the phone from my ear and stared at the screen. The wallpaper of me and my dad smiling up at me made me feel remorse.

Carol just wanted me to email her a place and time. That was it? No argument, no demanding me to go? I was actually confused, but Tucker's presence made me quickly forget when he came to stand next to me.

"You okay?" he asked, meeting my eyes.

"Yeah, I am." I gave him an innocent smile, making all my thoughts of Carol disappear.

"Good, because I'm ready to show you what I have planned for Brad's big mouth."

I softly giggled at him, causing a piece of my hair to fall in front of my eyes. Tucker slowly raised his hand and tucked the stranded piece behind my ear, dragging the tip of his finger across my cheek. My breath hitched again deep into my stomach. I found myself stepping closer to his body, not wanting the touch to end. Why was the feeling so strong for him to give me my first kiss? I wanted it so badly. Was it wrong for wanting it so bad?

I sure hope not.

Of course, the thought of Tucker giving me my first kiss made me drop my head in embarrassment and start scuffing the toe of my boot on the carpeted floor.

"You've got to watch, though. Brad's not lying down on the ground," Tucker said to me before leaving my side.

I turned to face the table, watching Tucker walk around to the other end to where Rachel and Brad were talking. Both were holding pool cues in front of their bodies, swaying them back and forth in front of their faces.

"Excuse me, man," Tucker said. Brad faced his body towards Tucker's back. My eyes went to Tucker's face as he slowly leaned down onto the table. His fingers curled around the pool stick as our eyes locked again and he winked at me. Tucker pulled the pool cue back once, twice and the third time, he went just a little too far and hit Brad right in his nuts.

Brad grunted and went down for the count, holding his manly parts. I immediately started laughing at the sight of him dropping down on his knees, moaning in pain.

"Dude! What the hell was that for?" Brad moaned out. Rachel started laughing and rubbed the top of his buzzed cut head as he leaned on her leg like a puppy dog in pain and wanting attention.

Tucker pointed a finger in front of Brad's face and said, "Be nice to Gabs."

I laughed harder, very content with Tucker defending my honor. I honestly didn't see that coming;

he was my knight in shining armor. I put my cue on the table and went to Tucker's side. I reached up and wrapped my arms around his neck, laughing over his shoulder. I saw Rachel's eyes widen as I hugged him.

At first Tucker was stiff and didn't do anything to embrace me. When I started to ease my arms from around his neck, I felt an arm wrap around my lower back and press me closer.

I mumbled, "Thanks, knight," and pulled back. He had the biggest smile on his face, his dimple deep as it could possibly go in his left cheek. I couldn't believe my own action as my hand came up to trace the dimple. The feeling that shocked throughout my body felt so intimate and new to me. His smile slowly faded and his blue eyes softened, almost breaking my heart with the way he was looking at me as he slowly leaned more into my touch. Had no one touched him this soft and intimately before?

Tucker suddenly pulled out from our little bubble and stepped back. His eyes went cold and dark as he looked over my head. I turned to see a bald African American man standing at the top of the stairs. He was dressed in an all-black suit and wearing a gold pinky ring, his gold watch just peeking out from his black jacket. I turned back to Tucker who was still staring at this strange man, but from the look on Tucker's face, I knew the guy he was staring at was dangerous.

Brad kissed Rachel on the cheek and she gave him a playful shove. Then he slapped his hand on Tucker's shoulder.

"Come on, man, duty calls," Brad said, snapping his fingers at Jett who kissed Jade and walked towards the scary man. I watched Tucker for any kind of sign that I should step away and let him pass me, but his face was hard as stone, his lips pressed together in a strong line.

I stepped back from him when his angry eyes flickered at me as I moved away. I almost wanted to run in the opposite direction, but his hand reached out to grab my wrist and pulled my body back closer to his.

His tall body framed over mine, almost acting like a protective shield as he stood right in front of me. If I leaned into his chest, I knew that my head would fit perfectly underneath his chin. He looked down into my eyes as his hand came up to softly brush my cheek again, sending rapid chills down my spine. I definitely had never felt like this before.

"Will you meet me tomorrow at *Times 3*?" Tucker quietly asked me.

My conscience was screaming at me to say yes, but I couldn't get the words to come out. My head started nodding in agreement. My breathing went uneven as he leaned in. His lips were so close to mine; I shut my eyes, waiting for him, but he just said, "Night, Gabs."

And just like that, Tucker was gone.

As the three of us walked the short distance home, Jade rambled on about Jett and everything about him. Rachel kept looking at me with her wide green eyes almost falling out of her head. I found out more about Jett in the last five minutes walking home than I knew about Tucker. My thoughts drifted to him again as his name came to mind. I still couldn't quite tell what the look on his face meant when the strange man at the coffee shop interrupted our game of pool.

Learning to play pool with a guy was the way to do it. Sometimes, Tucker would lean on my back and move my hands on the cue to hold it better. I went along with it. When I touched his dimple and sadness spread across his face, my heart started to break for him.

"And he owns his own tattoo shop." Jade's words hit me, bringing me out of my thoughts as we approached our building.

"Who does?"

"Gabs, who do you think? Jade hasn't shut up about Jett since we left the coffee shop."

I looked at Jade who was standing in the middle and she blushed. Her pale skin turned bright pink as I caught her looking down at her shoes.

I leaned in to add, "I did see him kiss you."

"Shut your mouth, Gabs."

I giggled as we walked into our apartment building with a polite "Thanks" to Michael; he just nodded as he murmured, "Ladies," and tipped his hat to us.

After we made our way into the elevator, Jade started talking again – mostly nonsense about Jett – and I remembered that Tucker had told me where to meet him tomorrow.

"What's Times 3?" I asked, looking at the two of them.

"A club, Gabs. Duh," Jade answered me and Rachel nudged her shoulder.

"Why?" Rachel asked as she looked at me.

"Tucker told me to meet him there tomorrow. Oh crap, he didn't tell me what time, though." I chewed on my lower lip. He didn't tell me a time – now what?

"It's okay, Brad filled me in. They're going there around eleven. I already told him we'd be there." Rachel smiled at me. So I would get to see him. My conscience was jumping up and down in my head at the thought of being around him again. I was happy at that.

Once we reached the apartment, Rachel and Jade both got ready for bed and headed to their rooms for our first night here. I hadn't unpacked a single piece of clothing. I had no idea what to wear to a club – just the thought of seeing Tucker again made my blood race and my heart feel like it was going to pound right out of my bony chest. I unzipped my two large suitcases of clothes and dumped them right on the bed. I started flinging clothes around left and right, trying to find something that would be club ready. I had nothing, no surprise there. I had Carol as a mother for nineteen years.

Oh, Carol. I had so many mixed emotions for her right now. She raised me for nineteen years, paid for all my education, and my ballet lessons. I didn't agree with her most of the time we were together but yet she helped me achieve my dream. I'm here which means one more step closer to starting my classes at Juilliard.

Sometimes she was a cold hearted person but other times, she *was* there in her own way, even if it didn't come out nice. I didn't want to be that hateful stepdaughter that most stepmothers dreaded getting in a marriage.

My stomach flipped on the automatic switch, I had my body set to whenever I started to stress out about Carol. Feeling the bile coming up the pit of my stomach and hit the back of my throat in a rush had me racing to the toilet in a matter of seconds to throw up my coffee mixed with Chinese food. The smell of coffee mixed with my stomach acid made me sicker. The throw up wouldn't come out, it was stuck. I had two options. One: let it sit in the back of my throat until it settled down. Two: use my fingers and force it out. In the end, I used my fingers. I gagged into the toilet bowl, tainting it with my mess of problems. I rested my arm on the rim of the toilet and laid my head down, before I knew it, I was sobbing.

My soft cries echoed in the white porcelain bowl, when I felt a hand rubbing my back. I jerked up quickly and tried to recover myself, swiftly wiping underneath my eyes and turned to meet Jade's ice blue ones. No longer having black makeup on around them, she looked like a blue eyed angel.

"Damn, I knew you were just as messed up as I am." Hot tears ran down my face as I cried into my hand. Jade already knew about my problem within a day of living with me. I have been doing this for a couple of years now and not even Isabelle knew. Jade dragged me up and put me in front of the sink, she shoved me hard by the back of my neck, almost putting my head in the running water she turned on in the sink.

A cold cloth was placed on my neck and I continued to cry softly to myself. Jade pulled my hair up into a high ponytail to get the falling strands out of my face. No one has ever done this for me.

Taking care of me and being there for me at a time of need when I needed someone who could understand me. Jade handed me a new toothbrush, I watched as she headed into my room and shoved all my clothes off the bed to pull my covers back. I spit out the suds and rinsed, in just a couple of quick steps Jade pulled me back into my room and to the side of the bed and pushed me down to sit.

"Get some sleep, we've got a shitload to talk about tomorrow chick." Jade left my room. I tucked myself in and sleep quickly found me.

The alarm on my evil phone was going off on my nightstand. I roll over to put a pillow over my face to help drown out the annoying sound. My bathroom door bursts open and my pillow is tugged off my face. Rachel was standing there, her hair in disarray.

"Shut the devil thing off before I break it," she said through clenched teeth and then threw the pillow back at me and slamming my bathroom door.

Rule number one, Rachel was not a morning person. I could tell she enjoyed her sleep. I shut my alarm off and padded into the bathroom to brush my teeth again. Rachel was in the shower, steaming up the mirrors. Grabbing a towel to wipe it but it speedily fogged right back up. I really didn't need a mirror to brush my teeth so I didn't clear it again.

Jade came in leaning on the door frame, her smoking black makeup back on around her eyes. She was still dressed head to toe in black again but wearing this very cute white hat on the back of her head.

"You look cute," I tell her around my tooth brush.

She shrugged. "Thanks, I made coffee. Get dressed, and come out to the balcony."

I went back into my room where my clothes were everywhere. If Isabelle were here, she would probably hate me for destroying a room so fast. I put some of the clothes back on my bed, contemplating what to wear.

Rachel came in my room and sat on my bed wearing only a towel with her hair dripping wet.

"We're meeting my mom at Bloomingdale's in an hour."

Hands on my hips, "I don't know what to wear."

"Just jeans and a shirt will be fine. Do you know what you're going to wear tonight at the club or do we need to get you club clothes?"

I nodded, "I definitely need club clothes, just nothing provocative I guess."

"I'll think of something," Rachel said as she runs her fingers through her red wet hair then ringing it out on a pile of my clothes.

"Hey!"

Rachel giggled, doing it again.

"Whatever. What's Jade going to do?" I went back to my mess of clothes.

"She has to go meet with the people in her orchestra, plus she hates shopping and she buys everything in black anyway."

"I have to meet Carol for lunch too." I found a pair of jeans and tossed those on my bed. Now for a top.

"Cool," she said and I looked coldly at her, "or not," Rachel mumbled under her breath.

"Sorry, I just don't know yet."

"What's that supposed to mean, Gabs?"

"It's a long story and if I get it any of it straightened out at lunch, I'll let you know." I pulled on the jeans and a baggy pink shirt that hung off one shoulder. I padded over into the bathroom and brushed my hair out to pull it up in high messy bun.

Rachel walked behind me going into her bedroom dropping the wet towel in the process. I saw her reflection in the mirror and noticed she had a tattoo on her lower back, right above her butt. It was gorgeous, a beautiful, colorful butterfly with things curling around it in black.

"I didn't know you had a tattoo."

Rachel faced me exposing her breast in my direction and I quickly turned my head. I never saw a girl naked before and being in the same room, to be honest, it made me uncomfortable.

"It's okay, you can turn around now. I'm dressed."

I turned back as she walked into our shared bathroom. She wasn't dressed; she was only wearing a black bra and a matching thong when she stood right next to me. I didn't know where to look. If I looked at her, would that be considered creepy?

"I got my tramp stamp when I was eighteen, but totally regret getting it though. If I make it to L.A. with my acting, I couldn't do sex scenes, unless they caked it with makeup to cover it."

I applied very little make up when Rachel masked her face up with her own. "I could never get a tattoo. With my ballet, your body has to be perfect and getting a tattoo is just asking for trouble."

I watched her carefully put on bottom liner along with some along the top, shimmery browns with a hint of purple made her green eyes jump out from her beautiful face. She loaded her lashes with mascara and applied red lipstick to complete her look. She was beautiful.

I went into the kitchen and found Jade resting her hip on the counter sipping coffee.

"Took you forever."

Jade poured me a cup of coffee and I sipped it. I gagged on the taste. It was bland and didn't taste good. Jade snorted then passed me the cream and sugar. I loaded my coffee with sugar and little cream until I liked the taste.

"Come on, it's balcony talk time."

Taking my hand, we made it through the living room and out to the balcony. Jade pulled out her cigarettes and handed one to me, like we've been doing this for a while. This time when I inhaled the smoke, I didn't choke. I still got a little dizzy but it quickly ventured on its way. We sat in silence as we smoked together. I never pictured myself as becoming a smoker. I never really enjoyed the smell as I past someone on the street as they blew the smoke out. They taught us in school that it was all peer pressure and shouldn't give into it. Jade wasn't pressuring me though, she handed me one and I gladly took the stick. When we put our butts out and tossed them over the balcony rail, I picked up my coffee and started taking slow sips, savoring the warm taste, letting it warm my belly.

"Gabs..."

I looked up at Jade, she had her eyes closed with a saddened look. Her brows scrunched up together like she was trying to find a way to talk to me without hurting me.

"I know that you threw up on purpose last night." I took deeps breaths as she spoke those words to me. They were just has hurtful as if I told my dad that heartbreaking news. My stomach quivered and my knees started to bounce with my shaken nerves. I anticipated what she was going to say next and I was scared that she would reject me for what I do.

She let out a breath, "I cut."

I had to remember to take deep breaths as she spoke to me about the reasons why she cuts. The pressure from her stepmother, her father not loving her, the nights when he got drunk and yelled at her for looking like her dead mother. She also explained that's why she wears the black makeup around her eyes, she disguises herself, to hide the pain for her dad, and that's all she told me. She didn't need to go into any other sort of detail about her dad not loving her. I'm sure he loved her, just showed it differently.

Jade's stepmother, Stella, didn't sound like a very nice person. She actually sounded ten times worse than Carol, which was very surprising. I didn't even think that could be possible. Jade told me that Stella called her mother a failure so many times for taking the chicken-shit way out and ending her life. Jade smacked Stella's face when she said that. Stella then called the cops and pressed charges against Jade because she was eighteen. Jade spent the night in jail. Her dad wouldn't even come get her.

"I cut to help the pain that I carry. I know it's not the smartest way to deal with it, but it's the sting that comes with it. Instead of yelling at Stella, I hide in the bathroom with my razor blade and slowly cut on my wrists. My dad saw it first and threatened to put me in a mental hospital, so I started cutting where he couldn't see it."

Jade pulled up her black long-sleeved shirt until she was at the top of her shoulder where she struggled. At first I didn't see anything like on her wrist or the top of her arms but when she turned her body sideways and showed me the back of her arm above her elbow, small lined cuts were there, about ten rows of red lines.

Tears formed at the corners of my eyes and they slowly slipped down on my cheeks. I quickly wiped them away before Jade could see them. My heart broke for her, Jade was in pain like me and didn't know how to let it out without hurting anyone, but yet, it still would hurt everyone the longer we both held it in.

"I haven't done it though since I left. I don't know jack shit about making yourself throw up, but I know it's not healthy and I'm hypocritical in that department because I know what I do isn't healthy."

No, it wasn't.

Jade's words sliced and diced my heart as I listened to her. I couldn't explain the way I was feeling at this moment. Carol wasn't as bad as Stella but she sure was right up there, with her nastiness and step monster material.

Jade and I had another cigarette right before Rachel came out to the balcony. She sat down on Jade's arm rest and wrapped her arm around her shoulders then gave a kiss on top of Jade's head, in a loving sister way.

"Gabs, my mom is here," Rachel said while Jade tossed me her pack of cigarettes that I barely caught through my shaking fingers.

"Trust me, if you're going shopping with Rachel and her mom, you'll need them." Jade winked as Rachel playfully smacked her arm causing Jade to wince, but I only saw it.

"I thought we were going to meet her there?" I asked.

"She wanted to come get us instead," Rachel shrugged at me.

Passing our door man Michael with his very polite greeting of *Ladies* to us. I giggled like a school girl at him with a nod.

A silver Range Rover was parked out on the curb as we made our way outside the apartment building. The nice mid-September sun was beaming in warmth and the door of the parked car opened before Rachel and I even came close to it.

"AH! Rachel baby!"

A tall Barbie of a mother came rushing out of the car and contained Rachel in a very big hug, knocking Rachel off her feet and landing right on her butt with the Barbie on top of her. Michael came out in a flash, helping them up to their feet as they giggled to each other.

"My baby, I've missed you so much."

"Golly mom, I've been gone one night, chill out," Rachel joked.

The Barbie looked over at me with a warm smile and walked towards me. Her tight jeans and orange tube top so low, she almost could spill over if she jumped me as she did Rachel.

"You must be the ballerina Rachel told me all about. You could be a ballerina, you have that look." Her green eyes sparkled at me as she pulled me into a small hug.

"Nice to meet you Mrs. Dawson."

"Oh come on girlfriend, please call me, Trish."

"Okay, Trish."

"That a girl. Come on, let's shop."

And shop we did. Trish was a shopaholic, every store we went into she had to buy something, even if it was the smallest thing, and she had to buy it. We had to stop at the Range Rover four times because we couldn't carry all the shopping bags.

"Gabs, you *have* to buy this," I turned to see Rachel holding up a hanger with what looked like a tiny piece of fabric. The color was very pretty, in its dark deep purple color.

"Is is a top?"

"Yeah, try it on."

"No way," I shook my head, feeling my cheeks move.

Rachel didn't listen to me as she pushed me into a dressing room. I sat on the little seat in the corner and stared at the purple top, chewing on my bottom lip. Do I try it on? I debated back and forth with myself.

I groaned at my conscience and finally tried it on; I wasn't going to come out of the room though. Rachel would just have to wait until tonight. When I stepped out, Rachel whined at me for not coming out of the dressing room, I shrugged.

She held out another hanger at me, this one was a black mini skirt. "You'll need a bottom with that top." I snatched it out of her hand, knowing that she was right.

We shopped all day long, Rachel told Trish about the apartment and her school schedule and how excited she was to start Juilliard with me. I was ecstatic as well. Finally being in an actual ballet studio with other ballet dancers my age, gave me the chills and nerves started up in my stomach. I couldn't help myself but be nervous, I couldn't explain it. Rachel told her mom about the guys we met last night at the coffee shop and right when she was going to say something about Tucker, my phone buzzed in my pocket. I frowned to see it was Carol calling me.

"Excuse me," I said to Trish in the middle of Rachel's story.

"Hello."

"Abigail, you never emailed me a place and time." She used her Carol tone, the one that made sure you knew you did something very wrong and made you want to hide.

"Sorry, the time got away from me." I rolled my eyes at my little fib.

"Don't make excuses Abigail."

"I'm not," I snapped at her and Trish looked at me with worried eyes.

"Meet me at Café Tortella in twenty minutes before brunch is over." And she hung up the phone. Nothing pissed me off more than when Carol hung up on me. I angrily shoved my phone back in my pocket and stomped my feet back over to Trish and Rachel.

"I have to go meet Carol for lunch, Rach."

"Okay, you're done, right, Mom?"

"No, but we can drop you off."

Rachel rolled her green eyes and Trish copied her. They looked just alike when they both did that. The car pulled up to the Café and I already saw Carol had a table outside. Her perfect legs crossed in her crème colored pant suit. Her hair perfect as usual too.

"Thanks for the ride," I told Trish.

"You're welcome, doll and don't forget your bags." Trish handed me my bags of clothes I bought with the little number Rachel insisted I buy for tonight to meet Tucker.

I climbed out of the SUV to make my way towards Queen Bee. She didn't stand up as I approached her side. Her perfectly shaped manicured fingers were just laced together. I immediately started to shift from the heels of my feet to my toes. I know I got so nervous over the stupidest crap and it's one thing I hated about myself.

"Abigail, sit down."

I grumbled, "Give it a rest Carol."

"Abigail. Sit." Her tone was nothing but sharp and firm with me.

She knew she still had over some sort of power over me and I hated it. I tossed my bags over on the seat next to the one I plopped my butt into.

Carol slowly leaned forward, "Abigail, we need to discuss us."

I rolled my eyes at her, "Why?" I asked, crossing my legs under the table.

"Stop rolling your eyes at me. It's very unladylike. Your father and I agreed together, we wanted tell you about Shannon when the time was right. So far, the time has never been right. You had your practice for

Juilliard auditions, your father is always working, and I was busy myself. It just never came up."

I asked myself, how you could leave behind a little detail about someone that they weren't your child. I slumped back into the metal chair and let Carol continue on.

"I loved your father while he was still married to Shannon. I had to respect his wishes that he wasn't going to leave her for me. I couldn't force him to leave her and I wasn't going to pressure him into it either. He made his choice and gladly walked away from me."

"How come you can't have children?"

Carol inhaled a breath at my words, hitting a soft spot.

"After your father left, I met another man who didn't treat me well, hit me, raped me, and used my parents for money to buy drugs. Then I got pregnant and my father forced me to get an abortion or he would cut me off from the family. He told me if I got the abortion, he would take me back in. So, I got the abortion but I bled too much afterwards because, it's not like now days where it's quick and easy. When your father and I got married, we tried to get pregnant, but I couldn't. A doctor told us I had a lot of scarring and it wasn't possible to carry my own child. I know because of the mistakes I made, I could never carry a child of my own."

I watch as Carol drops her head, her hand coming up to rub her forehead. I heard a sniff and saw her shoulders bounce as she silently cried. I was frozen in my seat; I couldn't move to go to her. I just sat and watched her cry. I'm sure any woman would be heartbroken to find out they couldn't carry a child. I know I would be.

"I didn't want you to turn out like I did and disobey us. I wanted to shelter you, protect you from all the evil that's out here in this world. I tried and it all fell apart the moment I laid my hand on you in the kitchen. I should have never had done that, and I apologize and I hope you can forgive me."

She tried to protect me. That statement replayed in my head, she tried to protect me. It was making sense, how could one protect a child and have that child live in fear of them?

We didn't say much to each other as we ordered and ate our food. I couldn't eat; I pushed my food around my plate like so many times before. I was still contemplating what Carol had to told me. She went off the deep end, was in a nasty relationship that didn't end well and had an abortion. Carol had a freaking abortion. I knew with what she told me that back then, you had to be very wealthy to get one done, and now some doctors will do it just because. I didn't have anything to say to her; I had to think about what all went down today. Carol paid for our lunch and I decided to walk home, to have time to think about Carol had told me. I knew my apartment wasn't too away from where Café Tortella was, only a couple of blocks at the most.

My shopping bags started to feel heavy the more I walked. I passed a cute little book store that caught my eye, so I retraced my steps and made my way inside the cozy little place. I looked at the rows and rows of books, from children's books to the romance covers. When I pulled a book from the shelf showing a guy with long hair and a woman's 1800's dress falling apart at the seams. A guy cleared his throat, as I gawked at the cover with my mouth hanging open.

"I call those books, bodice rippers."

His voice startled me as I quickly put the book back on the shelf, as if I just got caught stealing. More books fell around my feet as I dropped my shopping bags. During the messy process, I bent down to pick them all up as the stranger did the same for me.

"Thanks," I mumbled.

"You're welcome."

I smiled, remembering that certain voice that was imprinted in my brain.

Tucker

I looked up and met his blue eyes with a disheveled piece of hair in his eyes. He was wearing a black V-neck shirt and dirty ripped jeans across his knees. His smile was priceless, making his dimple show. We stayed crouched down just staring at one another. He was really so cute. He grabbed my hand to help me back up. I smiled and looked down at the ground.

"Hey Gabs."

"Hey Tucker," I glanced back up to him with a wide smile, "what are you doing here? Stalking me?" I playfully ask, my bad way of flirting.

"Actually, I saw you from across the street, came to say hey."

"Well, hey."

As nonchalantly as possible, I turn back to scan more books. I can still feel Tucker standing behind me. Nervousness filled my stomach as I looked around and he still wasn't moving. I pull out a couple of historical books and read the backs. Tucker was still standing there, motionless. I wonder what's going on in his mind as he watched my back, not speaking to me. I re-read the same lines over and over again on the back of the book, not grasping the meaning or the story line. I peeked over my shoulder to see Tucker just staring at me, watching over me as I decided on a book. I smiled and turn back.

My conscience screamed at me to do something, flirt, talk, smile at him. While I debated with myself, Tucker spoke.

"Are you coming to the club tonight?"

"Maybe," I tried to flirt with him setting the book back and picking up another to start fake scanning, "why, you want me to go?"

I softly hear footsteps come up behind me, his chest barely touching my back, light as a feather.

"I most definitely want you to be there." His knuckles brush my upper arms, and I catch my breath. My hands started to shake as I tried to hold the book up to pretend to read the back. But truth be told, my vision started to go blurry because I was staring too long in one spot, taking in the feel of his fingertips on my flesh, concentrating more on my breathing, trying so hard to even it out. But it wasn't working. How badly I wanted to lean against him.

His breath hot on my earlobe as it travels down the front of my neck causing me to shudder. Giving in at my body was wanting, leaned back onto his chest. I turned my head, our mouths a hair follicle away from each other.

Oh, I want his lips to kiss me. His blue eyes blaze so hot into mine, I find myself leaning forward towards him. But he pulled back and stood up straight, slightly moving away from me.

"I'll see you there then."

Tucker turned on his heel, and left me. Now, I was gawking at him as he left the bookstore, with this odd feeling racing through my veins. Man, what's the matter with me? I've only known the guy for a flippin day. One part of me was screaming, too fast. Slow down. But the other part was thinking about his gorgeous blue eyes, his smoldering smile with that perfect dimple in his left cheek and all I wanted to do was run my fingers through that thick mess he called hair. All my thoughts about too fast went right out the window and the little devil on my shoulder jumped for joy.

Chapter Six

I sat on the toilet as Rachel teased the crap out of my hair and every time I said "ow" or whined from the evil pull, she would smack the top of my head with the brush. I ended up spilling my guts to both Rachel and Jade about Carol. Told them everything, well...except for my purging. Even though Jade already knew, Rachel didn't and I was going to keep it that way.

I explained about Carol not being there, and the pressure she always put me under. Then about yesterday and how my dad told me about Shannon. Every time I thought about my birth mother, I would grab my necklace and slide it back and forth on the chain. I wondered what kind of mother she would have turned out to be. If she would have put pressure on me or just let me be my own person. Rachel gave me a small frame that fit the size of Shannon's picture and I put it on my nightstand.

Rachel pulled my hair again and I screamed.

"Oh baby, knock it off," she scolded me, "you're being a wimp, even Jade doesn't complain when I do her hair."

"That's because I don't let your nasty hands touch my hair."

I giggled as Jade entered our bathroom and climbed into the tub, crossing her ankles with her arms around the rim, making herself right at home in the jetted bathtub. Jade still hasn't changed to go to the club.

"Why aren't you dressed yet, Jade?" I asked, as I looked around Rachel and she hit me again on my head with the damn brush, obviously telling me to hold still. "Gah, would you stop hitting me?" I whined.

"Hold still and I'll hurry faster," Rachel argued back at me while I glared at her.

Jade chuckled and stared up at the ceiling, "I feel so bad for you right now."

Not coming to my rescue, Jade just sat back in the whirl tub and watched Rachel dress me up like her own personal Barbie doll. When my hair was done, make-up was next. I opened and closed my eyes so many times they were starting to dry out. She put many coats of lipstick on my lips, then stuck a piece of toilet paper out and told me to blot.

Wide-eyed I asked, "Huh?"

Rachel rolled her eyes at me, "Open your mouth." I did and she put the toilet paper almost in my mouth, "Now smack your lips together," and when I did, my lips stuck to the toilet paper.

Rachel patted my shoulder, "Okay, now you're done."

"Good," Jade mumbled under her breath, "I can't watch anymore."

My butt was seriously completely numb from sitting here for too long. I stood up and looked in the mirror.

Holy, crap.

My jaw dropped in awe as I took in my new look. My blonde hair was in long loose curls with some poof. I'm guessing that's why she would tease my hair then brush it out a million times. My make-up was heavy on my eyes, but made the caramel color stand out. I must admit, I looked good, really good.

"Rach, I'm pretty," I smiled, the red lipstick making my pale skin and teeth stand out.

"Freaking gorgeous. Now let's go," Jade got out of the tub and left the bathroom.

"Yay," Rachel clapped her hands in approval, "now, go get dressed," She jostled me in the direction of my bedroom. Then I remembered the outfit Rachel insisted I buy.

Oh crap.

I pulled out my shopping bag containing my still tagged clothes and dumped them on my bed. I held up the very short black skirt and purple tube top. I really didn't want to wear this; what if I fell out everywhere?

Oh boy, I was suddenly very nervous to go out into public and wear this, but I had to pull up my big girl panties and suffer through it.

Wait. I paused in the middle of tearing off a tag, what panties should I wear?

"Rach!" I yelled and looked at Jade, who smirked at me. I knew she was thinking the same damn thing I was.

"Yeah?"

"What a...what underwear should I wear with this?"

She laughed at my question, causing Jade to laugh and collapse down on my bed.

"Hey guys stop, I'm being serious here," I put my hands on my hips and let them cool off as I started taking my shorts and shirt off.

"Oh Gabs, you're funny," Jade exclaimed at me.

I ignored her; if they weren't going to answer my question, then I had no choice but to wear my black panties. I pulled them out of my side dresser drawer when Rachel snapped them out of my hands.

"You're not going to wear the grandma panties; I actually bought these for you while you were at lunch with your mom." Rachel's finger held up four different colored thongs and matching bras hanging up by a hanger.

"Wear the white thong, and no bra with that top. We'll meet you out in the living room."

I dressed in the very little amount of clothing that I bought today. And I've never worn a thong before, it felt like a pure wedgie up my butt, but whatever. I pulled on the purple tube top and every time I pulled it up higher on my chest, it rose higher on my belly and more skin would show, but when I would pull the bottom down, the top would go lower, showing more cleavage then anything, and I wasn't wearing a bra.

I groaned in defeat by a stupid piece of clothing that was fighting with me. I couldn't put myself in a bad mood; I was going to go see Tucker.

I went into the bathroom one more time to check myself out. I couldn't believe the work Rachel had done to make me this beautiful. I lacked in the beauty department, not that I was an ugly person. I just didn't get how to use makeup. I loved the way the dark color brought out my caramel eyes, the red lipstick with my pale hair and skin, was just beautiful; I smiled. My outfit on the other hand, was the least amount of clothing I have ever worn, but the skin tight purple top, brought out the skinny curves at my sides, and the black mini skirt made my skinny white legs look super long. Shoes, I'm missing shoes.

"Rach! What shoes?" I called out while walking out of my bedroom. Seeing Jade on the couch all ready to go, Rachel stood at her feet holding up a pair of purple pumps that matched my top perfectly. I slipped on the shoes, which were taller than what I was used to.

"All right, let's go." And we left the apartment.

We took a taxi to the club Times 3. I've never heard of it, but Rachel and Jade raved about it, telling me it the hottest club in New York right now. I still pulled at my top up and every time I did Rachel would swat my hands away and I would grunt in disapproval. Rachel then explained that she gave up on primping Jade because Jade would either throw the clothes away or just burn them. Burning designer clothes, just saying it, broke Rachel's heart and I just giggled at the face she made. It was heartbreaking seeing her bottom lip, pushed up over the top in a big puppy dog frown.

The club had a long line out front, but as Rachel walked up to the big bouncers and tossed her red hair over her shoulder, baring more skin. "Hey guys. How long's the wait?"

The two men just look at each other. "How about a dance later, when I'm not working?" The bouncer asked and then winked.

"You got it," Rachel clicked her tongue at him and he pulled the red rope free to let us in. The club was pounding away at the speakers, with music I was definitely not used to. Jade grabbed my hand to lead the way over to an empty table that faced the dance floor. The lights were fogged over and went in every direction while the bodies flooded the dance floor, grinding on each other. I have only seen this kind of dancing in movies, where the guys and girls ground all up and down on each other, with their hands on their butts.

"Hey, Hey, Hey." I turned as Brad, Jett and Tucker came to our table. My eyes went straight to

Tucker's as he sat across from me, which made me somewhat upset, as I wanted him next to me. He still wore the same outfit as before in the book shop, his hair was styled and flung over to the side. His eyes found mine as he just stared at me across the table with the little light flickering between us. The more he stared at me, the more I wanted to walk over to him and sit next to him. Of course, I couldn't, I didn't have the nerve yet. I looked back over at the dance floor and leaned on the metal railing, when the first round of drinks showed up at our table. Rachel and Jade lifted their drinks up and clinked their glasses together with Brad's and Jett's. Tucker sat still like me but he's eyes were now on the dance floor.

"Gabs!" Rachel yelled at me.

I leaned in closer to her, and even though we were sitting right next to each other, I still had to yell, "What?!"

"Drink this!" She tried thrusting a drink at me and I shook my head. I was only nineteen, way under the influence. Rachel glared at me and thrusted the drink back at me. Giving in under peer pressure, I took the glass and took a sip. It wasn't that strong of a drink, but I could tell when the alcohol hit my stomach, causing it to burn my stomach lining.

The last thing I wanted was to sip on it. I gulped the rest down in five seconds flat and cringed my face. I heard a chuckle and looked over at Tucker; he was smiling and still watching me. I smiled at him, his blue eyes were so intense and a strong pull started to happen between us. I couldn't tell if he was making me feel this way or the alcohol, but either way, I wanted him.

Jett stood up, pulling Jade along with him, and Brad and Rachel followed leaving Tucker and I alone.

The four of them went on to the dance floor and started dancing, getting lost into the bumping music while fading in the crowd.

"Do you want to go dance?" Tucker yelled, but I didn't answer him; I just made my way over to the dance floor, hoping I was being sort of seductive, because that's what I was shooting for.

The alcohol sure did make you brave when you would drink it. The things peer pressure does to you.

I made my way onto the dance floor to let my body sway to the rap music. The only way I knew how to dance was up on my toes with straight legs to very soft, slow music. This music was different, so I just let my body move to the beat. My eyes were shut and my hips were moving back and forth when I felt a large pair of hands on my hips from behind me. I turned to face him, but when I opened my eyes, expecting Tucker, I was shocked to see that it wasn't. It was the African American who was at the coffee house. I tried to pull away, but he was a lot stronger than me and kept me in place. When I got ready to yell, he pushed a finger on my lips to silence me. I started to panic and shake. What was this man going to do to me? I didn't want to stick around to find out. I started to fight him, pulling my arms away when he locked both my wrists behind my back.

His face was pressed up against my cheek as he spoke into my ear, "Stay away from Tucker – this is your warning," then gave me a little push, causing me to stagger back on my high heels into a group of people. Someone turned me around and I stared into the eyes of Tucker. I shoved at his chest to make him let go of me. I didn't understand why that man told me to stay away from him; it was the last thing I wanted. I didn't know anything about him, though. I was still shaking when I realized I was actually afraid of Tucker. He could be everything the news cautioned every girl about; a rapist, a murderer, a criminal. I tried to fight against him, but he wouldn't let go.

"Let go of me!" I shrieked as he grabbed both of my wrists in his one hand.

"Gabs, stop!" Tucker yelled.

"Stay away from me!" All the thoughts of what he could do to me were making me more uneasy. I had to get away.

"Let her go, Tuck!" Jett yelled from behind me and Tucker immediately let go. Jade wrapped an arm around my lower back and tugged me out a side door where smoking was allowed. I was trembling from Tucker and from the other guy who caused it all.

Quickly, Jade lit up a cigarette and handed it to me. "It'll help calm your nerves."

I puffed on it. It did help the shakes go away. When I finally felt calm enough to talk, I faced Jade who was smoking her own cigarette. "Who was that guy, Jade?"

"Jett just said he's Brad's second boss, whatever that means. Jett is talking to Tucker about it, I guess."

"So what does that mean?"

"How the hell should I know?"

Jade and I finished our cigarettes in silence and I was stubbing mine out when Jett walked outside. His black hair hung in front of his eyes and he chewed on his lip ring.

"I'm sorry about that, Gabs. That's Brad's second boss; his name is Jeremiah and Brad owed him some money, so he was looking for him," Jett explained to me while rubbing the back of his neck. His brown eyes almost felt like they were pleading with me to believe him. Jett wasn't the type to lie; he was more Jade's style and tells you how it is. But then again, I only just met this group of guys earlier yesterday.

"What does Brad do?" I asked.

Jett let out a breath and stepped next to Jade. "I can't say. It's not right, though. You can trust Tucker; he's a good guy. Tuck helps Brad out when he can. You could be something to him, ya know? He likes you."

The squeak of the door opened as Tucker stepped outside. My eyes locked with his and whatever that Jeremiah guy warned me about went good-bye. But I had some answers to find out. There was something about Tucker that I wanted; I couldn't quite tell what it was, but whatever it was, it was strong. I wanted him. Tucker walked towards me and held his hand out in front of my face. Not even thinking, I put my hand in his and he pulled me to him. The strong attraction was back between us. I felt if he would just hold me, it would all go away as if he was my shield. I wanted that. Who cares if I just met him? When you know, you know, and you should never let go.

"I won't hurt you, Gabs. I promise," he reassured me, and all I could do was nod at him.

We walked back inside the noisy club; the music was louder than before. We made it to the dance floor when a song came on that was familiar to me. I heard it in one of the stores with Rachel today. I couldn't remember any of the words; I just remembered the whistle part. I turned in Tucker's arms as he placed both of his hands on my hips to sway to the rap music. My arms went up around his neck as we started to move together while the beat played.

Every time the whistle came, Tucker would whistle in my ear, sending rapid shivers down my spine and chills up my bare legs. I pressed closer to him as his hands roamed around my back, not going any further than my lower back. I felt his lips pressed against the crook of my neck and shoulder, and I was lost in him. I couldn't believe something this strong was happening so fast.

We were so close, I couldn't tell where he ended and I began. Having him this close to me made me forget everything that Jeremiah guy warned me about him. Sooner or later, I would find out what he meant about Tucker, but not right now. I just wanted him as close to me as possible. My hands never left Tucker's long hair; it was soft to the touch. My fingernails scraped his scalp as he bit into my shoulder. My legs went to jelly and he pretty much had to hold me up. This was amazing; I had no idea dancing could feel this way. His hands got a little daring as he moved them down to my butt to press me closer.

We continued to dance for at least five more songs, just grinding on each other. His hands were all over my body, from my butt up to my shoulders and every time he passed the sides of my breast, I would get chills that would spike down my back, leaving goose bumps on my hot skin. The club was getting hot because of all the bodies crowded on the dance floor. I really wanted some air and a drink; at this point, I didn't care if it had alcohol or not.

I motioned with my hand up to my mouth, indicating to Tucker that I needed a drink; he nodded and led me off the dance floor. I scanned the club, looking for Rachel and Jade, but couldn't spot them. Tucker placed his hand on my lower back to have me follow him to the bar. A couple of guys were fighting and they got heaved out of the club at us. I stumbled and Tucker protected me as best as he could. I stumbled again and he pushed the group of wild men off me.

Tucker waved his hand up to get the bartender's attention, ordered his drink, and then looked at me. I nodded and he held up two fingers. The bartender was fast at making our drinks; each had a slice of lime. Once we had them, we headed to the back door to go outside, and the empty space confirmed we were going to be alone with each other.

Tucker hopped up on the ledge and took a sip of his clear liquid drink; I also took a sip and winced at the strong alcohol.

"What is this?" I pointed to my glass.

He chuckled. "It's a Gin and Tonic. Don't you like it?" he asked, taking another sip of his.

Other than the lining of my stomach burning off, I guess it was something to get used to. I took another sip because I really needed something to drink.

"Come sit with me, baby girl." He patted the cement next to him. I hopped up as gracefully as I could in my mini skirt and high heeled shoes, then took another drink. I could feel Tucker's eyes on the side of my face as I turned to look at him and he smiled, which made me grin like an idiot.

"So, what's your deal?" he asked.

"My deal? What do you mean?"

He shrugged. "Give me the basics."

Thinking about what to tell him, finally I said, "I just moved out of my parents' house and into an apartment with Rachel and Jade. Umm..." I bit my bottom lip, trying to think faster. "I'm starting Juilliard on Monday."

"What's Juilliard?"

My head snapped sideways at him. "You're kidding right?" He shook his head at me, "Juilliard is one of the most prestigious schools for music, ballet, some acting, and artistic skills." His brows shot up at my statement.

"Wow." He really did seem shocked at my best explanation of Juilliard.

"What do you do?" I dipped my finger in my drink and poked at the sliced lime, then put my finger in my mouth to get rid of the stickiness. When I looked back at Tucker, he was staring at my lips.

I sucked in my bottom lip. "What?"

"Ah...nothing." He downed the rest of his drink in one big gulp. "I tattoo a little bit at Jett's tattoo shop, just apprenticing for now."

"You tattoo?

He nodded.

"That's awesome," I said, ecstatic. "I wish I could draw, but I wasn't so blessed in that department."

"It takes a lot of practice. Anyway, what are you going to Juilliard for?"

"Ballet."

"Really?" This time I nodded at him and smirked. "Now, it takes talent to do that... toe thing I've seen those chicks do."

I tipped my head up and let out a laugh. Boys... they would never understand ballet, not even my dad.

"I'm serious – that's awesome you can do that."

Tucker hopped down and tried to balance on the point of his Converse shoes like a ballerina. His knees were bent with his arms straight out as he tried everything to keep his balance up, but couldn't. I laughed some more at his effort. I had to give the man some credit here for trying, and I knew he was trying to impress me, which was so cute.

I smiled as I watched him until he finally gave up. He looked back over at me with his piercing blue eyes that made my knees quiver and the pit of my stomach get a wave of butterflies. Tucker walked back over to me to rest his hands on the tops of my knees. As a reflex, I sat up higher at his touch, straightening my spine as he stared at me. The electric pull was happening as my heart raced and my hands shook. I didn't even know what to do with my hands, so I just held them together, hoping he wouldn't notice how nervous he was making me.

He breathed out heavily, "You know how beautiful you are?" as his hands traveled a little more up my bare legs. My breathing picked up as I took in the sensation of this feeling that started to travel throughout my body. My eyes moved down to his lips and then back up. Tucker slowly moved his hand from my leg and tenderly brushed his knuckles across my cheekbone. My eyes drifted shut as I took in the feel of his soft fingers. When I started to open my eyes again, his face was a lot closer to mine and I started to lean in for a kiss. I felt all sorts of giddiness as I readied myself for my first kiss. Tucker leaned in more and I could feel his breath on my lips. Our lips were a fraction apart when the door to the inside of the club opened and Rachel stumbled out laughing with her arm draped around Brad, with Jade and Jett on their heels.

"Tucker!" Brad exclaimed and came stumbling over to Tucker to pat him on the back.

I sat up in a rush, almost falling backwards; Tucker grabbed my arms to steady me. "I'm just gonna get down," I smiled as his hands went under my arms while I slid down the front of his hard body. Just from that, I could tell he had a great firm frame, which I wanted to explore with my hands. Just the thought made me blush, I looked down at my toes and his finger tipped my chin back up to his face.

"Don't look down," he whispered and gently pecked my lips. I barely had any time to react when Rachel started speaking.

"Gabs, we're heading back to the apartment. Jett and Brad are coming. Are you, Tucker?"

I barely heard Rachel's words as I continued to feel Tucker's soft lips against mine. My fingertips came up to my lips to touch them – to remember the feel and the zing shock that was left there.

"Earth to Gabs?" Rachel whined and waved her hand in front of my face. Jade pulled it down back to her side.

"Leave her alone," Jade snipped.

Now feeling like a complete idiot, I came out of the funk that I was in. Everyone was staring at me like I was a crazy insane person touching my mouth. I looked at Tucker, who had a smirk on his face. It was stupid I was feeling this way. I bet that didn't even count as a real kiss.

"Yeah, that's fine," Tucker answered while grabbing my hand to lead us back through the club. We made it out front while Brad held a taxi. Rachel, Jade and Jett climbed in the back.

"Dude, you're gonna have to get another taxi," Brad told us, obviously seeing there wasn't any more room.

I piped up before Tucker could say anything, "It's okay, we're gonna walk."

We watched as Brad climbed in and the taxi took off. We started our walk not saying anything and we didn't hold hands; I kept my hands together and in front of me. I felt silly right now, walking with him when I was just happy that he pecked my lips. I had to say something to break the dreadful silence.

"Are you from around here?" I questioned, looking up at him.

"Bushwick."

"Aah."

I'd heard of Bushwick...all I knew that it was the worst part of Brooklyn. It was infested with drug dealers and gangs, people were always getting robbed, and there were frequent shootouts. That was why I always loved the main city of Manhattan; I felt safe living in it. Just thinking about going to Brooklyn gave me the chills.

"What about you?"

"My parents have a house over on Fifth Avenue."

"What do your parents do?"

"My dad is a Criminal Justice lawyer for the city and my mom...I mean Carol, doesn't do anything besides shop," I snorted. That was the best way I could describe Carol in a way that wasn't mean. I looked over at Tucker who was staring at me as we continued on walking.

"What?"

"You called her Mom, then Carol. Spill, baby girl," Tucker said as he reached for my hand and interlaced our fingers together.

Staring down at our hands, I started talking. "Carol is my stepmom."

"That's not so bad, having a stepparent. I would rather have a step than none at all."

I glanced up from our hands to the side of Tucker's face. He stared straight out in front of us, his blue eyes lost in his own thoughts.

"Do you like it there?" I wondered.

"Where?"

"Bushwick."

He let out a huff and laughed, "No, I don't, but it's the best I can do for right now."

We walked in silence some more, just holding each other's hands. I know I sighed a lot during our walk, reveling in the comfort the little gesture of handholding brought to me. I snuck glances up at Tucker, knowing he knew, but he only gave me a side smile; his deep dimple in his cheek was so cute when I caught a glance of it. I really wanted to keep talking to him; I didn't get how we were so close to each other dancing and getting along just fine while outside the club, but now we had nothing to say to each other as we walked home. Our shoes were now the only noise lingering in the air.

"Wanna play a game?" he asked, breaking our silence.

I looked at him with a slight smile. "A game?"

He nodded.

"Sure."

"Truth or dare."

I stopped as I took in his words of the game he wanted to play, "Are you serious? We're not in junior high here."

"Come on, live a little."

"Okay," I mumbled.

"So truth or dare, Gabs? I can picture you being a truthful girl." I chewed on my lip some more. If he wanted me to live a little, then I was going to shock him as best as I could.

"Dare," I said.

He stopped and glanced at me; our hands separated, but I kept walking with my head held high. I heard his footsteps pounding on the sidewalk as he ran back to my side.

"Dare?"

"Uh huh, unless you're the one who's scared," I playfully tossed back at him.

"Nope, I don't think you'll do it though."

Ha. I faced him and crossed my arms. "Try me." I tapped my high-heeled toe.

"I dare you to..." He stopped to think, turning his head to look at the street. I suddenly got scared that he would dare me to streak in the street in front of taxi or something like that.

"I dare you to... kiss me on the cheek," he said as he eyed me. That was easy; I could do it. It was only his cheek. I stepped towards him until I felt my toe hit the top of his foot. I cupped his face to turn his head, his skin so soft under my palms. I could feel his stubble beginning to grow, but it was more soft then stiff. Right before my lips collided with his cheek, he turned his head and smashed his lips to mine.

Sneaky little devil, my conscience told me.

Tucker's hands locked behind my waist to tug me closer to his hot body. His lips were soft as velvet and his tongue touched the seam of my lips, wanting in. I gladly complied. As soon as our tongues rubbed together for the first time, my knees went weak as my hands gripped onto Tucker's shirt. Passion surged through my body and my knees started to quake. The chills ran from the very top of my head to the very tips of my open toed shoes. One of his hands glided to my butt and I sighed into his mouth; his tongue was softer than his lips. I melted into his body as I enjoyed my very first kiss.

A cab drove by and honked at us as we slowly pulled apart from our little embracement. I pouted to myself when the kiss came to an end; my heart was racing, pumping my blood throughout my body, making me hot. Our bodies were so close, I could almost feel his heart beating just as fast as mine as we stood there, just holding each other.

"I'm gonna do that again before the night is over," he half growled at me, while sweeping my hair off my shoulder and tenderly pecking my tingling lips again. I was totally fine with that.

"Your turn," he murmured so softly, then left me with a quick peck.

We played the little game of truth and dare as we continued our walk to my apartment. I didn't want any more dares; even though Tucker moped at me. I just blushed and kept walking. Tucker said dare every time it was my turn. I dared him to do stupid things, like ask directions from people and wrap his legs around a light post like a stripper pole. He would drop his head in shame as I kept doing it.

"Come on; give me something good to do if you're going to dare me. You can dare me to kiss you." I blushed at his comment. I really wanted to kiss him again, too, but couldn't find myself to dare him to do it.

We rounded the corner to the block my building was on and Michael opened the door for us, nodding his head and saying, "Miss Abigail", and tipped his hat.

"Thanks, Michael."

"You have one of those door greeter people. He only didn't greet you, but totally said hey and then tipped his hat." I laughed out loud as I dragged Tucker into the elevator. The elevator ride was quiet while Tucker just held my hand. I couldn't stop thinking about his lips; I desperately wanted them back on mine. That's all I could think about. Why was I even debating that this was fast. Who cared?

I peeked over at Tucker as he stood in the elevator with me; the pull started to happen as we locked eyes. My chest rose and fell with each of my rapid breaths, trying to help me breathe. Tucker took one step towards me, before capturing my face to kiss me again.

Oh yes.

His tongue entered my mouth as soon as I opened up to him. I gripped his elbows as his thumbs stroked my cheeks, holding my face still as he devoured my mouth with his hot tongue. The ding of the elevator pulled us from each other as we made our way to my apartment door.

Jade and Jett were sitting on the couch. She was under his arm as he played with her long black hair.

"Hey," I said to them, their eyes not leaving the flat screen where a movie was playing. I jumped when the scary man with a chainsaw came out of nowhere, chasing a half-naked girl.

"What's this?"

"Texas Chainsaw Massacre," they both said at the same time. Tucker sat on one of the black chairs; their eyes continued to watch the horror movie.

"I'll be right back." But I don't think they even heard me over the loud scream from the naked girl getting hacked into pieces with blood spraying everywhere.

I went to my bedroom to change out of my little clothes and the shoes that were killing my feet. I had to get out of them. Whoever designed shoes like this was crazy. I threw on my black sweats with a pink tank top and made my way into the bathroom to wash off the makeup and brush out my long blonde hair. When I was done, I heard soft moans coming from inside Rachel's room. I listened then caught, "Oh, Brad!" from Rachel's pleasured mouth.

I gasped and covered my mouth, hoping they didn't hear me. Rachel was having sex with Brad. I rushed out of my bathroom and back down the hall to plop myself in the other chair next to Tucker. I couldn't stop hearing Rachel's moans in my head; I couldn't believe she was already sleeping with him. I thought stuff like that only happened in movies.

The roaring chainsaw made me jump out of my thoughts about Rachel's moans. I heard Tucker chuckle, and when I looked over at him, he patted his knee. He was obviously hinting I should sit on his lap, but my body froze and a horrid thought entered my mind: was Tucker here to get laid, too? Was he gonna use me? My eyes went to Jade who was staring right at me; she apparently understood the look I was giving because she stood right up and walked over to pull me out of the chair and outside to our balcony.

Jade shut the door and quickly sat down in one of the chairs, lit up a cigarette and then tossed me the box. I pulled one out and lit up, then sat next to Jade, tossing the box of cigarettes on the little table between us. She was quiet, which didn't bother me at all. I felt like I needed to clear my head a little bit. We both finished, and then flicked our butts over the railing.

"You ready to talk yet?" Jade asked me.

I turned my head lazily at her, "About what?"

"What freaked you out? I saw it in your eyes when Tucker wanted you to sit with him."

Just knowing that Tucker was still inside my apartment, sitting there all hot and by himself, made me feel bad that I freaked. "Rachel is with Brad," I whispered.

"So? What's the problem?"

I huffed, "I don't know, I guess I just wasn't expecting to hear it when I went into the bathroom. Then having Tucker here..."

"You think Tucker wants a one nighter?"

"Yeah, I guess I just freaked out," I explained, waving my hands all in the air.

"Pretty normal for a virgin."

I was stunned; I didn't even know how to process that.

"Jade, I know I'm different and new to all of this and...."

"Just let go, Gabs. Everything that you were taught by that step monster of yours – let it go. Let loose. So what if he's here to have a one nighter with you? At least it's something you can scratch off your list or something."

I shook my head vigorously. "I'm not that type of person, Jade. I like him. I want to get to know him and I don't want him to use me."

"And I won't."

Jade and I both turned to see Tucker hanging halfway out the door, listening to our conversation. Why did it feel like I just got caught with my hand in the cookie jar? We watched as Tucker stepped out of the doorframe and stood right in front of me. The night wind picked up, whisking his hair from one side of his head to the other as it drifted across his blue eyes. I really wanted to move the pieces away from his cute face.

"I'm going back inside to finish the movie," Jade told us as she stood up, patted the top of my head, then left us. Tucker reached for the cigarettes on the table and took one; he held the box out to me, but I shook my head. I watched him put the cigarette between his lips and it seemed like everything was in slow motion as the little light of the flame flicked on and he tipped his head back to blow the smoke out above him, the wind sweeping it away into the night air. Watching

Tucker smoke was the hottest thing I'd ever seen. I think I had drool dripping from my mouth.

His head dropped back down and he met my eyes. "Do you really think I'm going to use you for sex?"

The first thing I did was shrug like a girl in high school would. "I don't know you, maybe."

"Well, let's get to know me." He folded his arms again.

The first question I thought of was a main one I knew every girl wanted to ask a guy. "Do you have a girlfriend?"

"No, next."

"Married?"

"Nope," he said, taking a pull from the cigarette.

"How old are you?"

"Twenty-five, next."

My mouth dropped open; I had no idea he was twenty freaking five, he didn't look like he was that old. If I had to guess, I would say twenty-three at the most.

"You don't look twenty-five."

"I'm very immature," he joked.

I giggled and he smiled. "When's your birthday?"

"August twenty-third." He lifted his hand to take another drag and blow out the smoke high above him.

"Do you go to school?"

He shook his head. "No."

"Where do you live?"

"I already told you – Bushwick, Brooklyn."

"I asked where you were from before, not where you lived."

He let out a big breath. "You got me there. I live with my mom and her loser ass boyfriend."

From his tone of voice, I could tell it was a soft spot. Tucker eventually finished his smoke, and then sat down next to me.

"Have you ever been to jail?"

Tucker grabbed my hand, rubbing small circles on the top; he let out a breath and shook his head. I continued on asking Tucker ridiculous questions, and he repeated the process to me. I relaxed more and more with his enjoyment; he smiled and then his little dimple would show. Tucker stood up and smoked another cigarette as we laughed at the sight of Brad coming out to the balcony looking, well, satisfied with his short brown buzz cut and rumpled clothes. Brad sat outside with us as he smoked another one of Jade's cigarettes.

"Come here, baby girl," Tucker said as he held out his hand to me. I stood up to take the couple of steps and stood in front of Tucker. His hands rested on my skinny hip bones, and our hips fit nicely into each other's. He took another drag then flicked the butt over the rail, tipping his head back to blow out the last bit of smoke that was left. When his head came back down, our lips were so close together again, but Tucker didn't kiss me. His intense stare caused me to shudder, but his hands came up to rub my arms, like I was cold and he was trying to keep me warm.

"Let's go inside," Tucker whispered to me, lightly kissing me. He tasted like fresh cigarettes and it didn't even bother me. We turned to go back inside my apartment while Rachel met us at the glass door, wearing nothing but a long shirt.

"Hey Gabs," she greeted me with a smirk, passing us to go sit with Brad as he finished smoking.

We sat on the chair that Tucker was sitting in before and he pulled me onto his lap, rubbing his fingers up and down my arm. I felt so relaxed against him. I knew Jade was right; I really needed to let loose and become my own person. So, I laid against Tucker's hot chest and let him caress my arm with his fingertips. I jumped against him as the man with the chainsaw came back and hid my face in his chest as his arms enfolded tighter around me.

"You okay?" he whispered.

I looked up at him and nodded. "I'm not a big fan of scary movies," I admitted.

Tucker stood up from the chair with me still cradled in his strong arms, then he turned us to face the chair. "Grab that blanket."

Grabbing the blanket and he sat back down. He tried his best to cover me with the little throw blanket, but I ended up just putting most of it over my face. Tucker chuckled and slouched down; one of his arms was wrapped around me while the other was over my legs, and he rested his hand on my butt.

I wasn't uncomfortable as I thought I would be; I embraced the feeling more than anything. At the soft touch he was giving me with the leisurely strokes on my arm, I shut my eyes tightly and tried to concentrate on my rapid breaths that were coming on rather quickly. My body was starting to get hot, and I felt my face start to sweat from the little space between me and the blanket.

Couldn't stand to take the heat anymore; I ripped the blanket down from my face and gasped for the cold air. Tucker laughed at me some more. "There you are." Then he kissed the top of my head.

"I wondered how long you were going to last under there," he said while squeezing me tighter against him. My fingers found the drawstring to his hood and I weaved them in and out through my fingers. Every time my hand came up just a little bit, Tucker would quickly peck my knuckles.

I didn't care to watch the movie as I was pretty content with the way I was right now. I glanced up at Tucker, who was still watching the movie. My eyes took in the sight of his gorgeous side view with his strong jawline and high cheekbones while his blue eyes shimmered in the dark light as the movie flashed in them.

Suddenly, he smiled and looked down at me as if he knew I was watching him. Our eyes locked for a moment before his started to roam all over my face before finally landing on my lips. I bit my bottom lip as he stared intently at it, his hands gripping my butt and arms tighter with each passing second.

I no longer paid attention to the horror movie that played in front of us; I mainly focused on Tucker's fingertips. Up and down, ever so slowly, his hand moved to my back and tugged on the ends of my hair, then he ran his fingers through it, causing my eyes to get heavy and start to drift shut. The next thing I knew, I was asleep in Tucker's arms.

I woke up lying down on the couch with the small blanket covering me. The Saturday morning sun was blaring in the windows and my eyes burned as I tried to open them. I felt someone shift behind me and turned my head to see Tucker behind me, asleep. I smiled. He was just as gorgeous with his eyes shut as when they were open. I turned back and wiggled closer to his body; as I did so, he draped his arm over my side and laced my fingers with his.

"Morning, baby girl," he cooed in my ear and I shivered. "You cold?"

Feeling my face actually get warm, I mumbled, "No." I moved closer to his body and he groaned. I turned my head to look over my shoulder and our lips were so close together. Getting up the nerve to just move that fraction of an inch was eating away at my insides, my conscience pretty much yelling at me to do it. I stretched my toes to make me a little taller and I tenderly pecked his soft morning lips. His hand came up to cup my cheek with his thumb softly brushing my cheekbone. I closed my eyes and took in the feel of it.

"What you going to do today?" Tucker asked as my eyes opened back up.

I shrugged. "I don't have any plans."

The thought of spending the day with him made me feel so special. I wanted to spend more time with him. I had to admit, I was falling for him and I wanted to get to know him more.

"Do you want to come watch me tattoo today? Spend some time with me, get to know me?"

"Really?"

"Sure, why not? Jett lets me take the easy clients for now until I'm all done with the apprenticeship."

"That sounds great," I said while sitting up on the small couch. I looked back over at Tucker and giggled.

"What's funny?" he asked.

"You have like, no room," nodding at his smashed body.

Tucker looked down at his toes; he looked completely smashed against the back of the couch with absolutely no space on the tiny couch. It looked like barely enough room to breathe, let alone sleep with someone.

"Well, at least I got to cuddle with you, baby girl," he said and I felt my face heat up so fast at his words. I shook my head, trying to make a curtain out of my hair so he couldn't see me blushing.

Tucker grabbed me around my waist, to haul me back on him. "Get over here," he growled playfully, then he started tickling me. I screamed and giggled as his fingers pressed into my sides, and my legs kicked at his as I tried to get loose from his stronghold. I tossed my head back and connected it right with his face, hitting him straight in the nose. Tucker grunted out in pain, letting me go and sitting up, tilting his head back over the couch cushion.

"Oh, Tucker, I'm so sorry. Are you bleeding?" I stood, waiting for him to answer me. If he was bleeding, then I could get him something. His hands cupped his nose as I stood there impatiently, waiting to see if he needed ice, a towel, anything. I hoped he knew that it was an accident.

"Tucker," I whispered to him as I was starting to get a little worried, but then his hands dropped with no blood showing anywhere and he was smiling. He was smiling; my heart stopped racing and I could exhale again.

"Gotcha," he joked and grabbed for my hands that were clenched together at my sides. I let out a big breath.

"You scared me," I told him as he pulled me on his lap and kissed my hair.

"Sorry, I couldn't help it."

"That wasn't funny," I pouted as I poked him in the side, which made him jump and the top of my head hit his chin.

"Oww," I rubbed the top of my head and he kissed it. We sat together in silence until we heard footsteps on the hardwood in the hallway. We both looked over to see Jett and Brad walking to us.

"Tuck, Jeremiah called. We gotta go, say bye bye, lovie," Brad said as he walked past us to the front door, then left. Jett held back to wait for Tucker; Jade came out in the living room and Jett put his arm around her shoulders. I got off Tucker's lap and moved into the kitchen to turn on the coffee machine for Jade. I knew she loved her coffee and cigarette in the morning, plus it was our balcony talk time. It was becoming a thing of ours.

I stopped to think about what had happened since I moved out of my parents' house. I made two really great new friends that I was quickly becoming close to and Jade understood me in every way – if that was even imaginable – given the short amount of time we had known each other. Then we met the guys and Tucker, who I liked the more I was with him. He could make me laugh, and I even loved the little game we played on our walk back to my apartment as we got to know each other a little more. Then waking up in his arms felt like the cherry on top; his arms were perfect to be in, strong and masculine.

Moreover, I was falling for him. Despite the warning that I was given by that guy, Jeremiah, I didn't care. What wasn't there to like about Tucker? He was definitely cute and a good dancer, except for when going on pointe. I laughed at the cute little memory. Jade walked into the kitchen and drew me from my thoughts, and I opened up the cupboard to pull out some black mugs.

"The guys are getting ready to leave," she spoke, crossing her arms.

But before I could answer, Tucker and Jett were standing at the front door. Jade went into Jett's arms as I stared at Tucker. Even in the morning with his shaggy brown hair all ruffled up and messy with it flung over to one side, he was so hot.

"Come give me a kiss, baby girl."

My stomach dropped at his command, my eyes locked onto his and found myself walking straight into his arms. Both of his hands cupped my face as he pressed his lips to mine; our mouths opened for one another and as our tongues touched, I knew I was a goner. I found myself wanting things I never thought I would imagine, but if it was with Tucker, I didn't care. All my thoughts disappeared as we deepened the kiss and I was lost.

We slowly drifted apart. "Rain check on the tattooing and quality time?" he asked. I just nodded and he kissed me again.

Once the guys left, Jade and I made our way out to the balcony to have our morning time together.

Jade and I talked on the balcony until lunch time. She was head over heels for Jett. It was really cute the way they just talked all night, getting to know each other. They were exactly the same in every way. Jade even told me she opened up to Jett about all the problems with her stepmom and dad. She didn't, however, tell him about her own little problem. I still couldn't imagine someone doing that to themselves. We talked about getting help together. Of course, Rachel would be left out of the loop, but it felt good to have someone by my side about my bulimia. I hated myself for doing that when I would stress out. I knew it wasn't a good thing to do, and I despised it more whenever I did it. Not talking to Carol actually helped me; it felt like more of a weight was lifted off my shoulders.

A little while later, Rachel came out with a cup of hot chocolate and the worst case of rat's nest hair I had ever seen. Jade and I smoked while Rachel told us about Brad. Apparently, sex was all Rachel wanted from him.

"We have nothing in common," she told us over and over.

I was sad at the thought she wouldn't see him anymore since Jade was with Jett and I was with Tucker. It was something like right out of a book. I spent the rest of my Saturday afternoon out on the balcony, talking, laughing, and just having so much fun with my new friends, who were quickly turning into my sisters. We just connected. I would look at us and think, Rachel was the top, like the glue that would hold us together. Jade was our entertainment for the group. And I was the newbie, watching from the sidelines. The more we chatted and laughed, I found myself more open than ever.

I didn't hear from Tucker the rest of the day. I was really disappointed because every time Jade's phone went off, she would look at the screen and giggle. Tucker and I didn't even exchange numbers. It was simple; I was jealous. I even found Rachel giggling like a schoolgirl at her phone. When I asked her about it, she would tell us it was Brad, but that was it. Jade kept whispering to me that Rachel loved to play hard to get, and that was exactly what she was doing to Brad. She loved getting chased.

"Should we cook something tonight? I really want to try out the kitchen," Rachel told us. Finally getting up from our chairs outside, we went back inside. I checked my phone to see that it was no longer afternoon but six thirty. Once I noticed the time, my stomach growled. Jade and I smoked one more time, and when we were about finished, the doorbell rang. I turned to see Rachel letting Jett in the apartment through the glass windows, but no one else. Disappointment must have been written all over my face because Jade patted my leg with a smile.

"Don't worry. I'm sure you'll see him soon."

Jett came out with a wide grin at Jade, his black hair hanging in his face as he chewed on his lip ring. Just like a couple that has been together for at least a couple of months, Jade lifted her cigarette to him and he took it to finish it.

"I'm gonna go help Rachel," I told them, standing up from my chair. Jett blew out some smoke while reaching into his pocket, then handed me a folded piece of paper.

"Tucker wanted me to give you this."

I opened it to find little digits written down. I smiled to myself and held the little piece of paper so close to my chest. I didn't want the wind to catch it and have it be long gone. My inner high school girl cheered.

I sat on the couch and entered the numbers in my phone. I debated back and forth about texting him or just waiting it out, but I finally gave in and texted him.

Me: *Hey, it's Abigail.*

My legs bounced as I waited for my screen to light up and when it finally chimed, I was all sorts of giddy. I felt my stomach do a one-eighty turn, then slam down, giving me the worst case of butterflies.

Tucker: *Hi, baby girl.*

I quietly giggled to myself at the nickname. I had to admit, though, that I really liked it when he called me that. I stared at my screen, thinking about what to say next, but Tucker beat me.

Tucker: *Whatcha doing?*

Me: *I'm sitting on my couch*

Tucker: *That thing about killed me*

Me: *Lol...sorry : (*

Tucker: *Don't send me a pouty face*

Me: *Sorry*

Tucker: *Stop saying sorry. It's not your fault. I liked having you close to me*

My insides were on fire. I liked being with him, too. I couldn't tell him that yet, though. My phone chimed again.

Tucker: *When do I get to see you again, baby girl?*

Me: *I don't know. Rachel is cooking dinner. You wanna come over?*

I waited, really hoping he didn't think I was being too needy or anything. I really did want to see him again.

Tucker: *Wish I could, but can't*

Me: *Oh, okay.*

Tucker: *Don't be so sad*

Me: *I'm not sad :)*

Tucker: *Hahaha...Now I get a smiley face? Is Jett still there?*

Me: *Yes, he's outside with Jade*

Tucker: *Wish I was with you right now.*

I stared at my screen for the longest time. He wished he was with me right now. I wanted to jump up and down from reading that little sentence. I'm sure my face was bright red as my cheeks creased clear up to my ears from my smile. So I took a chance.

Me: *I wish you were here, too :)*

Tucker: *Oh, miss me do ya?*

Me: *Maybe*

Tucker: *Yes or no...there's no inbetweenie*

Me: *Inbetweenie? Is that even a word?*

Tucker: *Yep, right between a yes and no*

I barked out laughing and smiled like an idiot at my phone when Rachel came out of the kitchen.

"What's funny?" she asked while pointing the spatula at me.

"Inbetweenie," I giggled with a smile.

Rachel just shook her head and went back into the kitchen. We texted back and forth for a little bit, but when I sent my last message, he didn't text me back right away.

To help get my mind off my phone, I decided to help Rachel in the kitchen. Slicing up peppers, she roasted some chicken and we steamed some rice. I kept checking my phone, waiting. Nothing came again that night as we ate dinner. Nothing came as I helped clean up the dining room. Nothing came as Jett and Jade curled up on the couch and started the movie, *Chuckie*. What was with them and scary movies? I would never understand it. I checked my phone again before I hit the bathroom to get ready for bed.

Still nothing.

Chapter Seven

Tucker's lips were soft against mine as I tangled my fingers at the nape of his neck and then entwined them through his hair. His tongue caressed mine as he possessed my mouth in soft slow strokes. His tongue rubbed on the roof of my mouth, sending the strongest shivers through my body. I sucked in his bottom lip as he growled deeply in my mouth.

Now we were lying on the couch with Tucker on top of me, his thumbs tracing my cheekbones, brushing my hair off my neck. He broke our kiss and moved down behind my ear, causing me to moan and arch my hips forward to grind against him like on the dance floor at the club. His hand made its way down to cup my breast firmly as his hips put pressure down on my sensitive area. My hands found their way back into his hair, but he grabbed them and pinned them above my head, grinding hard in between my legs.

Tucker's lips were now on my collarbone, lightly biting me as he pulled my tank top strap down to softly kiss my shoulder. Moving across my chest to the other side, my nipples tightened and my toes curled at the sensation of his lips moving carelessly across my scorching skin. Excitement fluttered around in my stomach as he pulled my shirt down and moved lower on my chest.

My pelvis went upward as a hot, needy feeling started to make me quake at his desire for my body. Tucker came back and attacked my mouth in a hungry mode. I moaned as he growled in my mouth, his hips pushing down and grinding so hard against me.

Something was happening; as he pushed more and more, it became the most pleasurable feeling I had ever felt. He pulled back to look into my eyes, his eyes such a beautiful blue that sparkled. He bit his lower lip while pushing against me again, making me cry out as his forehead landed on mine and I started to combust. At the same time, a loud, obnoxious beeping sound was going off in the distance.

BEEP. BEEP. BEEP.

My eyes opened at a snail's pace. *Are you serious?* I groaned, but I didn't shut my alarm off right away, and that resulted with Rachel barging into my room to slam her fist on it to shut it off like she always did when it would wake her.

"Your clock is super annoying," Rachel huffed, tossing a pillow on my face. I left it there, because the coldness on my hot face was so refreshing from my dream.

Wow, what a rush.

If a dream felt that good, I couldn't even imagine what the real thing would feel like. A dead knock sounded on my bedroom door and a very dawdling Jade walked in, landing on my bed face first.

Her black as night hair feathered around her head as she mumbled "I don't want to go to school," into my comforter.

I yawned. "It won't be that bad," I grumbled in my tired voice that croaked like a frog.

"It's gonna suck."

Rachel came back in and smacked Jade right on her butt, causing her to yelp and jump off my bed.

"Get up, lazy." Jade tossed over her shoulder at me before she left my room.

I dressed in my black leotard and black stockings, then pulled on sweats with flat shoes. I got myself ready in ten minutes – pretty good for the first day of school. My hair was slicked back into the bun and when I came out of the bathroom, Jade rolled her eyes. I knew she hated my bun, but I had to wear it back. Rachel made coffee and bagels and then we were off to school.

"I have to wear it like this."

Jade rolled her eyes. "Whatever."

Michael had a cab waiting for us, but since we lived down the street, we opted to walk instead. We made small talk about the weekend; Rachel spilled her guts about her one nighter with Brad, and her face was red as she told us every detail. I think my face flamed up as well.

"I don't think we'll go any further than that, though."

"Can you go any further than that?" Jade snickered while I giggled.

"Shut up! You know, we won't carry on a relationship. What happened Friday was it. We have…"

"Nothing in common," Jade and I both said at the same time.

Jade quickly changed the subject. "You excited for your class, Gabs?"

I thought about it and supposed that other than being bat crazy nervous, I was a little excited. "I guess. Nervous is more like it."

"I know, my orchestra teacher told us that we will be playing your first ballet in a month," Jade told me.

"What are you practicing?"

"He didn't say. I'm sure we'll find out today, though."

Jade played the cello, but she explained that she would never practice at our place and if she were gone, she'd be at her parents practicing and we weren't allowed to come over.

"How are things with Tucker, Gabs? Brad told me Tucker can't stop talking about you," Rachel giggled at me and Jade gave her a playful push. I felt my face get warm as I gripped my strap to my gym bag.

"Leave her alone," Jade defended me.

"It's fine, we get along great so far. I like him," I nodded, smiling.

Tucker, oh goodness. Just thinking about his lips against mine made me want to skip school and find him to finish that wonderful dream that I was having.

Since we lived just down the street, it wasn't that far of a walk. We didn't have any classes together. Rachel was on one side of the building for acting classes, Jade was on another side with orchestra, and I was in the middle for ballet. We split up and of course, in the process of trying to find my first class, I got lost. I even asked people that were walking in the opposite direction where the ballet room was and they all ignored me. My sense of direction was terrible. If you told me to walk in a straight line while chewing gum, I would choke on my gum and possibly fall over my own feet.

The last bell rung. Running down a long hallway with my ballet bag slung over my shoulder and my class schedule in my other hand, I hoped I was at least headed in the right direction. I was watching the numbers on the doors so I wouldn't pass it. Right when I looked down, the door came up a lot faster than I thought.

I slid on the floor in my flat shoes, balancing myself with my arms, trying to stop myself, but I fell on my butt with my ballet bag hitting me right smack in the face. I bolted upright off the floor as fast as my body would go, getting dizzy in the process. When I crossed the threshold of homeroom, every girl at the barre was staring at me, including my new teacher.

"Look who decided to cause a ruckus and join us with her presence."

My eyes met the lady at the front, tall and skinny with very short black hair.

"Hello," I waved at her. She folded her hands in front of her and raised a brow at me. So far, this wasn't good first meeting.

"Get in line," she told me through clenched teeth.

Quickening my steps over to the corner where we stored our belongings, I shucked off my sweats and pulled out my ballet shoes. I stretched my toes back and forth, then slipped and laced them up tight. I walked over like I was taught to the barre with my head held high, toes pointed with each step. I ended up at the back of the line of the rows of girls, all dressed like me, noticing only one boy in our class.

"Now that all twenty of us are here, we can begin," my teacher barked. "You all have been selected to take my class for a special reason. You may think you are the best, but you're not. You are here to learn to *be* the best. Just because you've been accepted, doesn't mean you belong here. There are over one hundred ballet dancers this year, and I expect every one of you to claw your way to the top. I want you to cry, your feet to bleed, and for you to be sore and stiff."

The girl next to me dropped her head, almost as if she thought she signed up for hell instead of a ballet class.

"My name is Madame Ava; you will treat me with nothing but respect. You do not talk back to me when I give you direction or a command. You will be on time to class; if the music starts to play when you walk through that door, you will get a warning. You will come to class clean and well put together. Ladies, we have a dress code. Black leotard with pink tights, keep your hair tightly pulled back and off your face. No ponytails or braids; you make it the traditional ballerina bun. Boys will wear a white shirt with black tights."

The girl next to me grunted. "This lady is intense," she whispered to whom I didn't know. Madame Ava marched right over to us with elegance and beauty, but the look on her face with her blue eyes pierced the girl standing next to me.

"What did you say?" she gritted through her teeth.

Just from that approach, you could tell she was mad. I could feel the girl's body go hard and stiff as she stood next to me. Madame Ava stood there waiting for her to answer, but the girl said nothing. She started to shake and stutter, trying to hurry up. Madame Ava's face grew impatient and she started tapping her slipper on the wood floor.

"What's your name, miss?" she asked annoyingly. Her blue irises started digging into the girl's face. She wasn't giving in.

"Bethany," the girl's voice shook with each of the syllables of her name.

"Bethany what? Don't you know how to introduce yourself properly?"

The girl took in a shaky breath, "Bethany Rackham."

"Well, Bethany Rackham, you just got yourself a warning on the very first day of school. Switch spots." Madame Ava nodded at me. Bethany looked over in my direction with scared wide eyes and very slowly, we switched places.

"Good. Now shut your mouth and be respectful."

Madame Ava walked back to her spot in front of the class. I heard Bethany take a deep breath and I could just tell from the noise that she was going to break down very soon. Bethany was right, though; Madame Ava was gonna be tough on all of us.

"Dancers are polite to teachers, to guests—anyone who walks through that door. I expect one hundred percent respect. Any rudeness to teachers or your peers will dismiss you from class. We do not lean against any walls, the barre or the piano. If you do not know where to stand, ask me. Yawning, talking, whispering, or having any private giggle session will dismiss you from class. You are here to listen, watch and learn. When I ask a question, I expect you to say, *'Yes, Madame Ava'*. Are we clear?"

"Yes, Madame Ava!" we all called out to her and she nodded her head in approval.

I knew there would be a lot of rules. Ramón warned me before I even tried out for the Juilliard program.

"Jasmine," Madame Ava called out and we all watched as the beauty stepped forward to stand at her side. This girl was gorgeous, with her piercing brown eyes as she stared each one of us down. When her eyes landed on mine, she stared me down like something a popular girl would do in high school. This studio was hers and she wasn't going to let anyone take it. And I wasn't going to take her staring at me. I made it here; I deserve this just as much as she did.

"Jasmine here is a second year and one of my top students. If I am not here, I expect you to listen to her as if she were me. Is that clear?"

"Yes, Madame Ava!" we all announced together.

"Very good. Jasmine, you may return to the leading line." Madame Ava held out her hand, guiding her back to the front of the line. Jasmine strode with grace as she walked back to the barre. "I expect you all to line up at the barre. Same place as the day before. Jasmine is the head of the line. You do something wrong, and you can expect to be at the end of the line like poor Miss Bethany."

As a class, we all turned our heads in time in Bethany's direction. I shifted on my feet, but tried my best to keep my back straight and eyes forward.

"Let's begin," Madame Ava clapped at us.

We started with stretching—first with our left legs, placing them on the barre and then bending forward, touching our toes for a deep stretch. Holding that position for thirty seconds, we then switched to the other leg. Then we all squatted down on the tips of our toes, holding onto the barre with our hands, finishing with lunges on both legs.

Madame Ava made it to each one of us as we stretched and warmed up our muscles. When she made it to me, she pulled on my shoulders, straightened my spine, and lightly tugged on my bun to line my head up with my spine as straight as I could go.

"Now, all face me." And just like we are her little puppets, we all turned. "The first ballet we are going to practice for is *Swan Lake*. I expect all girls to try out for the part of Odette and Odile. It's going to be a tough part to play, with being beautiful one scene then evil the next."

My insides jumped up and down. I had been practicing my soul out for this dance. I worked on it just a couple of weeks ago with Ramón. Madame Ava started the music and gave us instructions to complete these turns with leaps.

Of course, Jasmine went first. Her position for a start of pirouette was perfect, her back perfectly straight with her stomach was tucked in. Her front arm opened with grace as she propelled her turn for a one single pirouette up on her toes, ending flawlessly with a quad pirouette.

The rest of the team did their turns of a pirouette, some losing their balance and stumbling. Madame Ava didn't even give them a second chance as she just moved onto the next person.

The closer Madame Ava got to me, the more I wanted to run out the door. I was afraid I would fall. I knew how to spin *en pointe* during a pirouette, but it was being under the pressure that had me so nervous. I started to breathe heavily, shutting my eyes and focusing on the sound that filled the room. The classical music of *Swan Lake* was very soothing as the violins played.

Madame Ava then chose that moment to clear her throat at me. I opened my eyes and she was standing in front of me. I held my breath. Her lips were pressed together in a hard line, her hands laced together, waiting just for me to begin. I stepped away from the barre and positioned my legs just like I was taught. My spine straight, head high and aligned with my back, my arms in a circle in front of me for balance, I turned *en pointe* to complete my quad pirouette. I ended nicely without falling and I smiled to myself for not messing up in front of class.

"Very nice. One thing, though," Madame Ava said to me while raising a brow.

"Yes, Madame Ava," I replied, slowly inhaling, trying to catch my breath.

As Madame Ava's eyes moved down my body, I sucked in my stomach and stood up as straight as I could go, locking my knees as her eyes finally rested on my feet. My toes were facing out with my heels together. That was how a ballerina was supposed to stand in line, but when I looked down, my drawstrings on both ballet shoes were sticking out and hanging off the sides. I shut my eyes and waited for the mortification to start in on me.

"Ladies and one gentleman, can anyone tell me what's wrong with her shoes?" she announced to the class.

I wanted to run and hide. This is what I was afraid of, being an embarrassment in front of my class; it's the last thing I ever wanted.

I heard Madame Ava call on the one person who I knew would want to give me the shaft.

"Jasmine."

"Her drawstrings on her ballet shoes are sticking out, which is a disgrace and not very polite to have happen while in class. The ballerina can trip and fall, hurting herself. Madame Ava, we wouldn't want that at all."

I looked up and over at Jasmine, her hand on her chest, acting like she really cared for my safety. Madame Ava's eyes rested on my face, my chest rising and falling with each passing second.

"This is a safety issue. Don't let it happen again." Then she moved on to Bethany. I peered over at Jasmine who had a smug smile on her face, like she owned this classroom, which pissed me off.

When class was over, I put my sweats back on with my flats. My feet were sore. I just wanted to go home and soak them in warm water with some bath salts. My phone chimed deep in my bag. Good thing class was over or Madame Ava would have had a huge fit. Opening my phone, I saw one new message from Tucker. I smiled at the warmness pooling in my belly and then my face flamed up at the remembrance of the dream from this morning. I opened the text:

Tucker: *Hey baby girl, hope ur day is goin good… thinkin of you*

I felt all giddy as I read his message over and over. I quickly replied.

Me: *Day is great. Class just ended.*

I waited for my phone to go off again, but it didn't. I stuffed it back in my bag and left the ballet room. My schedule at Juilliard was simple: one class and that was it, but the class was three hours long, Monday through Friday, so we were done by noon. I knew that Rachel's class was the same and we agreed to meet each other out in front of the building. I rounded a corner to go there, but Jasmine stepped in front of me, blocking my path.

The look that she was giving me was nothing but rotten; it was obvious she didn't like me. News flash, I wasn't a big fan of hers, either.

"You better not screw up this year's performance. Top of the line directors are coming this December and April for our biggest shows. So, next time, tuck in your stupid draw-strings before you make us all look stupid."

She then turned and left. I grumbled to myself. Yep, I didn't like her at all. I met Rachel outside, who was beaming with the biggest smile on her face. She was a very gorgeous girl with her long red hair and fair skin. I'm glad that I got to spend more time with her. Even though Jade and I get along really well, I wanted to be close with Rachel, too.

"What's with the big smile?" I asked while pulling my strap higher on my shoulder. She just linked her arm with mine and off we went in the direction of the little café across the street.

"I think I'm in love."

I pulled back to look at her. "What? With Brad?"

"Pfft, no. There's this really hot guy in my acting class, totally swoon worthy," she said as she dropped her head on my shoulder and we crossed the street. We ordered our drinks. I got a latte and Rachel ordered her hot chocolate, going outside to sit on the terrace to watch the cars passing by.

"What's his name?"

She shrugged while blowing on the hot chocolate. "I don't remember."

"Rach, how can you say you're in love if you don't even know his name?" I asked as I took another sip, waiting for her to answer me.

"Because he knows how to kiss a girl," she giggled.

"You kissed him?"

"Yeah." She acted like it wasn't a big deal. "It was part of a scene, Gabs."

Oh, yeah. Acting.

"MmHmm.."

"How are things with Tucker? I know you two are getting pretty close," she said as her brows did a little dance above her green eyes.

I tossed the idea around in my head. It was true, I wanted to get close to him, and he seemed pretty into me, too.

"It's going," was all the information I was going to give her about that. Rachel begged me to give her more details about kissing him. Plus, she saw that we snuggled and slept on the couch.

We talked about little things, mostly just getting to know one another. Rachel explained her mom and her love of shopping to me, but I already knew that. I witnessed it on Saturday. I told Rachel about Carol and went into more detail about our coffee afterward.

Rachel wasn't a big fan of Carol after I told the story of her smacking me the day I moved in the apartment.

"God, no wonder you were such a mess. I honestly didn't know what to do with you being so quiet and shy. I wouldn't have suggested watching the porn if I had known."

I shrugged, "It's not a big deal."

"It kinda is; I didn't know how strict of a background you came from. I know my mom loves you – said she couldn't wait to see you again."

"Your mom is so sweet. I wished I would have known my birth mother. I wonder if I am like her."

Rachel leaned across the table to pat the top of my hand. "I think she would be proud of you for getting into Juilliard if she loved ballet, and for dealing with that rude woman you call a stepmother."

I smiled at her and laughed a little bit, "I know for a fact that she would hate Carol."

"Ain't that the truth? When do you have to see Carol again?"

"My dad has a dinner for his firm on Saturday. I should probably go get a dress or something."

"Oh can we go shopping? I know a perfect little place that has the absolute best cocktail dresses."

I nodded, "Sure." If Trish loved to shop, Rachel did, too. Like mother, like daughter.

The bell rang across the street; last class was over. We took our drinks and walked back over to the school to wait for Jade. She came out with a beaming smile as well.

"Holy shit! Is Jaiden Monroe smiling?" Rachel asked.

"Shut up. It was a good day, and Jett is coming to walk me home." Jade's face flamed up red.

"Oh, Jett is comin'!" Rachel squealed at her, in a high pitched girly voice and clapped her hands together. "Honestly Jade, I've never seen you like this with anyone. What makes him so special?"

"He just gets me. I give him attitude and he gets all mad at me. Usually people just ignore me, then don't talk to me. Not Jett. He gets all upset and calls me out on my shit. I like that." Jade looked at me and winked. "We are going to go get some coffee so you guys can go home."

Rachel gripped my arm. "Gabs, let's go to that little store I was telling you about."

"Ha-ha. You get to go shopping with Rachel again. Do you need more cigarettes?" Jade started going through her bag.

"Let's go, Rach." I said, grabbing her hand and pulling her long legs behind me. Rachel blew a kiss to Jade.

The little shop Rachel was telling me about was actually really cute. It was very small and the walls were lined with dresses in every color you could imagine. Shoes were on tables in the center of the room with a big chandelier hanging above them. The back wall was full of clutches; most of the colors were very neutral. The dresses in the shop were black, brown, gold, and silver.

I looked at the racks of dresses, pulling a couple of yellow ones with a very open back. I really liked the soft yellow color, as it could go with a black clutch and black shoes. Or would that look too bumble beeish?

"Gabs!" Rachel called out to me and I turned to see her approach with her arms covered in dresses. I barely had two dresses in mind and she had a crap load.

"Wow Rach. You buying all those?"

She stopped, looked at her arms and said in a serious tone, "Ah, no. These are for you, dummy."

I giggled at her. I knew they were for me. Rachel had a blonde moment and didn't even realize it.

"Do you like the yellow?"

"Yeah, it's pretty."

"It's very *How to Lose a Guy in 10 Days* type of dress."' Rachel pulled it from the rack.

I raised a brow. "It's what?"

"Nothing, it's just a movie. We should watch it when we get home. It's not porn, though. Promise."

Rachel held up her fingers in the Scout's Honor sign. I laughed again and put the other yellow dresses back on the rack while Rachel walked up to the sales associate.

I don't know how many dresses I ended up trying on before they all started to blur together as one. Every time I came out of the dressing room, they started to look more and more the same. I finally chose an elegant, deep purple, silk gown. Rachel told me how skinny I looked in the silk material. It had thin straps with a deep V in the front and the back. I loved it.

That night, I didn't hear from Tucker. I was sad and I didn't want to text him because I wanted him to text me first. Yeah, I was totally sounding like a girl in high school. Rachel ordered Chinese again and put in *How to Lose a Guy in 10 Days*. It was a cute comedy and the guy was a hunk. Jade came home around eleven without Jett and went straight into her room. I cleaned up while Rachel went to go talk with Jade, mentioning something about seeming down when she walked in. Rachel could tell just by the way Jade walked into the room that she seemed sad. I was impressed; they were truly close, and was glad I could be a part of their friendship.

I locked up the apartment, changed into my pajamas, and padded into my bathroom to brush my teeth. While rinsing my mouth, my phoned chimed. I finished up and ran back into my room to see a text from Tucker waiting for me.

Eeep!

I slid my finger across my screen and saw a picture Tucker sent me of him in black and white. His pose was so cute. His face turned to the side with his hand under his chin, almost as if deep in thought, his other arm stretching out to take the picture. I giggled. Under the picture it said: "Thinking of you. Night, baby girl.'

My heart was racing and my breath sped up. I was falling for him and the cute little things he was doing to my heart. I set my alarm and went into a deep sleep, hoping that I would dream of Tucker's sweet lips on mine and the electricity I felt for him in my heart.

Chapter Eight

The next two days went by in one big blur. I didn't hear from Tucker or get any cute pictures of him to make my heart race. I wondered what he did during the day. I knew he said tattooing, but did that take up most of his time? Madame Ava was cracking down on us, and hard. It seemed like all she did was yell at us the entire time. I was sent to the back of the line three times for getting my stupid triple pirouette turn wrong. I kept losing my balance on the final turn.

"Abigail, that's gonna cost you a chance at any part if you don't get that down!" Madame Ava yelled at me over and over again.

Getting yelled at was the worst feeling. I felt like such a failure every time I did something wrong. And whenever I looked over at Jasmine, she would just smile, kept ahead of the class and holding the spot at the top of the line. Bethany and I were always at the back of that stupid line.

I hated the line.

Every day I saw Jasmine in the halls, she would either bump into my shoulder or pretend to collide into my side, laughing with her friends. I really wanted to pull on her stupid bun and spit in her face – not very ladylike on my part and Madame Ava would have my butt if I ever pulled something like that off. I couldn't help but hate the perfect turns and leaps she did in class. She did it with grace and perfection; I was jealous.

Rachel, of course, had the lead in the play they were working on. Jade was still drawing and playing the cello like crazy. Jade was hardly home the past couple of days, mostly because she didn't like us to hear her practice and when she was home, Jett was with her. I gave in and texted Tucker a couple of times, but never heard back from him. Thoughts came to my mind about him giving up on me because I didn't sleep with him that first night, but it was still new and I didn't want to be that nagging girl who he kissed once, and now wouldn't leave him alone.

"Abigail and Jon."

My head snapped up to Madame Ava; she was standing in front of me, hands together and waiting for me to do what? Oh crap, I was spacing. I didn't hear her instructions.

I straightened my spine. "Yes, Madame Ava?"

"You and Jon will perform a quick silhouette together. Perform the *pas de deux adagio*, with an *air, en l'*, then Jon will *jete* you up, and hopefully catch you. And you, Abigail, will end it with a triple pirouette. Understood?"

Oh Crap.

"Yes, Madame Ava," I nodded.

I didn't know Jon; he was the only boy in our class and we were supposed to do a silhouette together of what? The *pas de deux adagio* is something I performed with Ramón in my studio. It was a very slow dance with slow leaps, with him catching me and slowly turning us around while my legs were stiff and toes pointed. *Air, en l'* is in mid-air where Jon is supposed to *jete* me; in other words, catch me. I hope he does catch me because I have to do the one thing I struggle with: a triple pirouette.

I really wanted to pee my leotard right now!

"Now, Abigail!"

I gracefully walked into the front of the ballet room with Jon by my side. Everyone parted the line so we could see ourselves in the wall-length mirror. My feet were positioned opposite of each other, heel to toes and turned inward. The soft music of Pyotr Llyich Tchaikovsky, *Swan Lake,* played through the room, echoing off the walls. I shut my eyes as Jon placed his hand on my lower back and we started to move together. The leaps and leg placements were good. Jon stumbled a little when I turned too fast in his arms and I bumped into his side. The climax of the music was coming, and it was time for me to do my *air, en l'* where I leap. I thought to myself, *I just hope he catches me.*

I stepped away from Jon, and then leaped up into his arms. The landing in his arms was a little rough, which made him lose his balance and step back a little bit. I wiggled in his arms to help him get a better hold on me and he kept grunting like I was too heavy. Jon was tall and masculine, so you wouldn't think he would have a problem trying to hold onto me. We did some turns while I was still up in his arms and he ended it with one pirouette, and then let me down smoothly. I stopped and faced the mirror. I positioned my legs perfectly, one pointed straight out while the other was bent at the knee. I listened to the music, waiting for the ending to start my triple pirouette. It came; I went up on *en pointe*, turned sharply once, twice and on the third turn, I lost my footing and finished the turn way too soon with a loud thump on the floor from my foot.

I was out of breath; I needed to get that stupid turn down. I could do two, but struggled with three.

It was so frustrating!

"Abigail, you are done for today," Madame Ava said to me. I could hear how disappointed she was in me. We still had an hour left of class and I was done.

I couldn't fight with her; she gave a command and I had to take it. I nodded, "Yes, Madame Ava." Tears stung my eyes as I walked away from her and the rest of the group, who all lined back up at the barre.

Walk of shame.

I quickly wiped away a falling tear and sat on the bench where my gym bag was kept. I unlaced my shoes, rubbed my feet and popped my toes. I pulled on my bottoms to my black sweats and watched the rest of the class. I wish I could at least leave the classroom so I didn't have to watch perfect Jasmine do her triple pirouettes with elegance. It was eating me alive; the longer I sat here and watched her, the more I wanted to stomp out of class.

"Very nice, Jasmine," Madame Ava praised her over and over. Very loudly too, I might add.

The bell rang and I couldn't be happier to leave. I slung my strap over my shoulder to head out the door, but Madame Ava called out to me. I faced the room and people walked around me to leave me alone with her. When Jasmine walked past me, I made sure not to have my eyes down on the ground. I met her glaring brown eyes as she snorted at me with a "failure" under her breath.

"What was that?" I growled at her.

"You heard me. You don't deserve to be here if you can't do a simple triple pirouette."

I started to go after her to tell her she was wrong. I practiced and practiced. I did deserve to be here.

"Abigail." Madame Ava's voice stopped me from chasing her down to play school yard hair pull. I did the walk of shame back to Madame Ava, my head still high.

"Abigail, why can't you do that turn?"

"I can, I promise," I pleaded with her. "I can, Madame Ava, I promise."

She arched a brow. "Can you? You've proved to me more than twice that you can't."

A rush of feelings went through me. *Failure. Don't deserve to be here.* Those words rang through my ears, echoing in my brain.

"Look at me, please." Madame Ava's voice was sincere and I met her sparkling blue eyes. "Can you do it, Abigail?"

I nodded, feeling the tears start to burn my eyelids. I was trying so hard not to cry. "Yes, I can."

"Let me see." She stepped away from me and stood at the back of the room. I wasted no time to hold my spot here in class. I went back over to the bench, stripped off my sweats, stretched my feet back out and then laced up my slippers. I walked back to stand in front of the mirror. I angled my right leg down, and pointed my toes, my left leg bent, and ready to push up on my toes to go on *en pointe* to do the turns.

"Do one first," Madame Ava called out.

I nodded at her through the mirrors. I pushed up on my toes and softly turned, then closed my position. My spine straightened up and I waited for my next command.

"Very nice, now two."

I went back down into position, pushed up on my toes on my left foot, then turned once and twice, and then closed it with no problem.

"Very good. Now, three."

I went back into position and up on my toes and turned, once, twice, and on the third turn, I lost my footing again trying to close.

I bent down to rest my hands on my knees. I wanted to scream out loud and throw things. I wanted to throw a huge three-year-old tantrum and start stomping my feet. Small hands on my shoulder made me jump a little. Madame Ava was behind me.

"Close your eyes." I complied. "Listen to me, listen to my voice. I know that you're nervous here. I know that you see Jasmine as competition here." I opened my eyes and tried to turn to tell her I didn't want to make trouble with Jasmine, but she held onto my shoulders and faced me back towards the mirror.

"Shut your eyes and listen to me."

Once again, I shut my eyes and listened to her voice whispering in my ear.

"I know you think Jasmine is competition to you. That's a good thing; she's a very good ballerina, but I know you can do better. This pirouette is easy, but you think too much. You think about messing up, you think about falling and you will if you keep thinking about it. Now..."

Madame Ava grabbed my hands with hers and stretched them out horizontally from my body. She tapped my right foot and pushed my heel with her toes. I stretched my leg out and pointed my foot. Her hand on my left hip pushed me down gently to get me to slightly bend my left knee.

"Listen to my voice, Abigail. Remember to inhale deeply through your nose, exhale through your mouth." I followed her instructions on my breaths, slowly inhaling and exhaling. "Do one pirouette on the counts."

I counted in my head. One... Two... Three... Four... Five... Six and Seven. I pushed up on my left foot and turned. I did the pirouette with ease, and I felt more relaxed as I turned and closed the position.

"Keep your eyes closed and do two." Again, I felt more relaxed and centered with my turn.

"Now three, don't think about it. Just do it like the other two."

I felt as if I moved in slow motion as I pushed up on my toes and swung my right leg, I dropped back down and turned, then went up on *en pointe* again and turned. The third time, I turned and finished it, closing the pirouette perfectly like I knew I could. On the inside, I was screaming for joy that I didn't mess up again.

"Very nice, Abigail. You may go now."

Madame Ava went into her office and shut the door. I jumped into the air, so proud of myself. I did it!

I ran outside, dressed in my sweats once again, hoping I didn't miss Rachel and Jade. But everyone was gone except for one face I was more excited to see.

Tucker. He was here.

He sat on the ledge of the cement wall, smoking with his head down, wearing a black leather jacket while his legs swung back and forth. He looked pretty cute just sitting there in his own little world. I wanted to race over to him, but I just stood there in place just to watch him for a moment. I wondered if he would notice me watching him. As if he heard my thoughts, his head looked up and met my eyes; he smiled with his deep left dimple showing. I smiled at him and took my time walking over to him. His smile got bigger the closer I got to him. He reached for me when I was close enough and I more than willingly went into his embrace.

Tucker has a smell about him that I just couldn't get enough of. He smelled of his leather jacket, cigarettes, and spicy body wash or cologne. His hair was a big mess today and flung over to the side; he wore a white shirt with ripped jeans. No gray hoodie today, but I loved the leather jacket.

His hands came up to cup my cheeks. Tucker's blue eyes sparkled in the sunlight; they seemed bluer outside than when we were inside. I could stare and get lost in them all day long. I placed my hands on the outer side of his thighs and they moved up the more he pulled me closer to gently kiss my lips. Passion surged through my veins as his lips moved with mine, and his thumbs caressed my cheekbones as my legs wobbled beneath me. One of his hands moved to my lower back and slowly slid down to the very top of my butt to grip the top of my sweats, pulling me in closer. Our tongues tangled back and forth as the wind picked up around us. I shivered, but not from the wind; Tucker did amazing things to awaken my body on the inside.

He pulled back and breathlessly said, "Hey, baby girl."

I smiled at his swollen lips, red and plumped from our heated kiss. "Hey," came out in one breath.

Tucker hopped down, taking my bag to sling over his shoulder, then grabbed a hold of my hand. "I came to walk you home."

"Thank you, that's so sweet of you."

"How was your day?"

"Frustrating, but it got better at the end of class."

"Is that what took you so long?"

"Yeah, I couldn't get a pirouette turn down, so my teacher made me sit out the rest of the class and she helped me after everyone left. I thought she was definitely going to kick me out."

"A what turn?"

I giggled, "A pirouette turn. It's just a turn that ballerinas do on pointe." When he continued to stare at me like I was talking gibberish to him, I said, "Remember, up on pointe? Like you did up on your toes?"

"Oh yeah. Sorry, that stuff goes right over my head." Tucker whistled as his spare hand went flying above his head.

"I'm sure if you tried to teach me how to tattoo, that would go right over my head." I repeated his same action with my hand and the whistle. He chuckled and wrapped his arm around my shoulder then kissed my cheek.

When we made it to my apartment, I introduced Tucker to our doorman, Michael. Mostly, it was for security reasons, I told Tucker. I pulled him to the elevator, but he didn't walk with me. He pulled me back into his arms and pecked my lips.

"I can't go up with you," he told me as he set down my ballet bag at our feet.

"Why not?"

He let out a big breath, "I gotta go away for a couple of days." He brought our hands up to the middle of our bodies and kisses the top of my knuckles.

"Where are you going?"

"I can't tell you. It's a favor for Brad. I have to keep my phone off and can't call you, but I wanted to come tell you, walk you home and to do this."

Tucker's hands dropped mine to cup my face again and kiss me so deeply that my legs gave out. He pretty much had to drag me up against the cold marble wall by the elevator to keep my body upright as he pinned me against it. Tucker was hungry for my tongue as he ate my mouth alive. I loved it. His pelvis pushed hard into mine. He possessed my body with just one heated passionate kiss between us.

"God, Gabs. You do something inside me that makes me want to be a better person. You're pure. That's why I gotta go and do this: sever ties, pretty much. That's the only way I can explain it right now. I really like kissing you, though."

And he kissed me again before I could even ask him what he meant. This was more of a good-bye kiss, soft and sweet. I didn't want to let him go, but he pulled away and walked out of my building, leaving me breathless as always. It was already too late; I was falling for him so fast. I was in trouble. That night I did get a text from him saying, "Goodnight, baby girl".

Ballet class on Thursday went a little smoother. I think Madame Ava didn't want to call on me at all during our run through and practices for the *Swan Lake* auditions that were coming up in October. She explained to us again that she expected all of us to try out for the part of Odette/Odile no matter what. Even if we felt like we wouldn't get the part, she wanted us all to be there. I watched every girl in my class as a competition, which wasn't right. We were all here to support each other, but I was determined to get this part. Jasmine moved across the wood floor with grace as always. She was untouchable to everyone.

Class was over without Madame Ava yelling at me. Jasmine continued her stupid glares at me whenever it was my turn. I was waiting for Jade and Rachel outside when Jon came up to me. His blond hair was spikey, sticking straight up, and his brown eyes were warm. He had a great smile as well, with nice, perfectly straight teeth.

"Hey Abigail."

"Hi Jon." I smiled.

"I just saw you standing here and was wondering if you needed a ride or... anything?" He laughed nervously, shoving his hands deep in his pockets as he shifted from foot to foot. Before I could even answer him, Jasmine was at his side, linking her arm through his.

Of course Jasmine did her signature glare towards me with her own devil brown eyes. "Jon, we need to go," she said, smiling up at him and he smiled down to her. They were a couple? I didn't know that.

"See ya, Abigail." Jasmine pulled Jon away, but she stopped to look at me one more time. "Tell Tucker I said hey, though."

My stomach dropped. Tucker knew her? My chest started to hurt as I let the words sink in. I wanted to punch something. I was confused. I hated having that feeling where everything hurts from seeing or hearing something you weren't expecting, like a brick sitting in your stomach. My breaths picked up and I didn't even hear Jade's voice as she was saying my name to get my attention. I watched Jon open the passenger door for Little Miss Snob who knew Tucker. I really wanted to pull on her tight bun to rip it out of her perfectly shaped head.

Jade pulled on my arm so I faced her, but it was too late. The same thing that always happened when Carol frustrated me couldn't be stopped. The ache in my stomach turned over again and I felt my throat open up. I barely had anytime to launch my body over the cement wall Tucker sat on just yesterday, and I heaved up my stomach acid.

"Oh damn it," Jade grunted out. "Gabs, get up before Rachel see you like this and she flips a lid."

I was dizzy and nauseous, which made me sicker, but I managed to straighten out my body while Jade wiped my mouth off with the hem of my black sweatshirt, then shoved a piece of gum in my mouth. I chewed the mint stick mixed with my nasty stomach acid in my mouth and tried my best to swallow back my gross saliva.

"Who was the devil bitch you were talking to?"

Taking deep breaths, I replied, "Jasmine. She's in my class and she's Miss Little Goody Perfect Ballet Shoe Girl. I got offered a ride by a guy in our class and she came up, made him leave, and then told me to tell Tucker freaking hi!" I yelled at Jade, not caring about anyone around us and my rant. My arms were flinging around like a mad person. The one person who I just didn't get along with knew Tucker.

When Rachel caught up with us, we walked home. I was silent the entire way; Jade threw me looks over Rachel's shoulders, but I kept my eyes in front. I was quiet when I made chicken and peppers for dinner. I was quiet when we ate dinner; I even went out to the balcony to smoke by myself. Again, I never pegged myself as a smoker before, but right now, it calmed me down and helped clear my head. Rachel and Jade kept their distance from me; I was grateful. I needed the space for a little bit. I flicked my last bit of cigarette over the railing and went to my bathroom to shower. I heard the chime of my phone, but my body didn't react all excited to the noise, hoping it would be Tucker. I turned the water on all the way hot and let it beat down on my head. When I finished my shower, I brushed my teeth and climbed into my bed.

I laid in the darkness for a little bit, staring at my ceiling in my own little world. My phone lit up my room, showing the shadows on the walls. Reaching over to grab my phone, it was connected to the charger.

2 new messages from Tucker

I opened them; I didn't have to reply back to him, but I wanted to know what he said.

Tucker: *Hey baby girl ;)*

Tucker: *Just wanted to say hey, but you must be asleep. Night, baby girl.*

I swallowed a huge, dry lump in my throat. It took everything I had not to text back. Instead, I locked my phone and set my alarm then snuggled deep into my comforter, feeling very lost and confused.

Class the next day was good and I made it to the fifth spot in the line. With Madame Ava's help, I was able to perform the triple pirouette without any more problems. I did it every time with excellence. Every time I was upfront in class, I could always hear Jasmine do something to humiliate me: coughing, clearing her throat. I knew she was just trying to distract me in some way. Jon didn't talk to me during or after class; I didn't really care, though. If he was with Jasmine, then he was lost.

Madame Ava gave us the dates of the auditions for *Swan Lake*. Eight A.M. sharp and we were not to be late. If we were late, then that was it; we didn't get to audition. I put all the information in my phone calendar as a reminder.

Rachel, Jade, and I went out to lunch after class. Brad and Tucker were gone; Jett wouldn't give me any information about him when he met us there. I asked him once and he just said, "He'll be back. He always comes back," whatever that meant. I wanted to ask more questions, but every time I opened my mouth, Jade would either start talking or kick me under the table.

Jett invited us back to his tattoo shop along with Jade, but I just wanted to go home. Rachel hailed a cab and it took us back to the apartment.

"Isn't tomorrow your dinner with your dad?"

I nodded, "Yep, it sure is."

"Nervous at all?" Rachel asked, popping her gum and smacking it together.

"Nah, this is an annual thing he does at the end of the year." Undoing my tight bun and running my fingers through my hair felt nice. Rachel and I curled up on the couch together in our jammies and watched another one of the girlie movies she loved. Turns out, Rachel was a huge Johnny Depp fan; she looked up to him as an actor.

"He can play any part, even if it's creepy weird or serious acting. That man knows how to act."

I just shook my head whenever she brought that up. Jade came home late, but I was in bed, staring at the ceiling. Still nothing from Tucker, but that was okay. My brain was still confused on how Jasmine even knew I was with Tucker. Well, I wasn't with him. I just really liked him. But still, "Tell Tucker I say hey," ran through my thoughts. I had to ask him about it. Thinking about my approach made my eyes get heavy and then they slowly shut.

Chapter Nine

I did so many twists and turns in the shared bathroom, taking in so many angles of the gown I bought with Rachel. I had Rachel help me with my hair earlier; she did a beautiful job with the loose curls, then pinned it up on one side with the rest falling down on the other. She also helped me with my makeup, but didn't go too crazy like the night we went to the club. She used soft browns and a hint of gold and the gold matched the clutch purse she let me borrow.

I think I'm good and ready to go. Walking out into our living room, I spotted Jade out on the balcony on her cell phone; it was a really good chance that she was talking to Jett. Those two, I swear, were like peas and carrots; they were just perfect for each other. I knocked on the glass window and she turned; I waved bye and she gave me the bird.

A black limo was right outside the apartment building when I came out. Michael held open my door and helped me with my gown so it wouldn't get caught in the door. I rearranged my dress and sat on the leather seat next to my dad, and when I looked up, I spotted a person who I hadn't met or seen before sitting next to Carol.

"Abigail," Carol said next to the man, "this is Alexander Blair, and he'll be joining us at our table tonight."

I didn't even greet him before I turned and leaned into my dad to give him a side hug.

He kissed my cheek "How are you, angel?" I loved when my dad used my nickname. It always brought me some comfort, especially when Carol was hovering around me.

"Good. How are you daddy?"

"Fine. Miss you around the house." I playfully smacked his leg.

"No, you don't. I'm sure you're happy to get me outta there, so I don't play all that classical music," I snickered.

"It was quite enjoyable at moments."

"Yeah, sure, Dad."

The rest of the limo ride was a bit awkward, mainly because I didn't know Alex Blair. There were times when I caught him looking at me; I looked over at him and he would turn his head to look away. And when I looked at Carol, she smirked then patted his knee, which was weird. We pulled up to the hotel where my dad usually held his firm dinners. My dad got out of the limo first and held out his hand to help me, lacing my arm through his to have him lead us into the grand hotel.

We were the last to arrive, mostly because my dad was the guest of honor. Since my dad was the head of the company, we had to sit at the front of the room at a long table facing everyone. The hotel dining room was gorgeous as always, decorated in white and gold colors, with dim lights and tall candlesticks on each of the fifty tables, which were full of his employees and their spouses.

They all stood up and applauded us as we made our way to the front. My dad had to stop to shake some hands of his closest friends; everyone loved my dad. Carol loved the attention. I turned back and watched her smile and give a little pageant wave. Alex met my gaze and smiled. I turned back around as we made our way up the little steps and to our seats. My dad sat right in front with Carol to his left and me on the other side of Carol. Alex sat on the other side of me.

"Hello Abigail," he greeted me as he sat down. He voice was strong and his blue eyes shined when he smiled.

"Hey." Carol cleared her throat and I sighed. "Hello, Alex." I smiled back, and then turned to face the front as my dad stood up to the microphone at the end of our table. He gave my shoulder a little squeeze as he passed behind me.

"Evening, ladies and gentlemen," my dad addressed the crowd. He talked about the goals they set at the beginning of the year and how they achieved them. More applause echoed through the dining room. He went on about some profits and raises for everyone soon to come for the Christmas season. They all clapped some more, then his voice got serious when he brought up Alex's name.

"Alex Blair is new to our group and so far, he has won every case handed to him." More applauses. "Alex, come on up here," my dad announced and started clapping with the crowd.

My dad waved him over, but before he stood up, he turned and kissed my cheek. I was shell-shocked. He barely knew me and he kissed me? Ick...yes, he was very good looking, but that was just weird. My dad introduced Alex to everyone. Being only twenty-five and having graduated from Harvard Law a year ahead of his class, he was now the youngest Criminal Justice lawyer at the firm. He was making his way to the top very fast. He wasn't a bad looking guy; he was at least six foot two with short brown hair and intense blue eyes, and his black suit clung to his body. My dad clapped him on the shoulder and with the next announcement, my dad made the room explode.

"Alex and I are taking on a very big case. The Grayson case, as many of you know, has been a huge struggle. The couple cannot keep their stories straight, so the divorce attorneys had to get us involved. So, after a great deal of thought between my lovely wife and I, if Alex helps me win this case, he will become partner in the firm."

The dining room exploded into more cheers and applauses. After all these years, not once had my dad even considered having a partner in his firm. He usually just had Carol by his side. Alex looked back over to me and winked, causing my face to heat up in front of the room full of people watching us. I lowered my head and tucked a piece of loose hair behind my ear.

"Alex likes you, Abigail," Carol whispered in my ear. "He actually told me he would like to take you out to get to know you."

That was when it hit me: Carol was going to try everything she could to get me to go out with Alex. He was just giving me the time because my dad would make him partner if he did. I groaned. Of course that's what was happening. I rubbed my head in annoyance to Carol. I didn't think my dad would do something like this to me; he probably would flip if Carol did this on her own.

They were done with their short speeches and dinner was served. The food was delicious. Almost everyone came up to Alex or my dad to congratulate them and wished them the best on the Grayson case. I've heard my dad in his office, yelling at people to get their asses moving on this case, but they couldn't do anything because of the arrogant couple they were dealing with.

A slow orchestra sounded through the speakers when Alex stood up from the table and held out his hand to me.

"Abigail, may I have this dance?" His blue eyes bore into mine in a very charming way, which suited him with perfection.

"Umm..." Carol bumped into my shoulder, trying to casually turn to my dad in the process. "Sure." I brushed at the wrinkles that weren't really there on my long purple gown.

Alex led me onto the dance floor as his right hand was placed on my lower back. We danced in silence, not speaking at all. Yep, this certainly looked like he really wanted to get to know me, as Carol explained. Every time we turned and I saw my dad and Carol, she had her hand on her chest, like a proud mother, seeing her daughter dancing with something that wasn't even there. When we turned again and I faced the back of the room with the double doors wide open, by surprise, I saw Tucker leaning up against the door frame with his arms crossed over his chest. I immediately wanted to run to him. Alex turned me faster and faster as the beat picked up, but every time I was turned, I searched only for Tucker.

The kisses we had shared made me quiver at my knees, and I wanted to feel his lips against mine. I hadn't seen him or talked with him. I missed him. I knew that sounded weird because I hardly knew him, but something deep down inside me made me feel like that. I smiled every time we made eye contact, his body still leaning on the door frame. Once the song was over, my dad came up to cut in.

I hurriedly said, "I need to use the restroom first, Daddy," not letting him answer me as I made my way towards the front doors. Tucker saw me heading his way and back out around the corner. I came out, looking down the hallway and yelped when a hand came out to pull me into a darkened spot.

"Can I just tell you how gorgeous you look in that dress?" Excitement ran through my veins and made my heart pound until it felt like it was going to burst right out of my chest. Tucker was dressed in black pants, a white shirt, with his black leather jacket. His long hair was slicked all the way back and I wanted to run my fingers through it. He dropped his head down and rested his forehead to mine, our noses barely touching.

"You can," I whispered. He chuckled. His hot breath hit my face and I looked into his sparkling blue eyes. Tucker's eyes always sparkled when I stared at him. When he looked at me, I was the only one that mattered to him.

His fingertips brushed my cheek. "Gabs, you're gorgeous," he said, and then he tenderly kissed my lips. It was soft and slow, and his hands locked behind my lower back as the kiss deepened. I felt his tongue at the seam of my lips and I gladly opened. His tongue was smooth and soft against the roof of my mouth.

Man, he could kiss.

His hands roamed up and down my sides, the silk of my dress felt hot against my skin, sending chills up and down my spine. I groaned in his mouth as he deepened the kiss even more.

I could let him kiss me all day long. Hearing some people suddenly talking, which sounded like my dad, I pulled away, our lips making that smacking sound, and I stepped back from him. He looked at me with an irritated look when I did that.

"What?"

He raked his hands through his hair. "Why did you do that?"

"Do what?" I bit my bottom lip. I knew he was upset that I pulled away, which was stupid of me to do.

He took a step to me. "Let's get outta here."

"Tucker, I can't," I said, shaking my head.

His eyes were the saddest I'd seen. "Yes, you can."

Still shaking my head, I said, "No, this is for my dad. I can't just leave right in the middle of the party. How did you find me anyway?"

The thought suddenly entered my mind on how he found me.

"Okay, the line of contacts. Jade talked to Jett, who told me once I got back, and I came straight here. Just lie. Don't you want to come and hang out at Jett's house? Rachel and Jade are there already; they even have a change of clothes for you."

I knew I shouldn't leave my dad here, but I wanted to be with Tucker. I missed him. "I'll be right back." Before I left our darkened corner, Tucker pulled me back into his arms and gave me a hard kiss. My body fell into his as I kissed him back just as hard and when we separated, we were both out of breath.

Wow.

My legs could hardly carry me as I made my way back into the dining room. My dad, Carol and Alex were back at the table, having their desserts. I walked up behind my dad and put a hand on his shoulder to get his attention. I leaned down to talk into his ear, hoping he would be the only one to hear me. If Carol found out I wanted to leave, she wouldn't let me.

I thought of the first thing that came to me. "Daddy." He kinda jumped at my words. "I'm not feeling well. Rachel and Jade are here to take me home."

His face dropped a little. "Okay angel, feel better. Call me tomorrow." Then he kissed my head, I turned and quickly left the stand. I heard Carol call out my name, but I kept going.

I made it back to where I left Tucker, but he wasn't there. I picked up the front of my dress and ran to the front of the hotel and outside. I spotted him by the curb, holding a cab door open for me. I rushed over to his side; his dimple showing with his wide smile did wonders to my insides. But I lied to my dad. That was something I'd never done before. What did he do to deserve me lying to him?

I climbed in the cab and Tucker slid in next to me and put his arm around my shoulders to get me to snuggle into him. His fingertips tickled down my arm. I closed my eyes and enjoyed his soft touch as I melted into his side.

We made it to Brooklyn and the cab fare was expensive for such a short trip. I tried to pay, but Tucker wouldn't let me. I glanced around at my surroundings; I'd never been to Brooklyn before. It looked like the city except for the run-down buildings had spray paint on them along with broken windows. The streets were darker here than in the city.

A flashing bright light made me turn to see the sign *Jett Black Tattoos*. Now I knew the name of his shop, and it suited him really well. Tucker took me around the side of the building and climbed up the back stairs to Jett's apartment. Loud music kept getting louder as we reached the top; Tucker didn't even knock as we made our way inside. People were scattered everywhere, just like it would be at a night club. A couple of girls looked at me like I didn't belong here. I'm sure it was because of the dress I was wearing, but Jade was at my side sooner than I thought.

"Oh hell, you look awful," Jade told me as she took in my dress with her eyes.

"She looks gorgeous," Tucker said to Jade, and then kissed my cheek.

"Whatever Romeo. Let's get you changed before I throw up all over you."

I giggled and followed Jade to what I was guessing was Jett's room. Covering the walls were sketches of flowers, cars, babies—just random things. He could draw very well. Just then, a knock sounded at the door.

"What?" Jade yelled.

The door opened and Jett walked in. "Dude, what if Gabs was naked?" Jade said with attitude. Jett walked over and hung his arm on Jade and kissed the side of her head. They were cute together.

"I like your drawings, Jett." I looked at a close up of the little baby's fingers, which looked so real. It was absolutely beautiful. The tiny little fingers were so precious.

"That one you're staring at, I didn't draw. Tuck did." I gasped at the surprise. I knew he could draw, but something as beautiful as this was breathtaking.

"Come out when you're done," Jett whispered to Jade and tugged her along.

The party was in full swing when I was dressed in some jeans, Converse shoes, and a black top that hung off one side of my shoulder. I found Tucker, Jade, and Jett on the couch, sipping whatever was in the red plastic cups. I saw Rachel and Brad dancing together in the crowd of people in the living room. Tucker saw me and winked as he strode over to me like he was stalking his prey. I liked the feeling my body was giving off as he made his way over to me. We started to sway to the music and I let Tucker rub his hands all over my body.

After a couple hours of nothing but dancing with Tucker, Jade came up to us on wobbly legs and grabbed my elbow. "Gabs, Jett is gonna give me a tat. Come on," she slurred the last bit of her words and was trying to pull me away from Tucker's hot hands on my butt. I really wanted to just stay right here with him; I rested my head on Tucker's shoulder as his fingers moved in little circles on my lower back.

Tucker pulled away from me and started walking back down the stairs into the shop as Jett flipped on all the lights. Rachel hung all over Brad's body in the corner, looking like they had nothing in common, except for their mouths never leaving each other.

Tucker sat on a chair and pulled me into his arms. I snuggled into his warm scented chest. This was much better than the work party for my dad. Maybe a little lie was okay. Alex was intense to take in; the way he stared at me made me feel slightly uncomfortable.

Jade straddled a black chair and Jett tugged down her shirt off her shoulder, sweeping her long black hair off to the side. Tucker snaked his arms around my waist tighter as the buzzing sound filled the room. I started to bounce my legs, afraid for Jade and the faces she was pulling. Jett had on black latex gloves and stretched Jade's skin on her shoulder blade while black ink smeared in every direction as he wiped it away.

Tucker nuzzled my neck and held my hand during the process. Jade sat completely still as Jett worked. I knew I would be squirming in the hot seat. I stretched my neck up to see the work Jett was putting on Jade's body, but Tucker would hold me back when I tried.

"Let the master work. You'll see when he's done." Then he pecked my lips, which turned heated pretty fast as his tongue roamed in my mouth. Our chests pushed closer together as I wrapped my arms tighter around his neck, wanting him as close as possible.

We rested our heads together as our breathing tried to slow down from kissing each other. His hands rubbed up and down my sides, causing me to softly moan against his lips. He kissed me over and over again while Jade got her tattoo.

By the time she was done, forty minutes passed by while I sat on Tucker's lap, wrapped up in our little bubble of happiness. Jade stood up and went over to the long mirror while Jett held another up in front of her for a reverse look if needed.

The tattoo was a very beautiful lotus flower. The purple and white on the flower stood out perfectly on her fair skin, with green leaves floating on the bottom. It was gorgeous. Jade smiled into the mirror and flung herself into Jett's arms.

"I love it," I heard her say into his neck. Jett hugged her back and kissed her head.

"You want one?"

I faced Tucker, almost in a panic. "No."

Nudging my shoulder, he said, "They're fun," as he tried to convince me. I couldn't anyway. One, I had nowhere to hide it, because of my ballet. Two, Jade's faces didn't look like she was enjoying herself.

"No," I shook my head again.

Tucker kissed my cheek and stood up. He pulled me back up the stairs to Jett's apartment, but we passed his door and kept climbing another set of stairs, ending up on the roof. We were the only ones up there from the banging party happening in Jett's apartment below us. Tucker led me over to edge of the building and straddled the wall. I sat down in front of him and he held my hand. I watched as he laced his fingers with mine and I smiled at the comfort it brought me. The warming pull started to happen whenever we were together and alone. I looked up to see his blue eyes staring intently into mine and he leaned in to give me a soft kiss. I welcomed his lips on mine like I couldn't get enough of him.

His hands held onto my waist as he tugged me closer to him. We slowly drifted apart and gazed into each other's eyes some more. He pushed hair away from my face as he stroked my cheek, sending shivers through my body. I didn't want to be anywhere else at this moment.

"You're so beautiful."

I smiled at his reassuring words. I did feel so beautiful when I was with him; he made me feel so gorgeous and like I was the only girl for him. Even if it was just walking down the street holding my hand, he made me feel pretty even then.

"Tell me about Carol."

I was shocked he wanted to talk about her. "Why?"

"You said she's your stepmom; do you not like her?"

I took a deep breath. "It's confusing. Sometimes, she's fine, other times...well...most of the time, I can't stand to be around her. She's so demanding; I never know what mood to expect being around her."

"Have you ever told her this before?"

"No way. Just last week, I told her there would be traffic in the morning, because well, it's New York, there's always traffic and she smacked me."

Tucker's body went stiff at my words. "She hit you?"

"Yeah, it's the first time she's ever done anything like that, though. I think she feels really bad about it, too. She calls me more, wanting to meet with me, to have lunch or just even to talk with me on the phone."

"She definitely feels guilty then."

I looked at Tucker. "How can you tell?"

"She wouldn't apologize or do any of those things if she didn't."

Silence lingered between us, but our hands were still laced together.

"What about your mom? What's her name?"

"Victoria, but she goes by Tori."

"What does she do?"

"Ha! That's funny." I raised an eyebrow at him. "She does nothing, except sit at home with all her damn cats."

"In Bushwick?"

"Yep. Her boyfriend is such an ass to her, too."

"What about your dad? Isn't he around?"

He shrugged. "I don't know, he left us when I was little. Haven't seen him at all, not that I even want to; I hate him probably just as much as my mom's boyfriend."

"I've never been to Bushwick before. Is it close by here?"

Tucker pointed out west of us. I couldn't see anything except the street lights and buildings.

"It's about ten minutes that way, but you can never go there."

I faced him again. "Why not?"

"It's not a safe neighborhood. Promise me, Gabs, that you will never go there."

I nodded, "I promise."

His face softened as he cupped my cheek. I embraced his warm palm on my face. Someone below us must have opened a window because music filled our ears. Then we heard Rachel and Brad's voices; we peered down to see them out on the balcony and embraced in each other's arms as they slow danced to the soft song playing from inside the apartment.

Tucker pulled me up, pressing his hot body against mine, wrapping one arm around my lower back. The other arm guided my arms up around his neck and we started to sway back and forth. Tucker's breath was hot as it traveled down my back, then down my spine. I pressed closer to him, wanting to be as close as I could to him. My fingers found his hair and I threaded them through it over and over again. He kissed my neck as if he couldn't get enough of my skin there.

Jett had a couch on the roof, and after our little slow dance in our own Tucker and Gabs world, we made our way over to the seat. We sat together and Tucker's arm was around my shoulders; he occasionally kissed my cheek and whispered in my ear about how beautiful I was to him. He would move my hair back from my neck and kiss me underneath my ear on my sensitive spot. My head fell back on the cushion and I moaned into the chilling night air.

Tucker's other arm wound around my stomach, lifting the hem of my shirt to lightly drag his fingertips across my skin while chills racked through my body as if it was on fire. I burned for his touch. I wanted his hands on me, all over my tingling body that only craved him. As his teeth sucked in my lobe, my eyes slowly shut and my head turned automatically to seek out his mouth; he gladly met mine. Our tongues clashed against each other as my body pressed up against his side; my hands shot up into his hair and I pulled, making him groan in my mouth.

Tucker slowly fell back on the couch with my body between his legs, our tongues still going crazy for one another. Pushing my shirt up a little more, his hands were hot on my skin as they rubbed up and down on my sides. I don't know how long we were like that, just me laying there on top of him, making out like crazy, horny kids in high school. I couldn't get enough of his hard framed body.

Suddenly, the air between us shifted as my body wanted him in every way possible. I knew Tucker felt it change, because he broke our kiss and sat up, pulling me into his lap with a deep breath.

I sighed, wondering if I did something wrong. "What's wrong?"

Tucker's hand went to his forehead and moved down; he looked confused, but wouldn't tell me what was bothering him or why he stopped our kisses. He looked me in the eyes.

"I just want to hold you," he whispered to me, pulling me into him.

I smiled at him. I could give him that much. Come to think of it, I didn't know if I was actually really ready to give that part of me, yet. I mean don't get me wrong; I really wanted to, but I had only known Tucker for a week, and it wasn't my kind of style to jump bones already.

We lay back down on the couch, my left hand up with Tucker's right, our fingers lacing and twisting together in front of our faces. We tickled our fingertips against each other's as we stared high up into the night sky; this night would be perfect if the stars were noticeable, but that wouldn't happen in New York.

When I was younger, I always dreamed of the beautiful white stars in the sky and would think about my dreams; they were mostly about ballet. Everything revolved around my ballet; I wanted nothing more.

I sighed happily. "What are your dreams, Tucker?" Still thinking about the stars and my dreams, I was curious to see if Tucker had any.

"My dreams?"

My head nodded against his chest and he let out a breath, blowing my hair in my eyes.

"Oh, I don't know. At first, I wanted to leave this town and never look back. Go somewhere new, where no one knows me."

He words softly hurt my heart. Go away? To somewhere they don't know him? My head looked up to him and saw his eyes staring at our twisting fingers.

"What do you mean?"

His blue eyes met mine and he kissed my head. "Nothing, baby girl."

I laid there wondering about what he meant, which was probably about his mom and her boyfriend he didn't like very much. Tucker's other arm was behind my neck and he slowly started playing with my hair, running it through his long fingers. Then I remembered my thoughts about how he knew Jasmine, or how she knew him.

"Tucker?"

He didn't answer and when I glanced up at his face, his eyes were closed. I sighed as my eyelids started to get heavy. I slowly shut them, content to be in the arms of Tucker and fell asleep.

Someone was gently shaking my shoulder. Groaning, I opened my eyes to the bright outside sun and to Jade's ice blue eyes, and Rachel's red hair in my face. They snickered at me and Rachel whispered, "We gotta go."

I nodded slowly, not wanting to wake up Tucker. I lay on my side, my backside being pressed into Tucker's front. When I tried to get up, his right arm pressed me harder into his groin. I sucked in a sharp breath as I felt every inch of him being curved into my butt.

Jade rolled her eyes at me and Rachel started to giggle. I mouthed, "What" at them and that ended with Rachel falling on the roof's floor and her giggles turned into full on laughing. Tucker jerked awake behind me at the sound.

Well, there goes that.

The four of us made our way back downstairs through Jett's shop, where Jett held a taxi's door open for us. I started walking towards it when I was suddenly jerked back and lips crashed into mine. I immediately reacted to Tucker as our mouths opened in unison and our hot tongues met. I pushed up on my toes and kissed him back with everything I had. I enjoyed it, too.

Someone in the background cleared their throat with a quiet, "Ahem," but we kept on kissing. The cab honked when we finally pulled apart, and my heart was racing so fast and hard, it was almost painful. I blinked up at Tucker as he softly pecked my lips one more time. Jade pulled on my arm before Tucker could take me back into his embrace where I wanted to be.

"Jeez man, did you get her pregnant with that kiss?" Jett joked and Tucker playfully punched his shoulder.

Once we were inside and the cab pulled away from the curb, I glanced back at Tucker, expecting him to be standing there and watching the taxi leave, but he wasn't; he was gone.

I pulled my phone out of the gold clutch that Rachel had all night and checked it. I wasn't too surprised to see that I had twenty-three missed calls from Carol; there were no voicemails, just calls over and over again. I was not prepared to find her car at the curb of our building as our cab made its way back into the city and came to a stop out front.

Michael immediately rushed over to hold open the door for us as we climbed out of the cab.

"Miss Abigail?"

"Yes?"

"Your mother would like a word with you," Michael said to me while pointing over my shoulder. To be honest, I was not going to walk my happy butt over to her car just to have her scream at me.

"You can tell her to call me."

I passed Michael to join Jade and Rachel at the elevator and my phone started going off. I hit ignore twice as we rode the elevator up to our apartment. I was too happy to have spent the wonderful time with Tucker last night; I wasn't going to have her ruin my happy time.

Carol called my phone twice more as I stripped out of my clothes and turned on the shower. The ringtone echoed into the bathroom as I scrubbed my skin so hard, it was starting to sting from the hot water and soap. The more it rang, the harder I scrubbed my skin raw. It wasn't fair that she was doing this to me. I knew what she was going to say to me. She would hound me with all the stupid questions as to why I left my dad's dinner and didn't turn back when she called my name.

I soaped up my hair and washed my scalp, trying to get rid of the annoying ringtone in my ears. I stood under the spraying hot water until my phone finally stopped ringing, but another one started. I jerked my head out of the line of water to listen more carefully.

Yep, Tucker!

My insides squealed at his rock and roll ringtone. As I opened the shower door, my body was smacked with nothing but cold chilling air. I didn't even bother to look for a towel as I ran into my room and dived into my bed naked just to answer a freaking phone call from my hot crush.

I smiled as I hit the talk button. "Hello?"

"Hey, baby girl," Tucker's voice warmed my cold body as I wiggled into my white comforter.

"Hi." I could tell my voice purred at him through the receiver.

He chuckled and probably noticed, too. "What are you doing?"

Cold water dripped down my back from my hair and streaked down my sides, giving me the worst chills. I almost felt too embarrassed to answer him about me showering, but I really wanted to know his reaction.

"I was showering." My face flamed up as the words came out. I heard Tucker groan and shift in what sounded like a leather chair.

"Was showering?" he softly asked me.

"I was in the shower when I heard your ringtone." I giggled.

"So, you're like..." he cleared his voice, "in a towel?"

Oh. My. Goodness.

Did I tell him yes? Did I tell him no? A part of me was saying, "Yes, tell him you're covered up." But the other part wanted to play along with him. I wanted to tell him no to hear his reaction. I went for the plunge.

Taking a deep breath through my nose, I said, "No, not in a towel." I slammed my eyes shut so tight, thinking they would burst and my tiny veins and my eyes would bleed out.

"Gabs," Tucker growled so deep. My chills gave me stomach jitters as my head dropped on my arm, too embarrassed to say anything to him.

Even though I spent the night in Tucker's arms on another tiny couch, I wanted to be near him.

Tucker cleared his voice some more before he started speaking, "I was wondering if I could come over later and take you out to dinner. Then maybe, we could watch a movie?"

My heart leaped with joy. "Like a date?" I was trying really hard not to screech it out like a love struck teenager. I couldn't help it if I did, though. I was excited that he even wanted to see me again. My smile was starting to hurt my cheeks and my lip was going numb from chewing on it so hard.

"Yes, a date."

I started nodding my head as if Tucker were here watching me. "I would love to."

He let a rush of air, "Great. I'll pick you up at fiveish?"

I looked at my clock to see that it was twelve thirty. I had a good five hours to get myself ready. I knew that for my first date, Rachel would be more than willing to help me get ready.

"Sounds good."

"See ya, Gabs."

I hung up the phone without saying good-bye and dropped my head back down. Forgetting that I was still naked and on my stomach, I couldn't get the image of

Tucker out of my head: his blue eyes, that one deep dimple, his hot hands as they roamed on my body. Gah, and his kisses, I couldn't even describe the most wonderful feelings I felt when his tongue would seductively stroke mine. Yes, he was the first guy I'd kissed, but it was amazing. All my crazy thoughts of him made my mind dizzy; I shut my eyes and quickly fell asleep.

SMACK!

"AAAAHHHH!" I screamed and grabbed my naked butt that was burning with hot flames. I quickly flipped over on my back.

SMACK!

"AAAAHHHH!" My hands came around to my front and cupped my exposed breasts, then listened to Jade and Rachel laugh their stupid heads off from their ruthless smacks on my naked body. I grabbed one end of my comforter and rolled myself up in it very tight.

"Dude, did you just carpet roll in your blanket?" Jade snickered at me through her laughing breaths. I was able to get my hand loose enough to give her the finger at the top of my blanket.

"Gabs," Rachel burst out as best as she could, stuttering as she tried to get her words out. "We just wanted to come tell you that...that...that Tucker is here and waiting for you in the living room."

Oh crap.

I sprang from my bed and planted my feet on the floor. Surprisingly, I didn't fall on my butt as I untangled my body from my comforter and rushed to our shared bathroom. Ugh, my hair. It wasn't cooperating with the brush since I fell asleep with it wet with Tucker on my mind. I went right to work on the rats nest, but finally accepted defeat and just pulled it back into the bun Jade hated at the base of my neck. Not having any time to mess with the makeup, I decided on a little mascara and some of Rachel's pink lip gloss, and then raced back into my room to find an outfit.

Once I was dressed, I stopped; I didn't know if I should dress casually or dressy. But knowing Tucker, I went with casual. After pairing black skinny jeans with a gray sweater, I also pulled on my black knee-length boots.

My heels clicked on the hardwood floor. Rachel smiled at my appearance, Jade rolled her eyes, and Tucker's back was facing me. He slowly turned and met my gaze, his side smile showing his deep dimple. He fully turned and my face dropped: he was wearing a black dress jacket and a black button down shirt with a silver tie. He dressed up. He even had his usually messy hair slicked back and away from his eyes. He looked down to my toes and back up; I'm sure he was taking in my casual outfit.

"Ah, shit," he quietly said, then loosened his tie at the knot.

Jade smacked him on the shoulder. "That a boy, Tuck; you looked like shit anyway."

I giggled and Tucker tossed his tie at me, hitting me in the face. I put it on just as a joke, but that didn't stop Tucker from taking my hand and pulling me to the front door and out the apartment. We stood waiting for the elevator and Tucker placed his hand on my lower back to usher me inside. The heat from his hand was still hot through my jacket and I shuddered.

"You cold?"

I shook my head. My body felt the complete opposite. I was warm, too warm. I wanted his arms around my waist, his lips on my skin, and his body pressed against mine. The thoughts entered my mind at a sudden rush, I wanted more. Tucker knew how to kiss and I wanted more. I peeked over at him and he looked down at me; I bit my bottom lip and stared back.

"Gabs." He stepped closer to me and I turned my body to face him. One of his hands rested on my hip, and his other hand moved up to tug on his tie that was still around my neck. I pushed up on my toes and our lips met. That instant shock happened as our lips molded together as our tongues caressed in a long lasting kiss that I felt all the way to my toes. The electricity that I looked forward to every time Tucker was near my body – that feeling was happening right now, and I loved every minute of it.

Tucker broke the magical kiss that was racing through my hot veins. "Mmm...You taste pretty good," he growled against my mouth and I instantly melted all over again. I couldn't help myself as I pushed up against his body to kiss him one more time. I really didn't care if anyone else got on the elevator with us. I just didn't want to stop kissing him.

The cab stopped out front of a fancy restaurant that I had been to multiple times with my dad and Carol. Actually, it was Carol's favorite French restaurant.

Tucker stopped us from walking into the restaurant, taking my hand in his. "I wanted to take you somewhere special." he mumbled out, looking at our intertwined fingers.

"Hey, it's the thought that counts, right?" He met my eyes and nodded.

"Yeah, but you're probably used to things like this, though?" He was right; I was. We came here about every other weekend. The staff even knew Carol's favorite table and said hi to us by name.

I pressed up close to him. "Let's go get a hotdog and coke. We'll sit somewhere. That would mean more to me than a fancy restaurant."

Bringing our hands up and he pecked my knuckles. "Are you just saying that, Gabs?"

"No. That would make me happier." I smiled.

We walked to a vendor just down the street and sat on the steps of the New York Public Library. I loved the library; I just loved to sit down to read a classic book by Jane Austen. But it had been so long since I even picked up a book. Our hands still locked onto one another as we ate the hotdogs and sipped on our drinks in silence.

"Tell me more about yourself," I asked when I was done eating.

"Not much left to tell," he said, taking another bite of his remaining hotdog.

I nudged his shoulder with mine. "Come on, tell me something."

"Um." Tucker sat there and thought about it. "I really don't have much."

"Let's start easy then." I brushed bread crumbs off my jeans. "What's your favorite color?"

Tucker tossed his head back and laughed, "Really, that's what you want to ask me? I thought you would dig deeper than that."

"I don't want to make you feel uncomfortable. I just thought it was a start, and then we can move up or something." I felt stupid for asking that silly first grader question, but I couldn't think of anything.

"Black," he answered.

"Black?"

He nodded.

"Why?" I asked.

"Black has so many levels of color."

"But it's black, just black."

"You would think that, but I see it differently. When I sketch, I use pencil. You would think pencil has one color, but it doesn't. You can smooth it out, shade it, push lightly, and push hard so you have different shades. Black isn't like that. When I tattoo, black is the hardest color to work with, you gotta get it right or you're doomed."

Wow. I really didn't think about it like that.

"I just really enjoy drawing, always have. Becoming a tattoo artist is awesome. I already have some promising clients."

"That's great, Tucker." I took another sip of my drink and stretched out my legs. My butt was going numb from sitting on the cement steps.

"Do you want to come back to my place?" Tucker eyed me with a smirk. "Or we can go to yours," I threw in, mostly because I didn't want to force him to come to mine, but wanted to give him an option that we could go to his place instead.

"No, I don't want to go to my place. My neighborhood is dangerous; I've told you that, Gabs. You can never go there."

I peeked up at him under my lashes. "Even if you're with me?"

"*Especially* if you're with me." He took my hand and turned it over to place a small kiss on my wrist.

Why did he word it like that? I wanted to ask, but Tucker continued on.

"I know that doesn't makes sense, but one day, I hope I get to tell you." Tucker stood and took my hand to pull me up and we started walking back in the direction of my apartment.

"What about you, what's your favorite color?"

I laughed with him. "If I had to choose, pink."

"Now, why pink."

"Cuz it's cute." Tucker laughed some more. "What about a favorite food?" I asked.

"Hmm, food." He thought for a moment, "Pizza. It's super easy and really good."

Now it was my turn to laugh, "What about you, Gabs?"

How could I forget my favorite food? It was from when I was little, but that didn't really matter.

"Macaroni and cheese with cut up hotdogs." I smiled proudly. "Oh, and you can't forget the glass of chocolate milk."

Tucker scrunched up his nose and shook his head. "That sounds disgusting."

"Nope. So good, you're missing out." I poked him in his chest and he grabbed my sides hard, then I started laughing and he ended up tickling me some.

When we walked back into my building, Tucker suddenly went stiff at my side. He quickly pulled me into a darkened corner and covered my mouth with his hand.

"Shh. Just be quiet, don't talk and stay here, okay?"

I nodded. Suddenly I was scared and started to shake. What was going on? Tucker took his hand away from my mouth, softly pecking my lips and walked back out into the foyer of the building. Over by Michael was the African American guy from the coffee shop and club, dressed completely in black again with a gold chain glistening on his shirt. My eyes watched Tucker approach him with caution.

"Jeremiah, man. What's up?" Tucker did that hand shake with him and they huddled together talking.

"Where's that girl you've been hanging around with these days? You've never been a one woman man, Tuck. What's going on?" Jeremiah stood straight and stuffed his hands deep into his dress slacks. Tucker's eyes met mine from across the room and he shook his head. I thought maybe he was talking to me and telling me to stay still like he warned. But then I saw Jeremiah was leaning in, whispering in his ear. There was more whispering and more Tucker shaking his head, and then Jeremiah stepped away from him and walked to the front doors. But when he saw that Tucker wasn't behind him and was just staring at me, Jeremiah barked an order at him.

"Now, Tucker!"

Tucker's eyes didn't leave mine as he walked over to where Jeremiah was standing, then left the building with him.

I didn't hear from Tucker the rest of the week. I didn't know where he went or what he did. When I asked Jett if Tucker was at the tattoo shop working, he would just shake his head at me.

"Jett, should I be worried?" I asked one night as the three of us were outside on the balcony smoking.

"Just leave it alone, Gabs. You'll hear from him when he's ready."

More weeks went by and still nothing. Every time I made eye contact with Jasmine, she would just smirk at me. I still wondered where he was. The thought crossed my mind if Jeremiah said something to him to leave me alone.

One day after school, Jade, Rachel, and I were walking home and when we rounded the corner to our building, I was shocked to see Tucker leaning up against my building. I slowly approached him while Jade and Rachel went inside. My doorman, Michael, watched us from a distance. I didn't know what to say to him, so I just walked by. However, he did follow me into the building and into the elevator, up to my floor and out on our balcony.

I was sitting on the seat, pulling out a cigarette then handing the box over to Tucker. He flicked up a lighter and leaned to light mine, then his. Silence was the inbetweenie now. I kept my eyes moving around, trying not to let them land on Tucker's cute face. If they did, I was gonna end up back at square one. I was going to hold my ground this time.

"Gabs, I'm sorry I just left you like that."

I flicked the ashes off the stick while blowing smoke out at the same time as Tucker.

"Where have you been?" I kept my eyes downcast as I asked him.

"I can't tell you."

I snorted. Of course he couldn't tell me; that's what was so frustrating. One question that I was afraid to ask was if he was with her. By her, I meant Jasmine. Ugh, even her name irritated me.

I shut my eyes and braced myself for the answer I was going to at least get from this one question. "Were you with Jasmine?"

Flicking his cigarette over the rail, he then knelt down in front of me. Taking my hands in his, he said, "Gabs, look at me."

I had a hard time meeting his eyes, afraid he would tell me that he was with her and he didn't want to see me anymore. Just the little thought of that made my eyes sting and almost water down my cheeks. I took another drag and tipped my head up, careful not to blow smoke in his face. When I met his eyes, I really wanted to cry. His baby blues looked so sad. I really wanted to cry just from staring at him. He slowly reached up to stroke my cheek with the tip of his fingers.

"I want to tell you, but I can't. I hope you can understand that much. How do you know her anyway?"

My legs started to bounce with irritation. "She's in my ballet class at Juilliard. Told me one day to tell you hey. So Jasmine says 'hey'. Did you used to date her?"

"What? No." Tucker shook his head, making his hair fall in his eyes. But just like always, he raked his hand through it in a wild sexy mess.

I shook my head. "I don't understand. Is it me, Tuck? Am I pushing you away? I'm sorry that I've never had a boyfriend, that I'm a virgin. I grew up in a strict house with Carol and no friends. So I don't understand what you do when you're gone all the time. I'm sorry, but I don't understand why you keep going away."

"Boyfriend?" he asked and I looked into his eyes.

"Sorry, I didn't mean it like that. I meant guy, I've never had a *guy friend* like you. Crap. I'm sorry, just forget the whole thing." I bit my lower lip.

Stroking my cheek, he said, "Gabs, I just can't tell you right now is all. Maybe one day, okay? But not now. I really need you to trust me, though. Please?" His hand was so soft up on my face, tenderly dragging his fingers down to my lips.

"You're so beautiful. I've missed you, Gabs."

And then he kissed me. My inner self was still so confused.

Chapter Ten

Before I knew it, a month passed. Madame Ava was hitting us hard every day with the performance of *Swan Lake*. The auditions were tomorrow night and it was down to four girls—Jasmine, me, Sadie, and Mary—for the main role of Odette/Odile. Everyone was required to be there, but Madame Ava had a meeting with us to let us know that the bar was set high and that we are each other's competition. I didn't know the other two girls, as they came from different classes. Jasmine was still being a crap head to me every time we were alone together. She did stupid crap to me, too. Just the other day as I was walking to get my gym bag, she stuck her stupid slipper covered foot out in front of me, and I fell on my face. Everyone laughed and Jon was the only one who came to help me up.

I hung out with Tucker most days after class; he would pick me up right outside the school, and we would either go out for coffee at the little shop where we first met and play a couple of rounds of pool, or go to my apartment. When we would end up at my place, I had to admit, it was my favorite time with him.

And we would always end up on the couch, with Tucker between my legs, making out like crazy. I couldn't get enough of him and every day that I was with him, I wanted more and more. Today was one of those days. Tucker picked me up from Juilliard and we walked home hand in hand. The kissing started really fast, his hands roamed up and down my sides, barely touching underneath my breast. Every time he got closer, the more I moaned into his mouth. My body was getting greedy with want and need from him.

Tucker walked me backwards to the couch, but I wanted him in my bed. I had a hold of his face and pulled him back down the hallway and we stumbled into my room. This was it, I couldn't handle it anymore. I wanted him. My hands were going crazy in his hair as I pushed my tongue in and out of his mouth. I really didn't know what I was doing, but I knew he wanted me just as bad. His hands gripped my shirt while his fingertips grazed my hot skin as we tumbled on my bed. I pushed up on my elbows to the top of my bed while Tucker followed my lead and was between my legs.

My mind kept screaming at me, *Too many clothes! Too many clothes!* I wanted to strip him down to nothing; I wanted to feel his hot flushed body up against mine so bad, and I couldn't wait.

I was barely able to say his name, but it came out more like a moan. "Tucker..." His hands were under my shirt, making their way up to cup my breasts. I cried out at the sensation and the pleasure shooting through my stomach and between my legs. I arched my hips up, needing him.

"Oh Gabs, you're so hot." And his tongue dived back into my mouth, his words driving my body insane.

Reaching down between us, I grabbed him through his jeans, making him hiss through his teeth, sending tingling chills up my back.

"I want you, Tucker. I want you so much." I continued to rub him through his stiff pants. He suddenly stopped and rested his forehead against mine, then stopped moving his legs all together against where I needed him the most. Exhaling a deep breath through his nose and lightly kissing my lips, he started untangling his body from mine.

I grabbed his arm. "Wait, what's wrong?"

His eyes weren't sad, but filled with something else – regret maybe? "Not yet, Gabs, I respect you way too much to do that to you."

Of course being a girl, the only thing I heard out of that was that he didn't want me.

"You don't want me?" I felt like crying.

"No, trust me, I do. I very much want to get inside you like nothing else, but..." He picked up my hand and kissed it. "I just don't want to pressure you is all."

I had to admit, I was so frustrated with that. I wanted this; the last thing he was doing was pressuring me into something that I wanted just as badly as he did.

"Okay."

Tucker bent forward, looking straight in my eyes. "Okay? Are you mad at me?"

"No, never!" I jumped at him and he raised his hands up.

"All right, keep your panties on."

Looking up at him through my lashes, I teased, "What if I want them off?"

His breath hitched and he shook his head. "Gabs, don't tease me."

"What if I want you to take them off? Just like this..." Before I had any time to even think about what my next move was, I reached down and pulled my sweater up and over my head. I was now in my black bra. My heart was beating so hard, I thought Tucker could see my chest thumping up and down with each beat. He stared at me, and when I say stared at me, he stared. I should just take a picture for him.

His fingers came up and touched my bra strap on my left shoulder, slipping beneath it, hooking his finger and then pulling it slowly down. My hand reached up to take down the other side, thinking I won, but I didn't.

"No, stop." He put the strap back on my shoulder and kissed me softly. "Not yet, Gabs." he said against my mouth in a whisper. I sagged down on my bed.

"Okay fine." I undid my hair and scratched my scalp. That felt nice and relieved some tension that was going on in the room. I laid there in my bra and jeans and before I knew it, we weren't alone anymore. I heard Rachel, Jade, Brad, and Jett's voices as they all came into the apartment, laughing.

"Tucker! You dirty bastard, quit boning that ballerina and get out here!" Brad yelled.

"Trust me, there's no boning going on," I mumbled under my breath. Rubbing my face in annoyance as I sat up and swinging my legs off the bed, I picked up my sweater to slip it back on. I turned to leave my room once it was back into place, but Tucker stuck his hand in the back pocket of my jeans and pulled me backwards into him.

"Gabs," he whispered into my ear from behind me; I shut my eyes as his arms wrapped around my waist. "You don't know how badly I want you. I want your body beneath mine. Naked, covered in sweat from the heat of our bodies." His hands slipped under my sweater, which now felt like it weighed a hundred pounds and desperately wanted to be off my body. His pinky finger slipped into the waist of my jeans and my hands grabbed at both of his wrists, moving with him while his wonderful words filled my ears.

"I want you naked, quivering so badly you won't be able to find your toes. I want my tongue all over your body, your boobs, sucking so hard on your nipples, you'll cry out in pleasure. Even between your legs, Gabs. I want you every way I can, you'll be begging me to stop. And after I'm done, you'll be so exhausted that you'll sleep for days." Right after he said that, his hand moved up my stomach and slipped under my bra to cup my bare breast.

"Tucker." My head dropped back onto his shoulder.

"And this Gabs..." His other hand moved down on the outside of my jeans and rubbed me so hard where I wanted him. I moaned out loud, but that didn't stop his wicked words. "I will have this any way I can and it will be so good, babe." His hand tightened on my breast. "It will be so good, my body moving in and out of yours, you'll be lost. You'll want more and more, you'll be begging me, but not yet. I care for you way too much. You deserve it to be special, but all in good time, babe." He kissed my neck, stepped around me, and left my room to go join our friends.

Holy hell that was hot.

Eventually, I came out of my bedroom a huge hot mess. Rachel raised her brows at me while Jade and Jett smirked at me. I glanced out the windows to see Brad talking to Tucker while he smoked. Tucker didn't look very happy with whatever Brad was telling him, but when he caught me staring, he winked at me and smiled that wonderful Tucker smile. I felt my face heat back up again.

"Damn Gabs, why are you so flushed?" Jade tossed at me.

"Good news!" Rachel screamed out before I could even say something to Jade.

"What's that?" I walked around to the couch to sit next to Rachel.

"Remember that concert with *Avenged Sevenfold, Black Falcon?*" she said, snapping her fingers at Jade, not remembering the name of it.

Jade grabbed her snappy hand to stop. "Stop it, dumbass."

"Pfft...whatever. Jade got us three tickets and when I told Brad, he went and got three tickets, too. We're leaving in an hour, so let's go get ready." Rachel stood up from the couch, clapping her hands.

"Wait, a rock concert? Tonight?" I blinked up at Rachel then looked over at Jade who nodded.

"Yep, we got to get rock and roll ready. Come on, Gabs." And off we went.

Once again, I found myself sitting on the toilet and being all dolled up by Rachel. She teased the crap out of my hair, then brushed it down and pulled it up. She made me open and shut my eyes so many times, they started to feel dry. Once she was done and I looked in the mirror, the ordinary Abigail wasn't there, but a rocker chick was. My eyes were heavily blackened with eyeliner; my hair was pulled up on the top of my head in a very messy bun.

"All right, clothes. I know the perfect outfit just for you." Rachel went into her bedroom.

"I don't know if that's a good thing coming from you," I stated to her as I followed her into her bedroom. Ignoring my words, she started flinging clothes out of her closet like crazy. It was seriously raining clothes .

"Aww. I totally forgot I had this dress." Rachel pulled out a white short summer dress. It was really cute, very summery. I could see myself wearing something like that.

"Can't I just wear that?" I asked, nodding in the direction of the dress.

"Ha! No. This is special to me." Rachel carefully put the dress back in her closet and continued on searching.

"Here!" she called and threw a pair of black leather pants at me. "Here!" She did it again but this time it was a deep red tube top.

"I really want something that has straps, Rach. What if someone pulls it down and my boobs fall out?" I wave the clothes in her face. She tossed her red hair over her shoulder and just blinked at me.

"Wear a black bra and let the straps show. That would be hot."

"Ugh, whatever," I said and went into my room to change.

Rachel and I walked down the hallway to everyone in the living room in record time. Rachel wore a short black dress with her makeup and hair the same as mine. Brad whistled and pinned Rachel up against the wall to kiss her like there was no tomorrow. Rachel was hooking one of her heels around his calf.

Nothing in common, my butt.

Tucker came up to me and held my arms out to get a good look at me.

"I like this, but I prefer my ballerina Gabs." Then he kissed my lips that were caked in bright red lipstick, which got on his lips. I wiped them off as best as I could while he laughed.

"I can wear my ballet outfit." I giggled.

"That would be pretty sexy, but I don't think Rachel would agree." We both turned to see Brad shoving his tongue into Rachel's mouth and both of us laughed.

"Whatever, can we just go already?" Jade asked pulling Jett to the front door.

We took two cabs to Madison Square Garden for the concert. People were lined up and down the sidewalks, waiting to get in the doors. A lot of the girls were dressed like me, and they all looked at me with a glare in their eyes. Tucker received tons of *hey's* and *hi's* and that silly shake thing that guys do as we walked past them to stand in line. We didn't wait long. I enjoyed standing in front of Tucker with his arms wrapped around my waist, his chin resting on my shoulder, saying how hot I looked in my red top with my bra straps showing.

"I can see straight down your top."

I gasped and turned, but he silenced me with a kiss.

"I'm just letting you know how badly I really do want you." Then he would kiss and suck on my neck. The music got louder the closer we got to the doors. I suddenly was very nervous. I've never been to a rock concert before; I didn't listen to that type of music either. We gave the guard our tickets and walked inside. A bunch of tables were lined up with different shirts of the bands.

"Do you want a shirt?"

I shook my head, "No."

"Just think how hot you'd look wearing only a shirt from a rock concert we went to together. Of course you would be naked underneath." He winked.

Oh, now he's just teasing me.

We walked into the main auditorium, and I gripped Tucker's hand so tightly he had to tell me to loosen my grip or he was going to lose fingers. He laughed and I glared at him. Our seats were on the floor and about the tenth row from the stage next to the big giant sound speakers.

"These seats are awesome, Jade!" Rachel yelled at her and Jade gave her thumbs up. Then the lights went dark and the music started right up with Black Falcon. Tucker's hands tapped my hips with the beat of the drums.

When their set was up, Brad and Rachel went to get us all beers. I didn't really care that I was underage at that moment, I was having fun. Tucker left my side and went to a group of mean looking guys in the corner. The lights were dim so I couldn't really see what he was doing. It looked like some sort of hand shake, but Tucker looked in his open palm, then gave the guy something back. He did the same thing, but stuffed whatever Tucker gave him in the back pocket of his jeans and left rather quickly.

A plastic cup appeared right in my line of sight. "You shouldn't let your eyes wander sometimes," Brad told me in my ear. I narrowed my eyes at him and took a sip of the warm brown liquid. I actually enjoyed the bland taste. Tucker came back to me and slipped an arm around my waist and kissed my temple.

"Who were you talking to over there?" I smiled up at him and then the lights went back down to start another small band from Brooklyn.

"Just some buddies of mine," Tucker said, then kissed my head. The little band wasn't awful, but they weren't good. We sat in the chairs and watched the group go from okay to worse. People actually started throwing their plastic cups at them. I continued to sip on my beer.

"Don't set that drink down whatever you do, Gabs!" Tucker yelled.

"Why?" I asked, taking another big gulp of the relaxing, rich taste of beer.

"Someone could put something in it. Try and finish it; if not just give it to me and I will!"

I nodded at him, but surprisingly, I finished it on my own. The lights went black again and Black Falcon took the stage for a second time. They were awesome and played a total of seven more songs. One of the band members with a Mohawk kept coming up center stage with the singer. He shaped a V with his fingers and stuck out his tongue, wiggling it. The crowd went wild while Rachel screamed for him. I secretly think she wanted to get his attention.

They all were a sweaty mess when their set was over. Brad gave me another beer and I gulped it down faster than the first. I was having a blast with the loud music, dancing with Tucker who held onto my hips and would grind into my backside. I would push back on him and he would suck and kiss on my neck again. My arms went up to his hair to keep him in place behind me.

When it was time for Avenged Sevenfold to come out, the crowd went wild, including the boys and Jade. I covered my ears from the screaming girls that were behind me. They were screaming out something that sounded like mmm...Shadows. Out of all the music that was played here tonight, these guys were my favorite.

Tucker and I continued to dance, touch, and caress each other with the beat of the music. When the stage went dark and the fans started cheering like crazy, I thought that the show was over. Apparently not, because the band came back out and announced they would play one more song. It was my favorite so far, and a lot slower than the rest. Tucker sang along to the song called *Dear God*. His voice repeating the lyrics in my ear touched me deep down and awakened feelings inside me that I have never felt before.

When the concert was officially over, we all headed out of the building. Rachel announced she wanted to go to a bar to have more drinks just to relax. I immediately agreed with her. The high-heeled shoes were killing my feet; I really wanted to sit and needed another drink.

We walked to a bar that was across the street from the Garden, which was jam-packed full of people who were at the concert. We found an empty table in the back, but it only had three chairs. The guys sat and pulled us girls on their laps. I loved sitting on Tucker's lap; it made me feel protected. We shared a pitcher full of beer and two rounds of shots. I was feeling a lot more relaxed. Out of the blue, I turned in Tucker's arms and attacked his mouth in a hungry kiss. He wasn't expecting it at all and we almost fell over off the chair. When I pulled away from him, I noticed a body really close behind us and when I looked, it was none other than Jasmine.

"Hey Tucker," she called out to him; he did a quick glance over his shoulder and turned back rather too quickly.

"Shit," he murmured into my neck.

"Abigail, nice to see you." Jasmine smirked. A guy came up behind her and placed an arm on her hip. She looked up at him sweetly, turned and then left without another word. That guy wasn't Jon, but I didn't even know for sure if they were dating at all.

Tucker's body went stiff under mine. I tried to scoot off his lap, but he held my legs firmly, not letting go.

"We need more shots!" Jade yelled while raising her arm for a waitress.

We took our shots and I was getting buzzed. I checked the time on my phone, which also had four missed calls from Carol. It was one in the morning. I knew I had to get to bed; I had my *Swan Lake* audition at eight in the morning. No matter how hard I tried to get off Tucker's lap, he wouldn't let me. I finally was able to wiggle out of his hold and go to the bathroom with Rachel and Jade.

"Guys, I gotta get going," I told them in the quiet bathroom. Both Rachel and Jade were in the stalls while I washed my hands and fixed the smeared black eye liner around my eyes the best I could. Jade came out of the stall first and washed her hands.

"Why you gotta go?"

"I have that audition in the morning. I can't miss it." Jade stumbled over to dry her hands.

"Okay, we can just have the boys come over, too." Jade shrugged like it wasn't a big deal. But this was a huge deal to me; I couldn't miss it. I couldn't even be five seconds late for this audition. Madame Ava told us that if we weren't there by the time she played any music, she wouldn't only give us a written warning, but she would also shut and lock the doors so we couldn't get in the studio. Then I would be in deep trouble.

I opened the bathroom door and smacked right into Jasmine as she was coming in.

"Abigail. You seem like you've had a lot to drink tonight. Don't be late tomorrow." She walked around me and then the door shut.

I went back to Tucker's side without any other run-ins with Jasmine. That girl was everywhere; I couldn't stand it. We all had another round of shots, but I dreaded doing mine a little. We left the bar, all of us on wobbly legs; our group got two cabs to take us back to the apartment. I didn't remember much after that. I knew that Tucker and I had our hands all over each other, laughing, kissing, grinding, and all of the above things that couples do. Were we even a couple yet? We'd been out on one official date and now a rock concert. I wanted him to be my boyfriend, but I wouldn't even know how to bring it up. Our apartment was booming with loud music and we girls were dancing with each other. I looked at the clock on my phone to see that it was four in the morning.

"I gotta goda beds," I slurred, and fell off Tucker's lap. The room spun all around me with the laughter from everyone made me laugh. I think I may have snorted.

"Come on, you." Tucker scooped me up and tossed me over his shoulder. I slapped his butt.

"Hey. No touching," he said as he grabbed both my butt cheeks and squeezed. Tucker tossed me on my bed as I wiggled out of my borrowed clothes. I wasn't surprised at all when I watched him strip down to his black boxers and climbed into bed with me.

Oh wow. He's nice looking just in black boxers. Yummy!

Tucker snuggled deep in my back and once my head hit the pillow, I was gone.

BEEP. BEEP. BEEP.

I barely had enough strength to open up one of my eyelids as the blasting sunlight streamed in my windows and caused this throbbing pain in my head. A body pressed into my back. I sat up in such a rush that I got dizzy and my head hit the pillow again. Then I remembered.

"Oh Shit!" I screamed and threw the covers off me and all onto Tucker. I stumbled into the bathroom with my leotard and changed.

Oh, I looked like hell.

I hurriedly brushed my teeth and grabbed elastic for my crazy hair. I had to be there at eight sharp or earlier. It was seven forty-five.

"Bye!" I called back to Tucker as I left my room with my ballet bag and ran out the door. I ran my heart out to Juilliard, I was completely out of breath when I reached the front doors and ran down the long hallway that seemed like it went on forever. Jasmine was standing at the door with her arms crossed and one brow arched at me. She didn't wait for me and hold the door open, but rather slammed in my face. I pulled it open and the music was playing in the room. The other dancers were all lined up at the barre ready to go.

Oh crap. I'm too late.

"Abigail!" My back straightened at the shrill sound of Madame Ava's voice and I dropped my bag.

"Yes, Madame Ava?"

She came up from behind me, silent like a poisonous spider ready to attack at any given moment. "Why do you think I should let you audition today?" Madame Ava asked as she circled around me. Her hands clasped together at her back.

"I'm sorry, Madame Ava. I overslept."

She stopped in front of my face. Her eyes were just as cruel as Carol's when I disappointed her. "This is your warning, Abigail. Get in line right now and this will not happen again."

I let out a huge sigh of relief.

By the time I had my slippers on, I went and stood in the fifth position at the barre. Madame Ava told us that we were to perform a single dance of one of the most popular scenes of *Swan Lake*. Not only would we be judged on how we presented our face, but our posture, legs, arms, and while on pointe, too. One little thing we forgot or did wrong could cost us the part. I'd practiced my scene with Ramón so many times; I even had my triple pirouette down, perfectly, thanks to Madame Ava.

Jasmine went first, setting the scene high with perfect dance moves. People were actually in awe as her feet quietly hit the floor. No sound. That's what a perfect ballerina does – if you can make your feet move and hop with no noise as you land. Jon was next; he wouldn't get the main part, but he would be the dancer to be with Odette/Odile during the scenes that needed him. Sadie was after Jon and her moves were just about as perfect as Jasmine's, until the very end when she stumbled and had to regain her footing. She just lost it. Mary was next and she was probably the worst so far in the group; she lost her footing and had to start over twice. I watched as Madame Ava made it clear that she made a big X on the clip board.

Fifth in line and now it was my turn. I started out great; my middle was awesome and I ended my triple pirouette with grace and closed very nicely. Even with a pounding headache, I was quite proud. I loved when I was proud of myself when it was something I'd worked so hard to accomplish. We were excused into the hall as Madame Ava went through our names and decided who would best fit the part, saying she would post the paper on the door. I took off my slippers and grabbed my bag to go into the hallway. I spotted Tucker standing there with his back up against some lockers. His smiled faded when he saw me and held open his arms, into which I gladly went. Breathing in his usual

Tucker scent of cigarette and leather, I was so grateful he was here.

"Hey Tucker." I pulled away from him to see Jasmine standing behind us. He didn't say anything to her, but I heard his breathing pick up as I faced her. I crossed my arms over my chest, and Tucker took hold of my hips to press me into him.

"What Jasmine?" I snipped.

"Just wanted to say hi to Tucker." His hands tightened on my hips so I took charge.

"You said it. So what do you really want?"

Jasmine's eyes narrowed at me. "Geez Abigail, you don't need to be rude. You hear how rude she is, Tucker?"

"I'm not. I'm honest and honestly... I don't like you," I said, standing my ground. She might be the best ballet dancer in class, but Tucker was mine. I didn't want to share with her.

"I heard her," Tucker said behind me. That made me smile. "I like it when she's feisty," He said, kissing and softly biting my shoulder.

The door to the ballet room opened and Madame Ava stepped out.

"Abigail, may I speak with you?"

I pulled away from Tucker. "Yes, Madame Ava." I picked up my ballet bag and followed her back into the studio. She softly shut the door and faced me.

"Abigail, here's the list. I want you to read it first." She handed me a piece of paper. Why was she doing this? Did I get the part? Butterflies roamed my stomach as I read the paper. And that's when it hit me right square in my chest. My heart started to constrict with the worst feeling ever. Seeing the line up sheet of the parts, and it big bold letters it read:

Jasmine Carter: Odette/Odile
Abigail McCall: Understudy for Odette/Odile

My eyes filled with tears and gushed down my face, dropping the paper as if it was on fire, and then I ran from the room. I passed Tucker crying. I also passed Jade and Rachel who surprised me outside, but I still didn't stop. He chased me all the way home, yelling at me to stop. I eventually dropped my ballet bag in the process to run away from him faster. I pushed the button in the elevator, with Tucker hot on my heels. He appeared as the doors slid shut, his face flushed from the heat of the run, but I couldn't stop my feet. I made it to my apartment in one huge crying mess.

I wanted to be alone in the dark. I was so humiliated at myself. I practiced so hard for that spot. I wanted it more than anything and I didn't get it. Suddenly, my stomach did that nasty turn I dreaded. Running to my bedroom, straight in the bathroom right before my nerves set on edge, I threw up in the toilet. I hated myself for this. I hated the fact that I threw up every time I made myself get so upset. I sobbed in the toilet bowl as I threw up again and again until nothing came out, and my stomach cramped up as I took in deep breaths.

"Gabs?" Tucker called from in my room.

Oh crap. He can't see me like this. I hurried and flushed the toilet, but I was so sick to my stomach, I couldn't get up from the floor, being way too dizzy. I listened to his steps getting closer to the bathroom, then his shoes echoed on the tile and that's when he saw me. The *real* me.

"Damn, Gabs, what's wrong?"

I shut my eyes. I couldn't look at him. I was so ashamed of myself; I didn't get the part in *Swan Lake*, and now Tucker was here with me after I'd made myself throw up. I couldn't stop the tears this time.

"You're so pale. Are you sick?" Tucker pulled my body up and swept away the sweaty strands of hair that was stuck to my forehead. He practically dragged me over to the double sink and rinsed my face like a sick child, which was something I never had done to me when I was little and sick.

"I screwed up," I cried. "I screwed up so bad."

"Shhh...baby girl. Tell me what's wrong."

"I didn't get the part. Instead I overslept; I got drunk and partied all night long with you and I didn't get the part I've practiced for, for the longest time." My head fell on his shoulder and I cried. Tucker rubbed my back and tried his best to sooth my comfort.

"Is that why you were throwing up? Are you hung over?"

I didn't want to lie to him. He was already keeping things from me, and I didn't want to keep anything from him. I felt like I couldn't let the barrier grow between us.

"No, I did it. I do that when I get upset," I mumbled out, ashamed of myself.

"You make yourself throw up? Like an...eating disorder?"

"It's not an eating disorder. It was at first, and now it's just something my body does on its own. I hate it so bad; I feel like I can't control it anymore. It's taken control of me."

Tucker didn't say anything as I explained how it all started with Carol, the most evil stepmother anyone dreaded having in their life. It all started with my weight because Carol assumed I was overweight. Now I was here and it only happened when Carol got me so upset about something, I always found myself in my bathroom, hugging my toilet like a life support.

Tucker picked me up in his strong arms and took me into my bedroom. I let him strip me down to my leotard, but I had enough strength to change into something more comfortable. I climbed back into bed and I didn't care that Tucker stripped down to his boxers again just to hold me close as I silently cried.

I vowed to myself that I would be in that studio day in and day out. Tucker gently wiped my face. He kissed my cheek, the back of my neck and shoulder, still trying to bring me some comfort.

"Gabs, I'm sorry that I didn't take better care of you last night. I should have stopped and taken you home last night to let you rest. I know how important this was to you and I've failed you."

I cried harder but made no noise as he told me this. He was blaming himself that I was so upset at not getting this part. It wasn't his fault; it was mine for being so irresponsible and being out late, drinking, and having fun.

"I'm glad you told me about your throwing up thing, though." I had to laugh at the way he said that. "But promise me that you'll try and not do that. I know it can't be healthy for you." I just nodded my head to him and he kissed my shoulder over and over again. His fingertips lightly tickled my neck and back. I was so exhausted and didn't have any strength left. I was paying for what my friend and I considered fun by not getting the part I worked so hard for. I listened to Tucker's breaths and when they finally evened out, I fell asleep, feeling a little better and more comforted than I'd ever been in all my life.

When I woke up, Tucker was still there, so we talked some more about my little problem. Tucker told me to just breathe whenever Carol called me; she couldn't do any harm to me. That made me snort. He explained how dangerous it was when I did that to myself; he didn't want me to hurt on the inside and to talk to him whenever I needed to vent – said that I could trust him. The more I was with Tucker, the more I liked him and the feelings were just getting stronger.

That made me smile.

Chapter Eleven

I still couldn't believe I didn't get that damn part. I hated myself when I saw Jasmine's name up as Odette/Odile and I was the understudy. The thought of being the understudy irritated me to no end. I spun around and around in the mirror up on pointe, missing that last balance as I tried to position my legs just right at the end.

Stomping my foot as I grunted, the room echoed from my frustration. I wasn't getting it; the more and harder I tried, my body wouldn't complete my turn. I was getting so aggravated with myself for being the damn understudy!

Resting up against the barre, I hung my head. My eyes started to burn from my unshed tears. Carol will be so angry with me about this. I just kept praying that she wouldn't find out. She will hold it against me for a long time even if it was dead and buried, and she would always find a way to bring it up. Standing up straight, I went back into the middle of the studio.

"Breathe Abigail," I told myself, and shut my eyes one more time. I started inhaling through my nose, and exhaling throughout my mouth. Opening up my eyes again, I glanced at my posture as I went up on *en pointe* and stood there, taking in my body. I was staring at my boxed toes, making sure my legs and knees were locked and straight, my hands down at my sides before lifting them slowly, together and over my head. Standing on *en pointe* with my fingers locked together, I straightened my spine, raised my chin, and held my neck up high. This was one of my favorite positions to be in, up on my toes with my arms above my head. I shut my eyes and I was a little girl again, looking in on one of the ballet classes that made me want to become a ballerina.

I remember watching them as they slowly moved with beauty up on their toes. My body started to move with no music in the room, but with the music I heard that very day when I was little. From *The Sleeping Beauty* music to the *Pas D'action (Rose Fairy)*, I remember just like it was yesterday, with the soft violins, hearing their teacher softly mutter the count to them, listening only to her voice in my head. It wasn't Madame Ava giving me direction, or Carol yelling at me this time.

This was the time that was my favorite to dance. I felt free to do my own moves, to glide across the floor and leap into the air without a care about who was watching me. I just moved on how I felt. Most of the time I felt sad as I moved, but altogether it was one of my favorite times, being able to glide without anyone judging me on my posture. I could do it all on my own; now I could hear my feet on the wood floor in the ballet room, leaping into the air and landing flat on my feet. Knowing I landed it just perfectly, I smiled. My legs moved and I went up on pointe to turn over and over, and then tucked my right leg in to close the move in a graceful turn. My arms straight out as I bowed to no one...or so I thought.

I opened my eyes to catch Tucker's in the mirror at the front door to the class. His arms were crossed over his chest, he was wearing his leather jacket, black pants, and gray V-neck shirt, and he had a killer smile that I just loved every time I saw him. His hair was a mess, but I liked that, too; his smile was beaming, so I could see that perfect dimple in his cheek.

I suddenly felt very nervous that he was watching me. He pushed his body off the doorframe and slowly walked to me.

"You were beautiful, Gabs, and you even did that toe thing." I stifled my giggle and smiled.

"You liked it?"

His brows raised and his blue eyes widened at my words. "Liked it? Gabs, I loved watching you just now. Your eyes shut." He brought his hand slowly up and his knuckles slowly brushed my cheek. "You looked as if you were floating and I gotta admit, that toe thing is amazing. Can you do it again?"

This time I laughed as I went up on *en pointe*. Tucker bent down, resting his hands on his knees as he stared at my toes with intent eyes, studying my feet like they were the most remarkable thing he'd ever seen.

"Damn girl, doesn't that hurt? You are seriously right up on your damn toes." He pointed at my feet and I giggled.

"Yep, I'm right up on my damn toes." He straightened up as I came back to flat ground.

Placing his hands on my hips he asked, "Really though, doesn't that hurt you?"

I nodded. "It hurt really badly when I first started, but you get used to it with the stretching and doing it almost every day. Sometimes my toes still bleed and they bruise pretty badly; it can get ugly. I hate my feet, and you'll never catch me wearing flip flops."

Tucker cringed and shook all over as if he was in pain himself. I may have over exaggerated at that. "I also gotta tell ya that you look pretty hot in the black swimming suit you're wearing." Tucker was looking behind me, and I'm sure at my butt.

I started laughing so hard; my face flamed up and burned my cheeks from my smile.

"It's a leotard, Tucker," I smirked.

"Oh, you're such a smartass." Just then, Tucker grabbed me and held me up in his strong arms and I was able to wrap my legs around his waist. Laughing some more in his neck and inhaling his spicy scent of cigarettes and leather, I felt his lips touch the base of my neck and shoulder. His hands moved down to cup my butt to hold me up better and I locked my ankles.

I moved my face to stare at him in his sparkling blue eyes as he lightly kissed my lips and they tingled at his soft caress, sending shivers down my spine and into my stomach.

"I love hearing you laugh and seeing you smile," he said against my mouth.

I had no words to say to him, but the whole entire room shifted with this spark between us. It was something so special that it hit me hard – the right-in-the-gut sort of feeling. I'd never felt like this before and I didn't want it to stop. Leaning back down, I kissed Tucker again and sighed in his mouth. Our tongues swiftly danced as the goose bumps moved down my arms and legs. Turning our light kiss into something more serious, the one word that came to mind was...passion. Before it could get any hotter, Tucker pulled away and set me down.

"Now, I want to see more of your moves."

He slapped my butt and I shook my head. He wanted to watch me and I was so going to let him. I shut my eyes again and went up *en pointe* to start my entire routine over. I was able to forget about *Swan Lake*, Jasmine, Madame Ava and Carol, because Tucker was able to help me do so and become that person I wanted to be when I was little.

Tucker was just amazed every time I went up on my toes. I grabbed a pair of guy slippers and tossed them in his direction.

"Put them on," I giggled.

"Hell no. One, that's not my style and two, guys really wear these?" He held them up by a string.

I walked over and sat down, crossing my legs at my ankles and leaned back on my elbows.

"Yep. They even wear tights." I chuckled as I watched him pick them up with two fingers and tossed them over to the other side of me. My eyes followed them and when I turned my head back, my lips were met by Tucker's. His hand cupped my face as his tongue entered my mouth and I sighed. I let him take control over my mouth, as his body pressed into my side. I easily laid down on the cold wood floor of the dance studio. Tucker half laid on my body as his kisses became more possessive of my mouth, one of his legs moving in between mine.

"You taste so good, baby girl," he said, and I was lost in him. He gave my face pepper kisses down my lips to my neck and shoulder. My hands roamed in his hair and he moaned when I softly raked my nails down his scalp and the back of his neck. So I did it again, and I felt his body shudder against mine as he took my mouth again.

"Ahem!" I untangled my legs from Tucker and shot up to my feet, pulling Tucker up with me as I faced Madame Ava.

"Abigail." Her tone was more of a warning. "I thought you were practicing?"

I looked down at my feet and Tucker whispered in my ear. "Look up."

I met her eyes. "I was, but now I'm all done and Tucker came to walk me home."

She took a breath and jerked her head towards the door, giving us a pretty big hint that our sweet time was up and we needed to go.

"Could you excuse us, please?" Madame Ava asked Tucker.

"I'll be right outside, baby girl." He kissed my cheek then left us alone in the ballet room. Madame Ava slowly walked up to me. I held my ground, not letting my head drop.

"Abigail, do you know why I gave Jasmine the part?"

I swallowed hard. I really didn't want to talk about this. "No, Madame Ava." I really wanted to tell her, "Cause she's your favorite," but I held my tongue back.

"You were late. If you would have been on time, you would have received that part. The door was open and it closed. You were late."

That damn Jasmine; she shut the door, not Madame Ava. I left my eyes down cast.

"Maybe the boyfriend should wait on the sidelines."

My eyes went back to meeting hers. "He's not my boyfriend,"

Madame Ava grabbed my hands. "Then why is he holding you back from being the best you can be, Abigail?" Her blue eyes were honest and sincere. "Think about it." Then she went straight into her office.

I sat on the bench, hearing the class door open and Tucker walked in as I was unlacing my slippers. He crouched down in front of me, taking over and removing my slippers. He brought my feet up, rubbing my toes and the soles of my feet. The deep pressure from his artistic hands felt so good on my sore feet. He put my flats on and pulled me up.

Tucker and I walked home holding hands. This was a favorite moment of mine, just our hands and fingers laced together. Just from holding his hand, it felt as if a flame was lit on my skin and was sending chills up my arm. I smiled and looked at him through my lashes. He leaned in to kiss me, but Brad came running towards us screaming Tucker's name.

"Tucker! Tuck." His footsteps hit the concrete and stopped right into Tucker's side. He pulled on Tucker's shoulder, whispering in his ear. But I wasn't stupid and pretended to ignore them. I heard every word that was exchanged.

"Tuck, man, I need the money now."

Tucker let go of my hand. "Dude, what the fuck?" He pulled Brad away by the collar and slammed him up to the brick wall of my building. I stepped back, but kept watching with wide eyes.

"How much, Brad?" Tucker growled.

Brad's eyes looked at me then whispered in Tucker's ear. I couldn't see Tucker's face, but he slammed Brad's body into the wall harder than the first time. I didn't need to see his face to know he was pissed off. He was starting to scare me from the force he used on Brad's shirt and body.

"Tucker, let him go," I said as softly as I could, and when he glanced at me over his shoulder, I added, "You're scaring me." He immediately let Brad go and swept me up in his arms.

"I'm sorry. I'll make it up to you," he told me in my neck and kissed my cheek. Tucker turned back to Brad. "Let me drop her off and I'll meet you at the shack." Brad nodded, then took off to cross the street and head into Central Park.

We started walking again and stopped at my front door. "What's the shack, Tucker?"

He quickly pecked my lips. "Don't worry about it. But I gotta go, baby girl,"

I pulled away from him. "That's okay. Just go and call me later, okay?"

"You won't be mad at me?" He raised a brow.

I gave a playful shove on his chest. "Nah, just don't scare me again."

Tucker gave me one more quick peck and off he went in the direction Brad was headed. I walked in the foyer a little shaky from Tucker's rage. I didn't like seeing him like that. That side of Tucker wasn't a pleasant one.

"You alright, Miss Abigail?" I turned to see Michael standing there holding a phone. "Do I need to call the cops?"

My eyes went wide. "No. It's just a misunderstanding."

Michael nodded and put the phone back in its cradle. "I've seen the way he looks at you, Miss. He likes you."

I smiled at his kind words. "I like him, too. He needs to be put on the list. His name is Tucker."

"Right away, Miss Abigail."

As I made my way into my dark apartment, I didn't have to shout for anyone to know that I was by myself. Jade would either be on the balcony or in her room with rock music playing. Rachel was shopping with her mom. Seriously, those two could shut a store down with the way they love to shop. My phone started buzzing as I walked to my bedroom to get undressed from my practice. It was an unknown number on my screen, but I decided to answer it in case it was Tucker using another phone.

"Hello?"

"Abigail?"

My bag slid off my shoulder and a loud thud sounded into the phone. "Abigail, you alright?"

I bent down to pick up my bag and set it on my bed. "Alex?"

He cleared his throat. "Yeah, how are you?"

What did I say? "Umm...I'm good."

He cleared his throat again, and he sounded uncomfortable. "I wanted to see if I could take you out to dinner tonight?"

I thought about it for about two seconds as I unzipped my bag and pulled out my dirty clothes. "Umm...I don't think so, Alex."

This was getting awkward fast. How did he even get my number?

"Alex, I need you to sign these documents for me ASAP," I heard my dad say on the other side of the phone.

"Right away, David. Abigail, I need to go. Think about it and call me back at this number. It's my desk phone." Then he hung up.

Okay, that was just a little odd.

I didn't hear from Tucker for four days after he dropped me off and went with Brad. Even Rachel mentioned that Brad was being an "ass" (her exact words) and not texting her back. She even threatened that she was going to go get some other guy if he didn't text back. I didn't dare do that with Tucker and blow it with him. Rachel and Brad's relationship was weird. She claimed that they had nothing in common, but when they were together, they were glued at the hip.

Maybe they both needed to be tamed by each other. Jade and Jett were so cute together—they never fought.

There was one time when I witnessed them having an argument out on the balcony. I was coming out from my bedroom and saw them out there. Jade's arms were flying about while Jett had his arms crossed and watched her pace back and forth. She then pointed an angry finger at him and tried to leave, but he grabbed her and pulled her to him. He cupped her face and talked to her. I knew he wasn't yelling because his face looked too calm to be yelling. She then threw her arms around his neck. I went back into my room after that.

Every practice stung my heart. I watched Jasmine and Madame Ava work together as I sat on the sidelines and sulked. The orchestra came in a couple of times to play music because Jasmine complained that she couldn't picture the dance without the actual music to the scene. I rolled my eyes. There were a couple of times when Jasmine would sit next to me to take a break and rub it in.

"Oh man, I'm exhausted, but I'm perfect for this part," she told me while fanning herself. I got up and left while she snickered to my back. I went back to the classroom to gather my things and leave. I knew Rachel would already be out of class early; I would just go sit with her. When I walked outside, she wasn't there, yet. I hopped up on the cement wall when someone spoke my name.

When I turned, Alex was walking towards me in his gray suit, with a white shirt and black tie. He was also holding two cups from Starbucks.

"Abigail," he nodded and handed me a cup. Instead of taking a sip, I smelled what was in it.

Caramel filled my nose and I took a daring sip. I expected it to be hot, but it wasn't.

"It's a caramel iced coffee." I looked up at Alex. "Thanks. Never had ice coffee, it's pretty tasty."

Alex sat next to me, sipping his coffee. "What are you doing out of class? Your father told me your class was over at noon."

Oh, my dad.

"I'm an understudy for the main part, but I left early."

Right then, the bell sounded and Rachel was right at my side, looping her arm through mine and pulling me up.

"Gabs, who's your friend?" Rachel asked while nodding in Alex's direction. I hoped she didn't get any ideas to get back at Brad with Alex. Well...maybe that wouldn't be a bad thing.

"Umm...Rachel Dawson, this is Alex Blair. He's a lawyer at my dad's firm."

Rachel suddenly jerked me back and was right in my face. "That's Alex?" she whispered.

"Yeah, he brought me coffee," I said, holding up the Starbucks cup to her face.

Her green eyes widened "We gotta go."

Alex must have heard her because he stepped up behind us. "Abigail, I wanted to drive you home and possibly take you out to dinner tonight." He straightened his tie that really didn't need to be straightened at all.

"Sorry, dude, she's got plans," Rachel told Alex, pulling me along with her. "Okay, I don't like Mr. Richey Rich pants. He's an ass; I can tell just by his vibes."

I giggled "I definitely agree with you on that one. He called me a couple of days ago, and asked me out to dinner. Aren't we going to wait for Jade?"

Rachel shook her head, red hair hitting my face. "No, Jett is coming to get her."

We walked the rest of the way home in silence. What I mean is, *I* was silent. Brad called Rachel, who turned into a huge giggling mess. I pulled her elbow to get her attention.

"Has he heard from Tucker?" I asked aloud, hoping Brad would at least hear me. I could hear him talking, but Rachel soon shook her head. I was disappointed.

"Oh, baby. I'd rather have your body between my legs," Rachel said and I raced into the building, leaving her behind.

I woke up the next morning feeling a little refreshed. Today was our first show of *Swan Lake* but, since Jasmine didn't magically fall and break both of her legs, I was still the understudy. Nothing changed that. I stood at the side curtain, watching her move across the stage. Rachel and Jett were in the audience, but they mostly watched Jade play her cello. The show was a good start to the year. Everyone applauded for Jasmine as she took center stage to receive her big bouquet of roses. I didn't even know why I came; I wasn't needed at all. When Rachel, Jade, Jett and I walked to the apartment, I found Tucker out front with Brad smoking. Rachel squealed and ran into Brad's arms, wrapping her legs around his waist while he groped her butt. I smiled at them. I wish they would just admit their feelings to each other. They were perfect together.

Tucker approached me, but my body took over and copied Rachel's moves. I jumped in his arms. His scent filled my nose of leather and cigarettes. I missed him so much. He kissed me deeply and his tongue thrusted in my mouth, seeming to ache for mine. Tucker held me in his arms as we entered the elevator and moved into my apartment. He headed straight for my bedroom.

Oh Yes.

He tasted so good. My shirt was pushed up while his hands were all over my body in unison with his soft tongue. I tugged his leather jacket off his shoulders and he shrugged out of it while I raked my hands through his long hair. Somewhere in the distance, I heard a phone ringing. We ignored it, our lips not leaving one another's as his fingers pulled at my clothes. I sat up, pulling my shirt up and off my body, needing him skin on skin. Tucker's lips moved down across my collarbone and down between my breasts. My hands gripped his hair and pulled, causing Tucker to gently bite my skin. There was more moaning, more ringing, and then pounding on my bathroom door.

"Gabs!" Jade's voice yelled.

Again we ignored it. Then my bathroom door burst open with Jade and Jett walking in.

"Dude, get out!" Tucker yelled at Jett, probably because I was shirtless. Jade covered Tucker's mouth and looked down at me.

"Carol is in the living room."

I shot up out from underneath Tucker's body. His jeans were stricken with proof of how much he wanted me. Jade helped me smooth my hair down, which I didn't know Tucker had pulled out of my classic bun. Once I looked presentable enough, Jade shoved me out of my room. I heard Jett in the background, "Let her go alone, that lady didn't look happy to see me here."

Oh that sounded just great—a pissed off Carol. That's exactly what I wanted at a time like this. She didn't even wait for me to get to the living room before she started yelling at me.

"How dare you get the understudy in that ballet! Do you not care about your future as a ballerina? Because you're not acting like the girl that wanted to do this at all! Who was that man that was in here? I demand to know who is inside my home with my daughter! He is trouble, covered in tattoos." I couldn't answer her questions. I was a coward for letting her talk to me this way while Tucker was in my room. Carol stepped up to me. "You are an embarrassment to the family. To me, your father, his firm, everyone! Everyone is watching our every move, and you are letting them down. Shape up, young lady, or I will shatter your dreams like they weren't even yours to begin with." Her finger hit my chest as she walked past me. "And get rid of that boy. I don't want to see him back in my house again." Then she slammed the door behind her.

The tears streamed from my eyes so fast, I couldn't control them. Was I really letting all those people down? At my dad's firm, too? I didn't want that at all. Then that feeling in my stomach happened and I booked it to my bathroom, shoving Jett aside as I barely made it to the toilet.

"Shit!" Jade yelled and came to my aid. I sobbed in the toilet.

"Dude, she alright?" Jett asked of anyone in the room.

My cries echoed in the porcelain bowl more and more as my stomach emptied. "I got this, Jade." Then I felt his hands on my back, gently rubbing me. Once I stopped, Tucker turned me into his chest as I continued to cry.

"Breathe, baby girl. I know it hurts, but breathe." He soothed and, comforted me, letting me cry into his shirt.

I met his eyes. "I'm I a....fail...ure...Tucker?" He wiped my face dry and kissed my forehead.

"No Gabs, you're no failure. She's a bitch for talking to you like that. I tried to come out, but Jett held me back. Don't you ever think you're a failure."

He hugged me to his chest so tight, I gasped for breath. Tucker continued to tenderly talk in my ear, reminding me to breathe. I concentrated on my breath, as if I would be dancing and remembering to breathe out evenly. It helped... a lot. Tucker stayed with me that night and the next day, but had to leave me for three weeks, saying he couldn't explain, but hoped I would understand. I didn't. I never did. I just hoped the scene with Carol didn't run him off.

Chapter Twelve

Jade and Jett were spending more and more time together. The night of the rockin' concert, Jade came home beaming because Jett gave her this necklace with a little black skull covered in diamonds and wearing a gold crown. It was so cute how she acted about it, and whenever Stella or her dad called, she would slide it back and forth on the black chain.

It was a nervous habit, just like mine. Jade went through about a pack of cigarettes when Stella called, keeping Jade on the phone forever. Jade smoked; I threw up. Jade was right when we first met; we were both messed up in our own way.

I was just getting ready to start making something to eat when the doorbell rang. I wasn't expecting anyone tonight, plus our doorman, Michael, didn't call to let me know who was here. I padded over to the door and opened it to find Tucker on the other side, looking gorgeous as ever, wearing black jeans with his usual gray hoodie and black leather jacket. His hands were deep in his front pockets, and his hair was in the messy style I loved and missed. My heart literally dropped into my stomach when he gave me that side smile with his deep dimple. "Hey Gabs." I loved the sound of his voice. He stepped up to me with our eyes locked, and he slowly put his hands on my hips. Our breaths mixed with each other's, making my face heat up at the soft touch of him. Sliding his hands ever so slowly to lock behind my back, he pulled me into a deep embracing hug. My hands snaked around his neck and as I locked my fingers together to hold him close, my fingers brushed his long hair.

Oh, how I've missed him.

I shut my eyes and listened to our hearts pounding into our chests, his heart thumping against mine, causing butterflies to roam throughout my stomach. I felt his lips so close to my neck; his breathing was deep, and I could feel the air from him flowing down my neck and under the back of my shirt. I shook against his body and he chuckled. Tucker pulled away from me, staring deeply in my eyes. I could feel his energy radiating off him; I wanted him to kiss me, to make me his.

"Michael let me surprise you," he told me as his hands rested back on my hips.

I smiled. "I see that."

The heat went up the back of my neck and flamed up my cheeks at the embarrassment that I talked to Michael like a giddy schoolgirl having her first crush. I was going to have to have a little talk with Michael. I didn't think he would actually tell him, but I did owe Michael a big thank you for letting him come up here to surprise me.

"I do have a surprise for you, though," Tucker told me as he tucked a piece of loose hair behind my ear. Tucker loved when my hair was down, so he could run his long fingers through it.

"You do?"

He nodded, "Yep, grab your coat – it might get cold."

I turned and ran down the hallway to grab my coat, then rushed back so Tucker wasn't by himself too long. When I came back out to the living room, I found Tucker standing in front of the large windows, staring out over Central Park. I had the sudden urge to go up and wrap my arms around his stomach and put my chin on his shoulder, maybe even kiss his neck. The man was a delectable piece and I was falling fast and hard for him. My feelings for him deepened to my core the more I was with him. Tucker turned around at the sound of my footsteps coming up behind him and gave me the side smile.

"You ready?"

I gulped, but managed to nod my head. Why all of the sudden did I have major jitters to be alone with him? I could do this. Tucker closed the space between us, tucking yet another loose piece of hair behind my ear and slowly dragging his fingers across my cheek and down my neck. My eyes shut, taking in the softness of his thumb caressing against my jaw. I sighed and Tucker's hand dropped from my face. I opened my eyes to his soft baby blues.

"Come on gorgeous," he said, as he threaded his hands with mine to pull me out the front door of my apartment to the surprise he had waiting for me.

We made our way to the elevator and Tucker placed my arm in his, grabbing a hold of my other hand as butterflies roamed my empty stomach. I peeked up at him through my curtained hair to stare at his face. I kept on staring at him and suddenly, the air shifted around us. It was as if a fan was on high and whipping our emotions all around us.

The ding of the elevator brought me back to get my feet moving and follow him inside the little cubicle, but when I did and I found myself pushed back into the back wall, Tucker's lips collided into mine. My mouth opened and I accepted his tongue as it stroked mine. His breath was hot as it melted my insides; my left ankle wrapped around his shin and the kiss deepened. My fingers were at the back of his head. Tucker's hands moved down from my waist to my butt in seconds; I pushed my hips at him and he broke away from me.

"I will never get enough of kissing you," he said as he kissed the tip of my nose, and then attacked my mouth again. I moaned as he possessed my mouth with his desirable tongue. I heard the ding of the elevator, telling us we were at the lobby floor, and I pulled away from him.

Tucker rested his head against mine as we stood in place, trying to let the passion between our bodies cool way down, but we took too long. The doors closed shut and started back up again as we just stared into each other's eyes. Tucker's blue eyes just sparkled, making me feel nothing but happiness. The doors opened and I heard voices crowding on the tiny car with us, but Tucker didn't move away from me, still pressing my back into the wall, cupping my face. I slipped my fingers in the front pockets of his jeans and brought his body closer to give him a quick peck.

"Lobby?" someone said from the side of me.

I started to nod and Tucker said, "Yeah." Swallowing down hard, it felt like I swallowed my tongue; my mouth was so dry.

When we finally made it to the lobby, my face was flaming red from my smile as we passed Michael.

"Evening," he nodded at us as we passed him.

"Thanks, man," Tucker told him.

The night air was cold as November hit, and the wind was chilly. Good thing Tucker told me to grab a coat; even though I was wearing my white cardigan sweater, I still would have been shivering out of my mind. We started walking towards Central Park as Tucker held my hand.

My teeth chattered, "Where are we going?"

"It's a surprise," was all he told me as we crossed the street. We walked down a trail and made our way deep into the trees. The wind picked up and blew my hair all around my face; I even heard Tucker chuckle as my hair hit his face.

"I know it's cold and I'm sorry for bringing you out here." He shrugged out of his leather jacket and handed it to me, then he pulled off his gray hoodie, leaving him in a black, long sleeved V-neck. I watched him put his leather jacket back on, and then looked at me, waiting. But I didn't know why he was waiting. He nodded at my hands as I was holding his gray hoodie.

"Put it on."

I unzipped my jacket, shrugging it off, and then pulled the hoodie over my head and down my body. Tucker held out my silver jacket to slide my arms through. He then pulled the gray hood up and tucked my hair in around the sides, then pulled on the strings to tighten it around my face, and zipped my jacket back up.

"There, now you'll stay a little warmer," he said with a smile.

I stared back into his caring eyes and he leaned down to give me another kiss. "Thank you."

"Anything for you, baby girl. Your lips are getting cold; let's hurry."

We continued to walk around in Central Park. I was happy for the extra jacket because the temperature dropped within minutes. I learned that the faster you walked, the warmer your body got, so I picked up the pace. Tucker laughed and picked up his pace as well; the next thing I knew, we were running on the trail holding hands. I was laughing as Tucker chased behind me, suddenly letting go of my hand. When I turned around, he was gone.

"Tucker?" I called out, but the wind was too strong; it even sounded muffled to me as it was lost in the wind. "Tucker?" I started walking back the way we came when he jumped out from behind a tree and scared the living crap out of me. I screamed as he tackled me to the icy cold ground, then started tickling me. I kicked my legs and tried to wiggle out of his hands as his fingers dug through my many layers of clothing.

"AH! Stop..." I said, trying to take a deep breath. "Tucker, stop." He laughed at me as I settled down and straddled me. My teeth started chattering together, and you could see my breath as I huffed out the air from my lungs, trying to breathe. Tucker leaned down and kissed me. I could never grow tired of him kissing me, with his soft lips and hot tongue; if I had the choice, his tongue would never leave my mouth.

I was no longer cold when Tucker pulled away and climbed off of me. "Come on, before we get ourselves in trouble." I giggled and nodded.

We walked for a couple more minutes before we stopped outside of a little building that looked kinda like a green house. I stopped in my path of steps and observed it; the roof was glass and pointed at the top— just like something out of a movie. The walls outside were wood, but some were falling off and the green paint was peeling. It was very rundown. "Tucker, what is this place?"

He turned and cupped my cheeks, "It's just an old greenhouse; no one knows it's here. It's just us," he said, softly kissing me.

Tucker and I were going to be alone together; I could scream with joy, but then I was also very nervous. I remembered what happened when we kissed...something inside me starts to grow and awaken. I never want the kissing to end; I wanted it to take me places I'd never been before, and I only wanted Tucker.

As we reached the door, Tucker actually had to kick it in order to get it to open. Inside was all dark, but with the glass roof, we could easily see the sky and clouds.

Tucker faced me. "Shut your eyes."

I raised my brows. "You're not going to murder me or anything, are you?" I knew he wouldn't, but I was curious and I was joking.

"Never. I like watching you do that toe thing too much."

I giggled and shut my eyes. I could hear his footsteps move away from me. I wanted to open my eyes, but I'd let him surprise me with whatever he had planned. I heard a click which sounded like a fan starting up. Another click and the back of my eyelids flashed red with the light that now appeared. I still had my eyes closed when his footsteps were closer to me and he kissed my cheek. "Open your eyes," he whispered in my ear. I opened them to a room full of white Christmas lights covering the walls. I was lost for words. The little fan I heard was actually a space heater to help warm up the tiny room. Taking off my silver coat, I kept on his gray hoodie – mainly because it smelled of him.

There was a little card table in the middle of the room with two lit candles on it.

"Our first candlelit dinner," he said from behind me, and I smiled to myself. He knew I could care less for all the fancy things I was used to from Carol, so this was perfect.

"Tucker, this is beautiful." My hand went to my chest as I felt tiny tears form. The room was perfect in every way.

"Are you surprised?" I turned back to him and wrapped my arms around his neck. It was my turn to take his breath away with my kiss, but he didn't let it get out of control like I wanted it to.

"I'm very surprised."

"Good. Come sit down."

We approached the little wooden table. He had everything you could think of for a dinner date just like if we went to sit down at a fancy restaurant: white plates, silver utensils, and even glass cups. In the middle of the table between the candles was a silver bowl with a lid and a little candle underneath it to help keep the food warm. Tucker pulled out my chair and I sat down. He leaned over me to grasp the lid, "For my lady, her specialty, and because," he pulled off the lid to macaroni and cheese with cut up hot dogs, "it's the oddest thing I've ever heard."

I busted out laughing, "I can't believe you remembered."

"I wanted to make it for you. And for drink, you get this."

I watched as he filled my cup full of chocolate milk. He really did remember my favorite childhood meal. "I really can't believe you remembered."

Tucker sat across from me. "It's no big deal. Just thought you would like it and I gotta try it."

"I love it, Tucker." He met my eyes which were so filled with happiness, they sparkled. I smiled.

"Tucker?"

"Yeah?" He started filling up my plate, then his.

"Before we start, I wanted to know what we are."

He looked at me dumbfounded, like he didn't know what I meant, but being a girl, I was pushy, I guess. But I felt a little weird for asking. This night was going so well and I had to open up my mouth. But I wanted to know, too.

Then we sat in silence, which seemed like forever, but it was more like two and a half seconds.

"Are you...um...my umm..."

"Boyfriend?" he finished the sentence for me that I couldn't get out.

My face flushed. I did want to know what we were. "Well, yeah," I answered as I tucked a piece of loose hair behind my ear.

"What do you think?"

Are you kidding me? Now, I had to answer that. He answered a question with a question. So unfair. I wanted to be his girlfriend, but did he want to be my boyfriend? That sounded so childish to me, but I gave my honest answer.

"I want to if you want to."

Jitters made my legs shake as I waited for him to answer me. Yes, it was stupid to think so.

"I do." I let a big breath out that I didn't realize I was holding.

"I was gonna talk to you about it tonight. I want you to be mine. I kinda tell people you're my girl anyway."

Tucker stood up from his chair and walked over to sit on a stool that faced out through Christmas light windows. Something inside him shut down. I watched as he occasionally picked at his fingernails. My body was warm, so I pulled off his hoodie and his spicy smell left me.

Quietly walking over to him, I placed my hand on his shoulder; he looked up at me with dreading, sad eyes, just from sitting here thinking by himself, and I knew something was bothering him. My heart broke.

"What's wrong?" he asked, but he gave me a side smile as he pulled me onto his lap and I went willingly into his soft embrace.

"Just thinking about how lucky I am," he said, kissing my cheek. "My life has been hell, even now. But when I'm with you...it's different. You're all I want, just you. Everything around you just stops and it's just us against everything else. I feel like you're the only thing I have in my life that's good." He gulped, "I want only you. You're the only thing that's good for me."

I tried to move to take a look at his face which went from troubled to sincere. I loved how he just opened up to me. I only wanted to bring him comfort. Our eyes locked and I leaned down to softly kiss him. This small little kiss I was giving would change us; I wasn't going to stop it. I deepened the kiss and pressed myself closer to him, but it didn't feel close enough; I repositioned myself so that my chest was up against his. His hands roamed over my back and up the back of my head; he tugged just a little bit on my hair, which caused me to moan into his mouth. Tucker's lips were moving harder against mine as I took his every move, his tongue thrusting with mine—just like we couldn't get enough of each other.

Tucker's hands went from the back of my head to the side of my body, barely touching the sides of my breasts; his fingers were digging into my skin, pulling at my sweater, and sending chills up and down my arms. My own hands moved down between us as I started to push off his leather jacket. Once it fell to the ground, I started pulling at his shirt to show a little hair trailing from his belly button down to the hidden part in his blue boxers. I felt him quiver, so I decided to lightly rake my fingernails down his stomach and he shook with his own desire.

I pulled away from him to take a breath of air; I felt as if I had been swimming and held my breath too long, making me dizzy. I shut my eyes and rested my forehead against his as I pulled at his black sweater, and I opened my eyes to find his blue ones boring into mine.

"Tucker." His name on my tongue only seemed to turn him on more, because once again, he attacked my mouth. I pulled on the hem of his long sleeved t-shirt to pull it off; as it passed our faces, I saw a shadow on his right shoulder. I pulled back to get a better look, and what I saw amazed me. He had a tattoo that started at the top of his shoulder, curved around the back of his arm and down the front of his bicep. Three different lined directions morphed into one with this beautiful black tattoo.

Breathlessly, I said, "When did you get this?" I traced the lines with my fingers at the beautiful artwork. The design really brought out the muscle tone in his arms. Last time I saw him with no shirt on, he didn't have this. The black marks twisting were beautiful. Very Tucker.

He shrugged. "Jett likes a living canvas when he wants to practice," Tucker said as he nuzzled the inside of my neck, lightly kissing my skin.

"It's beautiful," I whispered, still tracing the lines up and down. I can't believe he did something like that. Just out of the blue and for practice. Tucker slipped my sweater down my shoulder to nibble on my collarbone; my head went his shoulder as we both fit perfectly together. "Tucker," I moaned, while wrapping my legs around his middle as he stood up from the stool.

"Hold on, baby girl."

He walked back over to the middle of the room, pulling me away from him to set me on my feet, then he went to the closet to pull out a bunch of blankets on the floor in front of the space heater, making a little bed out of it.

Tucker came back, staring into my eyes before grabbing my hand to lead me over to the little makeshift bed as we both dropped to our knees. His hand came up to cup my cheek as I felt his warm embrace; I loved having us skin to skin.

Before I could even back down at my next move, I grabbed the hem of my sweater and pulled it off, leaving me in my white cotton bra. His eyes roamed over my chest and down my breast as his took me in. "Gabs, we don't need to do anything you don't want to. I know that maybe you feel pressured, but I wanted to tell you, it's okay to wait." He gulped down hard. "I want you to know that; I have strong feelings for you and I don't want to rush you."

I placed my fingers over his soft lips. "I want this. Let me have this. Give me this one thing. Only you, Tuck."

I hugged him; just the feeling of our hot skin touching gave me chills. Yes, I wanted this. I reached behind me to unclasp my bra, letting the straps fall down my shoulders. Tucker pulled away and stared into my eyes as my bra fell to the floor between us. Not once did he look at my naked breasts. In a way, that didn't bother me. He wasn't checking them out like I'm sure other guys would, but he looked at me. It made me feel special, wanted, adored as if he was looking at *me*. I was the only one who mattered right now in his eyes.

However, Tucker's eyes finally did look down, giving me quivers. He leaned in to tenderly kiss me, his bare hands on my back with his nails gently digging in my skin. My hands went into his hair, slightly pulling. We started to fall back into the soft blankets. I reached between us to pop his zipper on his pants. He immediately started pulling away from me.

"Gabs, no," he tried pleading with me, his eyes caring and easy as he stared at my face. I didn't even want to answer him. I just wanted to touch, to feel. I continued my little journey between our bodies as I felt his hair on the tips of my fingers, and he was very much ready for me, as I was for him. He dropped his head against mine and he groaned out in pleasure as I unhurriedly teased him.

We slowly took our time; Tucker kissed me from my lips to my collarbone, between my breasts, in my belly button, across my hips. My hands tangled into his hair as he unsnapped the button holding my jeans together and slowly unzipped them. The sound of my jeans unzipping sent shivers up my stomach, awakening places that had never come to life, yet. My breathing picked up as I sighed, grinding the back of my head into the soft blankets behind me.

Tucker pulled my jeans down as they passed my hips, then they were gone. He kissed me down my thighs to the tops of my knees. I could feel his long hair on the inner side of my thighs as he moved down some more. The feeling was so exotic and new that my body craved more. I wanted more. I felt my left foot being lifted into the air, and I opened my eyes to see Tucker looking at my bruised foot and toes. I had to admit, I didn't have the prettiest looking feet because of my ballet. Embarrassed, I tried to pull my foot from his grasp, but he wouldn't let go; he just slowly starting rubbing the soles of my foot, then kissed each toe. He did the same with my right. I was in heaven.

We couldn't stop kissing. Our hands explored each other's bodies, caressing each other. Tucker pushed hair back from my face as his lips nibbled against my earlobe, his hot breath making me flush all over. My body was shaking with need from him; I wanted him more and more. The strong pull was back and my heart squeezed so much it hurt. Then it hit me like a ton of bricks; I was falling in love with Tucker. I smiled as I opened my eyes to the glass roof above us; it was perfect with the soft glow of the Christmas lights. It was the only light in the room and past the glowing glass was the moon, shinning bright above us. This night couldn't be more perfect.

I was in love with Tucker.

It seemed like we kissed and caressed each other's bodies forever. Then our underwear finally disappeared. Tucker pushed up on his hands, looking at me while his strong body settled between my legs.

"Abigail." I was a little taken aback with the use of my first name. Tucker never called me Abigail. My heart sped up as I took in a shaky breath. His blue eyes bored into mine with heat and passion as his next words struck my heart in every direction.

He let out a soft sigh, "I love you."

My eyes started to water with happiness, then slipped out the corners. He wiped them away and I laughed. I was so deliriously happy just from hearing those words I'd only heard before from my dad.

I cupped his cheek and pressed my lips to his. When our kiss was over, our foreheads were together with our noses brushing each other's. "I love you, too, Tucker," I said, and I meant every single word of it. He kissed me again, this time showing me just how much he wanted me. My body tingled as I thrusted my hips up to meet his, but he pulled back and broke our kiss.

"Are you sure?"

I nodded and Tucker slowly guided himself into me. The feeling was okay at first, and then it became foreign and unwelcoming. The unexpected burning sensations made me cringe up my face and hold my breath. I shut my eyes as I gasped for breath, but he kept going. The burning and pressure wasn't subsiding at all. I whimpered a little bit.

"Deep breaths, baby girl," Tucker whispered, as he pushed all the way in, until he almost rested inside me. My nails dug into his skin of his shoulders, which made him push harder into me and I cried out in pain.

Tucker brushed more hair away from my face, trying everything he could to soothe me, "Shhh...It's okay. I've got you." I started to shake uncontrollably, my breathing picked up way too much, and my heart was racing. The more I tried to control my breathing, more tears cascaded down the sides of my face and into my hair.

"Hey," Tucker whispered, "Look at me, Gabs."

Now more than ever, I felt so completely stupid for crying while losing my virginity. I thought it was supposed to be this mind blowing experience, and now I was crying like a big baby. I dug my palms into my eyes and applied as much force as I could to help take my mind off the pressure I was feeling between my legs.

"Gabs."

I pulled my hands away to look at Tucker. His shimmering blue eyes were glossed over, and I could feel his heart hammering into mine.

"I don't want to hurt you," he whispered against my wet cheek.

Suddenly, the unwanted feeling was no longer there as Tucker kissed my swollen lips. He started to move and I gasped again against his open mouth,

"I love you."

I focused on his words, driving into my brain that this wonderful guy loved me. He loved me. I wrapped my arms around his neck because I wanted him even closer to me, if that was even possible.

My hands glided down his back, slowly digging my nails into his skin. His hands tangled in my hair as he bit my bottom lip with each of his moves. And from that moment on, we were lost in each other's pace, as we made love for the first time.

Chapter Thirteen

I was so happy as Tucker and I laid there with our rapid breaths. My head was resting on his sticky chest, and his right arm was slung over my shoulder, barely touching my skin. Nothing at all could ruin this moment. Tucker kissed the top of my head for about the hundredth time when I finally got up on my elbow to look at him.

"Hey," he said with a smoldering smile, his deep dimple showing. I touched it with the tip of my finger,

"Hey."

"You okay?" I could hear the concern in his voice.

I sighed, "I'm perfectly happy and you didn't hurt me." I smiled while shutting my eyes and he pushed some of my hair behind my ear. I leaned into his hand. When I opened my eyes, I saw some bodies move past the glowing windows of the green house. Scared, I sat up quickly and covered my chest with one of the blankets, "Someone's here!" After I said that, the doorknob rattled—someone wanted in.

"Shit!" Tucker sat up fast, started pulling up his pants and tossed me my clothes.

"Better get dressed, baby girl; they'll come in whether you're dressed or not," Tucker said, zipping up his pants while I was still naked. More sounds from the door mixed with pounding made my heart race as I got dressed. Right when I pulled my shirt over my head, the door flew open and the cold November air came inside. Tucker pulled me up, holding my jacket when four guys came in, and Tucker went completely stiff in front of me as one of the guys held his arms out.

"Tucker, my main man," the guy said. He was one scary individual to me with tanned skin, light buzzed cut hair, deep brown eyes, and he was chewing on the end of a cigarette. "What you doing here, man? You don't look like you're out makin' me some dough."

I heard Tucker growl, "Drop it, Ethan. Not now, man." Then he gave me his hoodie and I slipped it over my head.

"Oh, you got ya a little girlfriend, huh?" I looked over at Ethan with a scowl.

"Oh, feisty thing, aren't you?" Then he took a step towards me. Tucker stepped up to Ethan, shielding me more.

"What's the matter, Tuck? You don't want to share this one?" Ethan asked. I pulled in a lungful of air. I knew that Tucker heard me because his shoulders went higher, blocking me from Ethan's glare.

"Oh, let me guess; he didn't tell you that we share women?"

I wanted to ask Tucker, but I couldn't; I couldn't even move out from around his body. I stared up at the back of his head.

"Shut up, Ethan. That was one time, man."

"Whatever, dude, you know you enjoyed it as much as I did. I wouldn't mind having a piece of what you got tonight, though."

Ugh, I had enough. I didn't want to be around them, especially this...Ethan. His strong, brown eyes burned into my brain as he kept staring at me. I backed away.

"Honey, don't you know that Tucker is too hot to handle for your cold hands? Now, you know who is hot?" Snapping his fingers, "What was her name, Tuck? Wasn't it Jasmine?"

Jasmine?

I had to get out of here, I needed to leave. But my feet were frozen to the floor boards. Out of nowhere, Ethan jumped towards me, trying to grab at me, but Tucker got in his way.

"Fuck off, Ethan." Ethan then grabbed Tucker by his collar and started yell whispering in his face. At the first opportunity, I turned to run out the door to make a run for it, but bumped into a tall, Hispanic guy instead.

"Whoa, look what I just caught, Ethan," he said, gripping the tops of my arms with force. "Is she fair game, Ethan?" I gasped and put all my anger into stomping on his foot; he let go with a grunt. I stepped back at the first chance I had, then he tried to reach for me again. I tried to turn away, but his hand caught my heart necklace, and the chain snapped like a piece of thread. I stopped to look at the guy's hand, which was perfectly still. I reached out to take it from him, but he pulled his hand away and held it up to his chest like it was his.

That. Is. Mine!

My anger boiled through my veins. This scumbag broke my necklace, which was my mother's, and now he thought he was going to keep it from me? Oh, hell no. The pit of my stomach felt as if it was on fire from my rage as I stepped up to him and smacked him across the face.

"That was my dead mother's, you asshole!" I yelled and snatched the necklace from his grip. Somewhere from behind me, I heard Tucker say my name, but I hurried out of the green house and into the cold night air before he could stop me. The tears streaked my face as I cried the entire way home. I didn't know if Tucker chased after me; a part of me wished he did, but my heart was so broken right now as

I held my destroyed necklace. I was also hurt from the mention of Jasmine's name. I couldn't believe Tucker touched her like that.

I made it to my quiet apartment in record time. Jade was sitting on the couch, watching some TV show as I ran past her in sobs, trying my best to cover my face.

"Gabs?!" she called out and I ignored her. I slammed my door shut and started stripping off my clothes. I had to get his smell off me, but it enveloped me like an air freshener. I put my necklace on my nightstand next to my mother's picture. I went straight into the bathroom to shower, and when I took my underwear off, I spotted the blood from the loss of my virginity. I didn't regret it; it was going to happen sooner or later anyway. I stepped in the line of scalding hot water when the bathroom door opened. I didn't want to see who it was. I stuck my head under the showerhead and let the pounding water beat my thoughts away.

In so many ways, I knew Tucker. And in many other ways, I didn't know him at all. He kept secrets hidden so well. I repositioned the nozzle down so I could rest my head on the cold, tiled wall. Once my head hit the tile, I started to sob uncontrollably. My knees started to shake as I cried. I loved Tucker, but not once had I ever heard him talk about Ethan before.

"Gabs," Jade's voice called to me.

Exhaling a breath, I said, "What?"

She knocked on the glass door. "Are you okay?" Her voice sounded so sincere and worried for me.

"I'm fine, just need a minute."

"Come out to our spot when you're done." Then she was gone. I wiped my face and let out a big breath; I knew that Jade wasn't a patient one—I had to pull it together and talk to her about it. I lathered my soap really well in my hands and started washing my body, then my hair.

I started to think about what Ethan said about sharing girls with Tucker; I cringed at the thought and grabbed my soap again to wash it all away. I hated the thought of Tucker being with other girls. But Jasmine? Really? I knew he had been with them before, but the thought of him and Ethan sharing one turned my stomach and I couldn't control it. The same feeling started to come up and hit the back of my throat. I cupped my mouth and raced out of the shower to the toilet and threw up all my anguish. The cold air in the room caused me to shake uncontrollably as I sobbed into the echoing toilet bowl.

I have to stop throwing up! I yelled at myself.

The breathing technique wasn't helping me. I breathed out; I cried. I sucked in air and the chills burned my flesh. I quickly wiped my mouth, then I went back into the shower to clean off the suds in my hair that I missed.

Jasmine. No wonder she kept throwing things about Tucker in my face. She already had him. I wrapped myself in a towel, brushed my teeth, and then ran a quick comb through my hair. Spotting my underwear, I scooped them up and tossed them in my hamper. I dressed in my one pair of thick dance sweats and padded to the balcony to meet Jade.

She had a black beanie on with her comforter on her lap. I was walking over to the other lounge chair when she tossed back the big blanket. "Come here, Gabs," she invited and she squeezed over to the side. We were both pretty little, so we fit together nicely in the small chair.

Taking off her beanie and setting it on my wet head of hair, she scolded, "You're gonna freeze with wet hair," then tossed me the pack of cigarettes. While I smoked, Jade gave me my space like always until I was ready to talk. Nothing was going through my mind as the slow three minutes passed by. Tucker did something dangerous when he wasn't with me; I got that much. I'd never heard of Ethan before—not even when I "wasn't" listening to Tucker and Brad talk on the sidelines.

"I had sex with Tucker tonight," I confessed out, while the smoke left my lips.

"Hooker." I snapped my head towards Jade as she giggled under her breath "Just kidding, Gabs. How was it?"

"It was okay; it hurt," I said, flicking the tip and watching the ashes fly away in the cold wind. I wished I could fly away just as easily sometimes.

"Usually does the first time, not so much after that." She nodded. "Is that why you were crying?"

"No," said as I stubbed out the butt and flicked it over the rail. "This guy, Ethan, came after we were done, asking Tucker if he was going to share me with him."

I felt Jade's body shudder. "Oh, that's nasty."

"I know! That's what I was thinking,"

The wind picked up around us and we pulled the blanket up to our chins and snuggled closer together.

"Then what?"

"Ethan asked if he was gonna share me like they shared Jasmine." I said her name with much annoyance.

"WHAT?!" Jade yelled and I jumped. I couldn't start the story right away; instead I sat there and cried for a little bit. When I was done, I started back at the beginning, from when Tucker picked me up to the throwing up in the bathroom, and even told her about our "I love you's". Being the good friend she was, she sat and listened to me spill my guts out. She nodded occasionally and agreed, but she always held in her opinion until I was done. That's why I loved talking to her so much.

"I can't believe it – Jasmine, of all people. But you know what I think?"

I was nervous to hear what she had to tell me. Was she going to say break up with him and never see him again? Because I didn't think I could do that. Taking a deep breath, I asked "What?" and shut my eyes, waiting for her answer.

"You love him and he loves you. That's all that should matter." My eyes snapped open.

"What?" My voice screeching at the end.

"What else do you what me to say? Gross, what a dick, that rat bastard?"

I held my hand up to silence her mouth and she smacked it away. Damn Jade, she always knew just how to push my buttons.

"Truth?" I looked over at Jade who was staring out in front of her.

I nodded and answered, "Yeah."

Right when Jade was going to tell me what she thought, we heard the door slam shut and Rachel's red hair went flying past the windows.

"Oh shit," Jade murmured

I tried to get up off the chair, but Jade held me back. "Let her cool off. Anyways, did you guys at least use a condom?"

Oh no!

We didn't. We didn't use anything. I smacked myself in the face right before Jade smacked me upside the back of my beanie covered head. The moment was right there, the sensations, the feelings, his lips on my body, my legs wrapped around his narrow waist as I drove my hips into his like a cat in heat.

"You didn't use anything?"

I shook my head at her. I felt the tears form at my careless decision, and Jade took me into her side.

"Okay, don't get all drama girl on me, just be careful next time. You don't want a little one running around and..."

My head snapped up. My conscience was screaming at me: *A baby? I didn't want a baby!* Then I yelled, "I don't want a baby!"

"Then think before you act, dumbass, and tell him to wrap it up."

I nodded and huddled into the chair some more with Jade. We smoked once more before our fingers felt like they were going to fall off. Jade joked with me, putting me in a much better mood. We were laughing as we walked back into the dark apartment and started down the hallway to Rachel's bedroom, when a dead knock sounded on the front door. I knew who would be on the other side of that door; I turned to Jade who left my side and the door to Rachel's room was closing.

I padded over and stood on my tippy toes to peek out the little hole to find Tucker on the other side. I rested my head on the door, and then I heard him.

"Gabs. Baby girl, please open the door. Just let me explain." My heart broke at the sound of his voice calling out to me.

Oh, I wanted to so bad. He touched Jasmine in an intimate way, but I knew that with just one look in his ocean blue eyes, all sad and looking at me, I would have no chance if I opened that door. I only saw myself flying into his strong muscled arms, just so he could hold me and tell me sweet things in my ear. I felt a thud on the door, wondering if it was his head. Squeezing my eyes shut as tight as they could go, I took a deep breath and straightened my body, ready to turn and leave him.

"Gabs, please. I don't want to lose you. Let me explain."

My heart sank and I opened the door. Tucker stood with his hands on each side of the doorframe with his head down. When he finally looked up, his brown hair looked like he raked through it a million times; his eyes were sad and filled with glistening, unshed tears. He reached out for me and just like I predicted, I flew into his arms. Inhaling the leather jacket scent mixed with the spiciness of him, I was lost.

"Jasmine was Ethan's girl a long ass time ago. It was something I only did once—it was nothing. She meant absolutely nothing to me." I cried into his shoulder as he told me this. Tucker's arms tightened around my waist. "Please, baby girl. I love you; I don't want to lose you. I love you."

And I was once again lost. I no longer cared about everything that went down with Ethan. I shouldn't have judged him for something he did before he even met me. That was his past, which shouldn't be brought up. You could end up only hurting you and the ones that meant the most to you. As we were still connected and walking backward into my apartment, Tucker kicked the front door shut and reached down to cup my butt as he lifted me up so I could wrap my legs around his waist. He carried me down to my room, shutting the door with his foot again, and we landed on my bed. He sat up, resting on his elbows as he stared intently into my eyes.

"I love you, Gabs. What Ethan said..."

I covered his lips with my fingers to stop him. "Shhh..." I whispered, then arched my neck up and pressed my lips to his in a tender kiss. We slowly pulled our clothes off and lay together in the soft sheets of my bed as we touched and caressed each other's bodies for the second time that night. We were slow and took our time with each other. Trailing lines of hot kisses up and down our bodies, he even tickled me a little bit. And this time, when it was time to have each other, we stopped before it got too far and I remembered Jade's advice. I didn't want a baby, and I'm sure Tucker didn't want one, either.

I woke up to the warm sun on my naked back. Fingertips traveled down my spine and back up They made a little circle over my shoulder blade, and then went back down again. My hands were under my pillow and my face was turned away from Tucker. I smiled when I felt his lips gently touch my shoulder.

"I love you," he murmured into my warm, sun-kissed skin.

Shutting my eyes as Tucker left the room, I didn't move as I listened to him in there, going to the bathroom, washing his hands, then coming back in. I still kept my eyes shut when he climbed back in bed with me; his fingers continued what they were doing. Then he stopped; my eyes slowly opened at the bright morning sun, my hair was moved over my shoulder and I felt a soft wet, sharp point on my shoulder blade.

I jumped at the surprise sensation pressing into my skin. "Hold still a minute, baby girl," Tucker whispered and I slowly relaxed and laid back down on my bed.

"What are you doing?" I asked into the pillow, smiling.

"Having fun, hold still."

I smiled, I knew what he was doing, and he was drawing on me. I felt the point press into my skin as little lines moved over my shoulder blade. Tucker stretched my skin and moved it around some more. I felt him blow his hot breath on my skin to dry it, then felt his fingertips go down my spine again, causing me to shudder. I turned my face over to look at him.

His long brown hair hung into his eyes, messy, just the way I prefer it. He stared at my back. "What did you draw?" He smiled instead of answering me. He met my eyes. I got up on my elbows and kissed his lips and he gladly kissed me back.

We spent most of the morning in bed. Holding each other and talking, I really didn't want to get up, or do anything. I had Tucker, and that's all that mattered. My head was resting on his chest when his phone chimed. He grunted and looked at it.

"Jett needs me to come in," he told me, kissing the top of my head while his other hand went through my hair for the millionth time today. Having him here felt so right—his touch, the feel of him pressed up against me, everything. I wouldn't want to be anywhere else.

I sighed and shut my eyes, "For how long?"

"I have two clients requesting me. Wanna come watch?"

I pushed up on my elbows, looking at his face. "Really?"

"Why not? You're my girlfriend," he said as he kissed my shoulder.

I didn't even think about answering him. I threw up the covers and booked it into my bathroom to take a shower. Of course I wanted to go. He's seen me practice; I wanted to watch him work. I caught a quick glimpse at my back. He drew the same black swirls on my shoulder blade like the pattern on his arm and up his shoulder. I smiled at the thought of having the same thing as him.

We took a cab to Jett Black's Tattoo and Piercing in record time. My hair was still wet from my shower. I refused to let Tucker in the bathroom with me while I got ready and when I was done, I let him shower. I couldn't find a shirt in time, so I just pulled on Tucker's gray hoodie.

I knew deep down, Tucker and I would have to talk about what Ethan said last night. Of course Tucker had been with other girls. Sharing them turned my stomach, but I focused on my breathing. I focused on Tucker's hand holding mine as we walked in through the front door. First thing I heard was loud buzzing sounds remembering the shop from when Jade got her first tattoo was different in the daytime.

My phone vibrated in the middle of Tucker's instructions from his clients and what they wanted. I rolled my eyes at the sight of Carol's name showing across my screen.

"Abigail?"

"Yes, Carol?" I answered into the phone

"I need you to meet me for lunch today, the hotel plaza, two o'clock."

I turned to watch as Tucker leaned over his client to get a better view of his back and the placement of the stencil. The guy approved and lay down on the table; that's when the buzzing sounded. I left the room so Carol didn't question where I was.

"Why?"

"Please just meet me." Then she hung up. I grunted, and stuffed my phone back into Tucker's gray hoodie I was wearing. I leaned on the door frame to watch Tucker do what he loves, tattooing. His strong arms rippling from the vibration of the tattoo machine, black gloves on, his hair in his face. He was hot to watch.

Sometimes, I could even see his tongue pressing on the inside of his cheek, like he was concentrating so hard on not messing up. He never did mess up. His work was so beautiful and real looking. He was that good. Even as just an apprentice, his client list was growing. Jett had to start telling people no because as an apprentice, Tucker could only do so much tattooing. Jett was even considering hiring another tattoo artist because he couldn't keep up.

"Alright man. You're finished," I watched as Tucker cleaned up the guy's back, wiping it over and over again until only the ink that was left etched in the guy's skin. I walked over to get a better look.

"What do you think Gabs?" Tucker asked as the guy got up from the table.

I loved it. There were three black skulls on his back. The biggest skull was in the center, with two smaller one on his shoulder blades. Black swirled smoke was in the back ground, making the skulls pop clear out of the guy's skin. Almost as if the skulls were 3D looking; it was awesome looking. Tucker's work was beautiful. He was so proud to give that person exactly what they wanted. The man then explained that he was the biggest skull and his two daughters were the smaller ones. He kept looking in the mirror and telling Tucker it came out better than what he thought. He also gave Tucker a generous tip and told him he's the only one allowed to touch him with needle and ink. I wanted that; I wanted something from him too. To always remember something I was proud of myself for doing. I knew just the thing too.

"Tucker." He looked up from cleaning his tattoo machine and putting the ink away.

"Baby girl," his voice serious.

"Would you give me a tattoo?" Now that had his full attention.

"You want a tat? I thought you couldn't get one because of your perfect ballerina body. You got in trouble for having strings out right?" He moved over to the sink and started washing his hands. I know he was trying his best to talk me out of it; he didn't want me to get in trouble. He already felt guilty enough about me not getting the part in *Swan Lake*

"What if we pick a spot where it stays hidden?"

Tucker faced me and crossed his arms. "I'll give you one if you really want one."

"I do and I want you to do it."

He pulled out the ink, put new needles on his machine. Now, here I was, lying on my back on the tattoo table. My shirt was up, my jeans unbuttoned, my hip exposed.

Breathe Abigail. I kept telling myself.

Could you blame me? Needles were going into my skin for a long amount of time. I'm crazy. Tucker's gloves snapped on his skin as he pulled them on. He poured more ink into the little cups and his machine went off. I jumped at the sound; it seemed nosier now that I was its victim.

"Okay Gabs, you ready?"

I let out a big breath through my mouth and nodded.

"It's not big and shouldn't take long, okay?"

"Yep."

"Love you."

All I could do was smile at him. I loved hearing those words come out of his mouth. He loved me, only me.

"I love you." I whispered out.

Then the buzz of the machine started. He stretch and pulled at my skin on my hip. The sting hurt at first, but slowly faded and went completely numb. Jett and Jade came into the little room and watched Tucker work. Jade grabbed my phone and took a picture of my face all scrunched up. She also made a little video.

"How you feeling Gabs." I held my breath as Jade put the phone right in my face. "Say cheese." She laughed. "Just think, it's like a little souvenir. Never know when you'll want to watch it."

"Come on you." Jett pulled Jade out of the tiny room of pain.

I heard a muffled chuckle from Tucker as the buzzing of the machine continued. He pressed harder in some areas and then wiped my skin. He was right, it didn't take long and before I knew it, I was done.

"Okay baby girl, all done. Sit up slowly and go look in the mirror."

I stood in front of the mirror stunned as I stared at my hip. It wasn't something big, nothing flashy, but so perfect that it brought tears to my eyes. The script was beautiful and the little surprise he put at the end, it made it that much better.

Juilliard

It was absolutely beautiful; the ballet slippers he added in gave it just the right touch. Something I would always remember, that I accomplished a dream to be a Juilliard Ballerina. I flung my arms around Tucker's neck.

"I love it Tucker."

I walked into the Waldorf Astoria to meet Carol, like I said I would. My hip hurt as my jeans rubbed on it. Tucker placed some gauze and told me how to clean it and should be as good as new in a couple of weeks. My first tattoo. I didn't feel any different, but it will always be something special that I did. Plus, Tucker did it too. That was just a bonus. I found Carol at a table, talking to someone and their back to me. The closer I got I wondered who it was, but didn't have to guess more than three times.

"Abigail." Carol greeted me in a happy tone that I wasn't used to. The person that was sitting with her was Alex. He stood up, wearing a black suit, white pressed shirt and red tie. His hair was styled just right, spiky and standing up in all the right places, and his teeth were perfectly white and straight as he smiled at me. He was a very good looking guy, but I knew someone that was better and he just marked my body. I giggled to myself at that one.

"Abigail, nice to see you again." Alex stuck his hand out for me to shake it.

"Hey there Alex." I greeted back and Carol huffed under her breath. I was in too good of mood to be taking her *huffing* crap. I was in love with Tucker; we proved it one another twice last night and once today. Nothing was going to ruin my fabulous day.

We sat, had drinks and talked of nothing that was important. And when I say *we* talked, I mean Alex and Carol. They chatted like it was no one's business. Carol didn't acknowledge me at all to join the conversation; I didn't care really, and my mind was elsewhere. Thinking about a long brown haired, blue eyed guy that did killer tattoos. My mind slipped to Tucker's hands on my body from the experience, his hands on my hip as he pulled and stretched my skin. Just the thought made my body quiver and I wanted him again. I couldn't get enough; I was addicted to him. I had to go to him. My body craved only him.

Interrupting their conversation, which they clearly were enjoying without me anyways, I pulled out my phone to check the time. Hoping Tucker will still be at the shop by the time I got back. "I'm sorry, but I have to go." Standing up from the chair.

"Alright, Abigail sweetie. Remember that Thanksgiving is next week and you are invited to dinner." Carol said with nothing but a huge grin and sweet baby talk voice.

What the...This is really getting weird.

"Okay. Bye." I rushed out of the hotel as if it was up in flames and had to make a quick exit. I took a cab back to Jett's tattoo shop, and Tucker was still there still tattooing. I walked in the crowded waiting room. Some girls that I passed rolled their eyes as I made my way to the back and into Tucker's corner. He was doing a giant back piece on a girl; it was full of flowers, popping with color. It was gorgeous. He stopped long enough to give me a kiss, dip the tip back in the ink then start up again. I was just happy right where I was and that was with Tucker. It felt right to be right here.

When he was done with his long wait of clients, we grabbed some take out and went back to my place. I tried seeing if Tucker would take me to his, but he just gave me that one look. You know, the one look where the answer is automatically no. Rachel and Jade were curled up together on the couch when we walked in.

"Hey!" I greeted them, making my way into the kitchen to start getting all the food out.

"Score! Gabs brought food!" Rachel screamed and came rushing into the kitchen then started pulling out plates. We gathered around the couch to watch whatever Jade and Rachel had on when we walked in. Tucker didn't say a word about the movie they had chosen. He did say if he ever saw this Jacob person in reality, he would tell him that he took his shirt off too much for a vampire movie. Us girls just laughed at him.

When it was time for bed, I invited Tucker to stay the night. Of course, he's a guy and said yes. We curled up and spooned together.

His body pressed against my back with an arm draped over me. "Tucker?" I started rubbing his arm and intertwining our fingers together.

"Yeah." He kissed the back of my neck, cuddling me closer to his body.

"Thanksgiving is next week. Do you want to come to my parents' house with me?"

From his movement on the bed, I knew he was sitting up.

"You want me to come meet your parents?"

I sat up with him, "Yeah. My dad and Carol." I smiled. Tucker didn't even hesitate to kiss me back down into the soft sheets of my bed.

I guess that's a yes.

Chapter Fourteen

I paced back and forth in my living room, biting my thumb nail as I waited impatiently for Tucker to get here. I was taking him home to meet my dad and Carol today, on Thanksgiving. My heart felt like it was going to pound right out of my chest as the minutes ticked by.

I went outside and smoked while waiting. It was becoming a habit, even without Jade, and when Tucker was with me, we both sat outside smoking together. I never pictured myself as a smoker; I didn't ever need to smoke but it's nice to know it's there for comfort. I left the balcony door open so I could hear that soft knock I've been waiting for the last hour. I ran back in, still holding on my cigarette as I answered the door to a very gorgeous Tucker.

"Breaking your own rule I see." he nodded to the cigarette in my hand.

"Crap!" I turned and went back outside, taking one more pull from it and then I stubbed it out in the ash tray. I went back into the apartment and stood back in front of Tucker. He looked so good in his outfit he'd chosen to wear. Black pants, black button up shirt, black tie with his black leather jacket—but his shoes were what made me giggle, he was wearing his converse.

My hand stifled my laughter; he looked like he was dressed to go to a funeral. He placed his hands on my hips to bring me closer to his body and I continued to laugh in my hand.

"What's so funny?" He smiled

"You're all in black," he looked down at himself and shrugged.

"Ah, so?"

"You look like you're going to a funeral, Tucker."

He raised a brow, "Maybe your dad will kill me for doing this to his daughter."

He pulled me to him and kissed me hard on the mouth. So hard that I threw everything I had back into giving him this kiss. Our tongues clashed together while I moaned in his mouth. Tucker's hands moved down to my butt, pressing me closer to him while my hands tangled in his hair. He bit down on my bottom lip and sucked it into his mouth and my body shook at the sensation. I pushed his leather jacket off his shoulders and then loosened his tie, tugging him backwards to the hallway.

All my nerves about him meeting my dad and Carol were suddenly gone. I had to have him right now.

"Gabs, were gonna be late," he tried to tell me around my mouth, but I didn't care. I pulled back to look at his face, his lips were swollen from our passionate kisses, his hair that was slicked back was now disheveled and his tie was loose at the knot.

Reaching down to the edge of my deep plum dress, I pulled on the hem, up and over it went then onto the floor. I stood there in my black lace panties and a matching bra. I was still in my heels and Tucker took a sharp intake of breath at the sight of me, making me smile. He suddenly attacked me, swinging my body over his shoulder and kicking off his shoes in the process. I screamed as he carried me down to my bedroom, smacking my butt in the process. I'm so happy that we are alone. We can be as loud as we want.

He tossed me on my bed while he removed the rest of his clothes in a rush, then landing on top of me.

Tucker kissed my worries away. This day was going to be just fine.

I helped Tucker straighten his tie inside the cab. I could tell he was nervous; he kept on joking that my dad was really going to kill him now for having sex with me before Thanksgiving dinner in his home.

"Knock it off. Just be the sweet Tucker I know you are," I kept repeating to him, then kissing him.

Walking in the front doors of my childhood home, nothing has changed since I've been gone. Maybe Carol got some new drapes in the piano room, but that was about it. The smell was the same as always; my heels clicked on the hardwood floor, servants busied themselves as we walked past them. I could hear my father on the phone in his study; I wanted to introduce Tucker to him before Carol. I knew my dad would like him, or so I hoped he would.

Grabbing Tucker's hand to lead him in the direction of my dad's office, Tucker's steps were beginning to harden the closer we got to the study. Once we were outside the door and before I had a chance to knock on it, Tucker grabbed my hand and turned me towards him. His face was scared; I could even tell and when he spoke to me, his voice shook.

"Gabs, what if he doesn't like me or approve of us?"

I tilted my head to the side as his sapphire eyes looked at the ground.

I placed my finger under his chin, "Hey, don't look down," reminding him what he always told me.

"Tuck, you have nothing to worry about; he's gonna love you," I cupped his cheek and closed his eyes. "I love you and that's all that matters. We don't need their approval to be together."

Tucker kissed me, but this kiss didn't turn heated. It was the type of kiss that was more of a comfort kiss. Kisses like this that Tucker gave me after a stressful day of school, or dealing with Carol.

Oh, Carol.

My stomach dropped at the thought of Tucker meeting and dealing with her; it made me more nervous than him meeting my dad. We broke apart when I heard my dad say goodbye and hang up the desk phone. I turned back to Tucker, "You ready?" He nodded. I knocked and waited.

"Come in!"

We emerged in my dad's office hand in hand. Tucker's hands tightened in mine and all I could do was wince at the slight pain shooting through my fingers as we approached my dad behind his oak desk.

"Daddy," I squealed out, but I think it came out more like a grunt because my dad looked up in a panic and Tucker's hand loosened.

"Abigail." He stood up from his desk and made his way around to me, hugging me in a tight bear hug. Tucker had a death grip on me as my dad rubbed my back.

When he was done, I pulled on Tucker's arm so he would be at my side. "Daddy, this is Tucker. Tucker, this is my dad, David McCall."

Tucker stuck out his hand ready to shake my dad's hand, "It's a pleasure to meet you sir," Tucker said. Surprisingly, his voice didn't shake at all.

Waiting for my dad to shake his hand, but he ended up clapping Tucker on the shoulder, "Tucker, my boy. Welcome to our home." And he gave Tucker a side hug. I let out a breath; I knew my dad would like him. Now Carol, she's a different story.

"You taking good care of my daughter?" My dad smiled at him.

"Yes sir."

My dad looked over the top of his glasses, "I already like you, because you call me sir, young man." My dad clapped his shoulder a couple more times before he let go.

"Well, I have a few more things I have to finish up before dinner. Abigail, why don't you go find your mother?"

I rolled my eyes at his statement of Carol being my mother. I showed Tucker around the rest of the house instead. He whistled in amazement every time we entered a different room, one being bigger than the next. I showed him my old room, which still screamed baby girl so I didn't linger in there for very long. We ended up in my old ballet studio; I was trying everything I could to keep Carol and Tucker away from each other, which was silly—I knew he could handle her if she got mean or something—but I couldn't handle her talking to him as if he were completely different from our family.

"This is your studio?"

I nodded, "Yep, it was a Christmas present to have it added onto the house."

He whistled as he walked up to my barre. I watched his face reflect in the mirror as he looked around. "Some present to give someone."

I shrugged, "Meh, I guess. It's always something big with Carol."

His eyes met mine in the mirror, "Can you dance for me baby girl?"

I bit my bottom lip and moved over to the stereo to turn on some classical music. He loved when I would dance for him; he always said how much it relaxed him as I moved quietly across the floor on my toes.

I kicked off my heels, stretched my feet and slipped on a pair of old ballet shoes I kept in the corner closest. Tucker cringed at my feet being bent all up as I stretched my toes up on pointe before I started.

"I can't believe that doesn't hurt you," he turned, leaning against the barre, crossing his arms, just watching me.

"Oh trust me, when I first learned, my feet would bleed for days at a time. It's nothing now."

I went stood in the center of the room and started turning, going on pointe a little bit, did a couple of leaps in the air, landing softly. You could barely hear my feet as they moved across the floor while Tucker just watched. To be honest, I loved when he watched me dance. He never critiqued me for something I did wrong. If my feet ended up together instead of apart, he never said a word, just watched me with quietness. I took my time with my little routine as my legs stretched and my toes pointed. When I was done, he had the biggest smile on his face.

He walked over to me, cupping my face, "You are so beautiful Gabs," then he tenderly kissed me.

"Abigail!"

I jumped at Carol's voice coming into the studio behind us, with her heels clicking piercingly on the floor. I turned and was ready for her to meet my Tucker. I wasn't going to hide him from her; he was too important to me.

"Hello," I greeted her. Carol looked so well put together for this special day for our happy little family. Her blonde hair was swept back and pinned up on one side, her beautiful earrings glistened in the soft light, and she had on a cream colored skirt and white blouse.

"Abigail, who's your friend?" her voice strange as she stared at me and not once did she look over at Tucker.

"Carol McCall, this is Tucker. Tucker, this is Carol."

Tucker stuck his hand out to Carol, "Ma'am, it's a pleasure to meet you," Carol's eyes didn't leave mine until I looked at Tucker's out stretched hand. She looked at him with cruel blue eyes while her face was hard and mean.

Whoa...What's her problem?

This wasn't a normal look for Carol. This look was of pity and disgust as her eyes raked up and down Tucker's body, but she finally grabbed his hand for a quick shake then dropped it as if would give her some disease.

"Tucker, do you have a last name?" She asked.

"Well, actually it's..."

"Here you all are!" My dad announced from the door way. Carol took that chance to leave us rushing past my dad with a polite, "Excuse me."

My dad watched her move down the hall, "Okay. Well, who's hungry?" my dad asked as I unlaced my shoes and replaced them with my heels.

We all met in the dining room. The long dining table held the glasses, which were shiny and sparkly as if they were new. The white plates were all around for four spots. My dad sat at the head of the table, Carol to his right like always, and I sat across from her with Tucker next to me. We all sat down except for Carol, who disappeared, probably to look over Isabelle's shoulder as she prepared dinner. I cleared my throat and shifted a little in my chair. Tucker placed his hand on my thigh; I met his eyes and smiled at him.

My dad asked, "So, Tucker. What do you do?"

He cleared his throat, "Right now sir, I'm a tattoo apprentice at my buddy's shop. I'm almost done, and then I'll be hired on as a full time tattoo artist." Tucker stroked my bare thigh. My face flushed.

I looked at my dad, "His work is gorgeous dad; very real looking."

My dad pushed his glasses back up his nose, "Tattooing? Have you ever thought about going to school for a real career?"

"Dad" I quietly snapped.

Tucker cut in, "No, it's alright. I understand sir that some people don't consider it a real job, but I like to draw, making it something permanent on people's skin. It's the thrill I get when the client takes the first look at that permanent spot that I just created and seeing the tears in their eyes. Something that will always be there, and for some people it soothes them to see the artwork. Brings them comfort."

Tucker couldn't have defended himself more perfectly; I was proud that he held his ground. I smiled at him which he gladly returned.

"Tucker, let's say you and my daughter get serious, talk about getting married, kids maybe. Do you think you can support them being a tattoo artist?" My dad rested his chin on his hands and stared intently at Tucker, waiting for his answer.

"Dad, I didn't bring Tucker here for you to give him a career change. And we're not getting married— no kids are in the picture."

"I know, I just wanted to know."

"Sir," Tucker cut in, "I'll let you know that I do love your daughter. I haven't thought about having kids, nor do I want to. I believe kids are meant for a special reason, to be born into a loving family when the time is right. I have no desire to have any anytime soon."

I couldn't have said that better myself.

I held Tucker's hand and watched his legs bounce under the table.

"You love my daughter?" We both looked up at my dad.

"Yes sir, very much." Tucker said bringing my hand up to kiss my knuckles.

I looked back over at my dad, "I love him too daddy." My dad did nothing at first but stare, and then he smiled. Carol's heels clicked on the hardwood as she came to the table with Isabelle at her side.

"Miss Abigail." Isabelle quietly said and nodded at me.

Tucker squeezed my hand more as Carol sat down across from us. The food slowly started to fill the table; there was everything from yams, mashed potatoes, all different kinds of veggies, cranberries and of course the giant turkey. And the rolls were to die for; I loved when Isabelle made homemade rolls.

There was little small talk between my dad and Tucker some more. I could tell he was relaxing a little more when they started talking about football and that they shared the same favorite team.

Pittsburgh Steelers.

I don't know much about football; I never understood the concept of tackling someone just to get a ball for a touchdown or anything else that surrounded the game. I did like the cheerleaders whenever I saw them on the T.V. Carol was very quiet during dinner; she didn't look over at Tucker or even acknowledge his presence. She just pushed her food around with her fork and sighed occasionally. Isabelle removed our dishes and brought out some pumpkin pie but banana for me.

I took a bite of the glorious pie, mmm...so good.

"You don't like pumpkin?" Tucker asked in my ear.

I shook my head, "No. I don't even like the smell."

"There are a few things you don't know about Abigail." Carol finally saying something, but to me, her words were hurtful.

Tucker's body straightened and cleared his throat. That made him uncomfortable. "What I know about her so far is good enough for me."

"Has she told you about Alex Blair?"

"Carol." My dad interrupted.

I met Tucker's eyes and shook my head again. "It's nothing."

"Alex is quite fond of Abigail. He's brought her coffee at the school, he's called her. They've even gone out to lunch not too long ago." Taking a bite of her pie and I scowled at her. Tucker let go of my hand and the doorbell rang. Isabelle scurried through the room to go answer it and who walked in next, I wasn't expecting.

Alex

His name was just as annoying as Jasmine's. Maybe I should introduce them. Alex walked in wearing his signature grey suit and black tie, his hair was perfect, wide smile with white perfect teeth. I groaned and turned away to face Tucker.

"Who's that?" He whispered.

This was going downhill fast.

My eyes sad as I answered, "Alex." I quickly reached for his hand but he pulled away.

"Tucker," I whispered to him.

"Alex, my boy. How the hell are you?" My dad said standing up from the table and hugging him like he did to Tucker earlier. My dad and Alex had small talk about a case and when they were done, Alex sat next to Carol.

This was awkward. I sat up straight and look at Carol, who had a smug smile on her face. That's when I knew she planned this.

"Tucker, this is Alex Blair. He's a lawyer at David's firm. Alex, this is Tucker, Abigail's friend."

"Tucker is my boyfriend," I snapped, defending Tucker.

Carol snickered at me, and took another bite of pie. I looked back over at Tucker who was staring at his plate, pushing crumbs around. "We'll see." She mumbled out.

I leaned into his side, "Can I talk to you alone?"

Tucker didn't even answer me as he stood up from the table with a soft excuse me, grabbing my hand and tugging me out of the room. I don't think he knew where he was going because we ended up in the grand piano room next to my ballet studio. He shut the door and faced me. The look on his face right now, was disappointing. He looked so torn, but how could you blame him? Finding out that I've had lunch with him from Carol then magically appearing here, today of all days, the one day I choose to bring home my first boyfriend.

"Tucker, I.." I tried to talk to him, but he silenced me with a hard kiss. There was anger in this kiss or it could be jealously? It was painful at the force of it. My hands grabbed at his hair and pulled, hard. He grunted at the sudden pain and kissed me harder, our tongues clashing in a heated wet mess. His hands were everywhere on my body, groping my butt, up my sides and forcefully grabbing my breasts, hard.

I shuddered at his touch, I craved it; I wanted it more than ever. He whirled my body around and pressed me up against the door, hooking his hand behind my knee, then lifting it to wrap around his waist as his hard-on ground into my center. His lips moved down to my neck, pulling the strap of my dress down to kiss along my shoulder line.

I moaned at his hard touch "Tucker."

"Gabs, I need you," he told me into my skin, kissing me.

"You have me, only me," I panted.

That was all Tucker needed to hear as his hand moved underneath my dress to tear off my panties. Literally, he tore my panties right off.

We sat on the floor with our backs still pressed against the door as we both tried to catch our breaths. Tucker held my hand; moving his finger in little circles, he carefully caressed my skin, acting as if I would break into a million pieces right then.

"I love you, Gabs."

I turned my head. "I love you too, Tuck. What brought that on?" I asked, rubbing my bottom lip as I tasted a little bit of rust.

"My lip hurts," I said as I pulled my hand away to see if there was any blood.

"If you would have been quiet, then I wouldn't have had to cover your mouth." He chuckled, softly kissing my lips.

"Mmm...do that again?"

Tucker laughed, "Again?" Then he wiggled his brows at me.

"No, dummy. Kiss me again."

Tucker complied with my requests and gave me the biggest kiss. Right in the middle of our tongues colliding, the door opened and banged against our heads.

"Abigail, get out here right now," Carol said, then slammed the door as best as she could with us against it.

Tucker cringed. "I don't think she likes me very much," he said, picking up my torn panties and stuffing them in his pocket.

I smiled at that. "She doesn't like anyone."

"Tell me about Alex. You've been out to lunch with him and when did he bring you coffee at the school?"

All good questions and I didn't have the answers. "Yeah, I'm sure it's Carol's doing. It's nothing, he's trying to become partner at my dad's firm and he…"

"She wants you to be with him, right?"

I shrugged. I knew that Carol wanted that, pushing Alex on me forcefully. I clutched Tucker's hand. "I think so, but I think it has to do with my dad's firm mostly."

Tucker cupped my face so I would look at him. "Can you promise me something?"

"Yes."

"Promise me. Promise me that you won't see him alone again? I love you; I don't want to lose you over him. He has money; I can smell it on him. He can give you things I can't right now."

He was talking silly talk. I didn't want anything but him, but I gave him my word.

"I promise."

We came out of the piano room and walked back into the dining room hand in hand. I wasn't going to let Carol push Alex in between Tucker and I. Carol stared both of us down as we took our seats and dead silence filled the room. The only noise that came was from the dang silverware scrapping against the plates. Tucker went on like nothing was wrong, having a slice of banana pie and fed me a piece.

Alex glared at Tucker the entire time, almost if he was trying to challenge him, but Tucker didn't notice. Well, at least I didn't think he noticed, and if he did, he didn't let it bother him. My dad ended up excusing himself to his study, tugging Alex along with him. I felt like I could breathe again with him gone. Carol remained at the table with us, watching like a hawk as we smiled to each other and held hands. I couldn't take it anymore; I was done and wanted to leave. Right when I was going to tell Tucker I wanted to leave, Carol spoke up.

"So Tucker, what do you do?"

He shifted a little at the sudden question. It seemed like "I want to get to know you, but really I could care less" talk. "I'm a tattoo apprentice, ma'am."

"Huh, how much does one make while doing that?"

He took a sip of water before answering. "Right now, ma'am, nothing. Unless the client leaves me a tip – then I get to keep that."

My stomach started to turn at the sight of Carol becoming the mean lady that she always was, digging for information on someone, possibly to hold it against them one day; that was the Carol I knew and hated.

"And how long have you been doing this?"

"A little over a year."

Her brow raised as I shifted in my seat. By Tucker's body language, he was getting uncomfortable. "And how long are you going to be doing this before you decide it's not something you want in life?"

Tucker wiped his mouth and placed his napkin on the table. "I love tattooing – watching someone's face as they see the beauty I just gave them is the best feeling in the world."

Carol rested her hands in her lap and sat back in the chair, "I think you're wasting your time."

My jaw dropped and I quickly got mad. How could she say something like that? To get a response out of him, out of me? For us to snap, to give her a reason to kick Tucker out?

"I'm sorry you think that way, ma'am," Tucker said back to her. I pressed my lips together and I started to shake from the anger boiling through my veins, not wanting to explode at her in front of Tucker. I stood up, still holding his hand, bringing him with me.

"We're leaving."

"Abigail, sit down. You're not going anywhere," Carol commanded, but I wasn't going to listen. I started walking towards the double doors to leave.

"Abigail McCall, if you leave, I'm dropping your scholarship at Juilliard."

I still kept walking towards the door, but Tucker pulled back, stopping me. I faced him, "Don't walk out on her," he said as he cupped my heated face, then kissed my forehead.

"That's so impolite to do that in someone's house," Carol said from behind us.

That's it! I angrily stepped up to Carol, challenging her while she just sat in the chair.

"What's your problem? You are going to take away my scholarship at Juilliard? You can't do that. That's *my* scholarship. I worked my *ass* off to get it! I'd like to see you even try."

Slowly standing up from the table, she stepped into the challenge I threw at her.

"You can't possibly be serious about this boy, Abigail. Does he know about the other boy I caught in the apartment?"

"That was Jett. That's Jade's boyfriend and the owner of the tattoo shop Tucker works at," I shot back.

Carol's blue eyes narrowed. "He doesn't work there. He can't take care of you; he doesn't have a job. An apprenticeship doesn't count as a job. He will use you because of the money your father has, and then he will leave you high and dry until you are nothing. He's trash, Abigail. This is it, Juilliard or else. Accept the consequences of the wrongful actions that you have made."

She was giving me a choice? Juilliard or else? Juilliard was something I'd worked on for as long as I could remember – something that had been my dream since I was little and saw the gorgeous ballerinas in the class room. I heard a door slam and when I turned around, Tucker was gone.

Carol grasped my wrist tightly, not letting me move my feet towards the front door.

"Don't you dare go to him, you have to stay here. He doesn't belong in our world, Abigail. That boy could never give you the things you need. He's lost! He's trash! Trash! Not for you!"

I wrenched my arm away; he wasn't trash.

"If he's trash, then so am I," I spat at her and she immediately dropped my arm.

With that said, I walked away from Carol in the dining room, leaving her stunned out of her mind. Angry tears streamed down my face as I approached the front door to go after him. I couldn't believe a day to be thankful turned into a day of crap. I thought this was supposed to be an exciting time when daughters brought home a boy – that it meant something special was going on between that couple. Well, at least that was what I thought.

I quickly wiped my cheeks when my dad came out of his study and I bumped into him.

Grabbing my shoulders to keep me in one place as I stumbled, he asked, "Abigail, what's wrong?"

"I have to go, Daddy."

His grip grew a little tighter on my arms. "No, you're not going anywhere. Come with me." I tried not to; I wanted Tucker. I wanted his arms around my waist and I wanted his lips against mine. I desired Tucker. I ached for him and Carol hurt him. Why couldn't Carol just accept the fact he was the man I loved and wanted to be with.

My dad guided me to his study, forcing me to sit down on the leather sofa that faced his desk. Alex wasn't in the room; I was sure he was with Carol, plotting out their next move against me. Deep down I was so afraid they were going to win and make Tucker stay away. Then I'd be as unhappy as Carol and be rotten to my own daughter. The thought of turning into Carol made a huge knot in my stomach. It was the acid forming, ready to come up. It took everything I had to keep it down. I focused on my breathing like Tucker taught me.

"Tell me what happened." I opened my eyes to see my dad leaning against the front of his desk with his arms folded.

I recapped what happened in the dining room – how I thought it was so unfair for Carol to do something like this to me. I explained how Tucker didn't bring me down, and how much I loved to be with him. I was sobbing in my hands when my dad came to sit next to me and he let me cry on his shoulder. He held me for some time before he spoke again.

"Tucker doesn't understand our world, Abigail. He comes from a background that doesn't make any sense to Carol. Yes, she did live it once when I first met her. I think she regrets going down that path more than anything, being with someone who treated her so badly – and it makes her that strict with you. I know it doesn't make any sense now, but wait until you have a daughter of your own and she might just go down that same path Carol went down – that same path you are heading down right now. You are nineteen years old; you can't be in love already, especially with the first boyfriend you've ever had, and I can tell you that I was shocked when I saw him standing here with you today. You guys act like you've been together for a couple of years, not a couple of months. Take your time in this world and find out who you are first, date around, concentrate on your ballet. I know how much that means to you. I know you wouldn't trade that for anything."

I looked up at my dad and took in his advice. He knows all about advice – I mean, he's a lawyer and gives it all the time to his clients. But is it worth it to take it and leave Tucker behind?

Chapter Fifteen

I walked home in a daze. I half expected to see Tucker when I came out of my parents' house waiting for me on the street, cooling off, but he wasn't. The November air was cold as I continued my walk home. Every once in a while, I would kick at the imaginary rock lying on the sidewalk as I scuffed my heel. I was only wearing my dress, with no panties I might add. I was cold from the wind.

My dad's words hit me hard as I kept rethinking what he said. Focusing on my ballet was the number one thing on my list. I went to the concert with Tucker, got drunk for the first time, and didn't get the main part in *Swan Lake*. I was paying for it by being an understudy for Jasmine. I didn't want to be the understudy every time I tried out for a part, and I wanted that main part with every show, not to be the girl on the side.

I was still in a daze when I walked into my apartment. Jade and Rachel were gone to their parents' houses and wouldn't be back for a couple of days. With the place being so empty, it would give me time to sulk in misery. My phone rang as I plugged it in the charger and I made my way into the bathroom to shower. I knew the ringtone; it would be forever burned into my memory. I knew I needed to think about what my dad said. He was right; Tucker grew up in a completely different world than I did. My phone rang two more times, and then silence left me all alone in the shower, leaving me to wash away the sins of my body that I committed in my parents' piano room. I really hated to think of it as a sin.

Even though I loved Tucker's hands on my body, deep down my dad's advice echoed in my head. I started to cry in the shower as I heard his ringtone go off again. He was looking for me. He probably already knew that I was home, but I couldn't go to him – not now – just a little peace of mind was all I needed. I scrubbed my skin until it felt raw, then I dragged my legs to bed and I quickly fell asleep.

My wonderful sleep didn't last long because of the loud banging on my front door. My phone rang throughout the night; his ringtone was starting to out *ring* my dad's choice of words. I ended up turning my phone off. Why? I had no clue. I was crazy for pushing Tucker away like this. I just wanted him, only him, but something was stopping me.

But those words, my dad's words. "You are nineteen years old; you can't be in love already. Take your time in this world and find out who you are first, date around, concentrate on your ballet. I know how much that means to you."

My ballet did mean so much to me. I wanted it badly, just as much as Tucker. I shut my tired eyes to have sleep claim over me once again. I didn't move for three days, not getting up unless to pee, which wasn't often since I wasn't eating or drinking anything. December first was next week and now that *Swan Lake* was over, we had auditions for *The Nutcracker* coming up. I wanted a Sugar Plum Fairy spot more than anything. As I dreamed of the beautiful moves of the ballet dancer to the soft happy music, I fell asleep again.

I felt my bed dip down and small hands rubbed my back. I slowly woke up and I already knew just by the hands that they were Jade's. Tucker probably called Jett, who called Jade – probably going through the line of our friends.

"Gabs, you okay?"

"I'm fine. Could you just go away?"

"Yeah, I'll go. But just so you know, Tucker is in the living room...wants to talk with you."

I shut my eyes so tight, they watered. "Just tell him to go, Jade. I'll call him later."

She sighed, "I'm doing this just once. Next time, you have to do it. I'm not getting in the middle."

I heard Jade's footsteps fade down the hallway and that's when the screaming started.

"GABS! Get out here right now!" Tucker yelled. I pulled a pillow over my head, trying to drown out his voice. Again, why was I hiding? Why was I pushing him away? I should be reassuring that we could work.

"Gabs!" He was right outside my door. I pulled the comforter up and over my pillow with my head still underneath it.

Coward.

Knocking on my door, he begged, "Gabs, what did I do? You've got to talk to me."

Gah, he didn't do anything! It's me! So tell him that, dummy.

"Just go away, Tucker!" I yelled through my layers of fabric, hoping he heard me. Instead, I heard my door open, then my blanket was ripped off me. The cold air hit my body like a bunch of hail hitting my skin, next was my pillow, and then I met very angry Tucker eyes.

"What the hell?" he asked.

I tried to rotate my body away from him. I couldn't look at him, but he grabbed my wrist and kept me in one place. I tried wrenching my arm back, but he wouldn't let me go. "Let go."

"No, not until you tell me what the hell is up. Was it that guy, Alex? Did he say something to you about us? Did he give you doubt? Does he want you?"

Tucker's words hurt me. It had nothing to do with Alex. I didn't like him. I didn't want him. End of story.

When I didn't answer, he got angry. "Do you want him?" he growled.

"What? NO!" I screamed sitting up. "How can you say something like that?"

"I don't know, you're not even talking to me. What did I do?" Tucker took hold of my shoulders to give a light shake.

"You're getting mad at me for not talking?" I scoffed. "You don't talk to me! You don't tell me anything about what you do or where you go when you're with Brad. Do I pester you about it? No! I mind my own business. So, you didn't do anything, Tucker. My dad just talked with me and I was just thinking."

His eyes softened but not much. "Thinking? Thinking about being with Alex? About dumping me for him?"

"No!"

"You'd rather have his body on top of yours? His hands touching you like mine do? Would you rather have his dic..." And that's the first time I'd ever smacked anyone before.

My hand stung and Tucker didn't look at me, but his face was turned away, and his lips were pressed together in a hard line, my hand print already showing up on his cheek. But when he finally did look back at me, his eyes were filled of pure hate and anger; it was something I hadn't seen in Tucker, yet. His pupils were dark like a storm just clouded over.

I pointed at him. "You do *not* get to talk to me that way. I already have to deal with Carol's smartass bullshit remarks, but you do not get to say things like that to me. Ever!"

Tucker backed away from me, finally letting me go. Could you blame him? I just smacked him. But he did not get to talk to me like that. I expected it from Carol, but not from him. We stared at each other as he walked back and out of my sight. I let out a choked sob as soon as I heard the front door slam shut and I collapsed into my bed again.

I didn't hear from Tucker. On the nights I was alone, I laid on the couch, crying. Flipping through Rachel's stack of chick flick movies, I put in the heartbreaking *Titanic* movie. I loved it. The classical music and the love that Rose had for Jack killed my insides, reminding me of Tucker and me in the same situation. I cried more when Jack died and Rose was left alone, but making a promise to live and fulfill her dreams without him. I rubbed my tattoo of my gorgeous ballet slippers and scriptwriting of the one school I wanted more than anything.

It had been a week since I'd smacked Tucker. I was so concentrated on working with Madame Ava and my Sugar Fairy Routine. I paid more attention in class and to Madame Ava's every word. I stayed later than everyone after class was over. Jon was my lift partner in a couple of scenes for another part. I was walking out of my practice room when Jon came up to me.

"Hey Abigail. I was wondering if you have a ride home."

"I actually don't live too far from here, so I'll just walk," I said, slinging my ballet bag over my shoulder. "Thanks though." I smiled, walking around him, then collided with Jasmine instead.

"What the hell do you think you're doing, McCall? Tucker dumped you and now you want Jon? You sure do get around."

My brows shot up. "What are you talking about?"

Jasmine's brown irises were nothing but mean as she crossed her arms over her chest. "Ethan told me Tucker dumped your ass."

I let out a little laugh, "Ha, don't believe everything Ethan tells you." I turned and walked away, but that didn't stop Jasmine from pushing me once my back was turned. I lost my balance by getting tangled up in my baggy sweats, landing hard on my hands and knees. I picked myself up pretty fast before she could do anything else humiliating to me. I turned to go after her, but someone held my ballet strap that was still attached to my arm.

"You've got some nerve, Jas," Tucker said as he came up from behind me. How long had he been here?

Jasmine took a couple of steps away from me. "Tucker, she was being quite rude to me. Again I might add that you have a poor choice in girls. "

He walked past me, past Jon and stood right in front of Jasmine. "You don't touch her, you don't look at her, and you don't go near her. You understand me?" Tucker growled at her. She shrieked back away from him.

"Yeah, got it."

He pointed at her. "You remember that when your *mom* wants to contact me or Ethan. Got it?"

She nodded her head so fast that her hair started to come loose.

Tucker didn't even give a sort of glance as he turned and left me in the hallway, which was the last time I saw Tucker for a while.

"Abigail, it's your turn," Madame Ava said to me in the giant auditorium of the Lincoln Center. *The Nutcracker* was the biggest performance of the Christmas Season. Not only did scouts come, but also producers from actual ballets on Broadway. This was my time to really shine. Not only was Madame Ava sitting at a little table in the audience, two other judges sat with her to help make a decision. She told all of us to get used to it, because we would have to face dancing in front of other judges all the time in the near future.

My stomach turned a little as I stepped out from my third position in line at the barre. Yes, I did make it to third in line. The line started with Jasmine, Jon and then me. Once I was in front of the class, I got up *en pointe*, and with my hands raised above my head, I started my sweet solo of the Sugar Plum Fairy. I did every turn with elegance and didn't hear my feet once on the wooden stage. I stretched my legs at the right time; I bent my knees at the exact time with the music. I turned slowly, leaped elegantly, and finished my triple pirouette just perfectly.

When I was done, I smiled to the judges and walked back to the barre. My nerves were shooting through my body so badly, I felt like I had to throw up, but I remember Tucker's words to just breathe.

Always. Just. Breathe.

That helped a little bit, but the feeling was too strong; it was coming – opening of the throat and there it was. I ran out of the room to the nearest garbage and heaved it all up – my nerves, my anxiety – everything. I quickly wiped my face, used the restroom to wash out my mouth, and went back into the auditorium.

"You alright, Abigail?" Madame Ava asked in the microphone. I just nodded and the auditions went on. Three more hours went by and we had to perform our solos again. Madame Ava explained we would have to do that sometimes in certain auditions. My stomach settled down enough to do mine again, and I remembered to breathe.

"All of you did an outstanding job. Go sit out in the hallway and we will call you out one by one for your parts. Remember, everyone will get a part in *The Nutcracker,* but we have chosen who would suit the best parts, okay?"

"Yes, Madame Ava," we called out as a class.

Once out in the hallway, I sat up against the wall and shut my eyes. I had the worst taste in my mouth. I rested my arms up on my bent knees and held my breath. This audition meant more to me than *Swan Lake*. This dance was so special to me as it was my favorite and Shannon's as well. I thought of my birth mother more and more the longer I attended Juilliard. My dad told me she loved ballets, which was something he always admired about her. I really wish she was here to support me.

"Abigail McCall?"

I looked up to see Madame Ava staring at me with a clipboard in her hands. I followed her back to the stage as she took her seat with the other judges. I started to fidget and shift from foot to foot. Madame Ava raised a brow and I stopped. I let out a rush of air through my nose and held my head high.

Then suddenly, I saw someone sit up straight in the back of the room. He had his gray hood on, hidden from view of everyone else, but he was here. Tucker. He was here. He came to watch me. He slouched down in the chair, pulled his hood off and ran his long fingers through his hair – that wild mess that I missed so much.

"Abigail, we would like for you to perform for us again," Madame Ava announced.

I nodded, "Yes, Madame Ava."

My slow music that I practiced to filled the auditorium. Bending my left leg while my right stuck out, I formed my arms in front of me like a circle. My fingertips touched each other and that's when I took off. My turns and pirouettes were perfect. My feet didn't crash loudly against the floor, and when I stepped *en pointe*, I did it with classiness. I remembered to smile for my judges while my head was held high and my back as straight as it could go. I closed better than I had practiced and I was very proud of myself. My music stopped and I walked back to the center of the stage. Watching the judges write some notes down, Madame's eyes never left mine. She broke contact with me when she was given a piece of paper.

Madame Ava stood up. "Abigail, we wanted to let you know the part you get in *The Nutcracker* is..." She stopped and studied my face. I had butterflies like crazy; I felt as if my stomach was in one giant knot. I tried my best to stay still as she continued to stare at me. "The main Sugar Plum Fairy."

And that's when the tears came. My hands covered my face as I silently cried. I did it. I freaking did it. I took my hands from my face and watched Tucker stand up from his spot and start clapping. The judges looked over their shoulders back at him, wide-eyed.

"WOO HOO!" Tucker jogged down the main aisle, climbed the little staircase to the stage and swept me

into his arms to spin me around and round. I took in
his scent that I missed so much – cigarettes and leather
filled my nostrils. Tucker was here. I was so happy
right now. I met his blue eyes and lightly kissed his
lips. He went stiff at first, and then gladly kissed me
back, hugging me tighter.

Madame Ava excused us. Tucker took my ballet
bag and we walked home, hand in hand. I couldn't stop
smiling. I got the part I wanted. I worked so hard for it.
I deserved it. I glanced up at Tucker – my sweet Tucker
who I missed so much the last couple of weeks, and
then I remembered the horrible thing I did to him. I
stopped mid-stride and pulled him to me. I had to
make it right between us so we could be happy again. I
wanted him.

"Tucker, I'm so sorry about hitting you."

He shook his head. "Gabs, stop." I put my hand up
to cover his mouth.

"Please, just listen to me. Okay?" He nodded so I
took my hand away. "What I did was wrong. I shouldn't
have smacked you. I know you were upset with me. My
dad said some things that made me stop and think. It
has nothing to do with Alex, I promise." Tucker's eyes
softened and I could tell he wanted to say something,
but I continued before he could. "My dad told me that I
was too young to be in love, but during our time apart,
I felt miserable without you. You don't know how much
it meant to me to see you there today. I loved having
you there, Tuck. I always want you there."

My last sentence came out more like a squeak. I
couldn't help but be miserable being away from him.
Tucker stepped up to me and cupped my cheek.

"I'm an ass, Gabs. A total asshole for the things I
said to you. I deserved what I got. It's just, Alex has
everything he can give you, and I don't have anything. I

don't even have a place you can stay at, or visit me. Nothing. I have nothing. You get that, right?"

My sight started to get blurry from his heartbreaking words to me. "That's not true, Tuck. You can always stay with me. You love me, that's enough for me. And I promise you, you won't lose me to Alex."

"You won't see him again?"

I didn't hesitate. "No," I said, shaking my head. Tucker didn't waste any time taking my mouth in a hungry kiss. We kissed as if we couldn't get enough, eating each other alive and putting all our passion into it. It was from all the time we were apart.

Tucker and I made nothing but sweet love to each other the rest of the weekend. We only stopped to eat, use the bathroom and then shower together. Jett had to pull Tucker away Sunday night because a tattoo client who refused to get tattooed by Jett. I went with him and sat by his side, just watching him work his magic on the skin. This client wanted a giant chest piece done, wanting it to look like his insides were falling out. Not my kinda of style, but Tucker's work was gorgeous as always. Tucker made the guy get up every once in a while to take a break. I sat in Tucker's lap as the guy smoked outside. Tucker's masterpiece was finally finished; he looked in the mirror and was in awe of Tucker's work.

"Tucker man, you've got serious talent. This is exactly how I pictured it on my skin, man."

The guy gave Tucker a huge tip and that was when Tucker's client list took off. Jett always had the shop open, but he told Tucker by state law, he couldn't hire him, yet; he had to have two years of apprenticeship with so many hours included. Tucker was getting frustrated and upset every time he didn't make any money while doing something he loved. He told me that he had already been apprenticing for a year and a couple months, with about five months left. Jett gave him what he could, but there were still times where Tucker had to leave me to go with Jeremiah and Brad. Whenever we saw Jeremiah, Tucker would hide me or tell me to walk the other way. He would never tell me why or what was said between them. They would talk and I would end up by myself. I would be mad at Tucker when I turned and saw him walking away from me, seeing him head towards Jeremiah instead. Of course Tucker always said just the right thing to sweet his way back into my bedroom and snuggle up with me at night.

I woke up today with Tucker gone and me alone in my bed. I shouldn't let it bother me too much, but it did. Today was my second *Nutcracker* rehearsal. Jasmine stayed out of my way during practice, but that didn't stop her in the hallway and after school when Tucker was late walking me home. She would continue on with the shove of her shoulder against mine or sneer at me while walking by. Jasmine never brought Tucker up around me. I still think that it was a little nasty about Ethan and Tucker sharing her. I tried not to think about it, because it just made me angry—that Tucker's hands had been on her intimately. I mostly thought about if Tucker's lips were on hers like he did to mine. If he made her feel the way he did to me.

Ugh! Not now.

It was one day from our first show. I was more excited than nervous. My dad called to let me know that he and Carol will be coming to the show, and would be there right on the dot. Tucker also told me that he would be there with Jade, Rachel, and Jett. Brad didn't promise me anything and just said if he could, he would be there. Practice came and went. Now

I sat in my dressing room with my hair and makeup being done. Sparkles covered my entire face and my white tutu and corset outfit laced in gold was perfect as ever.

When the red curtain went up, you could see the little girl and her cute little Nutcracker doll, and then the scene came alive with all the little laughing kids. This was the first time I even saw the kids. I knew they had their own practice room so that we could concentrate on our own scenes. When it was time for my entrance, the bright light on me pierced my eyes. I kept my head up high and simply smiled throughout my scene, moving across the stage with ease, just like I practiced.

Madame Ava came up to me when I was done. "Abigail, I think you could have done better than that. Don't you think?"

What?

"Madame Ava, I believe I did okay. Better than okay, I thought," I stuttered at her.

She arched a brow at me. "What did you say to me, Abigail?"

I let out a breath while my stomach turned in knots, making it feel like a brick was sitting in there. "Nothing, Madame Ava." And my head dropped to the ground. She walked away without another word.

I changed in my dressing room and went to go meet my dad and Carol in the after room where parents congratulated their sons and daughters. When I walked into the room, Alex was standing next to Carol, having a glass of champagne with her and laughing. My first thought was, "Where's Tucker?" I quickly searched the room for him. If he found out Alex was here, he was gonna flip. I spotted him in the dark corner with Jade and Jett talking to him. Tucker's eyes were set on

Alex's back, glaring daggers. I hope that Jett was trying to talk Tucker into doing nothing stupid.

As I approached my dad and gave him a kiss on his cheek, he said, "Angel, you were magnificent."

"Yes, Abigail, you did wonderful," Carol said to me. Alex took me in his arms unexpectedly and gave me a hug that took my feet off the ground.

"Abigail, you were absolutely beautiful." Then Alex kissed my cheek.

"Can you put me down, please?" He gave me one last squeeze that caused me to lose breath for a second. Once my feet landed, Tucker was at my side and grabbed a hold of my hand. I kissed his cheek and smiled, but that didn't stop his dirty looks to Alex.

"Tucker, good to see you again," my dad addressed while holding his hand out.

"Hello, sir." Tucker shook his hand.

I quickly turned to Tucker. "Ready to go?" He didn't look at me, still staring down Alex. But Alex found it amusing and chuckled softly to himself while taking a sip of his drink.

I yanked on his hand. "Tucker?" That did the trick and he finally looked at me. "Ready to go?" I asked again and he nodded. I swiftly pulled him from the room with Jade, Rachel, and Jett behind us.

Back at our apartment, Tucker exploded. "God! I can't stand that he was there. I can't stand him period!" Tucker paced out on our balcony while he smoked angrily, puffing smoke out all over the place and walking into it. I stubbed mine out and tried to go into his arms, but he pushed past me. I didn't like this side of Tucker that started coming out.

"Tucker, just stop."

"No! I'm not gonna stop. I don't like him, I don't like the way he looks at you or holds you. Touches you!"

"I get that, Tucker, and I told you that I didn't want him. I want you."

That did it. He stopped and engulfed me in his arms like I would disappear from him, and all that was going on stopped and we just lost each other in our tight embrace.

The morning of our next show, I was really sick to my stomach. Brad claimed that he had the flu a couple of days ago, hence, the reason why he didn't come. Rachel went to go see him and then she got sick right after. Jade joked to her while she was in the bathroom puking her guts out.

"You know, they should make tongue condoms so you can still make out but won't get the saliva flu." I laughed while Jade rubbed Rachel's back.

"Shut up, Jade," Rachel hissed, and then threw up again. I really hope it wasn't headed in my direction. That was the last thing that I needed.

Our next show was a hit. People swarmed the auditorium to see our performance. Once again, my dad, Carol and Alex showed up for my scene. Tucker wasn't happy when they sat directly in front of him. I could see it written all over his face. This time, Alex just played on his phone as I watched him from the side curtain line. People around him nudged his shoulder and he didn't put it away.

When I took the stage, I felt like I did my routine ten times better than the last. Then as we came out to the stage for our bow, I mouthed "I love you" to Tucker. He smiled and mouthed it back to me, but Alex raised his arm up and waved to me. I groaned, rolling my eyes. Sometimes, he just made this worse for me. At least I thought my dad would say something to him. Tucker was pissed at that and I saw Jett place an arm on Tucker's shoulder to hold him back. The show went better than the first and Madame Ava didn't point out my faults. She just told me to show what I showed them at my audition. I thought I was, but I would just prove to her the next time.

It was finally Christmas Eve and I was so excited. Just like a kid waiting for Christmas to come, when I asked what Tucker wanted, he wouldn't tell me – all he said was that he wouldn't be with me on Christmas. That was upsetting; I at least wanted Tucker to stay the night with me. So, Tucker cuddled with me and whispered sweet nothings into my ear on Christmas Eve as we watched the snow fall from my bed into the New York City street lights.

I woke up Christmas morning with the other side of my bed cold and a note on the pillow.

Baby girl,
Sorry I had to leave. Make sure you check under your tree.
Tucker

Tree? We decided against putting up a tree or any decorations. Rachel was going to be at her mom's and Jade went with her while her parents were in Russia. Jade didn't have a clue why they wanted to go there, and she plainly told them she wasn't going. One, because she doesn't speak Russian and two, she didn't have a good enough reason to go to Russia. Both good points if you asked me. I sat up too fast in bed, ending up really dizzy and incredibly sick to my stomach. I barely made it into the bathroom before I heaved up nothing but burning morning stomach acid. I immediately started to sweat and when I felt my own forehead, I was warm.

Oh crap. This isn't good. I was getting Rachel's grossed out saliva flu.

I barely made it over to the sink to brush my teeth and when I walked into our living room, the place was covered in Christmas decorations. Red and white lights strung up around the room. Dead center in front of the big bay windows stood a gorgeous Christmas tree with all sorts of different ornaments on it. I went back into my room to grab my phone, taking many pictures of the place and sent them to Jade and Rachel. They both texted back, telling me that they already knew, because they helped Tucker surprise me.

Sneaky girls.

One gold present sat under the giant pine tree with dozens of twinkle lights. I stared at them as some lights faded really gradually while others stayed on. The New York street below was covered in snow. I picked up the small box and tore apart the gold paper with the white bow just like an excited little kid. A velvet box remained in my hand; it was too big to be a ring box. I slowly opened it, and inside laid a little silver snowflake necklace with a sapphire stone in the middle. I gasped to no one in the room and my hand went to my chest as one tear fell down my cheek. It was gorgeous. My phone started ringing right after that and Tucker's name appeared.

"Hello?"

"Hey, baby girl."

I smiled in the phone. "Hi."

"Do you like your present?" His words hit me, then I looked around to see if he was somewhere in the room, secretly watching me.

Standing up, I said, "Are you..."

"No. I'm not there. Look above you."

I looked up to the beautiful angel at the top of the tree, and saw that a big gold bow held a little camera pointing down at me.

"What...what is that?"

"It's Jett's GoPro Camera. It's connected through wifi. I didn't want to miss the look on your pretty face as you opened your present."

My heart stopped. "Oh, Tucker." Looking back up into the camera, I mouthed "I love you" to him.

"I love you, too, Gabs." His voice made me miss him and I just wanted him here with me.

"I didn't get you a present," I confessed.

"I don't need anything, baby. I'm sorry, I gotta go, okay?"

"Okay, are you going to come ov..." I couldn't finish my sentence, asking if he was going to come over later. I cupped my mouth and ran to my bathroom and threw up again. I could hear Tucker's voice as he called out to me, asking repeatedly if I was there. I threw up again then collapsed on the cold tile floor with my phone in my hand. The cold felt so good on my burning up face. I barely had enough strength to put the phone back up to my ear.

"Gabs? Hello, Gabs?"

I shut my eyes, his words somehow made me dizzier. "I'm here."

"Are you okay?"

Feeling nauseated, I nodded instead of answering.

"Gabs, are you there?"

"Yeah, I think I'm getting sick. I've thrown up twice today already."

"Go lay down and I'll be there as soon as I can." Again I nodded and the line went dead.

I picked myself up to wash out my mouth. I caught a glimpse of Rachel's calendar on the side of the bathroom with a big red X on December fifteenth and on the eighteenth was an "End X" on it. I picked up my phone and pulled up the app that I used to keep track of my periods. I scrolled through it. I was supposed to start on the second, and today was Christmas and I just threw up twice.

Ummm...

I quickly put in the days I could remember of Tucker and I having sex, filling up the calendar with tons of pink dots. But we'd been using condoms. My inner voice told me that condoms are only ninety eight percent effective. I ran into Rachel's room and pulled out a box to read the precautions on the side. Yep, right there in bold letters. Condoms are only ninety-eight percent effective. I rolled my eyes at myself, but there were two times Tucker and I didn't use anything: the night I lost my virginity and Thanksgiving at my parents' house. Tucker told me he wasn't expecting to do that there. You could just call us horny dogs without a care in the world for that one.

I couldn't be pregnant. I couldn't be. There was no way. Could there?

Chapter Sixteen

According to the little app on my phone, it was saying that I could possibly be pregnant. What would a stupid app know? It didn't know my body. Tucker kept his word and came straight over to find me in bed. I didn't tell him anything about it, kept that information to myself in case I was wrong, very, very, very wrong. Tucker took care of me until late afternoon and then he said he had to go. He put on my new silver snowflake necklace around my neck.

"I'm sorry about the one that broke. Hope this makes up for it." He kissed my forehead and then left me. I didn't hear from him for the next three days. I was sick every morning after that, and as those three days went on, the more I started to convince myself that I was indeed pregnant. I couldn't stand the smell of coffee that Jade made in the mornings. I found myself staying far away from the balcony as Jade smoked outside. I was throwing up at least four times in the morning and brushing my teeth made it a tad bit worse.

We had one more show for *The Nutcracker*. We were at practice and I got really dizzy performing my triple pirouette, and ran over to the garbage can to throw up right in the middle of my scene. I really just wanted to lie down, and as if Madame Ava read my mind, she sent me home. Even though it was a short walk, I took a cab. I dragged my feet all the way up to the apartment. And when I walked in, Brad wasn't looking too happy, pacing back and forth as he rubbed his shaved head.

"I'm fucking dead, Rach I'm dead," he said over and over.

Rachel's green eyes were red and swollen from crying; I went straight to her side and pushed her hair behind her ear.

"Rach, what's going on?"

"Nothing. Brad's in a bind, I guess." She shrugged like it wasn't a big deal, but Rachel was crying – well, maybe not now anymore, but she had been. Something was definitely wrong.

"Rach, talk to me."

"This doesn't concern you, Gabs!" Brad yelled at me.

"Don't bring her in this, Brad," Rachel yelled back and stood up to get in his face. "This is your fucking fault, you deal with it!"

Brad turned and went to the front door, muttering under his breath, "I gotta find Tucker," and slammed the door.

I turned to Rachel. "Okay, what the hell just happened?"

Rachel pulled her red hair up into a high ponytail. "Brad owes money to that Ethan guy."

"Wait, how do you know about Ethan?"

"I heard you talking to Tuck about it one day. Plus Brad acts afraid of him. He's just freaking out; Tucker will help him, though; he always does. So don't you worry your cute little button nose," she told me as she tapped my nose with a finger. My phone rang, interrupting us; it was Carol.

I rolled my eyes. "This is not what I need right now," I told Rachel before I answered the phone.

"Hello?"

"Abigail, can you meet me for a quick lunch?" I looked at the clock on the wall; school would be just getting out, so I wouldn't have to explain why I was home. I was going to have to face her one day. My nauseous stomach would help keep my mind off her words.

"Yeah, I can." I picked at the imaginary lint on my pants.

"Great, see you," she chirped in the phone and hung up. She was in a good mood, which worried me.

"Lunch with the beast?"

I looked up at Rachel who was grinning at me.

"Ugh, yes."

"Well, have fun with that. Isn't your last show tomorrow?"

"Yeah."

"Oh, my mom wants to come – is that okay?"

"Yeah, sounds great. I gotta go before Carol freaks out that I'm late." I stood up from the couch and left, but outside of the door, I heard Rachel sniffle and softly start crying. Something was definitely wrong.

The cab dropped me off in front of the hotel. Right in front of the restaurant windows, I immediately spotted Alex sitting alone at a table, dressed in his signature pressed suit. He was flipping his silverware back and forth through his finger, while chewing on his bottom lip.

She did it again! She set me up with him! Ugh...frustrating woman!

I'd had enough of this, and I really didn't need to deal with this crap right now.

I walked into the grand hotel and to the right held its little restaurant; I hated these little play dates where Carol would set me up with Alex. Yes, Alex was very good looking and very wealthy, something Carol always approved of. I couldn't help but think of Tucker; I couldn't get him off my mind – his smile, the way his eyes would sparkle as he held me in his arms and tell me how much he loved me – to think that I might be having a baby with him. This thing with Alex had to stop.

Of course Alex was a gentleman and stood up at my approach. He pulled out my chair and I mumbled out a plain "Thanks" to him. I quickly looked over the menu while Alex did the same. For some reason he would never talk to me until we ordered the meal, but he never talked to me at all. Never get in the way of a man and his food. He put down his menu as the waiter in a pressed white shirt and black bow tie came to our table.

"Are you ready to order, sir?" he asked with a fake French accent. Even though I could speak French, my accent was always off. Ramón always told me that.

"Yes, I'll have the Sirloin, cooked medium with vegetables and she will have the... chicken pasta." Alex handed over his menu. I didn't remember making up my mind to have the chicken pasta.

"Wait," I told the waiter, "I'll have a Caesar salad with banana peppers and dressing on the side," I stated to him. The waiter looked over at Alex, which made me look at Alex, but when I did, I saw Tucker standing outside of the restaurant, staring at me through the big fancy windows.

My stomach dropped and turned with sickness and I knew it wasn't from the maybe pregnancy. He was just witnessing the one promise I made, which was now broken. I watched as Tucker pulled up his hood of his gray hoodie and stuffed his hands deep into his front pockets; he shook his head back and forth, looked back up to me one more time, then walked away. I abruptly stood up.

"Tucker," I mumbled out. I ran out of the restaurant, leaving Alex all by himself. I chased Tucker down the sidewalk and when I called out to him, he walked away faster.

"TUCKER!" I screamed as he turned up an alleyway. When I turned to follow, he was stopped and facing towards me, head down with his hands still deep in his pockets. I was very much out of breath as I approached him with caution.

"Tucker," I delicately said to him. I could feel his hot breath hitting my face; my eyes started to water as I watched the father of my possibly little baby struggle with what to say to me.

"What are you doing with him?" he growled out at me.

"I had to come, Carol set me..." But Tucker wouldn't let me finish,

"Are you always going to do what Carol says? I remember you telling me that you don't give a rat's ass what Carol wants you to do. Yet, here you are, having lunch with that asshole, Alex." Tucker pointed towards the front of the alleyway.

"It's not that easy, Tucker. I'm torn,"

Right when that one little word left my mouth, I knew it was a huge mistake. I wasn't torn, not at all. My body, heart and soul wanted only Tucker. So what did I mean when I said that?

I tried stepping towards Tucker; I had to tell him about the baby to get him to understand, but my feet were frozen to the ground and I couldn't move. Why couldn't anyone just let us be together? Something was always pushing us apart. Tucker made me so happy. He knew about my bulimia and helped me with it. Whenever I felt that wretched discomfort coming up my throat, I would turn to him and he would talk to me about how I was feeling. He was there; he would always have my heart, no matter what.

"Tucker, I..." I stuttered at my own words.

"I can't do this anymore, Gabs," Tucker whispered, but I couldn't stand not being close to him. I stepped closer until I felt my shoes hit the tip of his. My forehead inched until it hit his chest. I could feel his heart beating against my head, his breath flowing down the back of my jacket. The wind picked up with an cold icy breeze, and when I tilted my head up to look at Tucker, my eyes watched as snow started to fall.

Snowing while the sun now peeked out was a favorite of mine. "Ha, it's snowing, Tuck," I said. A tear slowly slipped down my cheek and he brushed it away with the tip of his finger.

"Yeah, it is."

Suddenly I felt my heart get warm with the way he was looking down at me. He had the most gorgeous blue eyes. I always found myself lost in them. Tucker leaned down to kiss me. I loved when he would take control to kiss me deeper. His arms wrapped tightly around my waist as I pushed up on my toes to be at his level. I couldn't get close enough to him; my hands went straight into his hair and I pulled lightly, making him groan into my mouth.

"Gabs, I want you so bad," Tucker said breathlessly as shivers ran through my body. I wanted him, too.

"You have me, Tucker, only you."

Then I slammed my lips back to his. My words were very true. I wanted Tucker more than anything. He was right there with my ballet; that's all I wanted. He pulled away from me to look deep into my caramel eyes. More snow started to fall, causing me to shiver, I didn't know how it was possible, but he managed to pull me closer to him.

"Come back with me." I dropped my forehead to his, our noses touching as he softly kissed my lips.

"I can't, Tuck."

"Ugh, why not?"

"I have to go back and talk with Alex. I'll tell him again that I don't want to be with him; I've told him enough that he should finally get the hint this time around. I promise to meet you later. Tomorrow is the last show of *The Nutcracker*, you coming? I have to talk to you about something."

He pulled away from me and I fisted my hands in his shirt to keep him closer. "I don't know, Gabs," he said as he scratched the back of his head. "Will Alex be there?"

I couldn't lie to him; whenever I had a show and my parents came, Carol always dragged Alex along.

"Probably yes." He pulled all the way away from me this time.

"Damnit, Gabs. No!"

Unshed tears stung my eyes. "I'm not going to fight with you about this."

"Just go back to Alex, Gabs. I'll see you later."

Tucker turned on his heel and left the alleyway. I covered my face with my hands and cried into them as the snow slowly fell around my feet. I couldn't chase after him now, even though my heart protested otherwise. I made my way back into the restaurant and to Alex's table. I felt so nauseous to my stomach, feeling like I was going to lose it all over again. Alex shifted uncomfortably in his seat, making me squirm as I looked up at him. He blue eyes were hard and fierce with anger that I had left, which wasn't very lady like on my part.

"Where did you go?" Alex asked.

"I saw someone outside who I had to talk to." The waiter brought out food to our table. Laying down my napkin, I took a sip of my untouched water and started pitching my lettuce with my fork.

"Who?" Alex pushed at me, but I stayed silent. He knew it was Tucker; he just wanted me to admit it out loud. "I know it was him, Abigail. That Tucker guy you think you love."

My head snapped up. "I do love him, Alex. I don't know how many times I have to tell you it's him that I want. Not you."

"He can't take care of you, Abigail, he's just..."

"You and I, *we* can't be together. I love him, not you," I said to him but he ignored my words and continued on talking to me about the firm and a case he was working on with my dad. They were taking on a really big case with some drug dealers in the city. I sat there, motionless in my seat; I poked at my food, wishing Tucker was here with me instead. I couldn't stand being away from him or us fighting; I just wanted him to hold me. Was that too much to ask? Alex finished his food and I barely touched my salad. I did, however, eat the banana peppers, which tasted so good to me.

Alex cleared his throat, "Abigail, are you listening to a word I'm saying to you?"

I stuffed another pepper in my mouth. "No, sorry."

"I said, I want to take you to Paris when you're done with school in June," he stated again and I almost choked on the pepper seeds.

Taking a sip of water, I said, "You want to take me to Paris?"

He nodded at me while taking a gulp of his water, and then smoothed out the tablecloth as I shifted painfully in my seat. "Why Paris?" As I met his gaze, he smiled, his blue eyes fierce and hard but sparkling in the light – but not as much as Tucker's did when he smiles, with the sunlight hitting his face, while he's smoking and shirtless.

Ha, what a dream.

"I talked with your father and he's given me his blessing for us to get married,"

"What?" My fork clattered on my plate, "Married? I don't want to get married, Alex."

"Yes, you do, every girl does," He shrugged like it wasn't a big deal.

"Well, sometime in the future, yes, but right now, no."

I couldn't even think about getting married, especially to Alex. I could be pregnant with Tucker's baby for crying out loud; there was no way I could deal with this. I quickly stood to my feet, almost knocking over my chair backwards if it wasn't for the waiter passing behind me.

"I can't get married to you, Alex, I don't love you."

"I don't love you, either, but I think we could fall in love at some point." Alex claimed, wiping his mouth with the white napkin. I couldn't believe he just said that. No girl or woman would ever go for that type of thing. Plus, he's trying to force me into the situation. This has Carol written all over it – pushing Alex on me like this when he didn't want to marry me anyway.

Where in the hell was all this coming from? All I knew was that I had to have some words with Carol and I had to find Tucker. Like, now!

Chapter Seventeen

I found Jade in her room when I got home, headphones on with not a care in the world, but my world was crashing down around me, and I needed her. I collapsed on her bed, but totally missed the edge and fell on the floor with a loud thud.

"Ouch," I cried.

I stayed on the floor as Jade leaned over to look at me, pulling out her earphones, "What's the matter?"

Grabbing a piece of hair to run my fingers through, I then started braiding the little piece and quietly mumbled out, "I think I'm pregnant." I shut my eyes, waiting for her to answer. Counting to five in my head, I peeked up at her. She was so still, like a statue staring off in the distance.

Whispering "Jade" finally got her to blink a couple of times and look at me.

"Umm, have you told Tucker?"

I shook my head against the comforter and kicked off my shoes to curl my knees up under my butt. "Carol called me to have me meet her. Alex was there instead and Tucker saw. He got mad and left, I chased him down, and he left me in the alleyway and I went back to Alex and..."

"You dumbass. What's wrong with you? You know you're blowing it with Tucker by hanging around Alex, right?" I stood up and lay on Jade's bed.

I nodded my head, making my hair go staticky. Of course I knew that and it killed me. Why wouldn't the world just leave us alone so we could be happy? Just have everyone shut the hell up.

"I've been around the shop with Jett when Tucker is there; all he talks about is you. About how beautiful you are. Your hair, your eyes." I silently cried in the white comforter. I was becoming such a cry baby. I really needed to stop. "Why are you still laying here?"

I glanced up at Jade who had a smug look on her face. "Don't look at me like that. Get. Out."

Jade pushed me off her bed and my butt hit the floor. Hard.

"Ow, Jade," I whined.

"Get outta here and go find him. Right now. Don't blow this with him. He's a great guy, someone who balances the two of you just right. Now go and don't come back until you've told him."

Jade was right. I had to tell him; he had a right to know. Even if he was mad at me. He's the only one I've been with; I couldn't keep this from him. I should have told him while we were in the alleyway.

I headed straight for Central Park. I would try there first to see if I could find the green house. That's where I knew he went with Ethan. I pieced that together myself. I half walked, half ran down a pathway when Tucker came out of the trees, looking very much pissed off. I screamed, almost falling backwards.

"Tucker. How did you find me?" I asked as I brushed hair out of my face.

He pulled out a pack of cigarettes to light one up. "I followed you."

I watched him blow smoke out around him; he was somewhat hidden behind the soft cloud and I couldn't make out his expression. "Why were you following me?"

"Because I don't like Alex. I knew you were going to go to him sooner or later."

My heart started to break. "Tucker, I've told you. I don't want him. When are you ever going to see that?" And then Tucker blew up.

"All you want is Alex. You don't fucking want me, all you want is him! I saw you two together! Your face fell when I caught you red-handed."

I had to remember to breathe. "Tucker, how could you say that? You know how much I want to be with you. I'll only choose you; I fell in love with you. Alex only means something to Carol, not me," I yelled at the end, my fingers hitting his chest out of anger.

When was he really going to get this through his thick skull? I really only wanted Tucker in my life. I felt whole being around him. He never pressured me. I watched Tucker pace back and forth in front of me. He took a couple of puffs and stopped pacing. His face tilted up to the afternoon sky and he breathed out, smoke coming out of his nose like a fire breathing mad dragon.

Right now, I don't even have the nerve to tell him about the baby. I couldn't bear it if he didn't believe me. Deep down, I knew that he would. I was such a chicken.

"Tucker," I managed to squeak out. I stepped towards him, but he stepped back, not meeting my face.

"Gabs, you want to be with me, but I can't if Alex is prancing away in front of my face. You know Carol doesn't like me and yet you still hang around me." He eyes burned into mine and he took one step towards me. Tears were falling down my icy cold cheeks and his thumb caressed the watery trails away. "I'm sorry, but I can't be with you if Alex is in the picture."

I let out a big breath against his palm, "Are you breaking up with me?" My heart slowly started to break, piece by piece and my guard started to build up around it. Just like I would do around Carol when I would disappoint her, I would just go into a different world, alone. I glanced up at Tucker, his face hard as stone as he thought about what I just asked him. Our bodies were so close together and my body just reacted like normal, fisting my hands in his shirt. I can't help my body as I push up on my toes and softly kiss his mouth, but there's no passion in the little kiss. His lips were set in a hard line, his hands coming up to give me a little push on my shoulders, making me step away from him.

"I'm sorry, Abigail, we can't be together. I can't see it happening. It's just not gonna work."

Shaking my head, I said, "You don't mean it,"

"Yes, I do. I can't give you the fucking life you live! We're not good together anyway. You're spoiled daddy's girl who gets everything handed to her left and fucking right. I can't stand people like that! I never had much money and I still don't, but what I have is a start and it's not going anywhere near you!"

My jaw dropped. "What's that supposed to mean?"

"I don't want you!" he screamed as his hot angry breath hit my face, blowing my hair back.

That did it; my heart just shattered into a million tiny pieces and it could never be fixed again. Tucker didn't want me. The first guy I fell in love with didn't want me. Carol was right; even my dad warned me about Tucker not staying with me.

"He doesn't believe in our world, Abigail."

I started backing away from him, his breaths were harsh to my ears. Some joggers rushed past us as I quickly turned around and started running away from him. I expected Tucker to call out for me that he made a huge mistake, but he didn't; he let me run. I came out of our hiding spot in Central Park and raced to my building. Michael didn't have time to even open the main door for me.

"Miss Abigail?" he called out, hanging up the desk phone, but I ignored him.

The elevator dinged open as I made my way inside in too big of a rush and crashed into the people coming out.

"You alright, my dear?" An elderly lady asked me, but I couldn't answer. I just needed to put as much distance between me and Tucker as possible. I hated him right now. I couldn't believe he actually thought I would go with Alex. Alex was boring, not me. I couldn't even tell Tucker about the baby – our baby. My hands went to my stomach and more tears cascaded down my face. I felt so alone. I couldn't believe this was happening to me. Would Carol force me to get an abortion like her dad made her? I couldn't do it. I was so much stronger than that. I didn't care if it destroyed my ballet career that I so desperately wanted. It was my dream to be doing this, but I couldn't kill something that we created together.

The elevator dinged and I stumbled off. I opened the door to the apartment to Jade and Jett on the couch. He had his acoustic guitar on his lap, playing for Jade while she sang to him. They both looked at my teary eyed face. Just seeing them sitting there like a cute couple made me sick, and I raced to my shared bathroom and threw up. I heard the door click shut and small, very familiar hands started rubbing my back.

"You didn't tell him, huh?"

I just cried into the toilet like I had many times before.

"Are you sure you're even pregs, Gabs? Maybe it's just stress. You know how you get when Carol upsets you."

"I'm six weeks late, Jade. Tucker was so pissed at me that Alex was coming tomorrow with my dad and Carol. He said, "I see the way you look at him. You want him." I couldn't finish telling Jade the awful things he said to me. I flung my body on the cold tile floor, not caring if it was dirty or not.

"I know Rachel has a pregnancy test in her drawer."

Jade went into Rachel's room and came right back with it already unwrapped.

"Here, pee on it and we'll know for sure,"

Jade thrust the white stick in front of my face. I unzipped my pants and sat on the toilet with Jade still in the room. I didn't care that she was with me. I clicked the cap back on, flushed and sat the test on the counter while I washed my hands.

"What's Rach doing with a pregnancy test?" Drying my hands, I turned and faced Jade, too afraid even to glance down at the devil white stick that held my pee.

Jade shrugged. "Meh, had to go buy one the first night you slept with Tucker. Remember when she came home that night and ran past us while we were outside?"

I nodded.

"Well, she was late and totally flipped out. She told Brad and they got in some big fight but my guess that it was stress. She got her period a couple of days later."

Oh poor Rachel. I had no idea she went through something like that and I didn't know. I would have been there for her if she would have needed me. Three long minutes of my life passed by and Jade just held my hand and waited.

Jade pulled out her phone. "It's time."

"I can't look," I said, covering my face with my hands.

"Come on, Gabs, if you're going to have a baby, then you can't be the baby. Now look." Jade shoved me over and I looked down to see the two blue lines.

Positive.

Even though I already knew, I was still shocked. I started breathing too much; it was too much. I couldn't control it. I was hyperventilating so bad, I was starting to get a panic attack. Tears spilled over my hands as they ran down my face as I screamed.

"Hey, hey, hey, Gabs, Look at me." But I couldn't look at her. I was so shocked about this. It was true. I was pregnant – nineteen and pregnant.

My cries were now loud as I screamed in the bathroom. Jade pulled me into her arms to let me cry on her shoulder. We huddled together on the bathroom floor until the sun went down and I passed out on Jade's lap on the dirty bathroom floor.

I woke up still on the bathroom floor, my head still resting on Jade's lap. I glanced up at Jade, moving slowly so I wouldn't wake her. She looked so at peace with her eyes closed and resting her head against the cabinets. I was so emotionally tired from all the crying, and I was sure the pregnancy as well was making this huge mess. I walked back into my room, digging through my purse, finding my phone to plug it in. With some hope, I wished Tucker would try to get a hold of me. But my phone showed no sign of him trying to reach me at all. My heart broke a little more. A part of me wanted to call him, scream at him, yelling that I was pregnant at the top of my lungs, but I couldn't. I heard groaning coming from the bathroom and the front door closing at the same time.

Rachel walked in my room with a very satisfied look on her face. Once again, her hair was a complete rat's nest.

"Dude. Do not, I repeat, do not let me sleep on the bathroom floor again!" Jade rubbed her butt and stretched out her back.

Rachel scoffed, "What the hell are you doing sleeping on the bathroom floor?"

Before Jade could even say anything, I cut in. "I got a little food poisoning last night. It's nothing. My phone buzzed and I picked it up to see Carol's number, my dad's, and Alex's. For one, I was not calling Alex back. I could ignore Carol, but my dear, sweet dad did not deserve to be ignored. I dialed his number and talked with him for a few minutes. Hearing Carol's high heels in the background, I kept my dad talking so she couldn't take the phone away. That didn't always stop her, though. I told my dad that the show started at eight and I would see him and Carol there, then quickly hung up the phone.

I felt bland; that was the only word I could think of to describe how I felt right now. Bland, tasteless, dead. I just had to get through tonight and try and make it not such a disaster moment in my life. The rest of the day went by in a blur. I sat and listened to Rachel talk about the most amazing night with Brad and how he actually took her out on a date. They stayed at Jett's on the couch, but she didn't care. Rachel didn't say anything about Tucker. She didn't mention his name once; I wonder if she even saw him. Noticing the time, it was time to get ready to go. Rachel left to go meet her mom and said they would meet us at the Lincoln Center. I was excited to see Trish; I missed her spunk.

I stood up and starting brushing out my blonde hair to pull it up in the usual bun. The cast would do my makeup when I got there. I wondered if Tucker was going to be there. He said he wouldn't step foot into a room with Carol, is she was going to have Alex was with her and dangle him in my face. I dressed all in black and Jade met me at the front door with my silver coat.

"You're coming?"

"Wouldn't miss it. I texted Ray; she's already there with her mom,"

I nodded. More people were coming and I just kept worrying about if Tucker was going to be there. Deep down, I knew I had to acccpt the fact that Tucker probably wouldn't be there.

"When did Jett leave yesterday?" I asked, shutting and locking up the front door.

"Right after you started throwing up. He said he was going to find Tucker, make sure he doesn't do anything stupid."

"You didn't tell him about the baby, right?'

"Gabs, no!" she snapped at me. "That's not my place, okay? That's between you and Tuck."

Michael had a cab pulled over as we walked into the cold winter air. The night was cold as we bundled closer together and climbed in.

"This is the last show right?"

"Yeah, last show," I said as my teeth chattered together.

"You sad?"

"No, I don't have to deal with Jasmine breathing down my back and trying to push me out of the way the entire time, and Madame Ava..." I stopped; I had mixed feelings about Madame Ava. I praised her so much for all the help she had given me. She had been tough, but sometimes you need tough love to grow a little.

Rachel was standing at the curb with her mom in tow, who looked gorgeous as always, but with the weather taking a turn and with the frosted cold air, surprisingly Trish was dressed from head to toe.

Rachel grabbed my hand, pulling me to the side and cupping my face.

"Where's Tucker?" Her green eyes were wide.

I didn't want to talk about him. "I don't know Rach." I tried to turn my face from her grasp, but she just wouldn't let me go. I could feel the tears starting to come, stinging my heart all over again at the lost of him.

"Brad is flippin' out, he can't find him."

"Then that's his problem, not mine." I was able to get loose of her hold, but as I tried stepping around her, she blocked my path. Looking at me dead in the eyes, I could see that they were very serious eyes.

"Listen, Gabs, Tucker is in trouble; he's in trouble for trying to help out Brad."

My heart sped up. "What kind of trouble?" I asked, now that she had my full attention.

"I don't know, something to do with Ethan. I only know Tucker was helping Brad out then Tucker took off. Brad said to keep you, Jade and I off the streets."

What the hell? None of this was making any sense. Rachel was talking in riddles to me. "I don't know what to tell you, Rach, but I don't know where Tucker is. I have to go perform, see you inside." Taking off and leaving my little group of friends at the curb, I raced into the Lincoln Center. The inside wasn't crowded, yet. The show started at eight and it was only seven. I had one hour to try and find Tucker. Pulling my phone out as I made my way to the dressing room, I stopped dead in my tracks when he answered, barking in the phone.

"What do you want?" I gasped in the phone at his response.

Shutting my eyes, I took a deep breath to form words. "Tucker, where are you?" I pleaded to him, hoping he would respond. "Just tell me where you are."

"Why do you care? I told you that I didn't want you."

I leaned up against a wall. I really didn't want to fight with him. I needed him. "Tucker, stop, just please tell me where you are? I'm scared." Tears formed and fell. I was thankful I didn't have my makeup caked on my face, yet.

"You shouldn't be scared – you have Alex and his money to protect you."

His words were hurting me and he didn't even know it. "Tucker, *stop* with the Alex stuff. I told you, I don't want him; I want you, only you." My voice cut off at the end and I cleared my throat.

I heard him take a deep breath and say, "I'm in Central Park," I had his location now. He gave in. Everything was going to be okay. I started walking towards the dressing rooms with my phone still up against my ear, but neither of us was speaking.

"Gabs."

I wiped my face. "Yes, Tucker." Shutting my eyes, I listened to his voice that I missed so much already. I wanted him near me right now, holding me tight in his strong arms, keeping me safe.

"Are you coming tonight?" I hoped he would say yes. I needed him more than ever right now, just to have him in the audience where I would dance just for him. He loved watching me practice my heart out. He didn't judge me as I would make little mistakes. He would just sit there all quiet, watching me. He always said he liked it when I would go *en pointe* on my toes – didn't know how I could stand it. The memory pulled from me as I tried to teach him one day. We laughed; I even tried to convince him just to put on the guys' ballet shoes so he could try. I remembered him answering me with, "That's not my style." I waited on the phone for him to answer me and when he did, I wasn't expecting it his words at all.

"I love you." Then he hung up the phone. He didn't even let me say it back to him. I loved him so much and I couldn't even tell him. At the last minute, before heading into the makeup room, I sent a quick text.

Me: U don't know how much I love you, Tucker. I hope you come 2night, I need you.

I watched the little word "sending...," then saw that it went through. Stripping my coat off, I sat in the chair as one of the cast crew started caking my face in makeup. I just held my phone, waiting for it to vibrate, but nothing came.

I was dressed in my white leotard and tutu with gold trimming with my crown on the top of my head. I was all ready to go. Big deep breaths...didn't matter how many times I perform, I will always get nervous. The lights in the audience began to flicker, meaning ten minutes and everyone should take their seats. This was my last dance in the *Nutcracker*. I was pretty sad about it. As I stood at the side of the stage, I scanned the crowd for a certain pair of eyes that only watched me. I dreaded it when Alex would come to watch me in my happiest moments; I'd rather have Tucker here.

The lights went dim and the slow orchestra started to play, telling everyone that the show was starting. I sat down on the floor and started my stretching routine when Madame Ava stopped at my feet. I glanced up to see her serious face and piercing blue eyes, her mink wrapped around her elbows and in a black gown; she looked beautiful.

"Abigail, this is the last show of the Christmas season." I swallowed hard, hoping that she wouldn't get mad at me for something already. The show hadn't even started, yet. "You've done very well so far, and I wanted to let you know how proud I am to call you my student."

I was shocked – not once through this entire ballet process had she ever acknowledged me. I watched her turn around and leave. Jasmine was standing behind her and gave me the famous death glare she always gives.

"Alright, come on ladies and gentlemen. It's time!" Our stage manager yelled as he tried gathering us around him. Walking over to our circle and standing by Bethany, our stage manager reminded us not to make certain mistakes like we had in the last show.

It was the same as always; if we got lost at all, we would count in our head, then repeat the moves from a dancer from the side. The lights dimmed all the way down and the music of the opening song began to play with the little kids enjoying the party. I watched the kids dance with each other, holding hands, dancing in a straight line up, then back down. I felt my throat close up and held in a sob that desperately wanted out. I covered my mouth with my hand to hold it in as best as I could. I think that was the first time I took in my pregnancy; I had a little innocent baby inside me. My hands rested on my lower abdomen as I continued to watch the party scene.

I scanned the crowd one more time, along the back. There was still no sign of him. I didn't have to look at the seated crowd for the familiar faces of my family to know that they were here; I knew they would be. But I did anyway. I found Trish, Rachel and Jade— all three spotted me and gave me a little wave. All I could do was smile back. Jade's face dropped and turned to look at the back of the audience; she met my eyes and shrugged.

About six rows in front of them I spotted my dad with a smile on his face as he watched the same little children dancing; Carol was next to my dad with a hand on his arm and her other hand grasping her necklace, and Alex sat next to Carol, and was on his phone. I groaned in frustration, which was so annoying; I knew he didn't want anything to do with me. He just really wanted to be on my dad's good side and to become a partner in his firm. There just wasn't any chemistry between us, but Carol didn't see it that way; she saw exactly what she wanted – me being taken care of. I could understand her trying to protect me, but my heart wanted what it wanted.

"Abigail, go," my stage manager growled over at me.

Time for my entrance, I walked gracefully with my head held up high as the role of the Sugar Plum Fairy would. Arms out, head high, then I stopped in the center of the stage. If Tucker wasn't going to be here, then I was going to give out the best performance tonight. I focused on the wonderful soft music and remembered to keep my head high and smile happily.

I was proud of myself for not missing one leap. When I jumped; my feet were together when they were supposed to be. I went *en pointe* and not once did I lose my balance. My smile got bigger and bigger on my face as I landed every move with grace and elegance. The room was so quiet when the music was stopped. When it was time for intermission, I padded over to a chair and sat my tired butt down. I felt so different right now—more relaxed for some reason. I put my heart into all my turns. While going up *en pointe*, I thought of Tucker doing it that night at the club, in his Converse shoes, and then when he was at practice with me. Someone handed me a bottle of water and I took the longest drink from it, finishing it in thirty seconds tops.

Madame Ava spotted me and made her way over. "Abigail," she breathed out, her hand hitting her chest and she dropped her head. I heard her take a deep then slowly let it out. When she looked back up at me, she had tears in her eyes. "You did absolutely beautiful out there. It has been your greatest performance yet." Her voice went high at the end. "Come here," she said, holding her arms open up to me. Getting up from my seat, I walked right into them as she embraced me in the tightest hug. "I'm so proud of you," she said, patting my back and I was lost in her arms. The hug didn't last long and she quickly pulled away from me to look in my eyes once more, then she was gone.

We finished the entire Ballet with the closing dance with everyone, then lined up to all bow for our wonderful audience. Roses were tossed on the stage with cheers as I stepped forward to curtsy on the pointe of my toes. The claps only grew louder as Madame Ava walked up to my side and handed me a huge floral arrangement of brilliant red roses. The smell of the fresh flowers was strong as I smelled them; I loved roses. I bowed one more time to the audience and made my way back in line. I saw Jade, Rachel and Trish (who by the way was staring at the back of my dad's head) standing proudly and clapping their hands off. Of course, Jade being Jade, she tossed me her middle finger high in the air. I just grinned more at the wonderful supportive people in my life.

I sat in my dressing room, staring at the one missed call I was dreading. Tucker called me five minutes ago and he didn't leave a voicemail. I tried calling him back, but no answer. I angrily tossed my phone on the dressing table and started washing the mountain load of makeup on my face. The more I thought about Tucker not showing up, the harder I scrubbed my face. My fingers dug into my eyes; the pressure helped. By the time I was done washing my face off, I pulled my hair out and furiously brushed through it, pulling on the little strands, causing me to wince at the pain at my scalp. I pulled on my outfit I wore over here and when I put my shoes in my bag, a knock sounded at my dressing room door.

"Come in!" I shouted, still gathering my things. The first person I saw was Rachel with a big gorgeous smile on her face as she walked towards me with open arms to embrace me in the biggest hug possible. She squeezed me so tightly, I had to tap on her shoulder to get her to let go. When she pulled back, her eyes were filled with tears. "Gabs, you were absolutely beautiful tonight. You danced like an angel."

Jade pushed her out of the way so she was now in front of me. "I'm supposed to give you this." She handed me a folded white piece of paper. I quickly opened it to see Tucker's script sitting on the inside.

You were so beautiful tonight.
I love you
Tucker

He was here, he saw me. My heart sped up as I read the lines over and over again. He was here. I looked around when I could and didn't see him at all in the audience; I wonder where he was hiding.

"You ready to go?" I looked up to see Rachel, Jade and Trish staring at me. I was just standing there, holding Tucker's note he gave to Jade. I really wished he would just be with me instead of leering in the shadows. We were walking down the hall, talking about the ballet, and Rachel and Trish were raving on and on about how it was the best one yet. Trish even mentioned to Rachel that my dad was a 'hottie.' Jade's eyes didn't leave the side of my face as she watched my every move, as if I was going to break down any second. I was so used to it by now; it never surprised me anymore when I would catch her.

"Abigail!" I turned to see Alex, strutting his stuff as he speed walked to me with a smirk of a smile—the smile I would rather see on Tucker's face. He grabbed my hands and held them out, forcing my arms to go around his neck as he hugged me. I went stiff and pulled back.

Ugh...I was started to get pissed off. Why wouldn't he just leave me alone?

"You did beautifully tonight," he said, smiling wide while he shifted from foot to foot. He did that when he was nervous, I noticed; he did that a lot in front of my dad.

Forcing a smile, I mumbled, "Thanks," chewing on my lip. I had nothing to say to him. The air around us in the small hallway was starting to get thick and very uncomfortable. Jade snaked her arm through mine.

"Well, see ya around, Al," quickly pulling me away.

"It's Alex," he called out, but we just kept on walking.

Chapter Eighteen

Once we were outside, we said our goodbyes to Trish at the curb of The Lincoln Center. Trish hugged me, told me how well I did, and that she was proud, and how she would love me always like another daughter to her. She thanked me for letting her come tonight, and I deeply squeezed her back like a daughter would hug a mother.

I still thought about Tucker and why he didn't let me see him tonight. I had to dance and let Alex watch me move across the stage when all I wanted was Tucker's eyes. I think Alex played on his phone more than he watched me. I wanted so desperately to tell Tucker about the baby.

Oh, our little innocent baby.

Just at the thought, I placed my hand on my belly and sighed. Jade looked over at me with raised brows and took notice of my hands.

Jade knew my situation I was in with Tucker; I couldn't even call it a situation. I was pregnant with Tucker's baby. I wanted Tucker more than anything, body and soul. Rachel raved about Brad and something he did for her that was "so cute and heartwarming'.

"We are getting closer. I can see us becoming an item." Jade and I both smiled at that. The night was cold. New Year's approached closer and closer every day. I pulled my silver jacket tighter around my body. I only had five more months of school left. If I did the math right, our baby will arrive around August, which made me not be able to go back to Juilliard the following year.

"Gabs?"

Jade's voice pulled me out of thought about our baby and school when I kept walking when they stopped. "What?"

I looked back at them and their eyes were set on something in front of us. I turned to see a group of guys walking towards us, saying profound things about the girls in front of them. They said Jade's name, but not Jade, they said Jaiden. I started stepping back. Rachel grabbed my hand.

"Hey girls! Where you off to tonight?" one of them called out

And that's when we took off in a different direction. They chased us, hearing their footsteps hitting the pavement behind us, gaining on our moves. We turned down an alleyway in hopes for a shortcut to our building, but it came to a dead end. When we turned back, the men crowded the opening. Their harsh breaths were coming up to us, sounding as it was echoing off the brick walls of the buildings between us. One of the men who was bald was right in front of my face and I slowly backed up. Jade grabbed my hand, pulling me back further until I was in the middle. The group of guys circled around us like prey. "I like the red head." Rachel gasped. Now we were shoulder to shoulder in a triangle shape, holding each other's hands, each one of us just watching them.

"I like the blonde," one Hispanic guy said about me. I gave him a death glare, but I didn't scare him. The look he gave me made me want to run and hide.

"Wait, I know this chick," the bald one said and pointed a finger in my direction, "Yeah, that's Kyle's girl."

"Kyle?" We three said in unison.

"Yeah, Kyle Tucker. That son of a bitch owes me money. Well, his buddy Brad does anyway." He shrugged. I heard Rachel suck in a deep breath.

"Just leave us alone, you dick," Jade spat at them and they all laughed. Their laughter echoed throughout the darkened alleyway, just like out of a scary movie with the dark shadows and evil lurking voices.

"I like a girl with a mouth – makes them harder to train," the Hispanic man voiced at us, then lunged for Jade's arm. Rachel screamed. We tried to pull her back to our little triangle safety zone, but his hold was much stronger and she was ripped from our fingers.

He had his arms snaked around her as she screamed and fought like her life depended on it. The bald guy, who called Tucker by the name of Kyle, was standing in front of me. I had every nerve in my body demanding to do something to get out of the situation we were in with this unknown group of guys.

I had a sudden impulse to do something, so I spit in his face, trying to distract him, to make him not see my next move. I then kicked his shin as hard as I could in my flat shoes, grabbed Rachel's hand and ran towards Jade to help her get free. He grabbed me around the waist, fisting a handful of my hair and wrenching my head back hitting his masculine shoulder. Then everything in that moment stopped— now moving in slow motion as I felt something cold and sharp pressing up against my throat.

Oh holy shit, he has a knife.

Horror surged through my body as I started to hyperventilate, my breathing picked up quicker with every beat of my heart and I went completely still. My fingertips left Rachel's as the guy snarled out words in my ear.

"Hold the fuck still or I swear to God, I'll slit your throat so fast you won't have time to say any last words." Pain radiated throughout my scalp as he pulled harder and I cried out.

"Now, be a good bitch and tell me where Kyle and Brad are." His breath hit my face, smelling of pure death and body odor.

"I don't know a Kyle," I stated. He pulled harder on my hair, stretching my neck up some more. I held my breath, trying so hard not to breathe so the knife wouldn't cut me.

"Oh, I think you do. He's your little boyfriend. He goes by Tucker," the man rumbled in my ear and moved some hair back from my face to peck my cheek. I flinched away from his revolting touch and chapped lips against my skin. His breath smelled so rotten, I wanted to throw up.

"Tell me where he and his friend are and then I'll let you go." He pulled harder on my hair and I screamed at the pain surging through. I swear it felt like my hair was going to snap any minute.

Tears pricked my eyes, and I cried, "I don't know where he is, I swear". I heard Rachel scream somewhere in the background behind me. Then I heard more stumbling around, more screams, her high heels pounding on the pavement, more screams, then a crashing into a dumpster. Silence. It was quiet for a good four seconds.

"JADE!" Rachel screeched out. Jade kicked her legs and clawed at the guy trying holding her. I bawled just watching her fight against him. I couldn't see what was happening to poor Rachel, hearing only the sounds of her cries.

"Now, if you don't tell me, my friend really likes redheads. He's knows just how to treat them." Sobs escaped my mouth as Rachel's screams continued to call for Jade and I.

"GABS!" Rachel grunted as I heard her face get slapped multiple times. You will never forget the sound of slapping skin when it was forced upon you with strength.

"RACHEL!" Jade screamed back, and still tried kicked at the man who was holding her in place. More grunts and harsh breaths from Rachel behind me made me turn into full on crying, soaking my shirt, while I listened to Rachel scream helplessly for us, but we couldn't do anything to help her.

"I really don't know. Let her go," I pleaded with the bald man. I looked at Jade, who was staring behind me at Rachel, now in full struggle to break free, still clawing away. But the man was still stronger.

Jade kept screaming, "Let her go, you bastard! Let her GO!" Her black hair whipped around in the night air.

The guy was back at my ear, wiping my face with his spare dirty hand. "Come on, gorgeous, just tell me and I'll have my friend stop," he cooed, his breath smelling of rotting eggs. I let out a breath and the blade pressed harder against my skin with the swallow of my throat. I had to go up on my toes to help get rid of some pressure. He pulled harder again with my hair wrapped around his fingers. I thought I felt the breakage happen as the hair pulled apart from my aching scalp. My tears cascaded freely down my face.

"I..." But before I could tell him, *I don't know*, I saw a quick flash of Jett sneaking up behind the man who had a hold of Jade, then he hit him over the head really hard. He fell onto the wet pavement, knocked out cold.

"Ah, they send the good friend to help." I tried to move away but the knife pressed harder. "Where are they Jett?"

Jett pulled Jade behind his body to shield her, but Jade pulled on his shoulder and whispered something in his ear. A sneak attack, maybe. But I watched Jett's body go hard and his dark eyes went cold as the dark night when he looked at me, already knowing what Jade just told him. My one secret that was now out of the bag and now Jett knew. I shut my eyes and let the tears fall on my icy cold face.

Jett held up his hands, and stepped a little closer to us. "Listen Skinner, the girl doesn't know where Tucker is, so...just let her go." Jett stepped closer and the guy constrained me harder to him. I was almost on the point of my toes, he had me that close to him. He pulled harder on my hair, causing another shriek from me. Jett was losing patience with every second, his face growing red with anger the more time passed. His dark brown eyes were black.

Rachel stopped screaming as we stood in silence. Jett and Skinner just stared at each other while I struggled to breathe. The knife pressing a tad harder and I whimpered. I thought of all the good things that had happened in my life so far, wishing Tucker was here—wishing I told him about the baby. To tell him that I love him always. I started to sob at the sudden thought of not getting the chance to meet our little baby that we created together. Even though our baby was an accident and unplanned, I knew deep down it was all going to be okay.

I kept trying to look around, looking for an escape route when suddenly I was let go and pushed forward so hard, I started falling on the wet ground on my hands and knees. I grabbed my throat and held my hand to see of any evidence of blood. Trying to catch my breath, I wheezed for a couple of seconds as I held my throat.

Jade crashed down in front of me. "You okay, Gabs?" she asked as she pulled me up. I turned around in a rush to see Tucker and Jett pin the guy to the ground. Tucker then straddled him, punching his face over and over again, one cheek then the other.

The guy had a knife and he was going to stab Tucker with it. I had to warn him. "Tucker!" I screamed and moved to go next to him. But Jade pulled me back and my eyes couldn't leave Tucker's rage as he beat the living crap out of the guy who wasn't moving when I heard sirens headed our way.

I ran over to Tucker to yank on his shoulders, to get him off the man who laid there unconscious. Jett and Jade followed me. Tears streaked down my face as I heaved on Tucker's gray hoodie. "Tucker, stop!" I yelled and surprisingly, he did. His breaths were strict as his angry blue eyes stared me down. I glanced down at his hands, noting that they were extremely bloody and he had cuts that needed tending, too. But that didn't stop Tucker from enveloping me in his arms.

"Gabs," he kissed my head. "Are you okay?" Cupping my trembling face to look at him, still a shaking mess, I nodded.

I just wanted him to hold me, bring me comfort in some way. The next was inevitable; I didn't even see it coming as the guy Tucker was beating the crap out of pushed the both of us off him. We fell on the cold ground. He started running towards where Rachel was. My eyes followed the guy's moves as he ran to their directions in slow motion, and Jett ran past us as we scrambled to get up. Rachel was running back to us.

Her nose and lips were bloody, and her right cheek was flaming red.

"Gabs," Jade grabbed my hand as we ran towards to get Rachel. Taking in her face, I wanted to comfort her and hold her so badly.

"You owe me, Tucker!" The guy screamed at us, then hit Rachel in the stomach. Jade screamed as Rachel's body slowly crumbled to the ground, holding her stomach. My hand went to my mouth as I watched poor Rachel's body dropping to her bent knees and she was gradually going limp to the ground. Jade caught her head before it hit the pavement and started to sob on her chest.

When I finally made it over to the two of them, the little knife that was held up against my throat was now in Rachel's flat stomach. Her bright yellow shirt spotted with darkness. I shook as I pulled out my cell to call the cops.

"911 dispatch."

"Yes, we need an ambulance, right now!" I screamed in the phone.

"What's the problem, miss?" the very annoying dispatcher asked me. I couldn't get out my answer fast enough, so Tucker took my phone. I dropped to my knees and grabbed Rachel's hand, feeling more of my own tears escape. I rubbed her hand on my cheek and kissed the top of it.

"Rach," I squeaked out. Rachel tried to say something, but it came out in gurgling noises with a small amount of blood coming out the corner of her mouth. Jade quickly wiped it away.

"Don't talk, Ray," Jade cooed. Seeing more blood seeping through her shirt, Rachel's body started to shake and quiver. Jade pulled off her jacket to drape it carefully over Rachel's stomach, hiding the ugly knife.

More sirens sounded as Tucker and Jett huddled around us. Watching Rachel gasp for breath with each passing second, I was so scared for her at this moment, each passing second was so valuable for her. Each of her cold breaths she made clouded around us from the cold. Her body shook. I just wanted the cops get here faster to help her. Her eyes got heavy. Oh please hurry. Her eyes fully shut.

"Ray, you stay here with me, I need you," Jade cried out as Rachel's eyes started to drift open but slowly closed again. I held my breath just watching her, waiting for her to gasp for air again, waiting for her body to continue to shake.

"Ray!" Jade shook her body for her, "help her!" Jade looked at me, her black makeup smeared all down the front of her cheeks as we made eye contact.

"Help her, Gabs," she pleaded at me with sad puppy dog eyes. But there was nothing I could do to help save her. I dropped my head and let more tears fall, and I collapsed on Jade's shoulder and wrapped my arms around her. We held Rachel's head as we both cried out for our loss of our dearest friend, Rachel Dawson.

Chapter Nineteen

When the cops surrounded our little group, they hauled Jade and I off Rachel's body. Jade clung to me for life as we both watched our friend being lifted onto a gurney and into an ambulance. Jade's tears didn't stop soaking my neck as I tried to soothe her. One cop came up to us, asking questions to which we didn't know the answers. Rachel was gone, just like that, gone. Tucker was behind Jade, trying to pull her away from me, but she held on.

He whispered in her ear, "Jade, Jett wants you," He tried again to pull on her, finally getting her to let go of my jacket and she went into Jett's arms.

Tucker held me, as the police continued to ask questions. I stared at the ground where a dark spot was at, knowing that's where Rachel died. Jett leaned on the side of the building across from us, holding Jade close. She looked like she was asleep, but I think she was trying to tone out all the conversations and chaos around us. When we first met, Rachel acted as a protector to Jade, telling me she was her sister. I couldn't imagine what Jade was going through right now.

Another cop car pulled up to us with a mean looking cop glaring at Tucker. "Shit," Tucker whispered in a voice that only I heard. The cop made his way over to us. "Tucker, I told you, if I had to deal with your shit again, I'm taking you in. Let the girl go," he commanded. I went stiff.

Take him? No.

The officer's hands were on Tucker's arms, trying to pry him from me, but I wasn't going, "No," I cried, trying to stay in Tucker's arms – trying to wrap his arms back around me. I finally had him back and now they were taking him.

Another cop came up to help, pulling me off Tucker. I watched as other cop turned Tucker around to slam him into the brick building and handcuff him. The cop digging in Tucker's front pockets pulled out numerous clear plastic baggies. I noticed some had white stuff while others had a darker looking green. I looked over at Jett who stood there watching as well.

"Jett, do something," I pleaded.

Jett shook his head and placed his face down by Jade's. I struggled against the cop as they started walking Tucker to the patrol car. They weren't going to take him; this wasn't his fault. Feeling my rage ready to boil over, like a pot of scolding hot water on the stove, I stomped as hard as I could on the cop's toes and heaved him off me. I ran like hell as soon as his arms let me go. I made it to Tucker before they pushed him in the backseat. I wrapped my arms around his neck to breathe in the scent on his neck.

"I love you, Gabs."

I wanted to tell him that I loved him, too, more than ever, but other words slipped from my lips instead, "I'm pregnant."

His body went taut and he pulled back to look in my eyes. The cop holding Tucker tried to push me out of the way as he tried again to put Tucker in the backseat.

"What?" he whispered, trying everything in his power to not get over powered by the cop.

I nodded at him with my head down so he couldn't see my tears as they fell. I kept repeating in my head. *Please don't be mad. Please don't be mad.*

The cop tried again and Tucker growled out, "Dude! Chill out, Daniels, okay?"

The cop stopped and Tucker kissed me. "You're sure?" I nodded again as I stared into his gaze.

"Found out yesterday." I shrugged and tried to give him a smile, but couldn't. "I took a test with Jade. It was positive."

The other cop who held me came up and grabbed me firmly on my shoulder. "Come on, miss. I'm taking you in on assault on a police officer."

"What?!" Tucker and I yelled at the same time.

The officer holding Tucker starting telling him his rights, and I heard, "Kyle Tucker, you're under arrest for drug paraphernalia."

The other officer grabbed my arms and jerked them behind me, slapping handcuffs around my wrists. Tucker fought against the other cop, but he over powered him and shoved him inside the cop car, then slammed the door. I was being dragged away to another car while Jade was screaming and trying to follow, but Jett held her back. Instead of fighting, I went willingly in the cop car. I watched as Jade cried out for me as the car pulled away from her.

The trip to the station was nerve racking, I never pictured myself being arrested for insulting an officer. The first thought I had was to call my dad as soon as I got there, to help me, but what about Tucker? Would he help him or blame him?

Pulling into the police station, they didn't run my fingers through the black ink to get my finger prints on file. They walked me through the police station, but in the crowd ahead of me, I saw Tucker being manhandled by Officer Daniels. He pretty much tossed Tucker around like a rag doll, then finally shoved him in a seat and handcuffed him to a desk.

I was walked over to a wooden bench in a little hallway across the room. This place smelled awful, like a gross, sweaty gym, that hadn't been cleaned in a long time. A female cop uncuffed my hands, but cuffed my left hand to a side rail, not saying one word to me, then left.

My eyes frantically searched for Tucker sitting at the desk. I started to get a little nervous being here by myself. I never saw myself being arrested and in a police station. I looked at all the faces in the little room. Cops were talking to different people at every desk as the back door that Tucker and I came through burst open with about five cops and one rambunctious bald guy.

Wait.

That was the guy, the one who held me hostage. The guy who stabbed Rachel, that was the guy. I stood up fast to get away from him, but the chain of the cuffs dug into my skin. I winced at the sharp pain, making me sit back down. I was annoyed that I couldn't rub it better. When I looked back up at the passing group, the bald guy was staring at me while smiling. That bastard was smiling at me for killing my friend. I wanted everything in my power to go up to him and smack that dirty ass smile off his rotten face. But when the group passed, my eyes were directed straight to Tucker's across the room; his face was pale, he looked sick as he dropped his head down. I wanted to go up to him and just hug him.

"Abigail." I flinched at the sound of my father's voice. I didn't even hear his approaching steps as I sat cuffed to a bench. I was afraid to look up. I kept my eyes down cast and stared into his shiny black dress shoes. My eyes started to sting, my bottom lip started to quiver and I bit down, trying hard to make it stop.

"Abigail," my dad whispered, and I knew he was waiting for me to make eye contact with him. I couldn't. All I could do was stare down at his perfectly shined shoes, that looked brand new and straight out of the box. I sniffed and that unleashed my tears; they fell freely from my face. I knew my dad was so upset with me right now, finding me here where he put criminals to justice, this place that I didn't belong in; I felt like such a failure at this very moment.

He placed his fingers under my chin to tip my face up, but meeting his warm brown eyes only brought on more sadness to me. Wearing his glasses, I could see the hurt I'd put him through right now as I stared into his brown disappointing eyes.

He snapped his fingers and pointed to my one cuffed hand. "Joe, would you please?" A little round fat cop, that clearly sat at a desk, walked up to uncuffed me. My dad held his hand out and I took it. We walked down a short hallway. Turning quickly to see if Tucker was still at the desk, we rounded a corner, but all I saw was cream paint.

My dad took me into a darkened room with one window. Two other cops were in there as well.

"Ah, David, you brought our witness," one cop said as we stood next them. They both smelled of strong coffee in their pressed uniforms. Coffee always reminded me of Jade; I wondered if she was alright, I would rather be with her right now.

"This is my daughter, Abigail." His hands cupped my shoulders. Both men looked at me and nodded.

"Let's begin, shall we?"

One officer hit a button with a loud buzzing sound and a door opening. Gazing around the room from the window, it was just like something off a movie; I was the person who stood on the opposite side of the mirror, invisible to the people on the other side. Bald men started entering the room, one by one, lining up in a straight line, all holding number signs. My stomach dropped at the very last guy, number six, the one from the alleyway, who hit my friend in the stomach with his stupid knife that had been pressed against my throat.

"Abigail, who stabbed Rachel Dawson tonight? Just say a number," one officer stated. My dad's hands still held onto my shoulders, slowly rubbing them.

"Number six." I raised my hand and pointed to the one bald guy who I would never forget – his face would always be burned into my brain. He would always be the man who killed Rachel.

"Very good. You may go now, David."

We left the little room and my dad held my hand as we walked down another hallway. The cream colored walls were lifeless with no pictures. Yelling from rooms made me flinch back into my dad's side. We passed the little room with the desks, glancing around rather quickly to see if Tucker was still there, but no one was sitting at any desks.

We entered a smaller room than the one before. I sat on one side of the little table while my dad sat on the other, propping his foot on his knee, relaxing into the seat as he examined a yellow file. Once in a while, he would rub his chin as if deep in thought. I looked around the small dark room with one light and no secret window. The silence was killing me; my dad had never been this quiet before. I sat on my fingers and let my feet sway underneath the chair, barely touching the ground. My dad cleared his throat and I looked back at him, meeting his stare.

"Abigail," he started and cleared his throat. "Do you know that Rachel died tonight?"

I dropped my head. I already knew, but I didn't want to even say it out loud.

"Look at me," he said and I slowly brought my head back up. "Do you know that Rachel died tonight?" he asked me again and I nodded in shame.

"Do you know this man?" He slid a picture of the bald guy towards me, but I shook my head.

"This is Spencer Harvey, also known as Skinner. Boyfriend of Tori Tucker. They are both drug addicts. Spencer was arrested two months ago for drug battery, assault, and robbery."

He took the picture back and put it in the folder. He flipped more papers and slid another picture towards me.

"Do you know this person?" Looking up to see a picture of Brad holding a little sign under his face—his own mug shot.

"Yes," I quietly answered

He cleared his throat again, "Tell me who he is."

I tapped the photo with my finger. "That's Brad. We've hung out with him a couple of times."

"With who?" He asked as he took the picture back and placed in the right spot where he got it from and turned more pages.

I shifted uncomfortably, "Rachel, Jade, Jett and Tucker."

"Ah, Tucker. You mean this boy?"

He slid a picture of Tucker across the table. It felt like he was moving in a slow wave and Tucker's still photo face stopped before my eyes. I rubbed my head; Tucker had been arrested before.

He lied to me, he *lied*.

My heart felt like it was just ripped out of my chest, stomped on, put through a shredder bin and taped back together, right after a dog peed on it. That was the best way I could describe my heart right now. I choked on a sob that got caught in my throat. My dad took the picture back and started talking to me, as if he didn't care that I was crying.

"Kyle Tucker. Twenty-five, arrested on the charges of: drug paraphernalia, robbery, resisting arrest, charged with trespassing, charged with giving a false name to a police officer, driving with a suspended license, charged with driving under the influence *with* a suspended license. Abigail, the list goes on, is this really the boy you wish to continue seeing?" He set the folder down and took off his glasses to rub his nose — something he's always done when he's frustrated.

I was in full on shaking sobs by this point. I rested my head on my arms on the table and sobbed. I bawled for many reasons at this moment; I cried for the Tucker my dad was telling me about, the Tucker I didn't know anything about. He lied to me about getting arrested; he told me he'd never been to jail for anything that night we played twenty questions on my balcony.

"Abigail, this is not the type of crowd you want to hang around with. His crowd is dangerous. Look what happened to Rachel tonight. What if that happened to you?"

I sobbed more into my arms. My heart was shattered. I had no idea who this Kyle Tucker character was – he wasn't the Tucker I fell in love with, that was for dang sure.

"Where is he?" I sniffed.

I waited for my dad to answer me. I had to find out why he lied, lied about everything, but my dad didn't answer right away. I sat there, shaking like a leaf, waiting for him to tell me. When I looked up at him, my eyes probably red from crying, he sighed.

"Right across the hall."

Standing up, the chair scraped against the tile floor as I moved towards the door. I was going to walk right in and demand answers, but I stopped once my dad placed a hand on my shoulder.

"Abigail, let's think before you act on this okay. Now, listen to me, angel." I faced my dad with nothing but anger written all over my face.

"Tucker is handcuffed to the chair. He knows he's being watched and videotaped, so he probably won't talk to you. There's a little camera in one of the corners; the light will be blinking, meaning it's recording."

I nodded, then gripped the cool metal doorknob. I was calm as he explained about the camera. I had to keep a low profile about the baby. I couldn't let my dad know just yet. He leaned in and whispered in my ear as I pushed the door slowly open.

"If you need me, I'll be right in that room." My dad pointed to the window; knowing he'd be across from me made me a little more comfortable.

The room was dark with one light on in the center of the small table. I glanced around to see the little black camera in the corner with a blinking red light. Tucker sat at the table, his hands cuffed behind him with his head down. I pulled out the chair and sat across from him, not looking up at me. Just like how I was with my dad, head down, not talking. I waited for him to look up, but he sat there, motionless.

"Tucker," my voice cracked in the dead silenced room. He slowly brought his head up and met my eyes. His happy blue eyes were now sad, lost. They broke my heart. I wanted more than anything to go in his arms, but I had to stay strong I had to ask the questions I wanted to know, find out who the real Tucker was.

"How come you never told me your name is Kyle?" my voice shook at my words coming out.

Silence

"You've been arrested before. Drugs right?"

Silence

I started getting antsy, my nails drumming on the table, waiting for him to talk.

"Do you do them?" Tucker snorted and shook his head no, then dropped his head back down.

More silence.

I leaned in on the table, "Tuck, you have to talk to me," I whispered.

Silence.

I could feel myself getting irritated. He was hiding from me. I stood up from the table and started to pace back and forth, something I did when I was mad at Carol or frustrated with Jasmine or Madame Ava. Tucker still didn't look up at me. I then found myself walking in circles around the little lit room, around the table, around Tucker, and he *still* didn't look at me. The more I waited on him, the more impatient I grew. I huffed air, I sighed, anything to get his attention and *nothing*.

Finally not taking it anymore, my anger exploded right out of me, like a pot of boiling hot water, and next thing I knew, I was yelling.

"Why did you lie to me?!"

Silence.

"You've been arrested for drugs; you've been arrested for DUI driving. How stupid can you be? My dad is the Criminal Justice attorney; he has like this big file on you, Brad, that Spencer guy and you don't have one word to say to me? Rachel is dead, she's *dead,* Tucker, and you can't even look at me?" I slammed my fist into my chest at the hurt I was feeling from all my disputes with him.

Silence.

Standing behind him now, the feeling I had earlier of hugging him was now gone and all I had left was hurt inside me. I wanted just to smack him upside the head to get him mad at me, something. Instead, I was quiet with my next words.

"Where's the Tucker I fell in love with?" His feet started to move. "Where's the Tucker who loves me? Where's the Tucker who holds me, protects me?" His body started to shift in the chair. "Where's the Tucker who doesn't give a crap what people think about us? Where's the Tucker who makes sweet love to me?"

I bent down on my knees to the side of his motionless body, head still down. Tears slipped from my eyes as I pleaded with him. I didn't care to wipe them off my face, I wanted him to see me cry for him.

"Where's the Tucker I love?" I reached up and turned his head to look at me. His eyes were closed and he was starting to shake under my palm.

My voice screeched out, "Tucker," and his eyes opened and bore into mine. They were red as his own tears streaked freely down his face. I wiped them away as fast as I could, but the more he wept, the more I found myself crying.

"Tucker, please talk to me," I tried again, as we stared at each other. I pushed his hair out of his face as he inhaled a deep breath and exhaled. I was surrounded by the scent of him. Our eyes not leaving one another, as he started speaking.

"My name is Kyle Tucker. I help deal drugs with my buddy, Brad Evans. Spencer Harvey is my mom's boyfriend. We call him Skinner on the streets. He's the one who had you, then stabbed Rachel. I want nothing more than to kill that son of a bitch for touching you. My mom is a drug junkie who could give two shits about me. I grew up with an abusive dad, who I'm named after. If you had an abusive dad like mine, you wouldn't blame me for going by my last name. I want nothing to do with him. Jeremiah is Ethan's right hand man; Ethan supplies us with the product and we go sell it, then bring the money back. If we're under the amount, Jeremiah steps in to bring us to Ethan at the greenhouse in Central Park. That very first night, at the club when Jeremiah touched you, to warn you."

My heart stopped at the memory of his hands on me, "Stay away from Tucker, this is your warning," His voice echoed through my ears.

"What product, Tucker?"

His eyes were so sad when the met mine. "Anything to everything. Crank also known as Crystal, weed, acid, X, heroin, everything, Gabs. Anything that pulls money in to Ethan. Brad is always in huge ass trouble and pulls me in to help him. Brad uses more than what he sells, always in a shit hole. I help him bring in money so Ethan doesn't go all crazy ass on him."

Tucker let out a big breath and started up again, "Ethan was pissed off that Brad and I were at the club and not out dealing. Jeremiah saw me with you and tried to scare you away. That pissed me off, so I went after him and yelled at him to leave you alone. Then Jett stepped in as Jade was pulling you outside. I told Jeremiah to tell Ethan to find another minion to do his damn dirty work and leave me the hell alone. That night at the greenhouse..."

His eyes shut as the memory of our first time together replayed in my head. The most wonderful night of my life, to let go and let Tucker have all of me, to touch, to feel for the very first time as he caressed my body, kissed my bruised feet, then slowly made love to me for the first time.

"Ethan was pissed that I brought you there, and he was pissed I wasn't dealing anymore. After you ran off, I tried to go after you, but Ethan pinned me down – told me if I didn't kick your ass to the curb, he would hurt you. I couldn't leave you alone after threatening that to me...I wanted to be there every second. I've been trying to cut ties, trying to stop dealing and taking his calls. Brad got a hold of me to tell me Skinner was out looking for me for payback, but he found you first. Now all this shit is happening. Gabs, I need you. Don't leave me, not when I need you the most."

His head dropped from my hands as I wept more. I couldn't believe Tucker, my Tucker was a drug dealer. He told me he loved tattooing more than anything. That all he ever wanted to do was be able to draw and print things people loved on their body.

"Tucker, I love you." I snaked my arms around his neck and hugged him. I embraced him to bring him comfort, I held onto him for the loss of our friend. We cried into each other's arms until a knock sounded on the door.

I pulled back from him to look into his red-rimmed eyes. I softly kissed his trembling lips, which turned a little heated with our passion for each other... I sat on his lap and put everything I had into that kiss. A squeaking door opened with someone clearing their throat. Tucker's body went stiff under my arms as I glanced over my shoulder to see Alex's tall frame fill the doorway of our little room.

"Abigail, your father is waiting," Alex stated, walking up to the little table, then sitting across from us. He flipped open a yellow folder like the one my dad had. Then he started talking to Tucker like I wasn't even there.

"Kyle Tucker, do you understand your rights as to why you're being charged tonight?"

Silence.

"Abigail, leave us," Alex said as he continued to flip pages over and when I didn't move off of Tucker's lap, he yelled, "Abigail GO!" and I jumped.

"Don't you fucking talk to her like that!" Tucker shouted back.

Alex glared at Tucker from across the table. Tucker being helpless and handcuffed, sitting there like prey, wasn't helping his situation.

"Listen, boy, you are being charged with murder here, and if..."

"What?!" I stood up, "You can't charge him with murder, and he didn't do it."

My voice echoing off the walls and my dad came strolling in the room. "Abigail, out now!"

"No, I'm not leaving him." More tears came out. I wasn't going to leave him. He just admitted everything to me. He needed me.

"Abigail," my dad growled out.

"NO!" I screamed, "Just let him go! He didn't do anything! Tucker helped me, Dad, he's not guilty."

My dad sighed, "Abigail, Tucker had drugs on him. We have to charge him," he told me and I went still. I turned to Tucker whose face was turned down. I stared at him, waiting for him to look up at me and tell me it wasn't true. But he didn't look up at me. He didn't tell me it wasn't true because it was...the baggies...the white stuff...

"Is that true? You were dealing tonight? Is that why you didn't come?"

Silence.

My heart broke for him and I found myself walking towards my dad's open arms. I glanced back over my shoulder. Tucker still had his head down as my dad shut the door. I crashed into my dad's chest and cried into his pressed white shirt and tie. He held me, rubbing my back, shushing me in my ear. I didn't want it to be true that Tucker had drugs on him when he came to me in the alleyway. Drugs were so bad; they did nothing but destroy your life. They ate away at your soul, killing your insides and all the people around you, destroying everything in their path.

I don't know how long I cried into my dad's chest, but I soon heard loud obnoxious high heels clacking on the tile floor. "David!" Carol shouted as she made her way towards us. Pissed off was all over her face when she stopped at our side. Her face was flaming red and her lips were pressed together in her Carol mad way. She then flew past us and went right into the room with Alex and Tucker. I stumbled out of my dad's arms and followed her.

Carol stood next to Alex and pointed an angry finger at Tucker. "You stay away from my daughter, you trailer trash worthless piece of shit!" she yelled.

My dad pulled on my arm to get me out of the room. Tucker was still motionless as Carol went on with hateful words that made me cry out for Tucker. He just sat there, taking every word.

"Carol, stop," I whined while I fought against my dad's hold. Carol walked around the little table, like I did earlier, her face still mad and angry as she stopped behind Tucker's chair.

"You are so low, Kyle Tucker. You don't deserve my daughter. You don't deserve anything, except a life behind bars, and that's where you truly belong."

I shut my eyes as I listened to Carol's hateful words to the man I loved, the father of my baby that was growing inside me. Carol straightened her body, then looked at Alex, "Do what you can to keep him away from us." She grabbed her clutch purse and left the room with me on her tail. Before I could grab her arm to have her face me, she turned on me.

"How could you be so stupid, Abigail?! How could you do this to us, to yourself? You know what that boy has done? You can't possibly want to be with someone like that!" Carol continued to yell at me in the tiny hallway of the police department. Every time I tried to talk back, she yelled more at me.

"You're just as stupid as he is!" she kept saying over and over. The more she yelled, the more I got mad. My dad, who stood behind me, kept on telling her to be quiet, but she didn't listen. She kept getting louder and louder with each sentence until finally, I lost it.

"Shut up!" I screamed, my arms flying in the air. "Shut up!" and she finally did.

Silence.

"This isn't Tucker's fault," Carol scoffed at me. "It's not, he helped me, us!" I screeched out.

"Abigail, Rachel is dead because of him. One of your friends died tonight. I know your other friend, Jaiden, is a complete mess right now. Trish is with her; you should see how miserable they are right now at the loss. And all you can do is stand here and defend someone who should be locked up? You don't even care, do you?"

"How can you say that to me? Rachel was like my sister. Tucker didn't have anything to do with Rachel dying. It was that...that...guy...Spencer, or Skinner, whatever his name is. He had a hold of me while two other guys had Jade and Rachel. Tucker came and beat up Spencer, who then took off and stabbed Rachel. Tucker isn't to blame!" I screamed the last words at her while I pointed back at the door where Tucker was.

"Abigail, do you even realize what you're getting yourself into with that boy? He can't take care of you. He's gonna use you, use your money, from us I might add, then he's going to dump you so fast. He's just like his father."

Whoa, what?!

"What are you talking about, just like his father?" I asked, confused at her statement.

Then, clapping echoed in the small hallway behind Carol. She turned and we watched a guy applaud to us as he approached us. His brown hair was long and greasy; he had a full beard with very raggedy clothes that needed to be washed or thrown away.

Carol stepped back and stood next to me, grabbing my arm and pulling me back to my dad and away from this stranger.

"Caroline, we meet again," the guy said, taking a bow. Just like something out of an old novel. Who bows nowadays?

Carol was silent, but my dad spoke up, "And who are you?"

"Ah, forgive me, kind sir." He stuck out his hand. "I'm Kyle Tucker, Sr."

Tucker's dad. He just said he hadn't seen him for a while. What was he doing here all of the sudden?

My dad extended around me and shook his hand. "David McCall."

"Yes, I've heard of you sir and is this your lovely daughter?" He eyed me and I took another step back, walking on my dad's toes.

"Yes, this is Abigail McCall and my wife Carol."

"I know Caroline all too well, as one might say." He said while raising a brow at me. "I'm looking for my son, Kyle Jr. Do you know where he is?"

"He's in there right now, meeting with a lawyer."

"He doesn't need a lawyer. Room number?"

My dad nodded in the direction. "The last door on the left."

"Thank you, Caroline. Nice to see you again." Then he bowed again and left.

Seriously, who bows?

"How do you know Tucker's dad?" I asked, facing Carol.

She stared right into my eyes. "He was the mistake I made, the same mistake you're making right now with the same Tucker bloodlines. He was the one who got me knocked up and then destroyed my life. I can't have kids because of that man. He is nothing but trouble. I found out who Tucker was when you brought him home for Thanksgiving. He's the spitting image of his deadbeat father. I could spot that face anywhere and his rotten offspring."

From the information I just gathered, Carol knew Tucker's dad from way back when. He had beaten her, gotten her pregnant, and then she got an abortion. Her parents made her. He was the guy, and he was Tucker's dad? My head started to spin; they shared the same long brown hair, same blue eyes. My stomach started to turn, but not from the anxiety I usually had when Carol was around me. It was from the baby. Our baby...the baby that comes from that same Tucker blood line. I started to get dizzy as my head swam around. My throat opened up and I spotted a trash can near the drinking fountains. I barely made it before I threw up all over the floor.

I slumped down onto the floor, death gripping the garbage can as my head started to sweat. My dad handed me a cup of water from the fountain.

"You alright, angel?" I just nodded, which upset my stomach some more and I emptied my stomach into the trash bin.

"Abigail, you should at least go to the ladies room," she snapped.

"Carol, stop it!" my dad barked with his narrowed brown eyes.

I swished the water around in my mouth to get rid of the acid taste in my mouth when I heard a vague voice coming up from the hall.

"You just don't learn, do ya? Stupid kid."

I looked up to see the two Tuckers walking towards us. My dad crouched down by my side, rubbing my knee, while Carol stood at my feet, tapping her foot with her high heel; the sound was irritating my head. And I was sprawled out on the floor with a gross smelling garbage can between my legs.

I spit the water out as I watched Tucker rub his wrists back and forth from where the handcuffs were placed. When he saw me in my current state, he didn't do anything. He didn't come for me to see if I'm alright; he didn't even give me that Tucker smile with the dimple.

Nothing.

"Well, Caroline, it was certainly nice to see you again. Let's not make it twenty years before the next visit, sugar." Tucker Sr. looked down at me. "You look pale, child, but pregnancy agrees with you."

He tugged on Tucker's gray hoodie and my mouth hung open as they walked right past us. And Tucker didn't even look back at me. Tears willingly went down my face as I watched him leave the building, out the front doors. He was gone.

My heart literally broke right then.

"Abigail, explain. Tell me this isn't true." Carol's foot started to tap faster as she waited for me to answer her.

I dropped my head down and cried into my shirt as my heart shattered. Tucker left me with his dad who knew Carol. Obviously, Tucker told him I was pregnant or he wouldn't have said anything. Tucker didn't even have the decency to look at me as he walked by.

I continued to cry my broken heart out at the loss of the man I loved and he just left me here while Carol and my dad fought.

Chapter Twenty

It had been three weeks since I saw Tucker, after he left me crying on the floor in the police hallway. Once my dad and Carol cooled down enough, they took me back to the apartment, which I was alone in. I cried myself to sleep that night, and then woke up with Jade curled into my side. Jade's shell was securely built up around her; she wouldn't talk to anyone except for me.

We were excused from school to help Trish with Rachel's funeral, which was not easy. Trish was the biggest mess of all that next day. She screamed at me, then Jade, while she threw Rachel's things all over her room, finally collapsing on the floor in an emotional mess. Jade and I stayed by her side at the mourning of her only child. Trish slept in her bed, curled up in Rachel's blankets, and then neatly folded her clothes into boxes. It only took Trish four screaming days when the room was finally emptied and Rachel's things were put away. However, Trish was ready to plan the funeral.

Rachel's funeral turned out to be so beautiful and peaceful. White and pink roses filled the church as the priest said a few kind words. Jade gave a very inspirational talk on best friends, and how this life didn't end but continued on, and how she would see her friends again. Rachel look so at peace in the coffin, her gorgeous red hair around her face on the soft white pillows, bright red lipstick on, which was Rachel's favorite.

Surprising everyone, Trish stood up at the pulpit to say a few words, the minister holding her hand the entire time for balance.

"Rachel had many dreams that won't get to be fulfilled in this life. But I know she is in a better place, where all her dreams can come true. Rachel was my baby girl, with so many accomplishments; she wanted to be like me." Trish sobbed into the microphone.

That's when I broke down. Rachel wanted to move to L.A. to start her acting career she worked so hard for at Juilliard and she wouldn't have that; she would never get that chance.

When the service was over, the pallbearers carried the coffin. Some ushered out Trish, who had a death grip on Jade's hand, but Jade wouldn't let go of me. Us three walked behind Rachel's silver coffin as we headed outside. At the back of the church, I saw Jett and Brad. To be honest, Brad looked like hell. He looked like he hasn't slept in five years. His eyes were swollen and puffy with bags underneath them. I personally think Brad and Rachel were getting closer and closer. Losing her probably hurt him just as much as us.

I kept my head down as we passed them, not caring to look for Tucker or not. I knew he wouldn't be there. I called him a few times, but the calls went straight to voicemail. Jade told me that Jett hasn't heard or seen Tucker since that night. My heart broke that I wouldn't see him again—that he was gone for good. I didn't want to believe it, but when each day passed and didn't hear from him, I started to believe that he wasn't coming back. He didn't want anything to do with me, or his baby.

The burial service was exquisite, with all the flowers from the church surrounding her grave site as her coffin slowly lowered into the ground. Rachel was ready to rest in peace. Trish cried out as she said goodbye to her daughter one last time, tossing a single white rose into her grave. Jade kept her arm looped through mine until we crashed on my bed together. We shut the world out for a couple of days, only answering calls from our parents. People from school tried to call, left us messages with their condolences. Jett sent over flowers for the both of us, but kept his distance. I sent him a text, telling him thank you for the flowers, and Jade didn't respond to him.

We were out on the balcony having our mourning time; while Jade smoked on the opposite side of me, I sipped on hot chocolate.

"I'm going to go see a doctor about my cutting. Will you come with me?" Jade flicked her butt over the rail.

I almost spit out my cocoa, "You sure?" I asked facing her.

She quickly wiped the tears from her face. "Yes. Rachel would have wanted me to." She sniffed and I pulled her into my arms.

Two days later, we were both sitting in Dr. Walter's office a therapist for Jade. When Jade told her dad, he was so happy for her, he cried. I was so happy for Jade. I controlled my binging to a minim, but morning sickness hit harder for me every day. Usually when I would talk to Carol, my stomach would twist and turn; when she would get a little out of control, I would race to the bathroom. Jade helped me by pulling the phone away from my ear and stuffing the little device under the pillow for five-ten seconds, then let me have it again when I got my breathing under control and the nausea settled down.

We grew closer every day, leaning on each other for support though this difficult time.

"Jaiden Monroe?" A lady asked in the waiting room and we both stood up. "I'm sorry, only Jaiden please." The lady announced, holding up a hand at me to stop.

Jade stopped dead in her tracks, "No, she comes or I go," telling her firmly and taking a hold of my hand.

The lady inhaled a deep breath through her nose, "Alright, come on."

We walked down the hallway with dimmed lights, touched up with a light colored gray for the paint and very colorful pictures hanging up on the walls. Trying to make you feel at ease I'm sure, but little did that work for Jade and I.

We entered a dark gray color office, with an older man sitting behind his desk, not looking up as he spoke.

"Ladies, please take a seat."

We both sat on the leather couch, holding hands. Jade's body went stiff as the doctor put down his pen from writing and finally looked up at us.

"Ladies. How are we today?"

"Fine." We said at the same time and Jade's hand tightened in mine.

"Well, let's start shall we?" He got up from his chair and moved around to the matching leather set in front of us.

Neither of us saying anything, he started. "I'm Dr. Walters." He sniffed then reached into his pocket for a hanky, blew his nose, which made me sick because of the sound, then stuffing his dirty hanky back in his pocket. Dr. Walters was a very much older man with white hair, thick glasses, and a very large belly.

"What brings you here today, Jaiden?"

"It's Jade for starters."

I stifled my giggle.

"My apologies Jade. What brings you here today?"

She looked at me with unshed tears, I nodded, "I'm right here," I whispered. Jade looked back at the doctor and let her words flow right out. Nothing was stopping her. She explained her mother's death, her step mother and how rotten she is. She even told him about her cutting, which brought her here, because our friend Rachel. She would have wanted Jade to have gotten help. Jade knew it was wrong to do it, but she embraced the pain. She went on about meeting Jett, how he's helped her along the way, but losing Rachel was something that hurt her so badly, she couldn't go through with it any more. So she decided it was time to get the true help she needed.

Dr. Walter's wrote some things down, clearing his throat then handed us a box of tissues as we were both in tears. I sobbed for Jade, with her being so strong at this moment for her. Plus, being three months pregnant wasn't helping my hormones. They came crashing down around me like a ton of bricks. When Jade felt like she was done explaining everything to Dr. Walter's, he turned to me.

"Abigail dear, you play an important role in Jade's life. You are like her security blanket. I see her holding your hand, looking at you for approval. You're her rock. How does that make you feel?"

"Good, because I feel the same way about her right now."

"Would you care to elaborate for me?"

"I have a problem binging, I'm a binger." I giggled at my new nickname. "I shouldn't say that I have a binging problem anymore, because I'm pregnant so now it's morning sickness."

"How far along are you in your pregnancy?"

"Three months or so. I go to the doctor in two weeks."

He wrote that down. "Good, congratulations."

"Thanks," I mumbled, then slouched down into the leather.

He slid his watch on his wrist up for the time, "I'm sorry ladies, but we went way over the hour." Dr. Walters stood up and reached out his hand, "Jade, you did very well for your first appointment. I hope you schedule your next one next week."

Jade smiled, "I will." and then shook his hand.

"Can you do me a favor though?"

Jade shrugged, "I can try."

"Come alone. There's nothing wrong with bringing Abigail along, but now that the first meeting is over with, I want to see how well you open up without her here."

She went hard at my side, "I can't promise you anything."

"And that's fine—just try."

Jade nodded, "Okay."

Then their hands let go, Dr. Walter's then turned to me and stuck his hand out. "Abigail, would you make an appointment for tomorrow with my receptionist? I would like to talk to you so more as well."

"Ummm....Sure."

He let go of my hand, pushed up his glasses, "Have a wonderful rest of the day ladies." Then he turned and went back to his desk.

We walked back down the light gray hallway and made our appointments. Mine for tomorrow at three and Jade's for next week. I liked Dr. Walters. He seemed like a very nice man. We will see with one on one time tomorrow though.

Three o'clock came a lot faster than I had planned, but I couldn't leave the bathroom all morning. I thought stress from Carol was bad, morning sickness was worse. Nothing agreed with my stomach, except for hot chocolate.

I haven't spoken to Carol about my pregnancy since the station. My dad called every day to check up on me, making sure I'm eating right, and asking how I'm feeling. I love my dad. He was the biggest supporter ever; I'm grateful for him. I know that he has told me about Carol being so disappointed in me. She tried to shield me, but yet, I followed in her steps, getting pregnant at such a young age. I'm not going her route though; I plan on having this baby alone if I have to, but getting an abortion is not my answer.

I entered the tall building where Dr. Walters was when my purse started to buzz. I dug around in my purse, trying to see the glow. I need to remind myself later to clean my purse out. I couldn't even find my phone. Having it on silent did help the problem either. But when I felt the rectangle device, I was shocked to see on my screen; 1 *missed call: Tucker*

I stopped walking as I stared at his name. When the screen went dark again, I got my feet to move to the bank of elevators. I stood in the elevator, holding my phone out, staring at the black screen. I didn't even know if I wanted to talk with him; it's been weeks since I've seen him. I tried calling him every day, but he never answered or called me back. I cried while I left messages, and only bringing up the baby once. I wasn't going to hold the pregnancy over his head. If he wanted to be here, then I'll accept that. It's sad to even think that I prepared myself for him not to be in this child's life.

The elevator dinged and I walked off. I debated back and forth about calling him back. Call him back and yell at him, call him and tell him to never call me again. Or just the simplest one was to ignore him. So I decided on just that.

I put my phone back in my purse and walked up to the receptionist desk. She looked up at me with a smile.

"Hi, I have an appointment at three with Dr. Walters."

"Okay, I'll let him know that you are here. Please, take a seat."

I sat down in the same leather chairs as yesterday, and my legs started to bounce, my nerves were going crazy being here by myself. I picked up a *Parents* magazine and flipped through it in record time, not even reading or looking at the pictures of the smiling babies. I took a deep breath and started the magazine over again, taking my time, not even paying attention to the little beep from my phone, telling me I have a new voicemail.

I pushed the thought aside and continued to flip, reading about being a parent is one of the greatest blessings someone could ever have. I read a testimonial from a lady. It was her third child and the worst case of morning sickness she's had. Her husband being there with the other two kids, then being there in the mornings, holding her hair back, getting a cold cloth for the back of her neck, and when she got back into bed, he went and took care of the other two kids.

Being a parent was this amazing thing that I should look forward to, but why is moving forward so hard, when one is by them self? I'm pregnant and alone, and the thought burned into my brain, then I started crying.

"Abigail McCall?"

Someone called out my name, but I didn't budge. I held onto the sides of the magazine and silently cried, watching my tears fall on the colorful papers of all the happy family stories.

I'm alone.

It echoed through my head over and over again, like a song stuck on repeat. Tucker didn't even care, that he left me in the police station, throwing up on the cold tile floor.

Just...walked right past me. Left me there.

I don't know how long I sat there crying, having a death grip on the magazine, until someone placed a hand on my shoulder.

"Abigail?"

It was the last voice I ever expected to hear and I flinch away from the touch. The magazine of happy families and wonderful, holding back the hair husbands fell on the floor and I held my head.

Alone

"Abigail. Please look at me."

I stopped crying long enough to look up and meet the blue eyes of my step mother, Carol, sitting right next to me. Her blue eyes were filled of sadness as she held open her arms to me. I went willingly. I needed to be held.

Carol let go and cupped my cheeks. Her eyes usually so cruel and mean, now were soft and caring. She pushed my hair back off my shoulder, "Meet me for drinks after this? There's a little place across the street. We have lots to talk about." I nodded. I agree very much, we did need to talk. I'm keeping my baby, I knew she would try and talk me out of it though.

"Abigail McCall?"

I looked at the lady calling my name then followed her down the same hallway as yesterday. I found myself on the same brown leather couch, with Dr. Walters in front of me, his hand under his chin, staring at me.

"Abigail, what has you so upset today?"

I sniffed and reached for a tissue, "I'm just emotional," I tried to play it off.

"Abigail, don't shut down. It's not fair to you."

I looked back up at him.

One breath, two breaths, and then three breaths.

I broke down and sobbed into the tissue.

"Abigail, let's talk about this. Obviously something is destroying you. You have to talk in order for me to help you."

"I'm pregnant. My boyfriend...or I thought he was my boyfriend was someone who I didn't even know. He lied to me from the beginning. Told me he's never been arrested, but he has—he deals drugs. My dad is a lawyer for the city and has this giant folder on him. The night Rachel died; I found out Tucker deals drugs. I'm not stupid; I know how dangerous that is. The Tucker I met wanted nothing more than to tattoo and he's so great at it too!"

I continued on my ramp page of anti-Tucker syndrome. I confessed about the bulimia, Carol, everything I could think of. When I told him about my purging, I was actually pacing in front of Dr. Walters. I went on about the stupid bullying from Jasmine, but she wasn't so much of a concern as Tucker. I ended up looking out the windows of his office, pulling on one of Dr. Walters leaves of his tall plant in the corner, while watching the traffic below me. Being up forty floors, I could get used to looking out a window like this every day.

"Tucker tried calling me when I got here."

Dr. Walter's cleared his throat. "Did you talk with him?"

I shook my head, "No, I missed the call, but I think he left a voicemail."

"Abigail, you need to listen to it. He could be trying to reach out. He doesn't have any family. You did say his mom could care less about him. Maybe while his dad was with him, he told him to leave you alone, maybe said to stay away. You have to hear him out on the other side here. He is the father to your unborn baby."

My head dropped with a thud on the window, the cars moving right below my eyes, straight down the building. I had a feeling the good doc would say something like that.

"I don't want to pressure Tucker into being a father. That's something he needs to figure out."

"I agree. In your situation, I think most men would do something like leave you with a child he could care less about. But from what you've told me, sounds like that isn't the case. Listen to the message, Abigail."

I turned and faced him, still sitting in his leather chair, yellow pad of paper on his lap, his glasses down on his nose just like my dad does when I walk into his office. I walked back over to the couch where my purse was and pulled out my phone. When I unlocked my phone, the little screen still showed:

1 missed call: Tucker

My eyes started to water again, taking a deep breath to help them stop them from falling, but it didn't work. A tear dropped on my phone as the screen went dark again.

"Go ahead Abigail. Listen to it." Dr. Walters was starting to push my buttons with the forcing. I unlocked my phone and dialed up my voicemail. While the lady talked on the phone, telling me I have one new message, his voice that I missed so much filled my ears.

Gabs, I'm sorry I haven't been around. I've been trying to lie low from everything that has happened. I hope you can meet me today. I want to see you and talk to you. I hope you can find it in your heart to call me back.

He sounded so nervous. I wanted to sec him, but another part of me didn't. Then all the what ifs filled my head. What if he didn't want to be with me? What if this. What if that. I wanted to pull my hair out. Instead, I just put my phone back and fell against the back of the couch, releasing a big breath.

"What did he have to say?"

I met the doctor's eyes, "Wants me to call him back, and wants me to forgive him."

"See, it's a start. Are you going to?"

I shrugged my shoulders and not saying anything else. Dr. Walters stood up and held his hand out, pretty much signaling that my time is up.

"Abigail, I hope you will come back for another session."

"Yeah, I will."

I shook his hand then left. I was alone in the elevator and let the rest of my tears flow freely down my face. People starred at me with raised brows, but their face sincere. I wiped them away with my as quick as I could when I reached the lobby. Again, I debated with myself on calling Tucker back. If I did, what do I say to him? I didn't want to be that girl who says one thing then goes crawling back to him just because he called me. My steps hit the outside and I started walking to the place Carol wanted to meet me.

I spotted Carol at the table, twisting her wine glass around with her fingers. Taking a deep breath I then went to her side. She smiled at my approach and right then, something changed between us. She gave me a sad smile at the corner of her mouth, and then I saw her eyes travel down to my barely showing belly. I wasn't showing at all, but you can tell I had a tiny little bump at the top of my jeans.

I sat down across from her and ordered a hot chocolate. We stayed silent until the waiter brought me my drink. Then we were left alone. Clattering dishes filled the silence between us as I blew on my drink to take a sip. Carol huffed, and then I glanced up at her.

"Abigail, why are you seeing a therapist?" She asked as her manicured nails drummed on the black linen cloth.

"I went with Jade to talk about Rachel's death among other things. He asked if I could come back today, so I did." Taking another soothing drink of my warm cocoa, letting it pool in my belly.

"I see. What about your condition? Have you given it any thought?"

I met her yes, "Yes, I'm gonna have the baby and keep it." That's what I wanted. I didn't want to give this up.

"I see," Carol waved her fingers in the air, signaling something behind me. I turned to see not something, but someone.

365

Alex made his way towards us, dressed in a gray pressed suit, his hair done nicely, and very gorgeous looking as usual. I faced back to Carol, "You called him? He's the last person I expected to see here."

She held up a hand, "Now listen to what he has to say, alright?"

I rolled my eyes as Alex pulled out the chair next to Carol's then sat down, his blue eyes piercing at me with the same look he always gave me. It didn't make my stomach twist and turn as if Tucker was looking at me. I hadn't see Alex since he was in the room with Tucker, yelling at me to get out. I couldn't even look at him. If you push past his good looks, Alex made me feel uncomfortable. And I was just going to find out how uncomfortable he made me with him being here.

"Nice to see you again, Abigail."

I smiled up at him, but I didn't have anything to say to him. He ordered his drink while more silence filled out little table. The waiter brought his drink, then Carol started talking.

"Abigail, Alex here has something he wants to say to you." She turned to him and my eyes met his.

"I know about your pregnancy. I want to help you keep your reputation up. I want you to marry me."

I huffed, "You call that a proposal? You certainly know how to sweep a girl right off her feet."

Alex then unbuttoned his jacket and reached inside in his coat pocket. When his hand came out, he held a little blue box that was every girls dream, setting it down on the table and pushed it towards me with his long fingers.

I sat back in my chair as if the box would burn me if it came near me. That's it! My conscience screamed at me.

Tucker knew he was lying to me. He knew I could handle it, as I thought about all the times things didn't make any sense while talking to him. He was trying to keep it from me. Protect me from him.

I glimpsed back up to Alex, his eyes were down, staring at the unopened box. I glanced over to Carol who was glaring at me.

"What?" I asked her.

"Don't be rude. Open the box." She jerked her head to the little blue Tiffany's box.

I couldn't open it. I didn't want to touch it. I couldn't, that would betray my heart of my true feelings. I couldn't do that to any man.

"Abigail," Alex got up from his chair, grabbing the ring box, and then dropping down to one knee. My nerves started up.

"Abigail, I know we don't know each other. I want to get to know you. Help you in any way I can. We can work together as a team. I will take care of you and your child, if you would just give me a chance. Marry me."

He opened the box. Nestled inside was a gorgeous, huge ring. The center diamond was at least four carats with little diamonds surrounding it. Alex's eyes were piercing blue as he asked me to marry him. But he did it wrong—he said the wrong things.

Carol put her elbows on the table, leaning closer to me. "Isn't it beautiful Abigail?

I stuttered, "It's overwhelming, but no Alex. Again, I don't love you and you don't love me. We..."

"Abigail, enough! You are being so disrespectful towards Alex and our family name. You deny him only because he isn't the father of your child. That boy cannot take care of you, he doesn't belong in our world, he can't do anything right. He'll only drag you down."

Carol's words stabbed my heart, deadly as sin. I wanted to swat them away like a dead fly. Even if it wasn't Tucker's baby, I still couldn't just marry someone else just because my reputation was on the line. This isn't the 1800's where that was the only option in life. There are tons of single teen moms in this world and I was gonna join them. I don't need Alex to take care of me.

"Think about it Abigail. I can take care of you." Alex said shutting the box and placing it on my leg. He stood up and left. I glanced at Carol who had a little smile on her face.

I walked home in a huge pregnancy emotional mess. Today had been so stressful. Pouring my soul out to a doctor I've only known for 24hours, Carol showing up in the waiting room; I actually thought maybe she cared enough as to why I was there in the first place...drinks afterward, and then Alex's weird proposal. The ring box was a brick in my purse, just sitting there, burning away at the seams. Carol didn't say anything to me after Alex left our table— I left first. I needed Jade; I needed to talk with her.

I decided not to call Tucker back. Three weeks was a long time to lie low from someone; I figured he could wait. I didn't want to crawl back to him after the first call he makes to me. I walked into my very quiet apartment and called out for Jade. Tossing my purse into my door my room as I heard some mumbled voices, sounding like she was on the phone when I walked into her bedroom. She sat on her bed wide eyed at me as I stomped my way in and starting shouting.

"Alex freaking proposed. He proposed!" Jade's brows shot up. "I can't believe it." I paced back and forth in front of her bed. "And what's worse, he gave me this huge blinging, blanging ring too! Not just some dinky little thing, but this huge diamond ring."

"Um.. Gabs, stop." Jade held her arms up.

"He got down on one knee and everything, right in front of Carol." My arms were all over the place as I continued to shout. I don't know if I was mad, angry, or frustrated, maybe all the above.

"And did I tell you the ring is huge, it's huge! I just stared at it, but Carol told me not to be rude, so I had to take it. You know how Carol is. I can't stand when she does crap like this. Said he wanted to take care of me, his baby or not. He doesn't care!"

"Gabs stop."

But I didn't listen to her. I kept going, rambling on and on about what happened just recently. Jade kept telling me to stop, I don't know why. She would hold her hands up and wave them. I'm sure she just wanted to throw in her opinion. Jade didn't like Alex, she was Team Tucker all the way. I don't blame her. With Tucker always gone, me being alone and pregnant, the more I wanted someone to lean on. Was that just the girl in me or was it all in the pregnancy? This was going to drive me insane.

"Gabs!"

I faced Jade, "What?!"

"Will you stop and listen to me for one damn minute please?" Climbing off her bed and taking my hand to pull me into my room. I couldn't believe my eyes as I saw Jett and Tucker sitting on my bed. Tucker holding the blue Tiffany box that held the ring Alex just proposed to me with. Seriously, could this situation get any worse?

Jade leaned into me. "He came over to talk with you."

The box snapped shut and Tucker chucked it into the shared bathroom, stalking towards me. His blue eyes were so angry looking, not soft and subtle at all. He reached up and I flinched back, his eyes went soft a mere second that I recoiled back. Then he grabbed my snowflake necklace and ripped it off my neck and stalked off around me. I started to go after him but Jett ran past me and they were gone and out the door. I dropped to my knees and cried once again into my hands. Jade hurdled over me, only trying to bring me some comfort, but it was nothing to compared to Tucker's strong arms.

I tried calling Tucker, no answer. I tried texting him, no answer. He did pick up the phone once; I could tell because I heard the tattoo machine, but he hung up on me. I get that he's pissed, but I'm pissed too that he wouldn't let me explain. I had my nights where I had to have Jade in my bed just so I would stop crying. I tried everything I could to talk Jade into calling Tucker so he would answer and then I would get on the phone. She told me no and then said he would just hang up on me. I stopped trying a week after he left my apartment.

I went to Juilliard a week later with one mission on my mind—facing Madame Ava. I had my usual bag of Andes chocolates in my hand; they were the only thing that I didn't get sick from and they had some sugar so I didn't get too sick. The day was gorgeous as the sun shined on my face and the snow was melting as I walked to Juilliard and up the front steps. It was a Saturday so no one was here, but Madame Ava lived in her class so I knew she would be here. I slowly walked down the empty hallway as I chewed chocolate after chocolate. Madame Ava's door was open with beautiful classic music playing in the background. I stopped to study her move across the room up on her toes, turning softly and slowly. She had her eyes closed as she danced and closed up her imaginary scene in her head. She was a very beautiful dancer, I'm so happy I got to see this part of her before I through in the towel.

"Abigail, what are you doing here?" She asked breathlessly with her hands on her hips.

"I wanted to come talk with you," I eased my way into the ballet room and sat on the bench were our ballet bags would go.

Madame Ava came to sit with me. "What about?" She took a gulp of her water and patted her face with a towel.

Might as well just spit it out.

"I'm pregnant." I hung my head in shame. I quickly unwrapped another Andes chocolate and stuffed it in my mouth.

"Don't eat so much chocolate." Madame Ava told me as she took the bag out of my hands. "You'll end up with high sugar in your urine and you'll have to do a 24 hour urine collection. Trust me, I know."

I giggled. I really didn't need to know that much.

"I'm sorry to hear this Abigail, I had high hopes for you."

"I'm sorry." I looked at her, her eyes were shimmered over. She looked beautiful.

"Don't be. You'll be an amazing mom. Young, but amazing." Then she pulled me into her side to give me a hug. She was right, I was young. I wish Tucker and I could have been more careful. But this wasn't a problem; I can solve this on my own.

Chapter Twenty-One

Today was my first doctor's appointment. I had found a doctor online that was very close to our apartment building. I had called Tucker before I left the apartment, but of course he didn't answer the phone. I left a message and gave the address of the doctor's office. I had to try and move on without him. I felt so naked without my necklace around my neck. My hand would always go up, but nothing would be there.

Jade sighed again next to me. "I hate doctor's offices," her knee bouncing wildly, up and down.

I quietly laughed, "Why?"

"They smell," she answered as she flipped through a magazine. I walked to the wall that was full of pamphlets about birth, circumcision, and cord blood. I picked up each one to look through at home. It's too soon to find out the sex of the baby. I'm only around ten weeks or so.. not sure on the exact date of when I actually conceived the baby.

"Abigail McCall?" A nurse called out.

I was weighed, which was one hundred and six pounds. While the nurse was writing my weight down, there was a board in front of me with tons of baby announcements. And some even the doctors holding the little babies. The nurse took us down into a little room where she took my blood pressure, made more notes. She clicked on the computer and asked me questions if I was sick with morning sickness, how would I rate the sickness on a level from one to ten (I said five) and if anything was bothering me so far in the pregnancy. I shook my head. Made more notes and then she left us.

"Damn, stupid doctors taking their stupid time." Jade kept mumbling out while flipping through more magazines. She was always so impatient with everything. She was the same way while we waited in Dr. Walters' office. I checked my phone, hoping there would be a text from Tucker that magically appeared and I missed the chime. Nothing came. I debated about texting him again, maybe he didn't get it.

Me: Hey Tucker, I'm at the doctors on 5ᵗʰ ave. Didn't know if you got my text earlier. Abigail.

Why did I put my name under it? Maybe he was done with me and no longer had my number, I thought to myself. Jade gasped and I looked at her from where I was sitting on the tall exam table with the noisy paper that crinkled with every move I made.

"What?" I asked

She turned the magazine for me to see a cute little baby boy sleeping in a pile of fluffy blankets wearing a cute little knitted hat. "This baby is so cute, have that one."

I giggled, "I don't think that's how that works Jade. My baby will look nothing like that." I stopped my words. My baby. I did say my baby as if Tucker didn't have a say if he even wanted to be in this child's life. I choked on a sob as reality hit me again about being alone with a newborn.

"Gabs, I didn't mean..." Jade started to get up to come to my aid, but there was a knock at the door and in walked in my doctor. She was very pretty and skinny, with her blonde hair pulled back into a low pony tail and green surgical scrubs. She sat at the computer and flipped through my chart.

"Abigail," She met my eyes. "I'm Dr. Shaw. How are you feeling so far?"

I nodded a little bit and wiped the corner of my stinging eyes. "Fine."

"Any morning sickness?"

"Some; nothing I can't handle though." I sniffed.

Dr. Shaw wrote that down. "You're under weight for your age. Are you eating enough?"

"Well, I'm a...well...I *was* a ballet dancer."

"Oh, I see. Keeping fit then." She wrote that down as well. "Your blood pressure is low as well. So, we will start you on prenatal vitamins as soon as you leave here. Some women get sick in the mornings while they take them mixed with the morning sickness. If you get sick in the morning while taking them, just take them at night."

I nodded at her.

"Do you know how far along you are?"

"Umm...I think around ten weeks or so. That's what the app on my phone told me. I'm not quite sure even when it happened."

"Is the father involved with you as support?"

I glanced at Jade, who shrugged. I looked back at Dr. Shaw. "I'm not sure. He's knows about the baby, but we are fighting right now. So I don't really know.

She wrote that down. Is she going write down everything I tell her? She should just take down my social and credit card number and she's golden. Dr. Shaw stood, "I'll be right back." Then she left the room, she wasn't gone for very long. She pulled in a giant machine with a computer monitor attached to it.

"Do you want to come over on the other side of the table?" Dr. Shaw asked Jade, who was completely silent as she made her way around to the other side of the exam table. "Abigail, please lie down and lift your shirt. This is just an ultrasound. We are going to look at the baby, make sure the dates line up, and figure out when your due date is."

I laid back, "Okay." Pulling my shirt up. I reached for Jade's hand as the Doctor shut the lights off and booted up the machine. It hummed for a minute and then the screen flickered to life.

"This might be a little cold. It's just jelly to help get a better look at the baby.

I was still as she squirts the cold jelly on my stomach and placed a small little device on top of the jelly, smearing it all over. I watched the screen, which didn't make any sense to me. It was black, then gray, and then something that looked like a black balloon with a white dot in the middle. Dr. Shaw clicked a couple of times on the keyboard and I saw the little white dot flicker a little and then a tiny sound echoed in the room. It sounded like a train with the way it sounded, choo, choo, choo, choo. Not stopping.

"That noise is the baby's heart beat and this flicker here," She pointed to the white dot with the flicker, "That's the heart beating. Very strong."

My eye's misted over and Jade squeezed my hand tighter. Dr. Shaw moved the device around on my belly some more then froze the screen again with a click of a button and that's when I first saw my baby very clear. The profile of its little body was perfect.

"It looks like a gummy bear," Jade whispered. I choked out a loud weep and covered my mouth as my tears spilled over and drifted into my hair. The heart beat sounded the room again and more tears cascaded down. Jade bent down and kissed my forehead, trying to calm me. She knew how heartbroken I am over this whole mess between Tucker and I. Hearing and seeing the baby just made me feel worse. I heard a sound like something was printing. I shut my eyes, to try to cool myself and the pressure from the device left my belly and the light turned on, flooding the room with light again and Dr. Shaw wiped up the mess on my stomach.

"Okay Abigail, all done. You can sit up now." Jade helped me sit up as I pulled my shirt down to cover my stomach. Jade stayed behind me and Dr. Shaw handed me a box of tissues.

"Can I ask what's made you cry?" I looked up at the doctor, whose eyes were filled with sorrow and my words just came flooding out.

"The baby is real. It's inside me, just...just...there." and I broke down. Jade came over and held onto me while I cried into her shoulder. I heard my little baby's heartbeat. It was so real, so perfect and so real. I started to laugh and sat back up. Now I was laughing? I was laughing, I felt happy. I heard my baby's heartbeat, that made me happy.

Dr. Shaw was right in front of me on the swivel chair; she softly placed a hand on my knee. "Abigail. I just wanted to go over some things with you about your baby. Feel a little better?"

I nodded, "Yes." And wiped my nose again. Grabbing my snowflake necklace and holding onto it while Dr. Shaw continued on.

"Good. Your baby is perfectly healthy and has a strong heartbeat. Take this prescription and get it filled for the prenatal vitamins. You due date is August eighth, which puts you at fourteen weeks, and the baby was conceived on November fifteenth or sixteenth. My nurse is going to take some blood from you, just to make sure you're healthy and for our records. Make sure you get you schedule to come back and see me in five weeks. Okay?"

Dr. Shaw handed me the prescription and little sonogram picture of my little gummy bear. "Yes ma'am." And then my nice lady doctor left. The nurse did a great job at taking my blood; one shot and she filled up six vials of my blood.

"What are you testing for?"

"We call it an OBP Panel. It's going to check your white cell count, along with blood type for our files, as well as a STD panel."

"STD? but...I've only been with one person."

"I'm sure you have nothing to worry about honey. It's just for our records to know that you're safe. We do it with all our patients."

The nurse wrapped my arm up and left the room. I looked at wide eyed Jade.

"Let's get out of this joint before I puke," she said, leaving the room without me.

On our way out, Jade pushed the button for the elevator and I remembered the day that the baby was conceived. "I know when I got pregnant." I announced to Jade.

"When?"

"The doctor said November fifteenth or sixteenth. That's the night I lost my virginity to Tucker, because the week after that, we went to my parents for Thanksgiving."

"All it takes is one time. I told you to wrap it."

I was silent the entire way home. Jade was of course probably texting Jett, her fingers moving a hundred miles an hour on that thing. I checked my phone once more for a text, nothing. I was starting to piss me off the longer Tucker ignored me. But maybe he was the kind of guy that would jump at the first chance he had about having a baby. A baby was a big deal. I remember that night I lost my virginity to Tucker, and then I came home to Jade and told her we didn't use a condom. I freaked about getting pregnant and we were careful ever since, but like what Jade said, all it takes is one time.

I tossed my jacket, keys and my phone on the kitchen counter. "I'm gonna go lay down for a little bit." I collapsed on my bed, feeling tired and so frustrated with Tucker, it was starting to give me a headache the more I thought about it. Jade kicked her boots off and climbed up next to me.

I laid on my bed and stared a long time at my little baby picture. Jade was asleep next to me. She couldn't really sleep in her room alone anymore. There were nights when she would wake me up with her cries and call out Rachel's name. Losing Rachel was hard, especially on Jade. She was lost without her. I heard a soft knock on the door of the apartment. I left the bed as quietly as I could so Jade wouldn't wake up. I had butterflies in my stomach with each step I walked towards my front door. I had a feeling about who would be on the other side. Hoping it would be the only other person that mattered to me in life, the one person who created this baby with me. My heart ached inside and out for Tucker to be with me at the doctors. Have him be there to hold my hand, kiss my forehead, and to cry with me as the little heartbeat echo through the exam room.

Taking a deep breath, I twisted the door knob and pulled it open to see Alex standing there on the other side. Looking clean pressed as always in his gray tailored suit, white shirt and black tie.

"Oh. Hey Alex." I greeted him as my stomach dropped in disappointment. The thought kept resurfacing in my head that Tucker is really gone this time.

"Can I come in? I want to talk with you." I didn't really feel like fighting him off right now. I stepped aside and Alex made his way into my apartment.

"I'll be right back, take a seat." I brushed past him to go to my room and closed the door. Jade would flip her lid if she found out Alex was here. She always had to remind me about him being a tight wad. I came back out into the living to see Alex standing where Tucker usually stands at the front windows staring out over Central Park.

I made my way over to the couch, "So what's up Alex?" He slowly turned towards me.

"I wanted to talk to you about my proposal. Have you given it any thought about it?" He walked over to the empty spot next to me and sat down.

I shook my head, "I'm sorry. I haven't thought about it very much to be honest. Still trying to work some things out, I guess."

"Has he even been around lately?" I knew where he was trying to get at with this small talk, something Carol would do too. Just use it against me and when I'm not expecting it, throw it back in my face.

"No, it doesn't really matter though. I'm gonna raise this baby, even if I have to do it by myself." I pulled the little throw blanket over my lap and played with the edges, waiting for time to pass slowly until he would leave.

"I was really young when I graduated early from college." I looked up at Alex's side profile of his perfect features that screamed GQ magazine. "People told me that I was going to be a big hot shot lawyer someday if I kept it up. I never believed them. My father pushed and pushed me into things I didn't want to do. He pushed me into law school, he pushed me to graduate early, and he pushed me into working for the top law firm for the city, which turned out to be your dad. David has been nothing but respectful to me. He talked about you a little bit, about attending Juilliard, about the way you danced across a ballet room."

My eyes started to water and the mention of my dad talking about me. I wanted to reach out to Alex for telling me these things. My heart started to break with the feeling; I wanted to hug him for some reason. And when he looked at me, his blue eyes were filled with hope.

"That first night I met you, firm dinner. You looked so gorgeous in that purple dress and your hair was perfect, you looked like an angel. There was this calming effect you had over me," He let a big breath out and shook his head like he couldn't believe what he was saying to me. "I've never felt like that before, all the stress from my father about everything, and then you came into the limo." He slid closer to me on the couch and looked me directly in the eyes. "I couldn't stop staring at you, your beautiful eyes. I just wanted to touch you, even if it was just a brush of your hand."

Now Alex's knee was brushing mine and his body shifted closer to me. "You are still so beautiful. You're perfect in every way, especially when you dance across stage on your toes."

My eyes started to sting and my body started to shake at how emotional I was getting. Stupid pregnancy hormones.

Alex leaning in closer, "I know that you don't love me and we barley know each other. But I'm hoping that you would give us a shot. Please don't tell me that I've lost you when I never had a chance at getting you." Alex whispered across my cheek. Our faces were so close all I had to do was turn my head and our lips would touch. Tears slipped out the corner of my eyes and down my cheek. Alex's hands brushed them away and turned my head towards his and he tenderly kissed my lips.

At first, I didn't kiss him back and he pulled away, whispering to me again.

"Please Abigail, give me a chance."

And this time, I pushed back to his mouth. His lips weren't as soft as Tucker's, more firm to the touch. It was nice to be touched, to be kissed again. That feeling that has been lost to me. Both of his hands cupped my face as his lips moved softly against mine. I moved my hands to his wrists and let Alex kiss me. When I felt his tongue touch my lips, I opened my mouth and let our tongues touch for the first time. There was no spark to this kiss, no electricity like when Tucker would kiss me. Is that what my life would be like if I married Alex? I continued on kissing Alex back, but I felt like I was searching for that magical spark that ignited my body up in flames like Tucker's kisses did to me. I dived deeper and deeper into Alex's mouth, still trying to find that one thing that made my body crumble to the ground.

I was desperately searching for it that I didn't hear a door open, and then softly click shut. I mean I heard it, but it didn't make sense for me to register or respond to the noise. Alex broke away from me and looked up over my head as my eyes tried to meet his. I turned around to see Tucker's face, red and angry, his fist were clench together at his sides.

"Gabs," Tucker whispered. Just the sound of his voice pierced my heart and what he just caught me doing. Kissing Alex, his one mortal enemy.

Explosion hit the room faster than I thought possible. Tucker took an angry step forward, Alex shot up from my side on the couch and they were in each other's faces.

"Who the *fuck* do you think you are?!" Tucker yelled. "Comin' in here, putting your mouth where it doesn't fucking belong!"

"I'm trying to protect her from you. You are nothing and just belong out on the street with the rest of those dogs you call friends! She deserves better than you," Alex screamed back. Tucker shoved at Alex's chest and he stumbled back. This wasn't good.

"You can't just swoop in here, wave your fucking money around and try to take what's mine!" Tucker yelled again. I stood up and faced Alex, placing my hands on his chest. I'd seen Tucker mad and I didn't want that for Alex. Plus, I'd had enough; I was about to blow up.

"Alex, don't, you'll just make it worse." Then I faced Tucker. "And you," I said as I pushed at Tucker's chest with my finger and he stepped back from me. "How can you just *swoop* in here and pee all over me, like you're marking your territory. Where have you been the last two weeks? Huh?" I stepped up to Tucker who was clearly pissed off. "While Alex has been trying to talk me into being with him, proposing to me, wanting to take me to Paris after the semester is over. Where the hell have you been? Have you been dealing again? You haven't called; you haven't done anything to be near me. Did you know I went to the doctor today? Did you show? NO! I sent you two texts to let you know where I would be and you didn't show!" I stomped my foot and shoved Tucker's chest. "You don't care!"

"How can you say that? I've been trying to cut ties with everyone I know so they won't put a hit out on me, so I can be with you and our baby!"

"You've been gone just to do that? Cut your stupid ties with your stupid friends? I don't believe you!"

"You should. I changed my number and everything after I went and talked with Ethan. That's why you didn't hear from me. I called your phone about thirty minutes ago and you didn't answer. Now I fucking know why."

"Don't use Alex as an excuse for me not answering a phone call. The fact is that you have been gone for two weeks, with no contact, I didn't know if you were dead or just ran with your tail between your legs. You left me at the police station, alone! I'm heartbroken, Tucker, and..."

"So you just want him then? He can take care of you and give you all that shit that I can't."

I stopped. "What?"

"You heard me." Tucker stepped closer to me and raked his hands through his hair that seemed longer than before. "You said he's been here, trying to convince you to marry him, to take you to Paris. That's what you want – money? To be taken care of financially? I told you before that I can't give you that. If that's what you want, I can't be the person to give it to you."

I took a deep breath, but that didn't stop the tears from sliding down my cheeks.

"You obviously don't care for Abigail if you're still hanging around those trailer trash friends of yours, and it's obvious you can't give her what she needs," Alex said from behind me, then placed his hands on the tops of my shoulders.

"Don't you touch her!" Tucker lunged towards Alex and I backed up into his chest, trying to keep the peace between them, but it wasn't working. I put my hands up in Tucker's face. That made me mad. I could no longer control what came out next.

"You don't get a say. You've been gone. GONE! When I needed you the most, you weren't there! You left me in the police station an hour after I told you I was pregnant. You didn't even look at me." I burst into angry tears from my rage. I covered my face with my hands and cried into them as if they were shielding the craziness from my life right now.

"Gabs," Tucker softly said to me and I heard his feet take a step on the plush carpet.

"Just go," I told him, my hands still covering my face. "Do what you're good at and leave me like you always do." I couldn't take it anymore. I couldn't look at him anymore.

"What?" Tucker asked.

"You heard her, she said to go." Alex's hands on my shoulders kept me still as a brick wall. I couldn't move. I couldn't do anything but cry.

"Gabs."

My hands came down, my eyes completely wet. "Leave!"

Tucker stopped and didn't say anything to us as I watched his angry footsteps stomping away from me, and then he slammed my front door. I fell into the couch, covering my face again to cry some more. Alex sat next to me, rubbing my leg; I could tell he was just trying to comfort me, but it wasn't working. I kicked Tucker out because I was mad and I *was* really mad. Seeing him brought back all those alone feelings I'd felt for the past month with being by myself. Jade was the one being by me as I threw up from morning sickness. I wanted what the article said when I was in Dr. Walters' office. The woman who was so sick, her husband took care of her, held her hair back. I wanted that so badly. Could Alex do that for me? I looked up at him and he just stared into my eyes. His blue eyes were sad, but he tried to give me a side smile.

"Alex, I'm pregnant with Tucker's baby. You could deal with raising another man's child?" I thought of Carol put in the same situation with me and my dad. Could Alex love this baby like his own? Or would this innocent child be neglected and get hurt like me?

His eyes moved to the floor, and then he nodded. "I could, but I can't do it by myself. I need you there with me. I think we could be good together; it could be a great thing, you and me. Come to Paris with me when the semester is over and I'll prove it to you. You don't have to give me an answer about the proposal, but come with me and let me prove to you that I am a good guy. I can take care of you."

On a whim, I nodded. "Okay," I agreed, and it was done. I believed that Alex deserved that much from me. I think he deserved a chance from me. It took a lot for a man to admit that he was willing to take care of a child that wasn't his. He wanted to prove to me that he could be by my side, even though it wasn't his.

Alex stood up, pulling on my hand to follow him. "I've got to make arrangements for our trip." All I could do was nod as we walked hand in hand to the front door. Alex stopped and cupped my face again as he leaned down and softly kissed my lips. I kissed him back, but there was still no spark. I had to admit, I was hoping there would be something there that time.

"I'll call you." I nodded again, biting my lower lip, and he left.

My back was up against the front door when I heard a loud clump down the hallway.

I jogged down the hallway and into Jade's room where she was throwing everything of hers into an open suitcase on her bed. Her dark band posters were stripped from the walls and ripped to pieces. Jade was in her closet throwing shoes, causing the banging I heard earlier.

"What are you doing?" I asked, walking in and almost getting hit in the face with a black boot.

"Get out, Gabs. I don't want you in here," she told me as I continued to walk in the room to make my way to her bed.

"Jade, what's going on? Why are you so upset?"

That got her attention really fast. She came bursting out of the closet with an armful of more black boots threaded with black clothes.

"I was asleep on your bed and my phone woke me up. It was Tucker, looking for you; he said he wanted to talk. He was right outside the building, so I told him to come up, you were here and just to come in. I figured you fell asleep on the couch or something. So, I came out to the living room to see Alex so close to you, it was sickening!" She stormed past me and tossed the clothes in the suitcase. "Then he kissed you. At first, I was thinking, "Oh, it's no big deal." then I watched you pretty much make your way into his fucking lap to kiss him back!"

"You knew Tucker was coming, didn't you? You knew he would see that when he walked in."

"Yeah, I knew. He had to know that you had your tongue down someone else's throat while pregnant with his baby!"

"He's been gone. I didn't know I would even see him again, Jade."

"Poor you and your pity party. And stop making excuses. Plus you knew that money talk irritates Tucker. You know how badly he wished he had money to take care of you. That probably hurt him more than anything." Jade zipped up her suitcase and headed out of her room.

"This isn't about the money! Where are you going?" I called after her.

"I can't stay here. I'm going to my dad's."

What? Jade hated being there. She couldn't leave me here. I grabbed her arm, trying to stop her. "Jade don't go, you can't leave me here."

"Sorry, Gabs, I can't stay here with you if you're going to be with Alex. You know it's because of your dad's firm, right? He's using you. Tucker loves you. So pull your head out of that rich snob ass of yours and do the right thing." She wrenched her arm away from my hold, and stomped out the door.

And once again, I was left alone.

Chapter Twenty-Two

More days went by and I didn't hear from Jade. I texted her countless times, but she never replied back to me. I knew that I messed up things with Tucker. Big time. I shouldn't have made him leave that day at my apartment when Alex was over.

The next day after Jade left, I ended up at my old house. Carol was ecstatic to see me and my little bump that barely showed. My dad just kinda grunted at me all night and didn't speak to me during dinner. Alex ended up coming over about an hour later and, as it turned out, he bought tickets for my dad and Carol to join us in Paris. That was just great and the last thing I needed in my life was to have Carol breathing down my neck and put more pressure on me about marrying Alex.

At dinner, I told them that I hadn't given my choice about whether or not Alex was the right choice of a husband. As we sat together in the living room, my dad said he wanted a word with me in his office. He'd never done this before, but I wasn't dumb; I knew that he wanted to talk about Tucker and what was going on. He knew I didn't even really like Alex, either. My dad knew something was up.

I eventually had enough nerve to walk into his office and sit in the leather chair across from his desk. He looked tired, taking his glasses off and pinching the bridge of his nose and rubbing his eyes, then letting a big breath out his nose.

"Abigail, tell me what's going on between you and Alex with no lies, young lady."

"Alex is a great guy, Daddy; I decided to let him take me to Paris after the semester is over."

"What about Kyle?" He sat his glasses down on his desk.

"Tucker came over yesterday to talk, but he walked in while Alex was over and we were kissing," I said, ending with the word kissing in a whisper. My dad just looked at me with nothing in his eyes. Just straight forward stared at me.

"Does he know about the baby?"

I nodded, "Yeah, he does."

"Do you want to handle this in court? I'm sure I can represent you so that you have full custody. Given Kyle's background, I'm sure it wouldn't be a problem."

I shook my head, "I don't want that. If he doesn't want to be around, then that's his problem. I'm not going to force him into being a dad, and if he doesn't want to be with me, I'm not going to force him on that either."

My dad cleared his throat, "And if he wants to be with you?"

I cast my eyes to the floor. I wished deep down Tucker would have stayed last night and I sent Alex away. It was too late now. I couldn't take it back.

"I wouldn't want anything more than for him to want to be with me."

My dad smiled at me and leaned forward, resting his elbows on his desk.

"Then don't you think you should go to him? Fight for him? I think he deserves that."

I thought about chasing him down after Jade left, but I was shocked that Jade packed up and moved herself out of the apartment. Tucker did deserve to be fought for and I was going to do it. Right now.

I got up from the leather couch and opened my dad's office door and collided with a solid chest of Alex.

"Excuse me, Alex." I tried to move around him, but he held onto my shoulders.

"I would like to talk to you outside for a minute," he told me as his blue eyes stared me down. But this was a different kind of stare; it was more along the lines of a "do what I say" kind of stare.

"Alex, come in here and let's talk. Abigail has to go home now."

Alex held up a finger to my dad. "Just a moment, David, I'll be right back."

Alex gripped my arm tighter as we walked by the living room and he tugged me all the way out the front doors and made me sit down next to him.

"What's your problem?"

"I need an answer."

"An answer for what, exactly? I already told you I would go to Paris with you."

"An answer to my proposal,"

My jaw dropped. "I told you, I don't have an answer for you. We don't even know each other. That's the whole point of going to Paris, to get to know one another."

I wrenched my arms out of his hold. I wasn't going to marry Alex and that was clear; I agreed to give him a chance and he was losing it pretty quick.

"Look," Alex reached into the inside pocket of his suit and pulled out the little blue box. Carol knew that I had it in my purse; she must have given it back to him. Alex opened it and my breath caught. The ring was very gorgeous, but I hadn't seen it since the day he proposed to me. It sparkled more now in the sunlight than it did in the restaurant.

"Abigail, I know that we have our differences, but I think we can move past that." He took the ring out of the box and moved down to one knee if front of me and grabbed my left hand. I tried to pull away, but he held on tight. "Abigail, just try it on, please." I didn't answer him as he slipped the cold metal on my ring finger. The diamond was beautiful, and with the other little surrounding diamonds, it made it even more gorgeous.

"Do you like it? If not, you can go pick something else out." I looked up at Alex who was smiling very big, but I pulled the ring off my finger and his smile disappeared.

"I'm sorry, Alex, but I have to go now."

I stood up and tossed the ring into the air as a distraction, and then I ran towards Central Park. I heard Alex shout my name, but I didn't stop. When I reached the corner to push the button to make the light change for me to cross the street, it felt like forever. I ran across the street and down the little path into Central Park. The park was huge, but the hidden greenhouse route was burned into my memory. I knew Tucker would be there. I yelled out left to people walking, letting them know that I was on the left of them and they moved.

My feet hit the pavement, making me hear every single step my feet made. I was out of breath, but I kept running. I didn't think about whether running would hurt the baby. I read somewhere that working out while pregnant was good and wouldn't hurt the baby. I ran up a hill then down and around a corner to the secret trail where I went back up a steep hill, then the green house came into view.

"Oh, thank you," I tried to cry out. I was happy I remembered where the green house even was. I jogged over to the door, not even bothering to knock. Ethan hung around here with his dealing buddies, but the thought didn't even occur to me as I opened the door. I'm glad I didn't stop, because Tucker was the only one there sitting in that same chair I cuddled in with him on the night I lost my virginity to him.

"Tucker." I brushed my hair out of my face and he looked up. He looked like crap with bags under his eyes, hair messy as always, rumbled up clothes too and that hot black leather jacket that I loved so much.

"Gabs." He got right up and made his way over to me. Our bodies crashed together and Tucker kissed me. He kissed me so hard and I loved it. I missed it. This was it, the spark that I missed so much.

"You're here," he said around my mouth, trailing kisses down my neck. "I thought I lost you."

"Tucker, I'm so sorry, I'm sorry." I found myself clinging to him with everything that I had. "I want you, only you," I cried.

"No, I'm sorry, Gabs. I'll quit everything. Dealing and just focus on tattooing, everything. I can't lose you and our baby. I promise you, I'm done. No more." I was crying so badly because I was so deliriously happy – that he would give that up for me and our child.

"Shh...baby girl."

Tucker kissed me again, begging me to open my mouth, using his tongue. His tongue stroked mine and I was lost in him. This was the kind of passion that Alex didn't have. Alex couldn't make my body surrender like Tucker could. Tucker's hands roamed all over my hot achy body. I wanted him. It'd been too long.

"Tucker," I cried out and he pulled my shirt up and off my head. I pushed his leather jacket off his shoulders and did the same to his shirt. I traced the lines of his tattoo that wrapped up and down his shoulder. His hands reached around and unclasped my bra, and I bit down into his skin on his shoulder. We were skin to skin and I missed it so much, I was hurting on the inside.

Nothing about this time was going to be slow. We both needed each other. I unbuckled Tucker's jeans as he tried pushing me down to the wood floor. I got his pants around to his knees as he kissed his way down between my breasts, circling his tongue underneath them and down lower to my navel. My hips arched up and he unbuttoned my pants to get rid of my restraining clothing. He kissed my tattoo as he pulled my underwear along with my jeans and then his hot mouth was on me. I cried out in surprised pleasure, tangling my hands in his hair and pulled. My nails dug into his scalp as he kept going. It'd been too long. I loved him. I missed him.

I was going to combust any minute; he didn't stop, just kept going. Then a bright light flashed behind my closed eyelids and I cried out very loudly before my body went limp.

Tucker climbed on top of me and attacked my mouth in need of passion for me. I kissed him back with everything that I had. The taste of myself didn't bother me at all. I took everything Tucker gave me.

"Oh Tucker, I want you. Give it to me...hard." I smiled and he kissed me again.

"Are you ready for me, baby girl?"

I nodded. "We don't even need to use a condom," I joked and he smiled as his body pushed into mine. I cried out at the wonderfulness of him back inside me. I'd missed him and never wanted to let him go. My legs wrapped around his waist like a vice grip. I wasn't going to let him go again.

"I love you, Gabs," he grunted into my skin.

"I love you, Tucker."

The only sound in the room was our skin clashing against our bodies, mixed with our moans around our crazy tongues. We both began to sweat very fast. I found myself begging against his mouth. That wonderful pressure began to build up again; the more I held my breath, the stronger that feeling got. I pulled at his hair as he bit my bottom lip and another flash of light exploded and I was once again lost in him.

Now, here I was two days later, sitting on my couch waiting for Tucker to come back to the apartment, and all I could do was stare at this magazine I was holding. Someone was across the street that day when Alex actually got down on one knee and slid that ring on my finger. Whoever took the picture was behind me. You could see the gray shirt I wore and Alex's smiling face as if he was the happiest man on the planet to be putting a ring on my finger.

The title of the magazine was: *Hottest Lawyer and Bachelor, No Longer a Bachelor?*.

And when you flipped further into the magazine, there we were again. The same picture was on the front and the side column read:

Hottest Lawyer of New York, no longer a bachelor as Alexander Blair gets down on one knee to propose to Abigail McCall, daughter of David McCall of McCall Firm. David McCall is a Criminal Justice attorney, who hired Alexander Blair right out of Harvard Law. Alexander Blair graduated early and at the top of his class. Insights from David McCall's wife, Carol, who was happy to announce the engagement of the two young love birds. "They are extremely happy to have found each other and they are a perfect match," Carol McCall tells us. They are planning a summer get away in Paris, France as soon as young Ms. Abigail McCall is done with her semester at Juilliard for Ballet.

And then the stupid magazine talked about my dad's firm and taking Alex on as a partner. I wanted nothing more than to tear up this stupid magazine to pieces, but I couldn't – I had to show Tucker first. He was just going to the store and then he was going to come back. Right? I grabbed my cell and dialed Tucker's number. It rang and rang, then finally went to voicemail. What if he saw the magazine and freaked? He could be gone. I panicked as I put on my jacket and raced out of the apartment.

The air was a little cold; the sky was cloudy as I made my way to the little store just down the street to where Tucker said he was going to go. I passed a newspaper stand that had that stupid picture up everywhere.

Yep, he definitely saw it if he passed by here.

I made it to the store and started looking around for Tucker or any sign of his gray hoodie. I started going down the aisles and back up again, still not being able to find him. When he wasn't in the store, I started walking back to my apartment. Hearing laughter down one of the alleyways, I turned to see a group of guys all in a circle. My heart sped up when I saw a very familiar gray hoodie standing in the middle.

"This gonna be enough, dude?" one guy said, examining the product in his hand.

Tucker nodded his head. "Yeah, contact Ethan if you want more."

When a gasp left my mouth, Tucker looked up and saw my face. The little store was in between my apartment and my parents' house. Their house was only about a seven minute walk from my apartment, but when you're running, it only took about four.

"Gabs!"

Tucker was chasing me; the last time I ran from him, he didn't, but this time he did. It started to rain lightly at first, but it seemed the harder I ran, the more rain came down.

"Gabs, stop!" Thunder cracked through the sky at the same time he yelled. My hair stuck to my face as I ran across the street, making cabs slam on their brakes and honk at me.

"Gabs, stop!" Tucker was gaining on me. I ran up the five stairs and into the house. The doorman saw me and let me by, knowing who I was. But when Tucker came to the front of the building, the doorman stopped him and then threatened to call the cops if he didn't go away.

"Gabs!" Tucker yelled.

I skipped up the stairs and into the foyer of the living room, past the kitchen, up another flight of stairs and into my old room. I slammed the door and made it just in time to my old tainted toilet and threw up.

"Abigail?" My dad's voice called out to me and I ignored him. I rested my head on the cold porcelain and heard my bedroom door open and then footsteps enter my bathroom.

"Abigail, what's wrong?" He gently rubbed my back and I cried.

"Daddy." And I flung myself into his chest and he held me as I cried and cried so hard I passed out cold.

I woke up with a little hand holding mine and rubbing my little belly, and I met Jade's wonderful ice blue eyes caked with black makeup. I sat up and embraced her so tightly and I heard the air leave her lungs.

"Gabs, you look like shit."

I laughed into her shoulder. "I've missed you, too!"

Our little reunion was interrupted when Carol came bursting in my room, mad as hell, too. She looked like she hadn't slept in days; her hair was disheveled and her clothes were wrinkly. Carol never let herself get this bad.

"Abigail, you need to start packing," Carol announced as she walked into my closet.

"What?"

Carol didn't answer me; I just heard my hangers banging around in my closet as she pulled my clothes from them. I got up off my bed and went to her. "What are you talking about, Carol?"

"Abigail. Enough!" she yelled at me.

I just stood there, wide-eyed. "No! I'm not packing until you tell me what's going on."

That got her attention. "I'm not going to let that...that...trailer trash, no good kid mess with your life. I won't have it. I will not allow it in my house under my roof. He already made you quit Juilliard, and for what? So he could leave you knocked up and alone to go deal drugs? No! I will not allow something like that to happen to you. Now pack!" Carol threw some of my clothes she had in her hands at me and stormed out of my room.

I dropped down to my knees in my closet. Why was everything in this stupid world ruining my chance with Tucker? It was ridiculous.

"Gabs," Jade called out to me, but once again, I was frozen and couldn't move. I heard her steps as she moved cautiously to me and started rubbing my back. I turned to her and cried into her chest.

"Jade," I mumbled

She smoothed my hair down my back. "I know, I know."

Did she know? Did she understand?

"Who called you to come over?"

Jade smoothed down my hair on my back, giving me the only comfort that was missing in my life right now. "Your dad did. Said that something was wrong. I passed Tucker on the way in; he was begging me to have you come out and talk with him. Gabs, tell me what happened now."

I sat up and wiped the fallen tears off my face. "He was dealing! After he promised me he was done. I can't be around that crap, Jade, I can't."

"Okay, drama queen, no need to shout. I'm right here," Jade said while pulling on her ear. I couldn't help the giggle that escaped my mouth. Jade leaned in and hugged me again.

"Jade, everything is falling apart. Everyone thinks I'm marrying Alex; it was in a magazine."

"I know, it's a shitty situation. Now listen to me." Jade cupped my wet cheeks and made me look at her in the eyes. Her soft ice blue eyes were rimmed with black eyeliner. "I love you, Gabs. Losing Rachel sucked, but I can't lose you, too. I'll go insane. This one time, I think you should listen to that step monster of yours. Pack and go with them, clear your damn head. Get away—I think it's best for you and the baby right now. All this pressure with, Carol, Alex wanting to marry you and Tucker, it's gonna kill ya." I couldn't help but laugh again. Jade ignored me and continued on. "The semester is over. I even talked with Madame Ava, too. She said she hopes to see you next year and wishes nothing but the best for you and come on, Alex is rushing this. They are trying to pressure you."

More tears ran down my face as I thought about Madame Ava. She was a brilliant teacher who made me a stronger and better ballerina. I would never forget her.

"Do you hear me Gabs?" I nodded in her hands. "Good, I'll help you."

Jade moved at a snail's pace with my clothes, putting them in my half-packed suitcase from Carol's attempt earlier. I heard a couple of sniffs from inside the closet as she gathered more of my clothes, and when I asked if she was crying, she yelled at me to shut up. Me leaving Jade behind was going to be hard on her; she needed to keep going, keep her head up high.

"Are you going to still see Dr. Walters?"

"Yeah, probably. I need to see someone if you're going to be gone. I'm gonna move out of the apartment; I can't stay there by myself."

I completely understood that. Not only would she be alone, she made memories there – memories that would drive her crazy. I reached for Jade and hugged her as tightly as I could, and for the first time, she hugged me back just as tight.

A soft knock sounded at my door, I quickly wiped my face and called out "come in" and my dad opened my door.

"You ready, angel?" he asked, pushing his glasses up his nose.

Well, I guess that sums it up about Carol already telling my dad that I was packing. I believed it was good for me to get away – get away from all the crazy things in my life. I wouldn't be gone forever; I couldn't keep Tucker's baby away from him. I wouldn't be that person to keep their child away from their parent.

"Yeah," I breathed out and Jade hugged me from behind again. I patted her hands and this time, I did hear her soft cries into my shoulder. "I'll be right there, Daddy."

"It's just like the olden days were a girl gets knocked up and they sweep her off to the country. Your parents are fast movers," Jade said.

I turned in her arms while we fell to the floor, just hugging and rocking back and forth. This time, it was me who cupped Jade's face to look at her – she had depression written all over it. My palms were soaked with her tears.

"Now you listen to me, Jaiden Monroe. You stay strong, no more hurting yourself, you have any problems, and I'm one phone call away. Okay?" She nodded. "I'm not going to be gone forever, just think of it like a spring vacation. I'll call you as soon as I land back in New York; you can even come get me from the airport."

"No, I'm not your maid service." I wiped Jade's tears and tried to fix her blackened makeup, but really, I think I was just making it worse. I hugged Jade one more time before she walked out my room. I walked down the stairs to the living room where my dad stood waiting for me; his back was to us and he was on the phone. I had to thank the Greek Gods that Carol wasn't with him. I don't think I could take her right now.

"Carol, don't you dare do that. No, you stop right now and you head straight for the airport. I'm not kidding, Carol, you...hello? Damn it."

I speed walked over to my dad, who was mad, and of course, it was Carol who pissed him off.

"Daddy?" He jumped at my touch on his arm. "What's wrong?"

He exhaled, "Nothing, Angel. You all ready to go?"

Something was wrong, as his face was flushed and his brows were beading with sweat. This only happened when he was mad or in the court room. He reached for my bags that Jade helped me with and we made our way towards the front door. For once, I was hoping that Tucker wouldn't be on the other side. He broke a huge promise to me.

On my dad's heels, with Jade holding my hand, I braced myself for Tucker's quick approach to me as we made our way out the front door. I held my breath as we took our steps out to the busy New York traffic with no sign of Tucker. I glanced up, and then down the sidewalk. Nope. He wasn't here. I even looked across the street to see if maybe he was waiting for me. Nope. Not there either. Inside I was happy that he wasn't here, but there was that tiny part inside that wished he was.

Ugh! I'm such a big mess right now. Back and forth, back and forth.

My dad loaded our entire luggage into the trunk of my dad's silver Bentley. It was the exact same as Carol's black luxury car. I faced Jade again who was biting the crap out of her bottom lip.

"That's a bad habit, you know." I eyed her swollen lip and she let if free from her teeth. Jade didn't give me a sharp remark like she usually does – just stared at me.

"I'll call you when I get there, okay?" She nodded and I hugged her again. "Unless you want to come with me, because I can hide you in my suitcase." She let out a small laugh.

"That sounds so tempting, but Carol is worse than Stella. So no, I'm gonna pass on that. But I have a gift for you. This is one of my favorite books and authors."

Jade pulled out a book from her purse with a violin on it; it was a beautiful cover.

"Thank you." I turned to start getting in the car, but putting the book in my purse quickly, I saw something that caught my eye. Reaching in, I grabbed something of Jade's – something that we both shared in the past and something that brought us together in the first place.

I quickly turned and said, "I think you'll need these." I tossed the unopened pack of cigarettes to her and she caught them. "I heard they calm the nerves." I gave her a wink and slid into the soft leather seats.

The drive to the airport seemed to take forever. My dad repeatedly called someone on his cell. My guess was Carol. That damn woman had a mind of her own and she wasn't going to let anyone stop her from getting in the way of what she wants. Only about twenty seconds after the car pulled out from the curb, my phone chimed and it was Jade.

Jade: Thanks for the smokes, my nerves are settled ;)

Me: Happy to have helped

Jade: Bow chicka wow wow

I laughed.

Me: lol...What?

Jade: Nothing, dumbass.... Call when you land and enjoy your reading material

Me: okay! Love ya

Jade: you too!

The traffic hit really bad on the bridge heading into The New York Airport. We sat for a good twenty minutes in the same spot. My dad was still calling someone on his phone while yelling at Jordan, our driver, to hurry and that we had a flight to catch. Poor Jordan – he couldn't move the traffic for the life of him. I sat back and flipped through my phone and stopped when I came across a picture that Jade took of me while Tucker was giving me my tattoo on my hip. My face was scrunched up in pain with the heel of my hands digging into my eyes.

Yep, that hurt.

Even though it wasn't a big tattoo, it still hurt. I stared at the scripted letters of 'Juilliard' in black ink with the little pretty pink ballet shoes. I wasn't supposed to get a tattoo, but before I even found out I was pregnant, I'd had a feeling this was going to be my one year at Juilliard. I wanted to make it a memory. It was the memory I wanted; now it was etched into me, so I would always remember what made me so happy once upon a time.

Traffic started to move again, but was as slow as could be. Our car finally pulled up to the curb and my dad rushed out.

"Jordan, the trunk!" he yelled around the noisy taxis.

The trunk popped while Jordan and my dad started pulling out our luggage. My phone started ringing with Tucker's ringtone; my stomach was a bundle of tied up knots as I answered it.

"Hello?"

"Where are you?"

I sniffed; I was going to cry just from hearing his voice. "The airport."

I heard glass shatter. "What why? Where are you going?" My dad took my spare hand and pulling me through the doors of the noisy airport.

"I'm going away with my parents."

"Fuck!" Tucker yelled loud enough that I had to pull the phone away from my ear. "Abigail, don't take my kid away from me."

I shook my head as if he could see me. "I wouldn't do something like that to you, Tucker."

"Yeah, you won't, but what about your dad, even Carol? They have power and money."

I glanced up at my dad who was staring down at me. I knew he just heard Tucker's words.

"Tucker, I have to go now."

"Not until you tell me where you're going."

We walked onto the escalators, heading towards security. "Paris."

Silence and then a soft knock on a door on Tucker's end. "Gabs, you leave the country, I can't come after you. I hope you understand that's the decision you're making." I heard the squeaky front door open as he hung up on me. I walked through the rest of security thinking about what Tucker told me. He couldn't chase after me if I left the country. He was right; I wasn't just making this decision for me but our baby as well.

"David McCall?" I glanced at my dad who was on his lawyer phone. "No, I don't think it's a good idea. Just leave her alone for now." He paused and I studied his face, his brows drawn together. Even I knew this wasn't good. "Listen to me; I don't care what she told you. We are taking her away for a little bit to help clear her head."

He was talking about me. I bet it was to Alex. My dad looked at me with an apologetic look and pushed his glasses back up his nose. We continued to walk through the airport to our gate as my dad still muttered into the phone. I fumbled on my phone and decided to text Jade to let her know that I got to the airport and I wanted to send one more text to Tucker.

Me: Tucker, I'm sorry. But I have to go. Bye.

My phone chimed back not even thirty seconds later.

Tucker: Don't do this, Abigail.

Tears slowly streaked down my face as I stuffed my phone into my purse. All I had now were memories of me and Tucker. I didn't want to leave him, but I felt as if I didn't have a choice. Carol and my dad held a lot of power over me. I knew that it sounded extremely stupid and a poor excuse, but my dad was a very powerful lawyer who could put Tucker away for a long time if anything happened to me or to his grandchild. My dad could be so ruthless and could convince any jury of anything. I found my iPod and put my headphones in to block out my thoughts, and of course, the one song started playing that reminded me so much of Tucker, *My Boo* by Usher. This song was us, in and out. My hand caressed my little baby bump while my dad held my other hand. The cover of the book caught my eye. I pulled it out, listening to the heartbreaking words as I flipped through the pages.

My dad tapped on my shoulder and took out my right earphone. "Abigail, you know how much I love you, right?" I nodded. "I'm doing this to protect you, angel. I don't want you to hurt from this boy. And you must know that Alex will be coming along with us."

"Dad," I groaned while taking out my other earphone. "I don't want Alex here. I don't want him. Can't you guys just stop it?" I was stomping my foot like a child.

"I know, it's all Carol's doing. Told him that we were heading to Paris early and he says he wants to come."

"Ugh, this sucks. Dad, he just wants in the firm. Don't you get that? He doesn't want me anymore than I want him. He just wants to be tied to you through me." My voice was getting louder with every word. I stood up from my chair and went to stand in front of the windows, watching the planes taxi around. I saw Alex's approach to my dad who stood up and shook hands with him. This was it; I was going to be forced in another situation I dreaded. I had to change it. The book was still in my hands as I continued to turn page by page, not really reading but just taking in the words of the author. It was then I read a paragraph, a paragraph that could mean a thousand different things to everyone.

"Fascinating how much life can change in twenty-four hours...how circumstances can draw two people together in the strangest ways. We're often so wrapped up in our own little minds, we fail to see the very thing happening around us, literally."
-Distractions by JL Brooks

Those words hit my heart with crushing force, turning my body inside out to help me see the bigger picture in my life. My tears leaked out and hit the cream pages. I looked back up at the moving planes.

Was I wrapped up in my own little mind so much that I failed to see the Tucker I wanted to see? I was failing to see what was happening around me. With Alex and Carol, she was trying everything she could to get me to marry Alex. He didn't even want me and I was having another man's baby.

I couldn't do this. Decisions had to be made.

Chapter Twenty-Three

It felt like forever, waiting for Carol to finally join us at the gate, my brain racking so hard in my head with decisions that had to be made right this minute. When she finally showed up, she looked flushed and out of breath. She was up to something. Alex barely talked to me as we waited. I didn't want to give the impression that I wanted us to become an item, because I didn't. I paced back and forth, waiting for our plane to start loading passengers; the longer I waited, the more nervous I got, and more thoughts entered my mind that I was making a huge mistake. I gripped the book as tight as I could; my knuckles were starting to turn white.

You leave the country, I can't come after you. I hope you understand the decision you're making.

Tucker wouldn't be able to come after me and that scared me. What girl didn't want a boy chasing after her? It was the true kind of love story when any boy would come screaming through the airport, looking for the love of his life as she was getting ready to board a plane. I wanted it. I wasn't going to get it, though.

"Good evening, ladies and gentlemen. We would like to start boarding for flight 4432 to Paris, France. We will start by boarding all first class passengers."

The lady over the intercom announced for our group to start boarding. I didn't move from my chair as Carol, Alex and my dad stood. Alex held a hand out to me and I stared at it. My time with Tucker flashed before my hands as I stared hard at Alex's hand. If I took it, this was it. I couldn't take it back. I put the book back in my purse and clutched the straps so tightly. I glanced at Carol who was glaring at me.

"Abigail, don't be rude." I started to shake from the anger starting to boil in my veins. I wasn't being rude. I was debating on a decision that didn't affect only me but my child too...Tucker's baby.

Carol walked over and shook my shoulders as if she was trying to shake me awake from whatever world I was in. "Abigail, I went to Tucker before I came here. I told him that you were leaving him. Marrying Alex, it's done. He doesn't want you. Now, get on that plane right now."

I sobbed. I really hoped none of her words were true. I didn't want it to be. I couldn't. I had to change it. Carol let me go with a little shove, but I didn't fall. I didn't belong here, not with Carol or Alex. This was no longer my world.

But he wasn't coming.

My heart was breaking for him to come to me, take me away from this world I no longer belonged in; I only belonged with Tucker.

"Abigail, come," Alex ordered to me, but I closed my eyes and tried to picture Tucker running through the airport.

"This is the last call for all first class passengers to board the plane," the lady announced over the speaker again.

"Abigail. Come, right now." Opening my eyes, I glared at him, the perfect Alex who everyone loved and adored. Alex, the perfect lawyer who didn't want anything to do with me, but wanted me to become a living object at his side. I wasn't going to do that. I pulled my phone out of my purse and slammed it down on the seat, making all my things scatter around everyone's feet.

No! I wasn't going to be a Carol! I screamed at myself and took off through the airport.

"Abigail McCall!" Carol yelled after me, but I couldn't stop; I wouldn't. I belonged with Tucker, even if he didn't want me. I needed him.

I left Alex, Carol and my dad at the gate to the plane and ran like hell through the New York Airport. I was passing people so fast, they blurred by. I jumped over some luggage that was lying right in the way of my path, but I kept on running and I wasn't going to stop. My feet hit the carpet of the mini security pathway for the first class passengers as a security guard turned around in my path and I collided into his strong chest.

"Miss, be careful," he growled as I passed his body. I dialed Tucker's number again as I stopped and waited in line for a cab, holding my phone up to my ear as my other hand rubbed my barely showing belly. The phone still rang – no voicemail was picking up, nothing.

Grumbled angrily, I hit the red button to disconnect the call.

"Abigail!"

Looking over my shoulder at the call of my name. Alex's face was red from anger as he ran towards me.

Crap!

I finally got a guy to chase after me in the airport, but it wasn't the guy I wanted. I pushed and raced through the sea of people waiting in line in front of me.

"Excuse me, emergency!" I yelled to get people to move. "Come on, people, move!" Some people pushed me back, called me a line cutter, but I didn't care, I just needed to get as far away as I possibly could from Alex. The look on his face wasn't pleasant looking.

The first taxi I saw had an elderly lady trying to get in it. I couldn't push her and take her cab, so I stopped and waited. People still gave me small pushes on my back while hissing at me. When I finally came to the top of the line, I looked back, seeing Alex pushing through the same crowd I just passed.

Crap!

Very quickly, another cab came up to the curb and I made my way to the guy holding the door, who tried to shut the door at my approach.

"No, no, no. Girlie, get in the back of the line." He pointed to the crowd behind me, some of them yelling, "Yeah!"

Breathlessly I said, "You don't understand, I'm being chased. I *need* to get out of here," I pleaded with the guy. Looking behind me again, I saw Alex gaining on me the longer I stood here. "Please!" I saw the guy's eyes move in the distance over my shoulder, then someone grabbed my arm, hard.

He spun me around. His blue eyes were deep with fury and dark. "Abigail, what are you doing?" Alex yelled in my face.

"Let go, Alex!" I tried wrenching my arm away from him, but he gripped harder on me and squeezed so hard I cried out in pain.

"Alex, stop! You're hurting me!" I cried and he ignored my cries, turning us around to start dragging me back to the front entrance of the airport. We bumped into people as I fought against his hold. People were gasping at the scene we were making, but no one was helping me. I twisted my arm, but he gripped harder. His looks were starting to scare me so badly; I knew he was going to hurt me. I yelped one more time as he bent my arm behind my back to hold me still. My shoulder aching, I ended up on my toes to help the burning pain in my shoulder.

"Alex, stop!"

"HEY!" someone called out. Alex and I both turned around to see the guy who was stopping me from getting the cab, standing off to the side of us. His fist cocked back and came swinging, hitting Alex right in the jaw. Alex went down, not letting go of my arm and I fell on top of him. Pain shot through from my elbow up to my shoulder, and I cried out. I looked up to see the man who hit Alex reach at me and I cringed back, afraid he would hit me, too.

"Come on, girlie." He suddenly scooped me up and jogged towards the line of cabs waiting. Another guy was holding the door open as the other slid me in the back seat and buckled me up.

"I'm sorry, girlie, that I didn't help you. Here," He held out some money for me to take.

I shook my head, "No, I can't take your money." Tears streaked down my face from the pain in my arm. The guy didn't listen and tossed the bills over the seat to the driver, "Take her anywhere. GO!" He slammed the door and the cab screeched away from the curb. I didn't dare to look back and see Alex standing at the curb.

"Where to, girlie?"

I looked up and met the cabbie's eyes in the rearview mirror. "Bushwick, Brooklyn please." I sat back and winced at the pain radiating up my arm. My cell rang and I fished it out of my pocket; I groaned when I saw Carol's name across the screen, deciding if I should actually take the call, or just toss my phone out the window all together.

"Hello?"

"Abigail, don't you dare go to him," Carol yelled. I had to pull the phone away from my ear at her screeching voice on the receiving end. "What are you thinking? You get back here right now!"

"I'm going, Carol, I love him."

"He can't take care of you or that baby of his. You know he can't! He deals drugs, Abigail. He's a loser."

I rolled my eyes. "Yes he can, and money doesn't mean everything, Carol. I want to be with him, it's him I choose," I snapped back at her. I heard Carol protest and some ruffles like someone was trying to take the phone away from her.

"Carol, enough!" I heard my dad yell, and then he came on the line, "Abigail?"

I got nervous, afraid he was going to tell me to come back as well, "Yes, Daddy?" I gripped the phone and waited for his response.

"Tell Kyle hello, and be careful."

"Daddy, I need his address. I don't know where he lives."

More tears shed from my eyes as I hung up the phone and stuffed it back into my pocket.

The ride to Brooklyn was very uncomfortable. I rested my head on the back and watched the passing buildings of Tucker's rundown neighborhood. If I had one word to describe Brushwick, it would be "scary". This was the scariest place; no wonder when I asked Tucker to take me to his home, he refused. He flat out told me, "You can't go there, ever." Now I understood what he meant; I was afraid of the group of people we passed on the sidewalk. I was afraid of the broken glass windows in the graffiti covered buildings.

When we came to a stop at his building, I was afraid to get out of the cab, but I couldn't stop myself now. I stepped on the sidewalk, placing my hand on my little baby bump as I made my way to the front door. I tried to open it, but it was locked. I saw the little numbers of the apartment number and read Tori

Tucker 416. I pushed the little button and the deep buzz sounded in my ears.

"Yea." A very descrambled female voice came over the speaker.

"Is Tucker home?"

"Who is this?"

"It's Abigail McCall. Is Tucker here?" I rested my hand on the brick wall, trying not to groan because of the pain in my elbow and shoulder. My hair curtained around my face as I waited. The door suddenly opened and a group of guys almost ran me over. One bumped into me and I hissed in pain. They turned.

"Oh, who you here to see?" one asked.

I had wedged myself between the door and a corner of the building. I shut my eyes and that's when I heard his voice.

"Hey!"

I opened my eyes to see Tucker standing there at the end of the pathway, wearing his gray hoodie with his hood pulled up. The guys parted around me as Tucker approached us.

"Oh hey, Tucker. This one yours?" The same guy that talked to me asked Tucker.

"Yeah, back off. She's mine."

My Tucker I fell in love with over six months ago was back, the father of our child growing inside me. A sob escaped my lips as I rushed over to him and crashed into his chest, crying on his shoulder as he held me tight against him. The other guys walked around us, leaving me be.

"Where have you been?" I mumbled into the fabric of his hoodie. "I have been trying to call you," I said as more sobs came out.

"I threw my phone at the wall and I just went to the bank. I thought you were at the airport; you were going to leave me. I thought I lost you for good. Gabs, let me explain what you saw. I'm not gonna lie. Yes, I was dealing, but I was getting rid of it all. I told them not to contact me – to go straight to Ethan."

I pulled back. "I know. I panicked. I'm sorry. I could never leave you, Tucker. I love you and I want to be with you. We are going to be a family." I took his hand to lay it on my little round stomach. "We want you, only you. I don't want anything else besides you," His hand rubbed my belly in little circles and his eyes filled up with tears. He looked relieved, almost as if a weight had been lifted off his shoulders. He let out a breath and looked at me in the eyes.

"I think this is yours." Tucker placed my now repaired snowflake necklace in my palm. Tears streaked down my face. He clasped it around my neck where it belonged. "Marry me, Gabs. Right now, no more running. You're mine and only mine."

I couldn't stop my head from nodding; I didn't even want a night to sleep on it. I wanted to marry him and make him my husband more than anything, and no one could stop me, not Carol, not Alex – nobody.

Tucker grabbed my hand as we ran to the moving taxi going down the street, and when we climbed in, Tucker said, "New York courthouse, please." I was all smiles as the cab drove us to the courthouse. I called Jade and told her our plans; she and Jett were going to meet us there to stand as our witnesses. Jett even said he had a surprise for us.

Tucker and I couldn't stop kissing each other, giving the cab driver a show all the way to the courthouse. His hand never left my belly, either. He rubbed it over and over while sighing in my mouth. And when he leaned more into my side and put some pressure down on my elbow, I winced and pulled back.

Tucker took a look at my elbow and shoulder as I told him everything that happened at the airport. I tried to bend in a way so I could see my elbow, but I couldn't see the gash, so he described to me.

"I don't think it's broken, but we'll get it looked at, I promise," he said as he kissed my forehead. I really didn't care if we got it looked at. I just wanted to get married.

We pulled up outside the courthouse and I spotted Jade and Jett at the top of the stairs. They both embraced us in hugs.

"It's about time you pulled your head outta your ass," Jade said in my ear and then whisked me off to the bathroom.

Jade had a white garment bag over her arm, which she handed to me while she unzipped it; inside laid a beautiful little white summer dress, which I knew well, and knew who it belonged to before. It was Rachel's dress.

"Rachel would have wanted you to wear it," she told me, brushing out my hair. Yes, she would have and she would be here getting me all ready with a cake load of makeup and pulling the crap out of my hair. I stifled a giggle at the memories I made with the mad redheaded girl.

Jade left my hair loose and I slipped in the white gown with matching white pumps. My heels clicked on the marble flooring as we approached a courthouse clerk who told us where to find the boys and the judge. The courthouse was all stone marble with deep dark wood for all the doors. Walking up to a metal detector, I went through it just fine, but Jade had trouble with her belt. A security guard helped us and then led the way to another door to another guard.

He nodded at us, "Miss Abigail, I presume?"

Breathlessly, I managed to get out a very quiet, "Yes," while death gripping Jade's hand.

"Right in here, ma'am." He opened the door with a big smile. The first person I saw was Tucker; he was dressed in an all-black suit and his wild long hair was slicked back, hands laced together in front of him. Anxiety raced through my body as I wanted to skip down to him. A judge stood up from behind his desk, dressed all in black with a white collar; I spotted Jett to Tucker's right and Jade held my hand as I walked the short distance to my knight, who I would always love and adore. Tucker's hand reached out for me and I took it as he pulled me tightly to his side, wrapping an arm around my back. My eyes couldn't leave Tucker's as the judge told us to repeat the vows, and he mouthed to me, "You're beautiful and I love you," through the entire process.

"Do you have rings, young man?" We both looked at the judge and we laughed. We didn't even think about the *rings*.

"No," we both said in unison, still laughing.

"Yes, you do," Jett announced from the side. Jade took my hand and pressed a cold circle in my palm, while Jett did the same thing to Tucker.

"Abigail." I looked at the judge. "Repeat after me, my dear," I nodded and looked back into Tucker's blue sapphire eyes and I repeated the judge's words:

"I, Abigail McCall, take thee, Kyle Tucker, to be my partner in life. I will cherish you and love you today, tomorrow and for always. From this day on, I choose you to be my husband," I said and slid the cool silver band onto Tucker's ring finger.

I heard a little sniffle from Jade and looked over at them. She was leaning up against Jett, her head on his shoulder, holding a tissue to her chest. I hadn't seen her this happy since Rachel died. I looked back to Tucker, who had the biggest smile on his face.

"Very good. Kyle." He looked at the judge. "Repeat after me."

"I, Kyle Tucker, take thee, Abigail McCall, to be my partner in life. I will cherish you and love you today, tomorrow and for always. From this day on, I choose you to be my wife." We both looked down to watch Tucker slide the little matching silver band on to my finger; it was perfect. Tucker cupped my cheeks, meeting his eyes that were glossed over with unshed tears of happiness. "Abigail, I promise to love you for always. To love our baby, to always be there for you, never to leave you, to take care of you, no matter what. I'll always be here, baby girl."

The judge cleared his throat, "You may kiss your wife, Kyle."

Then our lips collided for the first time as husband and wife. I couldn't be happier to have chosen the right man for me. I knew that Tucker was going to be the best husband and father I knew he could be. People in the little room applauded for us as we continued to kiss each other, so soft and tender of a kiss. One person was still clapping. I glanced back to see my dad and Carol at the door, my dad the only one applauding for us.

My dad walked towards us with Carol on his heels, and not a very agreeable look on her face. "Welcome to the family, son," he said and my dad hugged Tucker with multiple pats on the back. Carol walked up to me with a sad smile. "Abigail, if this is what you want, it's your decision. Not a great or wise one, but hopefully you'll learn one day."

"I'm happy. That's all that matters to me." I stood my ground with her. My dad engulfed me in a strong bear hug and dragged me away rather quickly to the side of the room. I looked back to Tucker and Carol, who looked like she was apologizing to him while Tucker looked really mad with his arms crossed over his chest.

"Abigail, I wanted to let you know that I fired Alex," my head snapped back to his face.

"What? Why?" I asked with my mouth hanging open. I hope it wasn't because I decided not to go with Alex to Paris.

"Airport security told me what had happened when we came out. I found Alex and fired him on the spot for treating you the way he did." He exhaled, "I'm so sorry, sweetheart," Then hugged me again, as he got a little choked up in my hair from his tears.

Tucker cleared his throat and my dad stepped aside, lifting up his glasses and wiping away the tears from his cheeks, "Sir, I plan on taking care of your daughter, more than you will ever know. I promise," Tucker told him and my dad clapped him on the shoulder.

"From father to new son-in-law, you clean up your act. That's my daughter and grandbaby. I expect you guys to be over every Sunday for dinner once that baby comes. You got it?"

"Of course, Daddy," I said kissing his cheek. My dad left Tucker and me in the corner of the judge's little office.

"Thanks for the call, Harry," I heard my dad say, and then hugged the judge. Of course, the judge called my dad. He probably saw McCall on the list and panicked, knowing how ruthless my dad could be; my guess is he called him right away to get him over here.

"Any regrets, Mrs. Tucker?"

I looked back into Kyle's warm blue eyes with nothing but love and no regret whatsoever. "None, Kyle, absolutely none."

"Kyle huh?" he asked, cupping my cheek and I nodded.

"Kyle Tucker. My Kyle Tucker," I said into his hand, and then I pushed up on my toes to gently touch my lips to his. I loved him and this is where I belonged, with him and our little baby that was on the way.

Epilogue

~Tucker~

Three Years Later

"This going to be enough?" I asked the manager of the new apartment building, that I just put a down payment on.

"Should be," he answered, clapping my shoulder. "Congratulations!"

I glanced up at the man with a wide smile. "Thanks." It felt pretty good to finally own my own place, something I thought would never happen. The manager, Saul, left me alone to take more looks around. It was a pretty decent sized place with two bedrooms, two baths and was clear across the city. Gabs would like it here; she sure would be surprised on how we could afford something like this, but what she didn't know was that while Gabs was going to the airport, Carol had a little visit with me, trying to pay me to stay away. Of course, I didn't have a chance to tell her to fuck off before my mother reached out and snapped the ten thousand dollar check from her spoiled rich fingers. I pocketed that money for a good three years, letting it grow in the bank so I could support Gabs and our family, just like I promised her.

My cell started ringing as I locked up the apartment door; I pulled out my phone to confirm it was indeed Mrs. Tucker herself.

"Hello?"

"Hey babe. You almost here? I'm so ready to be outta here." I could hear the rambunctious little kids in her studio, all ready to be done and go home.

Taking the stairs so she wouldn't hear the ding of the elevator, I said, "Yep, on my way. I have a surprise for you."

She inhaled a breath. Gabs always loved surprises, even if it was the smallest things. One more thing you could add to the list of why I love her so damn much.

"I'll be there soon. Be ready to go."

"Okay, I love you."

"I love you, too, Gabs."

I hung up the phone and skipped down the six flights of stairs. I hailed a cab and told him the address of the little studio Gabs ran with Jade. It was Jade's idea to start up the *Little Ballerinas*. Jade would handle the bookkeeping and Gabs would teach.

Jade and Jett were the awesome couple of the group – always smacking some sense into us when Gabs and I would fight. They were happy together and they were perfect. Jade still had problems with her dad and step mom from what Jett told me. And they didn't like Jett too much, either, but that didn't stop them from getting engaged. Jade started planning a rock and roll wedding – something Gabs wasn't happy about. She said she wasn't going to wear black to her wedding. While Jett and I were busy tattooing all day, Jade and Gabs were together, going to meet some doctor. Gabs didn't really go into any detail about why Jade went, but Gabs said it was helping with her throwing up thing. It was fine while she was pregnant; she only threw up when something didn't agree with her and the baby, but whenever Carol was around, that changed. Gabs told me that she felt she had control over it now and felt better about herself.

When I arrived at the studio, parents were there picking up their little children. Checking my watch to notice that I still had five minutes before Gabs class got over, I entered the building and walked down the little hallway to the five year old ballet class. I leaned on the doorway to watch as my beautiful wife helped the little girls bend their knees and keep their arms out in front of them, then back up without them falling.

My eyes scanned the room as I looked for a particular little girl somewhere. I found her standing behind her mom, holding her purple blanket in one hand and twirling her finger around in her blonde hair with the other. I whistled quietly to get her attention and when she heard me, she screamed out, "Daddy!" causing some of the girls to fall from being startled so badly. Gabs looked over at me with that same look I fell in love with four years ago. I winked at her, and just that easy, she blushed.

My legs were tackled as my little girl hugged them so tightly, "Daddy, up, up, up."

Reaching down, I picked up our gorgeous daughter. "And how is little miss Mia doing today?" I asked while giving her a kiss on her forehead.

"I'm mkay, Daddy. Mamma say she tired."

"Oh she is, huh? Well we better get her home then." I set Mia down and she grabbed my hand to watch Gabs close her class for the day. After Gabs found out she was pregnant, she quit her one year at Juilliard and went to the local college to get her teaching degree in dance.

Even though she had given up on her dream to have our daughter, she wanted to at least teach ballet. We did fine as a couple. David was livid when he looked at the books to see a ten thousand dollar check written out to me. He announced that he was done and

Carol divorced him a little while later. About a year after their divorce, Gabs had lunch with Trish, Rachel's mom. Gabs came home with a plan to set them up and they had been together ever since. Trish was still having a hard time dealing with Rachel's death, and Brad, too. I think it was hard on all of us. But David and Trish were good together. Skinner was sentenced to eight years in Ricker's for the murder of Rachel. Trish was happy he was put behind bars. My mom, on the other hand, wasn't.

After Skinner was sent away, she didn't have drugs right in the living room like before and I wouldn't go get any for her. I thought maybe she would stop and get clean, but going a couple of weeks being clean, then finally getting that amount you used to shoot up, will shut your eyes forever. And that was my mom; she never got a chance to meet our little Mia. Brad on the other hand went off grid after Rachel died. He got extremely drunk the night of Rachel's funeral and professed his love for the only redheaded girl who would only have his heart. We haven't heard anything from him since then. David even tried to a search to see if he was hauled off to jail or prison, but no such luck. Brad was gone.

David tried every Sunday during dinner to get me to go to college and work at his firm, even offering to pay for it, but I couldn't see myself being a lawyer. Trish would always smack his arm and tell him to mind his own business. Trish hated me at the beginning, but she softened pretty fast. Trish was very thoughtful when it was with Gabs or David. Trish even surprised the two of them by taking them to the cemetery to see Shannon's grave. I kept my distance, holding Mia with Trish at my side as David and Gabs held hands, saying some peaceful words with Shannon's headstone. Gabs and I visited her every Mother's Day.

"You okay?"

I looked up to see Gabs walking over to Mia and me.

"Yeah, just thinking." I smiled.

Gabs leaned down to put on Mia's jacket, but before she could, I cupped her cheeks and kissed her lips tenderly. Her eyes slowly opened as she sighed when our lips parted.

"I love you, Abigail Tucker, for always,"

She beamed the biggest smile. "I love you too, Kyle Tucker. For always."

"What bout me?" little Mia wined at us, pulling on the edge of my leather jacket. I loved our daughter – she was our best mistake. She was just the perfect mix between us; she had Gabs' blonde hair with my blue eyes. She was the most gorgeous little girl; she was going to kill the hearts of boys – if I let any boys come that close to her.

We closed down the studio and took another cab back to the new apartment building. My knee started to bounce with excitement; I couldn't help it, and I loved surprising her with just about anything.

Mia sat in the middle of us coloring and I watched my beautiful wife help her and hold the crayons for her. She looked up at me with a smile as I winked at her .Cupping her cheeks as she nuzzled my hand, she then gave my palm a quick kiss. Gabs reaching in her pink shirt to pull out the snowflake necklace that I had given her on our first Christmas still made me smile when I would catch her sliding it back and forth on the chain, kiss it and go back doing to whatever she was doing. She loved that necklace, and would never take it off.

After Mia was born, Gabs decided that she wanted another tattoo, but told me I could do whatever I wanted, as long as it was "pretty", she said. I drew out a beautiful little Mia face when she was about two sucking on a blue sucker. Blue drool was all over her face, but Mia was in heaven. I decided to place it on the top of her foot. At first she wasn't happy about it being on her foot; Gabs didn't like her feet, but I did. The things that she could do with those feet while dancing turned me on. Giving Gabs that tat took a good five hours; I wanted it to be perfect. When I was done and she looked at what I picked out, she cried for a good three days just staring at it. I also scripted out *Mia Shannon Tucker* underneath it. Now every time Gabs put on her ballet slippers, Mia can watch her dance. I loved tattooing; it was my passion and it paid our bills. We were just happy and with the money I saved, we now had our own place.

When we finally pulled up to the building, Gabs asked, "Where are we?" I shoved money at the driver before he could say anything. Picking Mia up and grabbing Gabs hand, we entered out new building. I was silent the entire way up to the sixth floor to our new place.

"Kyle, what's going on?" I looked over at her to see that her arms were folded across her chest and she was tapping her foot. That's the dancer part in her.

"You'll see," I said, as I tickled Mia.

She shook her head and rested up against me, wrapping her arms around Mia and I. When we made it to the apartment door, I stopped to let Mia down and held up a little copper key in front of Gabs face.

"This is for you, baby girl. Welcome home."

Her eyes widened and started to shimmer over with tears, unlocking the door to make our way inside our new home.

She stopped in the large living room. "We can't afford this, Kyle," she said, shaking her head and placed her hands on her hips.

"Yes, we can; I just put a large down payment on it."

She faced me quickly. "You what?"

"It's ours." And before she could protest, I took her hand to show her around the apartment. I showed her the two bathrooms, the spacious living room, and it even had a little balcony off our bedroom. Of course I mentioned to her that's where we would be having sex, too, and Gabs' face flamed up.

"Or you could plant flowers or something girly like that with Mia," I smiled, and she hit me in the shoulder.

We ended up in Mia's room when I was finished; I knew she loved the place, but was maybe just a little shell shocked that I actually went this far. She walked up to the one window in the room; she looked beautiful with the sun setting in front of her, with her blonde hair glowing. She picked up Mia to whisper something in her ear.

She bit her bottom lip. "I love it, Kyle, but where's the new baby going to sleep?"

My own eyes widened and my body froze as I took in her words,

Whispering, she said, "Tell Daddy, Mia."

My gazed focused on our daughter, "Mamma have baybay in tummy," Mia giggled then wiggled to be let down. She tried to escape the room, but I caught her and hauled her up and went to my wife. I embraced her in a hug and kissed her so deeply with Mia giggling the entire time. I had my gorgeous wife, my beautiful daughter, and now another little unexpected baby on the way. The world finally let us be together and life couldn't get much better than this.

If you or have any friends suffering from Cutting or Bulimia, or any problems with drugs, please contact:

http://teenlineonline.org/

Remember, you're not alone.

About the Author

Nichele Reese loves nothing more than to be snuggling up with her husband and little boy. Occasionally the two furry animals running around her house get some attention too. When she's not doing that, you can find her on her laptop, phone or reading on her kindle. On the side, she loves to study chemistry for fun....Can you believe it? For fun! Crazy girl. She also puts that into good use working in a Microbiology Lab where stinky bacteria grows. She currently lives in Salt Lake City, Utah with the freezing cold weather and the beautiful autumn leaves. This is her first Novel and she hopes you enjoyed it as much as she wrote it.

You can Email Nichele at:
AuthorNicheleReese@gmail.com

Nichele is currently working on:
'Dearest Gemma'
New Adult Novel
Coming Winter 2013

Some may call it fate, some call it a mistake. But I call it, my Dearest Gemma.

Emma Watsen wanted nothing but her college degree in Chemistry Science. Not caring about finding that one true love or being in the most popular sorority house. But James Murdock was the most popular boy, lead Quarter Back, he always got what he wanted and he wanted Emma.

No matter what the cost was. Even when Emma said, no.

One night can change everything in a blink of an eye. That one night will leave nightmares for Emma and everything around her will change.

That pregnancy test really couldn't be positive.

When Emma is faced with a courageous decision, that deals a lot with her future, she has to grow up faster than a regular nineteen year old. Decisions have to be made, but will they be the right ones? Her whole future is in her hands with that important decision.

Also to come in 2014:
Running From Fear- Brad Evan's Story
Hard Love- Alex Blair's Story

Acknowledgements

I've had so much help from so many great new friends that I have made along this journey. I can't thank them enough for all their kind words and inspirations to help me to keep going, to make my dream come true and finish my story of Tucker and Abigail. No matter how many times I changed my epilogue.

Janessa Osborne. Girl, I would be lost without your words of encouragement every day. No matter how bad of day I am having, I can always count on you to be there for me to make me laugh. I'm so happy to have met you and have you as my friend.

JL Brooks. Thank you so much for helping me with new ideas and always willing to brainstorm with me. I'll swap stories with you any day. Thank you so much for letting me use a quote from Distractions in here. That means so much to me. I love ya girl and I can't forget about Shepard ;)

Megan Myers. What can I say that you don't already know? We pretty much have the same mind in all things. I'm happy to have met you. Thank you so much for reading Juilliard and all your advice. You are truly my sister from another state.

Jaimi Mac, Nacole Stayton, Jenn Cole Bester, and Melanie Dawn. I love you sweet girls as my own sisters. Trusty worthy people are hard to find, I'm lucky to have found you. (((Hugs)))

Erika Taylor. Who always told me to never give up and to keep going.

Other BIG thanks go to, Kim Karr for taking me under her wing and helping me with re-wording, brainstorming and being able to handle my rambunctious phone calls. Also for putting me in the back of her book, Connected, to give me a great start to the writing world. You're amazing!

Nikki Sparks and Amanda Stone. Thank you for reading some of my lines when I was also stuck. You both have helped me improve on my writing and helped me understand a different way to express them. Even if it was just one word that helped me.

Holly Malgieri. What would I do without a Travis in a box? Hehe...You're so amazing, your blog is amazing and I don't know what I would do without you helping me with a blog tour! Thank you for always being there.

Michelle Valentine. I thank you for the Falcon Boys. They're one of my favorite guy bands. Michelle, I value our friendship so much. Thank you for all your advice in this community. I can't express how grateful I am to have met you. Thank you so much for letting me use them in my story. I will always treasure that.

To; Kelli Maine, Emily Snow, Katie Ashley, K.A. Linde, Gail McHugh, Kimberly Knight for taking the time to read some of Juilliard or Else and all your wonderful advice. I'll never forget you ladies. You don't know how much I look up to you as authors.

Anne Leigh for becoming one of my new sweetest friends. You're just an amazing writer who expresses herself perfectly in your writing. Your writing inspires me.

To my ladies in The Indie Chixx, for becoming my new buddies. I love you all!

To Audrey Harte. I get all teary eyed when I begin to think of all the work you've helped me with. I don't know where to begin. You helped me when I needed it most and when I almost gave up. Your advice on true edits completed this task and making my story 100 times better. We worked so well together and I take everything you showed me into my heart always to remember. You're an amazing editor with all that you've done for me and Juilliard. I can't express it enough to how grateful I am for you. Thank you so much <3

Angela at Fictional Formats. Thank you so much for squeezing me into your very busy schedule. Thank you for your patience and kindness and answering all my questions. You're one of the sweetest ladies I've ever met in this writing journey, even though we have only known each other in a short time. Thank you so much! ☺

To my greatest friend of all, Vanessa Churchill. You are my complete book partner. Thank you for believing in me to finish this. For reading for me and all things. You are a fabulous person and I'm so happy you're in my life!

My sister Melanie, for being the best sister a little sister could ever ask for. Carrie, my wonderful Mother. She always told me I could do anything, now I believe her.

Save the best for last. To my wonderful husband Brett and son ((Mini Reese)) for being so patient with me through this process, but still making me laugh every day. For dealing with me playing on the computer during the day, then working graveyards at night. For dealing with dirty clothes, no clean dishes and for letting me escape into the writing world in my head. I love you both so very much.

Turn the Page to read the first chapter in

Lucky 8

A novel by

Megan Myers

Due out sometime in 2014

Chapter One

It sucks when you work into the wee hours of the night and have no life outside of it. Then come home to an empty house, only to remind you that no one is there waiting for you, with the exception of my very hyper chocolate lab.

Yup, Clyde is the only man that hasn't left me, but I secretly think it's because I keep him cooped up in the house all day and only take him out on a leash. He has no way of escaping me. Even then, he still tries to take off and chase after those darn squirrels... I swear those damn things just like to taunt him for fun. One of these days I'll let go of the leash to let him run free and then we'll see if the squirrels act just as tough as they do now, but that's for another day, another time.

Right now, all I want to do is get home, strip off these damn scrubs, take a nice hot shower to wash off the remaining germs that I came in contact with and slip into my nice comfy pajamas that will be waiting for me. All snuggly and warm.

Pulling into my townhome complex and parking in my spot, number eight. Which is pretty funny if you think about it, because that number isn't very lucky for me. It's a torcher number; or a damn curse. It sucks owning a townhouse without a garage, if I had one, then I wouldn't have to look at the damn number every day.

Dragging my tired ass out of my Tahoe, wondering why I even bought such a big vehicle in the first place. I'm single, with no kids. Unless you count

Clyde, which I do, but a little sporty Camaro would had done just fine, but I've always wanted a Tahoe.

Of course, I didn't count on me still being single at the border line of my twenties. Okay, thirty. I'm thirty, but I like to round down the number. I always pictured myself being married to a hot Hollywood actor, living in the Hollywood Hills in a five million dollar mansion, with ten bedrooms and fourteen bathrooms, because I don't ever like to use the same bathroom twice in a week. Seriously, what are you supposed to do with fourteen bathrooms? Okay, who am I kidding? Those were my awesome dreams at night, but I certainly didn't picture myself still being single at this age.

I checked my mailbox before heading up the stairs to my door. Even before I reached my floor, I heard my sweet boy whimpering for me behind my red painted door to let him out so he can do his business. Still hanging on the hook is a very colorful Christmas wreath on the outside. Making a mental note to take that down, but I'm still within the timeframe to have Christmas decorations up, after all it's only January. So I'm good.

"I'm coming boy, just a second." I called out as I dug into my purse for my keys. Is it sad that I think of him as my child? Well, my four legged child, who is covered in fur, but he's still my child nonetheless. Putting my key in the lock and turned it to open up my door, I'm immediately greeted with happy barks and a wagging tail. If you listened really carefully you could almost make out a 'hi'. Yes, I think my dog talks to me, don't judge, okay. Tossing my keys and mail on the entry way table and bending down to let him give me wet kisses across my nose and cheeks, making me a slobbery mess.

"Hey boy, did you hold down the fort today?" After scratching behind his ears for a while and giving him kisses back, I straightened my tired spine to head into my living room.

Being the type of person that can't stand the quiet I flipped on the TV to the Rock music channel, so I could have it as background music. Listening to Rock music helps drown out all the little voices floating around my head screaming, "You're single." "You're all alone."

Walking into my dream kitchen while bobbing my head to *Whore* by In This Moment, I contemplate about making me something to eat. Rummaging through my double door stainless steel refrigerator to see that I had everything to make a good ole healthy salad, but putting that off since a glorious hot shower was calling out to me first.

Heading down the hallway to my 'suite' as I like to refer to it, I pass by all my photos my lovely best friend, Becky put up. I'm not very good at decorating, so I let her OCD ass have free reign with my townhouse when I bought it.

Of course, I had to pay for all the decorations, but I'll admit that she did a kick ass job with it, way beyond what I would have done, which would have been nothing. Plain ole boring. She told me before, "Rach, you have to have some color in your life since you have nothing else."

Dang, she really knew how to throw a low blow.

Finally giving in, I let her have her way. She was like a little kid in a candy store, running in and out of my house during the first few weeks with different paint swatches trying to find the perfect color palate. She highlighted the hallway with a beautiful cream color, which accented the red she painted the living room. She then added some of my favorite family portraits that I cherished so much.

Walking into my room, I kicked off my shoes and headed towards my bathroom to turn on my shower so it could start warming up. I love my shower. That's my place to relax and let all the stresses of the world, plus work go right down the drain. When I first bought this townhouse, there wasn't much that needed to be renovated, but the shower was the one place I splurged on by going all out and it's beautiful.

It's big enough to fit at least four people. Of course, I haven't tested that theory out, but it would fit six of me, and since I'm averaged size at five four and one hundred and twenty pounds, we'll just say four.

Any who, back to my amazing shower.

I chose eight by eight with dark mocha travertine tiles to line the walls with those little bitty light brown squares going around the middle to pull the nice warm look together. There's also a bench, you know to shave your legs and what not. What did you think the bench was in there for? *Dirty mind.* The designer had three cubbies built into the wall to hold all my shampoo, conditioner, sponges, face wash, body wash, you get the picture, to hold all my girly shower stuff. But my real love in the shower had to be all the shower heads. The first one; is a huge round silver rain shower head that comes out of the ceiling, and then there's a handheld one on the wall along with full body jets that aligned either side.

Honestly to say I love my shower would be an understatement. If I could find a legal way to work from my shower, I would do it in a heartbeat. But I can't so that's why I work at the hospital in the labor and delivery wing as a nurse. I've always loved babies, so to be a part of someone's family at that special moment is heartbreakingly beautiful. Well let's say nothing gets better than that, except my shower.

Stripping off my scrubs and tossing them in the hamper that's right outside my bathroom, I see that Clyde was already sprawled out on the bed calling it a night. He was so sweet to wait up for me and then crash. Like a typical man would do. Turning back into the bathroom that was now all nice and steamy, filled with smoldering mist so that I couldn't even make out my own reflection in the mirror as I stepped into the shower.

I lingered under the shower heads as the beating streams of hot water relaxed my aching muscles, clearing my mind of everything. Thirty minutes later I was putting on my favorite Aggie shirt that hits right in the middle of my thighs, perfect nighty shirt length. Glancing at the bed one more time to see Clyde was still lying there on his stomach sprawled out on his side snoring away. I know, strange for a dog to snore but he does, I've told y'all before he's like a kid.

Padding into the living room and grabbed the stack of mail from the entry way as I made my way to my couch. Pulling out my cell from my purse as I started sorting through my mail, it's usually a bunch of junk, since I pay all my bills online anyways. There's a formal looking envelope in the stack, so I fished it out first and slid my finger under the sticky flap. But what's inside was oh so very shocking! It felt as if my breath was stuck in my throat while my stomach dropped out of my ass as I scanned the lines over and over.

"What the hell? Why would he send this to me?!" I yelled while jumping to my feet, causing my wet auburn hair to curtain around my face, along with little droplets of water hitting the fancy cardstock.

Continuing to inspect the ivory wedding invitation with intricate calligraphy written on it, I read it aloud.

Mr. and Mrs. Michael Jones
Request the Honor of your presence
With the marriage of their daughter

Stacey Lynn Jones
to
Kyle Wayne Smith

Saturday, the Twenty Fourth of May
at two o'clock in the Afternoon at
St. Margarets Catholic Church

"You have got to be fucking kidding me." Quickly grabbing my cell and dialed my girlfriend, Becky. She answered on the second ring. "Damn it Rach, there better be a damn good reason you're call me at...two o'clock in the fucking morning. Geez two o'clock really?" Becky hissed at me through the phone. She's a girl that loves her sleep.

"Becky, you will never believe what I just got in the damn mail?"

She breathed a tired breath into the phone. "It better be a damn letter letting you know your death is near, because I'll kill you if this isn't a good enough reason."

I just loved how snappy she gets when I wake her up, "Beck, Kyle sent me a wedding invite to his and Stacey's wedding in May."

Hearing what sounded like Becky jumping up in bed, flinging the covers off of her, "Are you fucking kidding? Why the hell would he send you of all people an invite?"

Rolling my eyes, "Gee thanks for that, damn."

"Oh don't you roll your eyes at my missy, you know what I mean." How does she know when I'm rolling my eyes? "Yeah, y'all were hot and heavy for months, and then you dumped him and he immediately met Stacey right after. Now just six months later he's engaged, getting married in five and to top it off he sends you an invite. What is he trying to do rub it in your face or something? You know I never really cared for him and this just proves I was right."

I started pacing back and forth in front of my couch. "No this just proves I'm right, I'm nothing but a good luck charm for them. I'm the one they date before they meet 'The One'. It's like I train them, and then send them off like a teacher into the real dating world. Ready to fall in love and marry the one right after me." I stomped my foot in frustration.

Becky started rambling on about something, but I stopped paying attention. Trying to remember what happened to all the men that have come and gone in my life. See this is why number eight isn't my lucky number, that's the number of men I have dated that have gone on to find 'The One'. There's nothing against finding 'The One', I just hate that it was after they dated me. To make things worse they all have dubbed me their 'Lucky Charm'.

Yup, that's right. Just because they dated me and then the next girl (or guy) they dated, fell in love, then up and married them. Then to top it off they even had the nerve to send me their stupid wedding invites as a thank you for dumping their ass. Ugh, Kyle's wasn't even the first one I received.

"Rachel! Are you even listening to me?" Becky's rambling snapped me out of my thoughts.

"Oh... um... no not really, sorry." I admit "Hey I think I'm going to go ahead and call it a night, I just want to forget this whole day." Becky tells me bye and made me promise her that I will call her tomorrow before I go in to work.

I laid my head back on the couch and welcomed the cool feeling of the leather against my wet hair. Reaching for the remote I flipped through the TV guide until I saw my all-time favorite romantic movie, *The Notebook*. Selecting it in hopes it will keep my mind off everything crazy going on in my life.

The last scene I remembered before drifting off was Noah and Allie on the docks and he was telling her, it wasn't over. Before I knew it I'm waking up from the strangest dream, I dreamt about my very first ex.

I dubbed him, 'The Athlete'. He stood about six foot, great build, broad shoulders, the whole nine yards. See, he played football back in the day and worked out every chance he had after he finished his contract. His eye's where a pretty brown, pretty in a manly way, had slight stubble on his cheeks, which made the attraction to him even greater. I guess that's what first attracted me to him was his looks, I mean because honestly that's the first thing we see when we meet someone. Next, you get to know them and then you fall in love with what's on the inside, but looks are the first thing you notice. You know it's true.

Second thing I noticed; was that he was very sensitive and in touch with his feminine side. Now don't get me wrong, every woman loves a guy that can sympathize with them about things, but damn. Sometimes you want a manly man, a shoulder to cry and lean on, not have it be the other way around.

I remembered when I first started noticing 'the signs'. We were watching *The Notebook* one night over at his house. Okay that should have been the very first sign, because he picked that movie out in the first place. At the time I just figured he was being sweet because he knew how much I loved that movie. Noticing out the corner of my eye, that he was quoting each and every line from the characters, and then he cried at the end. Yeah, he totally cried. That's when the red flags started waving, with the loud blare horns going off frantically in my head.

I called it off the next day. To me I just didn't see us going anywhere, especially with his very feminine side. Sometimes I just couldn't take it.

Turns out I put him off women for good, because I heard through a friend of a friend that after I broke up with him, he had an epiphany and fell in love with a lovely man. No really, I heard he's rather *lovely*. They truly make the perfect couple; I've seen a few pictures of them together on Facebook *after* he sent me a friend request. What nerve.

First, I was kind of put off that I might have turned him gay, but then again you don't just wake up one morning and decide to be gay. I truly believe you are born that way. So that leads me to feel he was hiding himself all along, but we didn't sleep together so that was good. I think that would have been awkward anyways.

Hearing very odd sounds, I woke up to realize I had fallen asleep on the couch with some very awful amateur porn playing on my TV.

Gotta love HBO during the early morning hours. I thought to myself.

Squinting at the receiver with dry and tired eyes, blinking a couple of times to focus on the glowing blue numbers to make out that it was well after four in the morning. Untangling my body from my plum fuzzy blanket while picking up the remote to turn off the TV and dragging my tired ass down the hall and into my bed with my fluffy down comforter. Double checking my phone to make sure it was plugged in, along with my alarm set to go off in five dreadful hours so I could go back to work. I chanted in my head, 'I love my job, I love my job'

"Night Clyde," I mumbled while patting his head. He's still snoring away on his side. I rolled over to turn my bedside lamp off and fall into a peaceful dream that isn't filled with any of my ex's.